LICENSE TO QUILL

ALSO BY JACOPO DELLA QUERCIA

The Great Abraham Lincoln
Pocket Watch Conspiracy

LICENSE TO
QUILL

Jacopo della Quercia

St. Martin's Griffin
New York

LICENSE TO QUILL. Copyright © 2015 by Jacopo della Quercia. All rights
reserved. Printed in the United States of America. For information, address
St. Martin's Press, 175 Fifth Avenue, New York, N.Y. 10010.

www.stmartins.com

LIBRARY OF CONGRESS CATALOGING-IN-PUBLICATION DATA

Della Quercia, Jacopo
    License to quill / Jacopo della Quercia.—First edition.
        p.   cm.
    ISBN 978-1-250-05965-9 (trade paperback)
    ISBN 978-1-4668-6503-7 (e-book)
    1. Shakespeare, William, 1564–1616—Fiction.   2. Marlowe, Christopher,
1564–1593—Fiction.   3. Gunpowder Plot, 1605—Fiction.   4. Great Britain—
History—James I, 1603–1625—Fiction.   I. Title.
    PS3604.E4446L53 2015
    813'.6—dc23
                                                            2015035688

Our books may be purchased in bulk for promotional, educational,
or business use. Please contact your local bookseller or the Macmillan
Corporate and Premium Sales Department at (800) 221-7945, extension 5442,
or by e-mail at MacmillanSpecialMarkets@macmillan.com.

First Edition: December 2015

10 9 8 7 6 5 4 3 2 1

For Pamela, Annelise, and Prof. John M. Bell

Also for Erzsébet

Act 1

1593

Prologue

[Thunder and Lightning]

Three blood-covered riders charged into the darkness. The heavy drumming of their snorting horses shook the woodlands like thunder.

"Halt!" their dogged leader called to his companions. He reared his steed and raised his lantern. With restless eyes, the horseman probed the endless forest around him.

"What is it?" a second rider panted, his heart pounding. "Have we lost him?"

"No," declared the leader of the manhunt. "He is here."

"Where!" gasped the second.

"Where . . . ?" wheezed the wounded, barely conscious third man behind them.

Seated high in his saddle, the lead rider's eyes narrowed. He lowered his lantern, obscuring it with his cloak while drawing a small, shining blade from his belt. The patient hunter went silent and let his eyes readjust to the dark. Beside him, his winded companion breathed nervously. All he could perceive through the woods was a vast lifelessness. The dead of night.

And then . . . a grunt.

As quick as foxes, the two horsemen turned their heads. Their eyes raced across the black morass and onto a dark figure hunched in the grass. The creature's huge, hideous face was staring straight back at theirs.

Faster than the second rider could flinch, a throwing knife flashed through the air and struck the creature head-on. A wincing, earsplitting shriek shot through the night, upsetting both riders' horses. Amidst the cacophony of whinnies and screams, the lead rider lifted his lamp and spotted the silhouette of their fleeing victim. The horseman grinned and the chase resumed with two riders in pursuit of their prey, only now with a fresh blood trail to follow.

Still faint from his own wounds, the third rider limped onward.

"He is stricken!" the leader shouted. He leaned forward while spurring his fatigued charger faster. He thrust his glowing fist forward and unsheathed his sword in a wide swipe. The rider swung the blade like a scythe, itching to cut down his enemy. Within the fleeting evening's fading moonrays, the naked saber flashed like lightning.

"You are mine!" the horseman thundered as he moved in for the kill. *"You—"*

The lead rider saw the most unexpected distraction ahead on him: a head. A woman's face, wreathed in flame. She was staring back at the horseman through the forest's wooded halls.

"What on earth?" the rider whispered.

"What the devil?" spoke the second.

The horsemen pulled on their reins, coming to a stop inside a small clearing deep within the ancient heart of the woods. A crackling campfire bathed the glade in a circle of light, washing over the riders with intense warmth.

Beside the fire, two figures stood tall and resolute.

They were women. Young women, albeit different in age. The elder was taller with wizened eyes and a faint scar stretched across her neck. The younger had sharper, more striking features, and was holding a small babe to her breast. Both women had piercing gazes, for neither one displayed fear. They were unflinching, unblinking, and unaffected. Completely unafraid of the blood-soaked men before them.

Only the infant was moving.

"Who are you?" the lead rider spoke. "What are you doing here?"

"Killing swine," replied the younger in a faraway accent.

The two horsemen exchanged glances. Their eyes shifted this way and that: there were no pigs in sight. No knives, no spit, no chopping block; just a crucible in the fire. Puzzled, the lead horseman turned back to the women. "We chase a villain through these woodlands. An *assassin*," he emphasized. "Be you friends or not, this man is a murderer who can and will kill you. All of you." The rider's eyes briefly fell onto the babe. "Where did he go?"

The women glared at the horseman without saying a word. After this pregnant pause, the woman nursing the infant pointed off to the left. The hunter followed her naked arm to a thick bush at the edge of the clearing. A thin blood trail cut through the glade and into a shrub, where a crimson pool was forming under its thorns.

The lead rider's eyes widened. "We have him!" The horseman raced toward his adversary but then paused once he noticed his otherwise reliable partner's unusual absence. The leader turned around in his saddle. "Skeggs?" he called out.

The second rider was motionless, save for the quaking charger beneath him. Neither male wanted to turn his back on the women.

"Hoy! Skeggs!"

His startled horseman snapped to attention. "Aye, Poley."

The lead rider stared at his comrade in disbelief. "Have you gone soft in the head? Get your stupid arse over here! Now!"

The second rider obeyed.

As the two turned away from the women, the infant murmured and kicked. "Hush, sister. Hush," the younger woman soothed in an ancient tongue thought to be dead. Preoccupied, the men did not notice.

The leader leaped from his mount with a spring in his step, but Skeggs climbed down from his with great difficulty. He had been riding for so long that he had nearly forgotten how to stand. After regaining his footing, the horseman found his more experienced friend circling the bush. The lead rider's sword and lantern were raised.

"Get ready," the hunter whispered.

Skeggs's fumbling fingers found his dagger and rapier. The familiar sound of their unsheathed steel reawakened his confidence, and with callused hands, he followed his companion.

The riders surrounded the bush with their weapons fixed on its center, at which point the leader of the hunt gave a nod. He threw his lantern into the bush, breaking it open. Its fires found fresh kindling, and the bush was soon roaring with flame. As the fires licked higher, a deep grunt bellowed from beneath its branches. And then, screaming. The same high-pitched horror these horsemen had been hunting for hours. The riders waited anxiously as the burning bush roasted their opponent alive.

Then, a huge figure leaped out from the flames. It lunged straight at Skeggs with scorched skin and a blackened knife stuck in its face. Skeggs screamed and fell backward, holding the beast off with his sword while repeatedly stabbing it with his dagger. The two rolled on the ground amidst the foul smell of burnt hair and bacon until the master of the manhunt brought the fight to an end. He stabbed his sword through the creature, pinning it to the ground at its neck. He then seized his blackened knife's bloodied handle and yanked it, tearing half the creature's face off its skull. Unmasked, the poor player fell dead.

The beast was defeated and the manhunt was over. There was only one problem: this villain they slew was no man.

Skeggs scurried onto his feet while his partner stared at their opponent, aghast. "A boar?" said the second.

The lead rider was speechless. It was a large boar, but no man.

The two looked at each other, knowing full well that a lot more than their evenings were ruined. And unfortunately, things were about to get worse.

Skeggs looked away from his partner. "Poley!" he cried.

The lead rider spun around with his bloodied blade only to nearly drop it in shock. Both the women were gone, as were the men's horses. All that remained in the glade was their fire, for even the crucible had vanished. The men were as good as dead in the wilderness.

As the riders combed over the clearing with mad eyes, their third, wounded companion finally emerged through the woods. He sat lifelessly in his saddle with fresh blood pouring down his face. He fell from his horse like a dead man while his comrades rushed to his aid. He was still breathing, but barely.

"This is bad," Skeggs observed as he raised the wounded man's head.

"This is the worst job we've ever done," the leader confirmed.

"The man . . ." the injured rider groaned.

The lead rider crouched down and shook his head. "We lost him."

"But not all is lost!" the second rider promised the third. "Your master will take care of everything. You know he will! He said he would."

The third rider shook his head with hot tears streaming down his face. "God save me!" he cried. "I am dead! We are all dead!" The man sniffled and then shouted: "All will know me as the man who killed Christopher Marlowe!"

Once more, the two kneeling horsemen exchanged glances. "It

wasn't you," Skeggs assured his sobbing companion. "It was someone else."

The lead rider turned away in defeat. He was already dreading the creeping dawn.

Far off in the distance, an infant's cries filled the forest.

Chapter I

The Man Who Killed Christopher Marlowe

Marlowe was dead! There was no doubt about it, and no one knew this better than the man who had put a dagger through the late poet's heart.

The renowned playwright now known as Christopher Marlowe, deceased, was born in Canterbury in 1564. His parents were a cobbler and a Katherine who, little to her knowledge, had given birth to one of the most important babes in the country that year. Her boy was handsome in his youth and grew into an even more handsome man: tall, dark, and dashing with a wavy mane of brown hair, large brown eyes, and a thin mustache perched atop a mischievous smirk. Considering his many endowments, the young buck had plenty to smile about—or at the very least, to flaunt. Marlowe acted as if the world were a stage and he its star player. But in all fairness, who could blame him? Some men and women just seem to be born loving life, as was clearly the case with this ill-fated poet.

Before his death, Christopher Marlowe was the most lively person alive. He was strong for his frame, nimble, and as fit as a fencer. He had the agility of a cat, quickly graduating from climbing trees in his youth to scaling Roman walls and stone towers throughout

Canterbury. When no one was looking, he even enjoyed a grand view of the country from atop the highest points of Canterbury Cathedral. The boy was daring, but also generous, gregarious, and gifted with a mind as razor-sharp as his tongue. A precocious student, young "Kit" attended the King's School in Canterbury and Corpus Christi College in Cambridge—on scholarship, he would boast. By the time he was twenty, the bright lad was already a bachelor of arts, a master of six languages, and a Machiavel overflowing with ideas and ambition. However, the low rooftops of Cambridge soon proved a small summit for Marlowe. Like a conqueror, his thoughts turned to the Channel and how best to cross it. He wanted to climb higher and see farther than even he could imagine. He wanted an adventure. Fortunately, adventure found him in college.

The trouble started during Marlowe's fifth year, when his postgraduate studies were interrupted by frequent and mysterious trips to the Continent. The naughty rumor was that Kit planned to enter the priesthood, but the more accurate description was that Marlowe became involved "in matters touching the benefit of his country."* Specifically, the clandestine kind. War had broken out between England and Spain, and students of promise quickly became important commodities to the Crown. In 1585, Marlowe was approached in his dorm room by Thomas Walsingham, an intelligence operative not much older than he was. The young man offered Kit a unique opportunity to experience how the world worked during wartime in the service of Thomas's cousin Sir Francis Walsingham, Queen Elizabeth I's legendary secretary of state and spymaster. The eager young student graciously accepted, and so began Marlowe's little-known but life-changing semesters abroad.

Truth be told, Marlowe did enter the priesthood during these years, but it was more for the thrill and the money than for the wine

---

*John Roche Dasent, *Acts of the Privy Council*, vol. xv, 141.

or the women. He was an agent in Sir Francis Walsingham's extensive spy network as the war between Protestant England and Catholic Spain exploded. Now on Her Majesty's secret service, Marlowe crisscrossed the Continent under the guise of a Jesuit to gather intelligence about Spain's plans to invade England. This wolf in priest's clothes was in Florence when Mary, Queen of Scots was beheaded. He eavesdropped on the Vatican when Sixtus V granted Philip II papal authority to depose Queen Elizabeth. And when the Spanish Armada finally moved against England, it was Marlowe's contacts in Italy who provided the Walsinghams with the information they needed to destroy the great fleet. The war made Marlowe a hero to the most powerful people in England, and for his services, the scholar returned to his studies with friends in high places and more money than even a college student could spend.

So, how did such an upstanding young man ultimately find himself arrested for heresy, a capital offense? Simply put, Marlowe liked spending his free time getting himself into trouble.

After completing his education at Cambridge and "elsewhere," Marlowe quickly established himself as the most celebrated playwright in London—and the most controversial. His play *The Jew of Malta* featured a prologue delivered by the ghost of Niccolò Machiavelli himself. After that, he chose the seven deadly sins as his muses and Mephistopheles as his mentor for his inflammatory *Doctor Faustus*. His play *The Massacre at Paris* not only lived up to its title but contained a warning to the queen that the play might encourage murders—which it did. However, it was *Tamburlaine the Great*, a comedic discourse about the most brutal conqueror since Genghis Khan, that ultimately resulted in the brash playwright's inconvenient demise.

In the year 1593, someone in London began posting unfriendly comments about Protestant refugees living peacefully in the city. The bills were written in blank verse—Marlowe's favorite—referenced several of his most famous works, and were suspiciously signed

"Tam-berlaine."* Whether Marlowe was behind these vicious libels or not, a warrant was issued for his arrest on May 18. Two days later, the dramatist surrendered himself without any drama. With Sir Francis Walsingham dead and any chance of a pardon unlikely, the situation appeared grave for the ill-fated poet.

As Marlowe awaited his impending trial, torture, and death, he was taken to a Deptford establishment owned by Dame Eleanor Bull. The building was a safe house for government agents and its owner was well connected to the Crown. With London under lock-down due to plague, the otherwise teeming Deptford Strand was deathly silent and still.

It was May 30, 1593. The coroner's report said it was still daylight, but it was actually nighttime.

Christopher Marlowe's last meal was wine. Lots of wine.†

Three armed men guarded Marlowe as he dozed on his bed. They played backgammon on a table while the condemned playwright snored loudly behind them. All three guards at some point had worked for the Walsinghams. Robert Poley was the largest and most dangerous man in the group: a seasoned spy and double agent, and the English government's unrivaled expert on the London under-world. Sharing his bench was Nicholas Skeres, a con artist and saboteur who occasionally proved a reliable henchman for Poley. Together, the two had played key roles in exposing the Babington Plot, which ultimately cost Queen Mary her head. Ingram Frizer was the only man in the room who had never worked for the great Sir Francis Walsingham. His employer was Thomas Walsingham, the same operative who had recruited Marlowe at Cambridge nearly ten years before. Thomas had spent the greater part of the last decade foiling Catholic plots against England, but with his famed cousin

*"A Libell, fixte vpon the French Church Wall, in London. Ann° 1598°," Oxford, Bodleian Library MS Don.d. 152, flo. 4v.
†"Coroner's Inquest on Marlowe," William Danby, Coroner, 1 June 1593, PRO C260/174, No. 127.

dead, even those days were reportedly behind him. Frizer was nothing more than Thomas's business agent, and as he played backgammon that evening, he knew Marlowe's death would be a painful financial loss to his master. Thomas had been Christopher Marlowe's chief patron ever since they retired from the secret service. But then, how could anyone retire from the world of espionage without being dead?

There was a knock at the door, and the three guardsmen looked up from their game.

"Who goes there?" called Poley.

"Ale!" came a voice from behind the thick door.

"I pray you remember the porter?" Skeres teased.

"Of course I do," Poley snapped. "Skeggs, go open the door."

"I move for no man," Skeres scoffed. "And don't call me 'Skeggs.' I'm only Skeggs when I'm working."

"You are working."

"No, I'm not. I'm playing 'tables'!" Skeres smiled with a roll of the dice.

"The only thing you're playing is yourself for a fool, so get off your foolish arse and open the door."

"Even my foolish arse moves for no man," Skeres replied with a wink.

At an impasse, the squabbling guardsmen looked down to small Frizer, who sat cheek by jowl between the two larger men. The agent struggled on his bench. "I cannot move left or right."

"Then fly!" Skeres laughed.

Frizer grimaced as he pushed himself up from the table, careful not to bump his twelve-pence dagger into the silent playwright behind him.

"Morley, you still with the living?" Skeres asked while Frizer walked toward the door.

The dramatist snored in response.

"He's sleeping," observed Poley.

"Ah, sleep . . . Perchance to dream?" Skeres mused.

"Not while we're working," spoke the expert.

"Aye, there's a rub!" Skeres sang as he scratched at his crotch.

Frizer opened the door and a thin, dark-haired porter entered the room carrying four frothy beers on a tray. He placed three beers on the table and balanced the fourth on his tray as he waited for Ingram Frizer to sit. However, something made the otherwise indifferent third man go rigid. He turned his head and fixed his eyes on the window above Marlowe.

"What is it?" asked Poley.

"I thought I saw a horseman outside."

Poley and Skeres turned around and stared out the dark portal. An uneasy silence filled the room as the men listened for hoofbeats. However, the tension was diffused by one of Marlowe's loud snores.

"Morley must be dreaming about men on horseback again," Skeres snickered. "Come! Let's finish our game."

Frizer shrugged and returned to the bench, but as he was about to sit, Poley caught him. "Where's your dagger?" he asked.

Frizer felt his belt and found his leather sheath empty. Alarmed, the three men looked up at their mysterious porter.

The porter slammed the door and then smashed his last beer on the floor, causing an explosion that engulfed the whole room with thick smoke. Poley and Skeres leaped to their feet and drew their weapons with such speed that Frizer was accidentally slashed on the head by one of their rapiers. The agents coughed fiercely and stabbed their swords through the smog until a loud shriek filled the air.

"Marlowe!" a bloodied Frizer cried out.

The three spun around to see the window above the playwright thrown open. As smoke escaped from the room, their prized prisoner gasped helplessly from his blood-covered bed. Marlowe's face had been mutilated and Frizer's dagger was buried deep in his chest. Blood was shooting in streams with every pulse from the dying man's heart.

"Treachery!"

"Murder!"

"Morley!" the guards gasped.

The men rushed to his aid, but Marlowe twisted when one of them reached for Frizer's blade. The playwright gripped the dagger and writhed violently, spurting blood all over the guardsmen. Skeres and Frizer stumbled backward while Poley braved the horror up close. "Hold him steady!" he shouted. "Marlowe! Can you speak?"

The gored man tried to form words, but there was no breath left in his lungs. Only a sinister hiss seeping from the fleshy hole in his chest. And then, silence. The playwright's lips parted and his body went limp as the last of his life faded from the one eyeball he had left.

Christopher Marlowe was dead. Brutally murdered with a dagger. Frizer's dagger.

The three guards stared at one another in panic. Each one of them had Marlowe's blood on his hands.

At that moment, the wooden door behind the men was thrown open. A tall, hooded figure rushed into the room with a glowing lantern held high.

"Who are you!" screamed Poley while accidentally cutting Frizer a second time. "Show yourself!"

The dark figure pulled back his hood. The three agents recognized him immediately.

"Master Thomas!" gasped Frizer, who was now sporting two nasty wounds on his head.

"What are you doing here?" asked Poley while lowering his bloodied rapier.

"Might I ask you the same?" replied Thomas Walsingham. "Marlowe was marked for assassination this evening, and you dullards are letting his killer escape!"

"He's right." Skeres nodded, albeit out of confusion.

"I rode here as soon as I learned of the plot," Thomas continued with urgency. "You must pursue this villain! Take my lantern! Ride with all haste!"

"But master . . ." stammered a blood-soaked Ingram Frizer as he backed away from Christopher Marlowe's maimed corpse.

"Fear not. The queen's coroner will absolve you. Just find the assassin! Fly, you fools! Fly!" Walsingham shooed the men out of the room and smacked Frizer on the backside with his sword, inadvertently giving him a third and final wound for the evening. The trio leaped onto their horses and galloped into the evening, not knowing which direction would lead them closer to their unknown assailant.

As the three blood-covered riders scattered into the distance, Thomas closed the window above Marlowe and looked down at the deceased. The intelligence officer shook his head: the poor playwright was not even thirty. His right eye was horribly bloodied and more closely resembled a small liver. His other eye, agape and bloodshot, stared vacantly into the heavens. A single teardrop trickled from it. And then there was the knife sticking out of the foul-smelling wound in his chest: a deep cavity of red carnage that still gurgled with blood.

Walsingham fell to one knee and whispered: "Alas, poor Marlowe."

The dead man said nothing.

Walsingham furrowed his eyebrows and spoke louder. "I said: 'Alas, poor Marlowe!'"

Still no response.

Walsingham's eyes widened. He angrily twisted the dagger sticking out of the dead man's chest.

"*Ow!*" Marlowe winced.

"Enough with the theatrics." Thomas scowled. "The show is over. There is no more audience."

Marlowe grinned with delight as he slipped the cat liver off his face. "I am sorry, my friend, but I never performed my own death before. I figured it should be the death of a lifetime!"

"You'll have plenty of time to play dead where you're going,"

Thomas chided. He pulled his friend up by the hand so that the dead man could sit.

"Ah, Venice . . ." Marlowe sighed with the dagger still stuck in his chest. "Is the boat ready?"

"Yes, but we have to move quickly."

"Va bene." The sprightly playwright bounced up from his death-bed and removed the blood-filled pig's bladder hidden under his shirt. "These methods are malodorous," acknowledged Marlowe, who often used the same props in his plays. "Fortunately, my companions complained that I reeked of wine this whole evening! They'll suspect nothing."

"They'd better not," said Walsingham as he wrapped Marlowe's false dagger in a handkerchief. It was not Frizer's, but a duplicate with its blade broken off. For only twelve pence, such weapons were easy to come by. "And what of your assailant?"

"Oh, I'd nearly forgotten!" Marlowe stomped his boot twice. "Will! Take a bow."

Right on cue, a dagger slid out from under the bed. It was Frizer's missing dagger, and Thomas picked it up from the floor.

"Are you sure he's up to this?" Thomas asked as he smeared the weapon with blood.

"Of course he is!" assured Marlowe as he helped his attacker up from his hiding place. "He keeps his nose out of trouble, this one! Believe me, he'll be less of an arse-ache than I was."

"That's a relief, but I'm referring to whether he has the stamina for this. He won't fizzle out on his own, will he?"

"Such a doubting Thomas!" Marlowe teased as he handed Walsingham the pig's bladder. "Put your fears to rest for one evening. He's already rewritten our history! Give this man enough ink, and he'll rewrite our whole language." Marlowe clapped his killer on the shoulders while covertly wiping some of the blood off his hands. "He'll be a worthy replacement. He even scripted this little performance himself!"

Walsingham raised his eyebrows. "Really?"

"Of course! There's no way I could have staged my own death. Had I authored this, it would have taken me a fortnight to die!"

Walsingham nodded. "I don't doubt that. Now come. We must depart."

The comrades tossed a pouch of gold to Dame Bull on their way out the door and raced on foot to Deptford Dockyard, where a boat was waiting to take Christopher Marlowe into the afterlife. As the dead man boarded the barge, Thomas offered his former friend one last handshake. "It seems like only yesterday we were discussing what good you could do for this country."

"Yes, well. What good was it?" Marlowe sighed as he shook Thomas's hand.

Walsingham tightened his grip and narrowed his eyes. "Good enough." The man smiled. "Enjoy your retirement."

The poet bowed his head with gratitude for the second life he had been given. Not even England's own agents would know where Marlowe was going: exile in Italy. It was the best punishment he could have hoped for.

And then the poet turned to his killer.

The two fell into each other like brothers and shared a long, silent embrace. Their speechlessness spoke volumes about the times they had shared: every subject they studied, every song and sonnet they swapped, all the ideas they exchanged, and all the hopes they once harbored. All their love's labors, lost.

It was the end of a friendship, an apprenticeship, and a partnership for the ages.

"I don't know where to begin," choked the dead man.

His killer smiled. "No matter where you go, I hope you find a happy ending."

Marlowe beamed brightly at his successor. "To be continued!" he promised as he danced up the ship's plank. Without a moment to lose, Thomas signaled the skipper and sent the vessel into the

Thames to begin its race against the daybreak. Fortunately, the winds favored the men and their mission, and the ship drifted east until it was swallowed by the glowing horizon. The boat disappeared from all record, taking Christopher Marlowe with it, while Thomas Walsingham and Marlowe's patient killer observed from the dock.

"You will receive a stipend," began Walsingham to the silent assassin. "And the necessary license to write and perform your works free from censors. In return, you will report any activity you encounter of concern to the Crown. Failure to do so will result in your immediate termination. Understood?"

"Yes, Master Walsingham."

"'Master W' will suffice," Thomas puffed as he lit himself a pipe. "Marlowe said you have a publication pending. I assume this is for income until the plague passes?"

"It is," confirmed the killer, who had a wife and family to provide for in Stratford.

"What's the title?"

"*Venus and Adonis.*"

Walsingham nodded as the conversation became shrouded in smoke. "I assume the Stationers' Company has it?"

"They do."

"And is your name attached to it?"

"No, Master W."

Walsingham smiled. The young man was behaving precisely as he had been instructed. It was a welcome change from Marlowe. "It is now, master bard."

"Thank you," the assassin replied while masking his excitement.

"How do I spell your name again?" asked Thomas as he returned to his pipe.

The man who killed Christopher Marlowe handed Walsingham a small piece of parchment. The spy-chief looked down at the signature scrawled on it.

"William Shakespeare," he read.

Act II

1604

Chapter II

The Players

BRUTUS
Let's kill him Boldly, but not Wrathfully:
Let's carue him, as a Dish fit for the Gods,
Not hew him as a Carkasse fit for Hounds:

The bard nodded.

And let our Hearts, as subtle Masters do,
Stirre vp their Seruants to an acte of Rage,
And after seeme to chide 'em. This shall make
Our purpose Necessary, and not Enuious.
Which so appearing to the common eyes,
We shall be call'd Purgers, not Murderers.
And for *Marke Antony*, thinke not of him:
For he can do no more then *Cæsars* Arme,
When *Cæsars* head is off.

The bard stroked his short beard as he turned his gray eyes to Cassius.

CASSIUS

Yet I feare him,

For in the ingrafted loue he beares to *Cæsar*.

BRUTUS

Alas, good *Cassius*, do not thinke of him:

If he loue *Cæsar*, all that he can do

Is to himselfe; take thought, and dye for *Cæsar* . . .

Despite his best efforts, the playwright sighed softly. Those last few lines exhumed some old memories he preferred to keep buried. His thoughts turned to Italy and to his friend cast away there, but only for a moment. Nothing more than a brief blink in his mind's eye: *Is he still writing? Is he still laughing? Is he even still breathing? Surely he's alive. Surely! But that was over a decade ago.* . . .

The bard shook the thoughts from his head and returned to the matters in Rome.

TREBONIUS

There is no feare in him; let him not dye,

For he will liue, and laugh at this heereafter.

Offstage, the young apprentice James Sands hit a frying pan with a mallet. It did not sound much like a clock's chimes, but for the time being, it worked.

BRUTUS

Peace! count the—

"Be still a second," Cassius interrupted, raising his hand.

Brutus froze.

The soldiers and senators waited for the conspirator to continue, but instead, Cassius stared at his scroll in confusion. Young Sands struck his pan two more times. Once again, there was no response from the ancient assassin.

"The clock?" Brutus offered.

Cassius shook his head and turned to the lone man in the gallery. "Master Shakespeare?" he called.

The bard glanced at the empty seats to his right and his left. "Are you expecting me to throw something at you?"

"No."

"Good," replied Shakespeare. "There will be plenty of people to do that if you lose your place in front of a full house."

The players snickered as ancient Rome reverted back to the Globe Theatre during the summer of 1604. William Sly, who several seconds ago had been Roman senator Cassius, lowered the long, narrow scroll containing his stage cues and dialogue. "There is something wrong with this scene," he started.

"I agree," observed Shakespeare. "And I am looking at it."

An affronted Sly grimaced as the laughter around him intensified. "Will, it's the lines."

"There's nothing wrong with my loins," Shakespeare assured while crossing his legs, for in those days, the word "lines" was pronounced the same way as "loins." The playwright liked puns.

"Master Shakespeare . . ." Sly seethed. "You made an error. The script says a clock strikes."

Several actors checked their scrolls, but the bard did not need to consult his prompt book. He knew what he scrawled in there five years ago, so he simply stared at the dramatist. "Does that offend you for some reason?"

"Not at all," replied Sly. "But unless I am lost, clocks did not exist during the days of Julius Caesar."

In an instant, the snickering around William Sly stopped. None of the other players had considered this detail during prior performances or rehearsals. All eyes turned to Shakespeare, who went back to stroking his beard. "Is that a problem?" he inquired.

"In sooth?" asked the actor.

"By all means, please soothsay away!" The bard welcomed the challenge with an expertly feigned grin on his face.

Sly bowed his head. "Many thanks. William, you must admit this line sounds a bit out of place for that century. It'd be as if Caesar ordered his soldiers to ready their cannons and muskets."

Shakespeare meditated on this. "I see your point, Master Sly. Fortunately, I have a simple solution. A remedy that should help you throughout your career."

Sly raised his eyebrows. "What is it?"

"It's called 'acting.'"

An enraged Sly spit from the stage while the rest of the King's Men laughed. "You're a cheeky arse, Shakespeare!"

"And you used to be a fine actor!" The bard smiled. "What happened?"

"William!" Sly protested. "Do you not realize this error shatters the illusion of your play? As one actor to another, I must say that I find it distracting."

The bard looked at the empty theater around them. "Does this look like ancient Rome to you?"

"My dear sirs," leading man Richard Burbage interjected. "I believe our good friend, and *fellow shareholder* in this company, I might add . . ." Sly grinned. "I believe the pest does raise a fair point. I, for one, always wondered why we don cloaks and sabers for this play. Why not dress appropriately? We have ample bedsheets for togas."

Amused, William Shakespeare shook his head and simpered. "*Et tu, Brute?* My dear Richard, we have known each other for many years. This is the first time you have ever questioned my methods."

"Ah! And does that offend *you* for some reason?" the veteran player challenged.

"Oh, not at all," replied Shakespeare. "However, since it is too late for us to uncrack this egg, I think it is only fair that I address your misgivings. Master Sly, I put clocks in the play because it is the only reasonable way to denote the passage of time. Sundials do not toll at the top of the hour. And to the great Master Burbage, I truly am sorry to say this, but most of our regulars have no idea what togas are. If we dressed historically appropriate for this play, too many people would mistake us for ghosts. That would complicate things for Master Heminges over there, since he appears as Caesar's ghost in act four."

"Well, that still doesn't explain our choice of language," John Heminges countered. "Master Shakespeare, we have performed this play so many times in the king's speech. Why not perform it in Latin for once? It might make a fine novelty."

"Or a fine mess," the bard quipped. "I think we can all agree that more people believe in ghosts than speak Latin these days. While it would be interesting to explore the latter, it would ultimately alienate audiences we otherwise could attract. Besides, the bitter truth is that the Latin tongue from Caesar's day is extinct. Even if we tested your offer, it would still be built upon fantasy. Historical accuracy is simply impossible in this play. Artistic licenses must be taken, and since we are all licensed artists, I suggest we choose the route that entertains the most audiences. They are the ones who make our plays possible after all. I say we owe it to them, even if just as a return investment."

The amused players smiled in agreement, but William Sly was not ready to forfeit. *"Et tu, Brute!"* he challenged, taking a step forward. "If you're so timid of Latin, Master Shakespeare, then why use it in your play?"

The bard rolled his eyes. "Because it's *the-a-ter*!" he stressed. "At this very moment, every one of us is competing with every performer, peddler, and prostitute in London for our patrons' last pennies. And that's without bringing churches, public executions, or bear-baiting into the picture. Within this wooden O, you men are magicians and wizards armed with only your mouths! As long as my powers allow it, I will continue to write you only the very best spells."

"O, buzz, buzz!" Sly scoffed. "Why are we even rehearsing this play? It's not billed for performance!"

"That is true," Shakespeare acknowledged. "But at the moment, I am drafting a new play. Since it is a return to ancient Rome, I thought a quick reading of this one would prove helpful."

"Wait. . . . This is for your amusement?"

"No, it's for research."

William Sly's eyes widened. "Are we getting paid for this?"

The bard thought for a minute, and then offered the actor a bag of hazelnuts by his seat. "You're welcome to have some before you go."

An incensed Sly threw his scroll to the floor. "Blessed fig's end! I'm leaving! If anyone needs me, I'll be at the Cardinal's Hat!" The actor shoved his way off the stage.

"Master *Sly*," Shakespeare stressed, "just read the lines."

"Read *these* lines!" Sly shouted, grabbing his loins. The player slammed through the Tiring House and stomped onto Horseshoe Alley toward his favorite brothel in Southwark.

"Such a shame," the playwright sighed to the remaining King's Men. "He would have made a grand Cleopatra."

The players laughed as church bells tolled the hour throughout the city. "Master Shakespeare," his assistant Lawrence Fletcher entered. "You have an appointment this afternoon."

"Hmm? Oh yes." The bard stood up and clapped his hands. "I think we've caused enough trouble today." The actors retired to the Tiring House while Shakespeare turned back to Fletcher. "Whom am I meeting again?"

"John Johnson was his name."

Shakespeare's face twisted. "John Johnson?" he repeated.

"Yes, sir. Do you know him?"

The bard could not help but chuckle. "No, but that's the most made-up-sounding name I ever heard in my life."

Chapter III

The Play

A little less than half an hour's stroll from the Globe Theatre was a popular tavern on the opposite side of the Thames. Located on Cheapside between Bread Street and Friday, there was not a playwright in town who didn't frequent the place. The den was the prized pearl of the fishmongers' guild and served as proud home to the finest intellectual circles in England. Everyone knew everyone there, and no subject was too bold for discussion. The severed heads Shakespeare passed on his way across London Bridge served as stern reminders of this. Many of them lost their lives for schemes they plotted in the same fine establishment. To be counted among those severed heads was a statement as much to good taste as to treason, for never had there been a cavern quite like the great Mermaid Tavern.

Shakespeare smiled as he passed under the siren hanging over its door.

"Good greetings, Master Shakespeare!" called the barkeep, William Johnson.

"All of God's greetings upon you. How goes things, my friend?"

"All is well." Johnson smiled. "What can I get you, Will?"

"There should be a man waiting for me: a John Johnson. Do you know where he is?"

The barkeep's bright grin dimmed and his posture stiffened. "Oh yes. I know that one. He's upstairs. A large man with red hair. You won't miss him."

"Many thanks." Shakespeare nodded as he turned toward the stairs.

"William," called the barkeep.

The bard stopped and turned.

"Before you sit with this man, make sure you count the coins in your purse. I don't want to see you robbed by him."

"Oh?" Shakespeare replied with piqued interest. "What is he, a crossbiter? A drigger?"

"Something like that," the barkeep grumbled. "He'll probably say a lot of sweet things to you with that smart mouth of his, but I'll tell you right now that John Johnson is not his real name. I keep a record on everyone who comes in, and that red angler upstairs owes me money under *two* different names."

"Really?" The bard kicked out a barstool and sat. "And what names would they be?"

The gentleman the two Williams were discussing downstairs was indeed a tall, muscular man with a full head and thick beard of rust-colored hair. He sat alone in a corner beside a large glass window from which he had studied William Shakespeare since he stepped onto Bread Street. With the bard in the tavern, this quiet customer waited with a loaf of bread on his table, a plate of peasecods, a bowl of hazelnuts, oysters, two kippered fishes, and two tall beers he planned to share with England's most famous playwright.

"Master Johnson?" the bard greeted as he approached the table.

"Master Shakespeare!" The patron rose from his seat and the

two shared a strong handshake. "I appreciate you meeting me this afternoon."

"As do I." The bard smirked slyly.

"If I may ask: Do you prefer Will, or William?"

"Oh, what's in a name?" the playwright mused to the man he knew was not John Johnson, but Guido Fawkes. And long before that, before he had disappeared from the rolls at the Mermaid, Guy Fawkes.

"May I sit?"

"Please!" Guy Fawkes replied with a bow. "And help yourself to some eating."

"Thank you. I think I may."

As the two lunched and talked amicably about a wide range of subjects, the bard was impressed by his companion's composure. Fawkes seemed more at ease in this false face he wore than he did as that more serious fellow Shakespeare had caught spying on him from the window. Although William's smile was as sincere as when he stepped into the Mermaid, he assumed that intense glare boring down on him was Guy Fawkes's true self. With that in mind, Shakespeare could not help but admire the man laughing with him over drinks. Fawkes may have been a man of many faces, but he was also a uniquely gifted actor.

But alas, such a masquerade could not last forever. After dancing around the subject for two pints, Shakespeare asked: "So, what is this meeting about, Master Johnson?"

Guy Fawkes smiled and ever so slightly narrowed his eyes. "I am glad you asked, Master Shakespeare. I was sent here as a representative for my employer, Thomas Percy. He is a wealthy man of good standing who wishes to commission a play from you."

"Is he the gentleman who will be paying for this meal?"

"He paid in advance."

"How nice of him!" Shakespeare smiled as he leaned back in his chair. At the very least, this solved the mystery of why William Johnson had let the man through the door. "What type of play does your master want?"

"A tragedy. One set in Scotland."

The bard dropped the fish bone he was picking his teeth with.

"Master Shakespeare?"

"Scotland?" the playwright asked.

"Yes. Is that a problem?"

Shakespeare sat upright. "Not a problem. Just a challenge." The bard had never set a play in Scotland before. "Is this a historical piece?"

"It doesn't have to be. We want you to be creative with this. We want it to be something that shakes the very core of this country. Something revolutionary!"

The playwright was intrigued. "What are your specifics?"

Fawkes glanced around the room and then leaned forward. "My employer wishes to commission a tragedy about the abuse of power. About the misfortune visited upon those who pursue ill aims for ill needs."

"So, this is a political play," the bard clarified.

"Yes. But for the sake of security, you are welcome to take whatever creative liberties you wish."

Shakespeare scratched his short beard and squinted in thought. It sounded as if Fawkes's employer expected their play to attract the ire of government censors. But why? "If this is a political piece, then why set it in Scotland? Why not someplace safer, like a country far away and . . . less close to home?" The playwright shook his head with this last line, knowing that he could do better. He was William Shakespeare, after all. "Master Johnson, why Scotland?"

"Scotland is a mysterious place. It makes an appropriate setting for the darker subjects we hope you will explore in this drama."

The bard smirked incredulously. "Are you sure this has nothing to do with King James or his patronage?" The king's mother was the same Queen Mary who lost her head for plotting against Queen Elizabeth. But of course, "John Johnson" knew that. Everyone knew that.

"Master Shakespeare . . ." Guy Fawkes folded his hands. "My employer is a member of the Honourable Band of Gentlemen Pensioners. He is a dutiful man sworn to protect the king's life and honor, so, perhaps you are mistaken about whatever you insinuated just now. Such misapprehensions could get a man even as respected as you in trouble someday."

A threat?

Yes, a threat!

It was a veiled threat, but one as pointed as a dagger pressed against naked skin. Shakespeare *loved* these types of threats because they allowed him to test whether they carried any weight, or whether they were just bad acting. Since no man alive could spot a bad actor better than William Shakespeare, his mind went to work on Fawkes using the cards the man unconsciously dealt him throughout their talk.

The bard sensed something out of character in Fawkes's delivery. He wore a false name and face, but his confidence appeared to be genuine. Shakespeare understood that much: Guy Fawkes was a good actor, and he knew it. However, he exuded a different poise when he issued his threat. It was not bravado; it had to be confidence in his connections. The bard considered Fawkes's business partner: Thomas Percy, gentleman pensioner to His Majesty. Shakespeare knew it would be difficult for anyone to falsify such credentials and dangerous to attempt to, even if it was over drinks in a tavern. Thomas Percy had to be real, but why would such a person hire a man like Guy Fawkes? And why would Fawkes choose to meet in an establishment where he already owed an outstanding debt? Was it carelessness, or was Fawkes truly so confident in his employer that he no longer feared bartenders . . . or anyone else for that matter?

Since Shakespeare did not wish to find this out the hard way, he surrendered his cards even though he suspected Fawkes had won this round on a bluff. "I apologize, Master Johnson. I'm just curious why it has to be Scotland. The London crowd prefers exotic locations: Venice, Rome, Florence. . . . What makes Scotland so special? And what makes your employer so confident that his investment will be returned, if at all?"

Fawkes shifted his eyes and then produced a folded piece of paper. He slid it across the table with his finger pinning it down. "*This* will be your main draw. It is our only specific request for the play."

"Scotland is pretty specific," the bard parried.

"Not this specific."

The playwright furrowed his brow and looked down to the parchment. As he reached for it, Guy Fawkes seized Shakespeare's wrist. "Be careful who you share that with," the man cautioned with a tightening grip.

William Shakespeare stared straight into Guy Fawkes's eyes.

Beneath the table, both men had their hands on their swords.

Without breaking eye contact, the bard freed himself and took the paper. He unfolded it with one hand and examined it against his chest like a card player.

> *Double, double, toile and trouble;*
> *Fire burne, and Cauldron bubble.*

Shakespeare raised his eyebrows. "Your employer requires a play on the occult?"

"Not necessarily. All he requests is a tragedy set in Scotland covering the subjects we discussed. However you treat the stranger side of pagan history is entirely up to you. All we ask is that a group of witches say these lines at some point in the drama."

"Witches?" Shakespeare repeated.

"Yes. Three of them."

The bard froze. There was only one time in his career that he had accommodated such a strange request, and it nearly cost everyone at the Globe Theatre their lives. Although Shakespeare and his actors managed to escape with their heads, never before had the Crown more closely monitored the bard's every move. Informants combed his audiences, unfriendly faces began to haunt him throughout London, and his license to work free from censors had been revoked. It was a dangerous time to be a playwright in authoritarian England, and the last thing this one needed was to find himself in the same boat as Christopher Marlowe. If Fawkes had been sent to trap Shakespeare, the playwright knew he was already as good as guilty in the government's eyes.

The bard took a deep breath.

"Why does your employer wish to cover such a sensitive subject?" he asked. "Has the king's campaign against witchcraft gone unnoticed?" Such persecutions reached their greatest fervor in Scotland during the prior decade, and the Witchcraft Act of 1604 had been passed by the House of Lords only months ago.*

Still wearing his cheeky grin, Guy Fawkes brought the conversation deeper into dangerous territory. "Master Percy has many backers. It is necessary that he satisfies all their demands on this project."

"And which one of them wants me to write about witches?"

"I am afraid I am not at liberty to speak on their behalf. I only speak for Master Percy."

"And if I were to ask Master Percy in person?" Shakespeare thought it was time to play a bold hand. If he was to get any sleep this evening, he needed to know whether Fawkes's connections to the Crown were genuine or a farce.

Fawkes appeared hesitant for a moment but then nodded. "That could be arranged. But only if you commit to penning our play."

---

*"An Act against Conjuration, Witchcraft and dealing with evil and wicked Spirits 1604," I James 1c.12.

A mixed response. Shakespeare gained nothing from it.

Fawkes was *good*, he realized.

As the playwright mulled over this, "John Johnson" plucked the parchment from his hand and slipped it into a pocket. He then removed a leather purse from his belt and set it on Shakespeare's side of the table. The brown bag clinked of coins.

The bard studied the pouch and then looked back to its owner. "I never said I accepted your commission."

His opponent smiled with a wide grin. "You will. Consider it a mission from God." With those words, Guy Fawkes had completely removed his mask. Shakespeare could now clearly see the man before him, and this one was not bluffing. Fawkes had been holding all the cards all along. The deck was stacked in his favor, and he had just one card left to play.

Fawkes rose from the table while the stunned playwright remained seated. "My master works from a building owned by John Whynniard, the Keeper of the King's Wardrobe. It can be found adjacent to the House of Lords in Westminster. You have one day to comply with our request." He then put his hand on Shakespeare's shoulder, leaned close to his ear, and under the wide brim of his hat, whispered: "Go in peace, brother."

There it was. Guy Fawkes had made his play.

He knew something about William Shakespeare.

And on that note, with that gesture, the mysterious messenger departed.

Shakespeare remained at the table long enough to follow Fawkes from the window as the stranger walked out of the Mermaid and onto Bread Street. His large hat made him easy for Shakespeare to spot, and the tall figure walked with a comfortable gait. Once Fawkes disappeared into the London mob, the bard checked the leather purse left on the table.

The last time Shakespeare had had a conversation like this, he was paid in precisely forty pieces of silver.

Chapter IV

W

Shakespeare stood silently outside the Mermaid while his active mind was pulled in four different directions. About half a mile behind him was the Globe, where the playwright could begin work on his strange new play immediately. To his left was St. Paul's Cathedral, where he knew he could dispel every doubt Guy Fawkes raised by presenting the leather pouch in his palm as an offering. Straight ahead was a road that would take him to his apartment on Silver Street, where he could easily pocket the money and pretend his encounter with Fawkes never happened. And lastly, looming like a mountain over a mile of ramshackle rooftops to his right was the white and arresting Tower of London. The path there was filthy: an open sewer of rotting garbage, dead animals, and bad memories of the bard's last visit. The encounter marked the end of Shakespeare's relationship with Thomas Walsingham, who now not only enjoyed a knighthood but also his late-cousin's famous headquarters on Seething Lane. To go back there would be an act of self-mutilation, a reopening of every wound in the bard's body.

The playwright chose the right path and tossed his bag of silver coins to the first beggar he saw: a young girl on Cheapside who had been staring at him the whole time.

There was a knock on the tall doors of Walsingham's mansion, its portal a gateway to power beyond rival in the British Isles. The beautiful woman who served as its custodian was whispered to be Thomas Walsingham's mistress, but the truth was something much more shocking for the seventeenth century: she was his secretary. She, a woman! Her name was Lady Penelope of the great and noble House of Percy, but because of her silvery-blond hair, those who loved her and whom she loved knew her as "Penny."

She opened the door and just as quickly had the breath sucked out of her. "Will . . ." she whispered.

"Lady Percy." The bard smiled.

It had been more than three years since the two had last seen each other.

As was custom for the time, Shakespeare took the lady by the arm and moved in to kiss her, but Penny was not going to have any of that. She threw her arms around the playwright and passionately attacked his handsome face. "Penny!" He tried to speak, but the sound was smothered against the woman's lips. Only once Penny ran her fingers down Shakespeare's back did the bard manage to free himself from her embrace. The man was flushed, and the woman delighted. "Lady Percy," he repeated, reddened and winded.

"Still so formal." Penny smiled as she artfully blocked the entrance with her body. "Oh, Will, if only you knew how long I've been waiting to find you knocking on my doors."

"I hope the wait hasn't been too painful," the bard teased while straightening his shirt.

"Oh, no. Believe me, Will, you don't know what pain is." Penny stepped aside from the open doorway. "Won't you come in?" The playwright entered and Penny shut the door behind him so suddenly that it bumped into his buttocks and knocked his sword a few inches out of its sheath. "Please wait here while I make sure you two are not disturbed." Shakespeare smiled uneasily while Penny sashayed in her silk gown across the hall into her study.

And so, in the regal foyer of Walsingham Mansion, the bard waited. And waited. And waited, until Penny emerged from her room with a long line of stern-looking men behind her. They marched straight toward the playwright, who out of instinct opened the door beside him. Shakespeare bowed his head like a footman while absorbing angry glares from, one by one, the secretary of state, the lord high chancellor, the master-general of the ordnance, the sheriff of London, a trine of astrologers, and every other government official whose meeting the bard had unexpectedly interrupted. Shakespeare imagined the astrologers were particularly affronted for failing to see this coming. Penny watched from her study with satisfaction as her gentleman caller was subjected to this irate parade of politicians. Once the humiliation was over, Shakespeare shoved the mansion's doors shut and threw his back against them. The playwright was sweating, and the lady secretary was beaming.

"You may come in now." Penny beckoned with a gentle wave of her middle finger.

The bard exhaled and walked into Lady Percy's chambers. The lady sat down at her desk with a quill, and Shakespeare passed through a crimson door into Thomas Walsingham's office.

"Master W," spoke the bard.

"Master Shakespeare," the spy-chief acknowledged from behind his desk.

While Walsingham's attention was absorbed by a parchment in his hand, the standing playwright saw no harm in letting his eyes wander a bit. The ornate office appeared precisely as Shakespeare remembered it: an oaken fortress with armored walls that encased a vast archive of state secrets. Countless reports from cover agents throughout the Continent cluttered the room. Empty wineglasses adorned its tables atop encoded letters and cipher keys. An unusual brass device soon to be known as a telescope stood on a desk to Shakespeare's left. Large maps of the Netherlands and Spain festooned its walls, as did an unfinished, ever-changing map of the New World. A busy cloud of tobacco smoke hung in the air and descended in a silver string to a pipe on W's desk. A framed portrait of the late Sir Francis Walsingham by John de Critz loomed on the wall behind Thomas as an unspoken reminder of his family legacy in espionage. And on the wall to Shakespeare's right, a massive painting of the late spymaster's greatest achievement: the spectacular defeat of the Spanish Armada by English warships in 1588. It was a room with no windows, yet it offered a clear view to an empire. A British empire.

After this long silence, Thomas Walsingham at last lifted his eyes from his document. "You look the same," he observed.

"As do you," the bard replied with a soft smile.

Thomas sized Shakespeare down and up, then up some more. "I see you're still losing your hair."

The bard's smile faded.

"Take a seat," Walsingham ordered, and the playwright obeyed. "So, what's so important that it had to interrupt a private briefing?" The spy-chief set down his parchment and picked up his pipe. To Shakespeare's surprise, the document Walsingham had been poring over appeared to be nothing more than a drawing of a comet.

"Master W—" began the bard.

"Just call me W," Walsingham interrupted. "It will save us some time."

Shakespeare's jaw clenched. "Very well. W, about an hour ago a gentleman solicited me to write a play for Thomas Percy. Do you know him?"

"I'd be out of a job if I didn't," Walsingham scoffed with a snort of smoke. "He hails from one of the finest households in England, and my lady secretary is his distant cousin."

Very distant, Penny mused as she took notes in her adjoining office.

"There are several peculiarities about this commission that trouble me," the bard continued. "The representative employed an alias, John Johnson, but I know his name is Fawkes. Guy Fawkes."

Walsingham did not appear troubled by this information, but he did not appear disinterested either. "Continue," he commanded.

"The gentleman requested a play that I have no doubt would draw your ire. He wants a political play set in Scotland that dabbles in the occult."

Shakespeare expected the spy-chief to jump upon hearing this. Instead, W continued to puff his pipe. "Is that everything?" he asked.

The bard cleared his throat. "Actually, there was one last thing this man mentioned. Something he threatened me with." Shakespeare took a moment to choose his words carefully. "I think he knows about my lineage."

Walsingham's posture shifted. "So, he knows you're Catholic?"

The playwright scowled at the spymaster. "No. I think he harbors misconceptions about my family's religious history that could . . . potentially harm me and my loved ones."

"And your wife?" Walsingham prodded. The man knew all about Shakespeare's Catholic wedding to Anne Hathaway twenty-two years earlier, and how the ceremony had been "expedited" due to the significantly older bride's unexpected pregnancy.*

Shakespeare's eyes narrowed.

"So, you're afraid that someone threatened you, your loved ones, and your wife. Honestly, Will, I'm disappointed you came to me with

---

*"willm Shagspere . . . and Anne hathwey" (Bishop of Worcester's Register, Worcestershire Record Office).

this. It's not your style. You're an actor! Couldn't you at least pretend not to sound so pathetic? You're too old and bald for me to be fighting your battles for you."

The bard leaned forward, ignoring the spymaster's taunts. "W, does not this whole affair sound disturbingly similar to when I was approached by men from the Earl of Essex?"

This time, it was Thomas Walsingham's gray eyes that narrowed.

Three years earlier, Shakespeare's playing company was approached by representatives of Robert Devereux, 2nd Earl of Essex, to stage a one-time-only performance of *Richard II* at the Globe. The actors were offered an extra forty shillings for their labors under one condition: the play had to include a scene previously censored by the English government—a scene henceforth known as "the deposition scene."* Ultimately, Shakespeare let his personal politics cloud his judgment since he was bitter at Thomas Walsingham at the time. The bard believed the scene never should have been censored since his role as a government informant freed him from editorial oversight. As far as Shakespeare was concerned, Thomas betrayed their prior agreement by secretly monitoring his work. The bard agreed to perform the play as requested, uncensored, and without reporting it to "Master W," as was his duty.

The show was staged on February 7, 1601. The next morning, the Earl of Essex and his allies launched an unsuccessful uprising against the ailing Queen Elizabeth.

Although the rebellion was crushed and the guilty parties arrested, the conspirators revealed under torture how they plotted to use *Richard II* and its deposition scene to turn the public against the Crown. Since Shakespeare was Walsingham's chief informant in London's theatrical circles, his decision to stage the play meant the

---

Calendar of State Papers, Domestic Series, of the Reign of Elizabeth, 1598–1601, Preserved in Her Majesty's Public Record Office, ed. Mary Anne Everett Green (London: Longman and Co., 1869), 578.

English government had inadvertently financed and participated in an coup attempt against their own queen. The disaster may have unmasked the Earl of Essex as a traitor, but that did not absolve Shakespeare or his actors from the parts they played in this drama. The bard was immediately stripped of his status as an informant, his stipend was revoked, and for four terrible nights, he and all his actors were taken to the Tower of London for questioning.

Although everyone at the Globe Theatre was cleared of wrongdoing, the bard's error proved fatal for his relationship with Thomas Walsingham. The two had not seen each other since February 24, 1601: the night before the Earl of Essex was beheaded for treason. As a final punishment for their unique role in the coup, Queen Elizabeth ordered Shakespeare and his troupe to perform *Richard II* in a private show for her, in its entirety, including its infamous deposition scene. It was a terrifying experience, a sick charade concocted by shadowy figures like Walsingham and acted out by trembling players convinced they might be killed where they stood. When the accursed exhibit was over, the ailing Elizabeth rose from her royal chair, declared, "I am Richard II. Know ye not that?" and sent the men on their way. As Shakespeare locked eyes with his former friend and master, two of his actors fainted from the ordeal.

That was three years ago. Three years later in this darkened room on Seething Lane, Thomas had the same look on his face as he shook his head at the playwright. "Do you honestly think you can come back here and use a chance encounter as your redemption?"

"I am not seeking a reward," Shakespeare clarified in an angered tone.

"Yes, you are. I know you well enough to know your motives, Will, and whatever brought you here today was most certainly *not* love of country."

"The Globe Theatre is my country," the bard affirmed. "And my fellow actors are my countrymen. I will defend them with my life."

"As passionately as you defend your work?" Walsingham pointed with his pipe. "As passionately as your pride nearly destroyed this whole kingdom, including you, me, and all your precious actors? I doubt it. Much as I doubt your beloved 'countrymen' share the same love for you after your arrogance nearly resulted in their incarceration and execution for high treason. Was that truly noble of you? Was it worth risking their lives without their consent or knowledge just so you could preserve a few extra lines in some silly play?"

The bard was silent.

Walsingham rose from his desk and marched straight up to Shakespeare. "In all my years of service, I've never encountered an enigma as impossible as you are. You possess such remarkable faculties for understanding history's greatest villains, yet you are wholly incompetent at understanding your own allies. What do you think keeps these unruly isles afloat, William? Our king? You know better than most people how easily kings and queens can be deposed. Our faith? As far as I'm concerned, all the gods, new and old, are as dead as King Henry's six wives. Nay, William. The only thing keeping this kingdom together is what goes on in this room: everything my late cousin started and everything men like you and I have continued. You know the types of reports I receive every day." The spy-chief seized a fistful of letters and crumpled them in Shakespeare's face. "Every Catholic kingdom in Europe is plotting this country's demise! You and I are standing at the brink of oblivion in this office. Whether this kingdom lives to see a new century or whether it gets murdered in its sleep could come down to one missing letter, or a mistranslated word, or the unbelievable presumptuousness of one unthinking, unruly, uncontrollable playwright!" Walsingham threw his pages in a fury that blanketed the room. "You nearly destroyed us, William, and all those who would've ruled over our ashes would have heralded our downfall as God's own will!"

The bard kept his chin down but locked his eyes on his former master. "I am aware of my failings, and I like to think I paid for them. But while I admire your 'religious' zeal for your work, I am sorry that that same passion forced us to part ways."

"Who says it has? The door wasn't locked when you reported in today, Master Shakespeare."

The playwright paused and lifted his head with surprise. He squared shoulders with Thomas Walsingham, whose posture exuded nothing but confidence after that last remark. "Is that what this is?"

"Only if you're willing to go once more unto the breach," the spymaster replied, borrowing from one of Shakespeare's plays.

The bard narrowed his eyes but then smiled. As did Penny in the next room.

"Just because we monitor your work," Walsingham continued, "does not mean we are incapable of admiring it."

The playwright's smile dimmed slightly. "And what will it take for you to trust me with my work once more?"

"Only your trust in return."

The bard nodded, and W accepted.

"Very good. Welcome back, master bard."

Shakespeare offered a handshake, but Walsingham had already turned his back and returned to his desk. "The world is right where you left it. Make sure you don't keep any secrets from me this time around. If your suspicions are correct about your new employers, the only way we'll know the full extent of their plans is if you help them on their efforts."

"So, I should accept the commission?"

"More than that. I want you to find out everything there is to know about them: who they are, where they meet, and what their plans are for this play."

"Very well, sir."

"Also . . ." Walsingham began to write a small letter. "Since you've been away for a while, pay Bacon a visit before you go home."

Shakespeare raised his eyebrows. "Master Francis Bacon?"

"None other. Things have changed since you've been gone. Bacon's working at the Ordnance Office now—the Double-O." Walsingham set his quill pen aside and looked up at the playwright. "Go to the Tower of London and hand Bacon this document. Also, see to it that you don't give the man any trouble. You're not a blunt instrument or a petty informant anymore. You're a Double-O operative, so start behaving like one; even if it requires some of that famous 'acting' of yours."

W placed his seal on the letter and handed it to the playwright. Shakespeare accepted the document with a somewhat unexpected and renewed sense of duty. It seemed like another lifetime since he had last seen Walsingham's seal, never mind received it on parchment. The bard admired W's wax crest as the spy-chief looked the newly minted operative over.

"I must confess this business with the Scottish play sounds troubling," the spymaster noted, "but that's why I believe you're the best man to handle it. Don't make me proud, master bard. Make me right."

"I will," Shakespeare promised.

The bard emerged from Walsingham's office to find Penny writing at her desk. "It looks like I'll be seeing more of you," Shakespeare teased.

"*You will,*" she flirted back. "Good luck."

Chapter V

The Double-O

Ashort walk south-southeast from Walsingham's Seething Lane mansion, Shakespeare was assaulted by the sights and smells of the most magnificent yet menacing structure in London. There, jutting out of the city with all the majesty of a massive tombstone, standing strong as rock and white as bone, was the great and terrible Tower of London.

Erected by William the Conqueror atop the ruins of an ancient Roman settlement, the Tower served as stronghold to five centuries of English monarchs and despots. Located on London's easternmost perimeter along the Thames, the sprawling fortress was the city's best defense against an invasion. Its eponymous keep, the White Tower, stretched nearly one hundred feet in each direction and was crowned with four tall turrets atop its four corners. This enormous, boxlike stronghold was reinforced with Caen stone, Kentish ragstone, and local mudstone, and stood in the center of a grassy ward encompassing more than twelve acres of gardens, workshops, and palace buildings. This ward, or ballium, was enclosed by an inner wall fifty feet high and thirteen feet thick with thirteen towers for defense, an outer wall guarded by six more towers and twenty-eight feet thick, a reeking moat that bobbed with centuries of carcasses and human excrement, and a heavily guarded wharf along the Thames riverbank to its south. When viewed in full, the Tower of London was a fortified pentagon that served as the English government's administrative center: a royal palace, mint, menagerie, armory, treasury, prison, and torture chamber in one.

This particular afternoon, William Shakespeare had business with the Tower's Ordnance Office.

Colloquially known as the "Double-O," the Office of Ordnance was tasked by King Henry VIII in 1543 to serve as quartermaster to all the arms and wares in his military. They were the keepers of all the weapons, all the armor, all the gear, and all the gunpowder for the entire English army and navy. Due to the war with Spain and the subsequent surge in military spending, this body was expanded under Elizabeth I into a permanent defense board in 1597. Now empowered with new responsibilities such as research and development, this body remained headquartered at the Tower of London's Ordnance Office. It was this facility, the Double-O, which occupied the enormous complex of armories, workshops, and laboratories honeycombed throughout the Tower's inner ward. A scientific revolution was underway within these walls in 1604, and England's greatest genius was leading it. Francis Bacon, the first scientist in history to receive a knighthood, was now the Double-O's chief researcher, and his arrival was heralded by the clamor of ravens flying throughout the Tower.

Bacon was in his lab examining astronomical data when Shakespeare interrupted him. "Master Bacon," the bard greeted.

The scientist looked up from his parchment to see his least-favorite man in the hemisphere. "You . . ." Sir Francis Bacon gasped from behind his pointy beard. The scientist jumped up from his chair as his piercing eyes bored into the bard. "What are you doing here? This is a laboratory, not a drinking den! Get out of here!"

"He forced his way in," one of the Tower guards escorting Shakespeare explained.

"Then force him out!" Bacon shouted as he filled his arms with documents and threw a sheet over the enormous blackboard behind him. "This is a government facility, not a bawdyhouse! I will not tolerate this presumptuous pimp! He—"

"He has a letter," the guard interrupted. "He's refusing to show it to us."

"My apologies, Master Bacon, but something tells me this message was intended for your eyes only." Shakespeare produced Walsingham's letter from his shirt and offered it with a welcoming hand.

Bacon recognized the seal. "Where did you get that?" he muttered.

Shakespeare smiled at the disbelieving scientist. "From W."

Bacon dropped his papers and snatched the letter with hasty fingers. As he broke W's seal and examined the document, Shakespeare glanced at the chalkboard, which the scientist had only partially covered with a white cloth. One section stuck out to the bard if only because it had been a long time since he had seen anything written in Hebrew.

*כוכב אחד לשבעים שנה עולה ומתעה את הספנים

Shakespeare considered asking if Bacon was studying for his bar mitzvah, but instead the shrewd actor shifted his eyes back to the scientist just as he looked up from Walsingham's letter.

"Do you want this man arrested?" asked a Tower guard.

"Nothing would please me more," Bacon seethed. "Unfortunately, since it appears he is on assignment, I am afraid you will have to leave him with me." The scientist turned to the guards. "Have one of the stable hands ready Aston."

*Babylonian Talmud: Tractate Horayoth, Folio 10a.

"Yes, Master Bacon." The guards bowed and marched out of the laboratory, leaving the scientist and the playwright in peace. Only one of the two great thinkers seemed to find humor in their surprise pairing.

"This is a comedy of errors if there ever was one," the bard chirped, referring to an embarrassing case of mistaken identity involving both men and a young lady during a Christmas masquerade ball.* "Rest assured," the grinning playwright moved in and whispered, "I'm going to keep my mask *off* this time!"

With a steady hand, the unsmiling Sir Francis Bacon rolled up Walsingham's letter and pushed Shakespeare away with it. "This way, please."

"Walsingham said you had a few toys for me to play with," the bard mused as he walked through the lab. Somewhat childishly, he ran his fingers across every tool and trinket that caught his eye.

"This is the Ordnance Office, not a toy store," Bacon scolded as he led Shakespeare into the armory. After walking down a spiral staircase, the bard found himself in a vast corridor lined with innumerable weapons: swords, spears, daggers, axes, pikes, halberds, muskets, and even an eight-shot matchlock revolver. Shakespeare was itching to get his hands on the fine firearm, but instead Bacon picked a freshly forged rapier off the wall. "This will be your primary weapon."

The bard wrinkled his eyebrows in disappointment. "That's all?"

"Yes. Standard issue for all Double-O operatives. You simply—"

"Master Bacon," Shakespeare interrupted, "I know how a sword works."

"No, you don't, master bard. Not this one." Sir Francis Bacon stood up straight and pointed the rapier at a suit of armor. The sword emitted a fantastic explosion that knocked the armor against the

---

*Francis Bacon, letter to Lord Burghley, c. 1598, *The Works of Francis Bacon*, vol. II (London: D. Midwinter, W. Innys, D. Browne, C. Davis, J. and R. Tonson, A. Millar and J. Ward, 1753), 411.

wall, sending the surprised playwright jumping backward. Bacon stood tall and proud as the pierced armor came crashing down, as would have any unfortunate soul wearing it at the time. The inventor pivoted on his leather boots and presented the weapon to Shakespeare. "This is for duels you know you can't win. The rapier's guard contains two pistols, one on either side of its blade. To fire the weapon, you pull on this trigger built into its finger rings no differently than a musket. The sword only holds two shots, so make sure they count."

"And if I need more than two shots?" asked the bard.

"In such a scenario, I suggest you use the pointy end of the weapon." Bacon threw the rapier's leather scabbard in Shakespeare's face. "May we continue?"

Shakespeare slipped his old sword off his belt and replaced it with the rapier while Bacon guided the playwright into a large workshop. Its shelves were piled high with jars of powders, herbs, chemicals, and even the occasional body part suspended in liquid. One eyeball seemed to stare at the bard as if Shakespeare had just called out its name. Away from the shelves, a human cadaver lay on a table while eight men huddled around it, one of them dissecting its arm as part of an anatomy lesson. The playwright noticed a nearby copy of *De humani corporis fabrica* by Andreas Vesalius out, which he recognized by its illustrations. The book was open to page 184, which depicted a man flayed of his skin from every inch of his body, save for the top half of his face.* The figure's head was bent back and to the left as if appealing to the heavens for a quick death. His exposed muscles dangled from his body in some places, dripping like candle wax onto the Paduan foreground where he stood. Although Shakespeare was no stranger to such graphic violence in his plays, his imagination ran wild over this image of such an unfortunate fellow; a poor player per-

---

*Andreas Vesalius, *De corporis humani fabrica libri septem* (Basel: Johannes Oporinus, 1543), 184.

forming his last hour on the world's stage while wearing his own face like a carnival mask.

Bacon interrupted Shakespeare's mental trip by holding something up to his face. "An ordinary deck of playing cards—"

Startled, the bard snapped his head back to the scientist. "Say again?"

Unamused, Bacon stiffened his posture. "*Again*, an ordinary deck of playing cards."

Shakespeare stared at the deck, curious. "Are you expecting me to cut them?"

"If your life or your mission depends on it, yes." Bacon tapped the cards against a table and tore one in half, revealing a fine powder inside it. "These cards are rigid envelopes containing matter that should help you on any assignment. The spades contain poisons, the clubs gunpowder, the hearts healing salts, and the diamonds exotic spices worth more than the deck's weight in gold. Use them wisely. If thrown into a fire, the clubs will cause the deck to explode. It won't be a fatal blast, but it could burn down a building—or at the very least, cause quite the distraction for you."

"That should make for an interesting game of one-and-thirty," Shakespeare joked as he flipped through the deck.

"Your assignments are not 'games,' master bard, and your equipment are not playthings." Bacon then reached into his pocket and presented Shakespeare with an adorable bauble that resembled a small stack of gold coins with a clock face.

The bard had to suppress laughter. "Is it my birthday already?"

Bacon ignored this. "Master bard, what you are looking at is a watch: a portable timekeeping machine small enough to be worn or carried. I believe you are familiar with the story of the late Queen Mary owning a similar device?"

"Yes. It resembled a human skull." The bard smirked as he examined the elegant clock. "A silver skull. A fitting memento mori considering how she died, wouldn't you say?"

"If she possessed a watch like this one, it would have had a fatal impact on her. This ordinary-looking device is actually a powerful explosive. Pull out this winding pin here to activate the weapon's internal fuse. The device is designed to fragment, so make sure you take cover before it detonates."

"How much time will I have before it explodes?"

"About five to ten seconds after you remove the pin."

"No more? No less?" Shakespeare teased.

The inventor rolled his eyes. "Just try not to waste our time by blowing yourself up with it! Many hours went into making that machine."

"Master Bacon, you know I would never waste your time." The happy playwright pocketed the timepiece. "*Tempus fugit*, as the ancients say."

"You're more right than you know," said the scientist as he led Shakespeare deeper into the workshop. "We're in the midst of a technological war right now, and every second you bleed from me is time our enemies will use against us. The Double-O is a foundry where the future is being invented unrestrained by the dogmas of Romanism."

"I see. Just the dogmas of Protestantism," the bard mused as he leafed through a copy of *Daemonologie*, a book supporting King James I's witch hunts in Scotland and authored by the monarch himself.* The book lay atop a copy of German inquisitor Heinrich Kramer's *Malleus Maleficarum*, which argued witchcraft was practiced primarily by women due to their innate moral failings and "childlike" feeblemindedness.† The latter also detailed how to conduct a witch trial right down to whom to torture and how. Respectively, the two books served as the Protestant and Catholic churches' solutions to the growing menace of witchcraft.

---

*James R^X, *Daemonologie, In Forme of a Dialogie, Divided into three Bookes* (Robert Walde-graue, Printer to the Kings Majestie. An. 1597).
†Kramer Institoris Iacobo Sprengero, *Mallevs Maleficarvm in Tres Divisvs Partes*, 1580 ed. (Frankfurt am Main: apud Nicolaum Bassaeum, 1487).

Bacon slammed the books shut on Shakespeare's fingers. "It is neither my mission nor my interest to fear the powers of the occult. I prefer to decipher them."

Shakespeare snickered. "You believe such knowledge is within your power?"

"Knowledge is itself power." Bacon handed Shakespeare a small piece of parchment. "Commit this to memory."

A *B* *C* *D* *E* *F*
Aaaaa aaaab. aaaba. aaabb. aabaa. aabab.

G *H* *I* *K* *L* *M*
aabba aabbb abaaa. abaab. ababa. ababb.

N *O* *P* *Q* *R* *S*
abbaa. abbab. abbba. abbbb. baaaa. baaab.

T *V* *W* *X* *Y* *Z*
baaba. baabb. babaa. babab. babba. babbb.

"Well, it's certainly memorable," appraised the playwright. "However, the ending was a bit obvious."

"What you are looking at is a bi-literal alphabet: a new cipher developed for use by all Double-O operatives.* It's easy to remember thanks to its binary format, so you need not worry about deciphering symbols. This new method allows any user to hide whatever message they like in plain sight using whatever delivery system they choose: letters, poems, music, drawings, and even plays, if you wish it."

---

*Francis Bacon, *The tvvoo bookes of Francis Bacon. Of the proficience and aduancement of learning, diuine and humane. To the King* (London: Thomas Purfoot and Thomas Creede, 1605), reprinted in *The Advancement of Learning* (Oxford: Leon Lichfield, 1640), 266.

"But *of course* it can do that!" The bard spoke with a thick slather of sarcasm.

"Here . . ." Bacon groaned. He handed the playwright W's mysterious letter.

> Bacon
> *Willm Shakspere is back. Please equip him*
> *Accordingly.*
>
> > *In haste*
> > *Mr W.*

The bard looked at Bacon with a face full of confusion. The scientist responded by tapping his finger on the cipher page. Once Shakespeare recognized the pattern embedded within both documents, they fit like a lock and key in his mind.

> Bacon
> *Willm Shakspere is back. Please equip him*
> *Accordingly.*
>
> > *In haste*
> > *Mr W.*

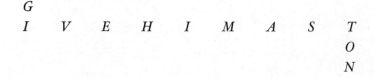

AABBA
  ABAAA BAABB AABAA AABBB ABAAA ABABB
AAAAA BAAAB BAABA
                    ABBAB
                    ABBAA

G
I   V   E   H   I   M   A   S   T
                                        O
                                        N

GIVE HIM ASTON

The bard raised an eyebrow and smiled at the inventor. "That was certainly nice of W." He handed both parchments back to Bacon. "So, what exactly is an Aston?"

"He's more than you'll ever deserve in your life!" sneered the scientist. He then seized a leather book and stormed out of the building.

The bard could not help but feel a little rejected as he followed the great Sir Francis Bacon out of the Double-O.

Chapter VI

[Enter Aston]

D espite the frequent friction between himself and Francis
Bacon, Shakespeare walked out of the Ordnance Office more
satisfied than if he had just won the state lottery. His new rapier,
watch, and playing cards cloaked him in a welcome sense of security, and although they seemed a bit excessive for his new assignment, the playwright was in no rush to give them back. Never before
had the bard seen or even dreamed of owning such fine weapons, and
that was before he set eyes on the even more stunning creation waiting
for him in the Tower stables.

"How's Bentley?" Shakespeare asked as he and Bacon crossed the
Inner Ward.

"He's had his day, I'm afraid. We had to put him out."

"To stud?"

"No, out of his *misery*, master bard. What you see here is all that
remains of the animal you failed to adequately care for."

Shakespeare froze in shock and stared at the leather book in Bacon's hand. "Bentley . . ." the playwright whimpered as he reached out
to his former friend. "How could you, Francis? He was a good horse!"

Bacon ignored the saddened Shakespeare and stood with his codex behind his back. His attention focused on the Tower stables, and for good reason. Once the bard discovered why, he could not look away.

Two squires approached the men with the most magnificent animal the playwright had ever seen. "This is your new horse," Bacon announced. "A Turcoman stallion; cousin to the Arabian. Sixteen hands high. His name is Aston, so make sure you call him that. He's trained not to cooperate under any other name."

"Unbelievable . . ." Shakespeare gasped. He had never seen a horse with such a shimmering coat before. The gray steed shined like Damascus steel, and his lean muscles more closely resembled knots of silver silk. He had a long, slender body, a gunpowder-gray tail, a straight profile with a wide forehead, and two large, soulful eyes as pensive as a monk's. The bard removed a glove and tried to stroke the steed's long neck, but Aston turned his head and snorted angrily. Shakespeare drew his hand back, much to Bacon's satisfaction. "Is he always so friendly?" the spooked playwright inquired.

Bacon continued his briefing: "He's lighter than the Neapolitan Courser, which should work to your advantage. It makes him a more difficult target to shoot or spear. Speed and agility will be your best defenses on Aston. Any armor would sap him of his swiftness, so you won't be given any."

"He's a bit thin, isn't he?" With its long back and high belly, the silver stallion somewhat resembled a massive greyhound.

"To the untrained eye, Aston will appear weak or underfed. It's all a facade. Beneath the mask, this horse is a charger with unrivaled endurance. You could cross an entire desert on him towing gear without him tiring. He's strong, fast, fears neither flames nor thunder, and Master Markham swears that Aston is the most intelligent horse he has ever trained."

"A horse of letters? That's adorable," the playwright teased. "Tell me, how smart is he?"

"Smart enough not to ask so many questions. Please pay attention, master bard." Bacon waved over a squire carrying a large leather saddle. "We have some equipment that should help you if you find yourself in trouble." Bacon opened a leather pouch on the saddle and removed a rough-looking iron ball. "This is a larger version of that timepiece we gave you earlier, only this one is designed to fragment without explosives. What you are looking at is a tightly packed collection of caltrops: small spikes designed to point upright no matter how they fall. Just push on this button to loosen them, and then throw the ball behind you as you gallop. The sphere will break apart and cover the ground with caltrops, destroying the feet or hooves of whatever pursues you."

"Bless my sole," the bard appraised with a smile the scientist did not return. "But wouldn't it be easier if I just lobbed the ball at the rider?"

"Just make sure you throw the weapon *behind* Aston, master bard. Also, the same goes for this. . . ." Bacon reached into a different saddlebag and pulled out a glass sphere filled with amber liquid. "Can you guess what this is?"

Shakespeare shrugged. "A suppository for the horse?"

Bacon narrowed his eyes and shook his head. "This is urine from a mare in heat."

"That was my next guess."

"'Twas not."

"'Twas!"

"Be silent, playwright. This is a weapon to trip your enemies. Shatter the glass orb behind you and any stallions on your tail will quit their chase. The same goes for their riders once they are thrown off their horses."

"That's not reassuring," observed Shakespeare, who was a keen student of military history. "Master Bacon, that trick is as old as the Song of Songs.* How do you know I won't be subjected to the same fate due to an unfriendly wind?"

---

*Song of Solomon 1:9.

"As I explained, master bard: you simply throw the sphere *behind* you."

"Understood, but don't you think some precautions should be taken?"

Bacon's face changed. "What precautions?"

Shakespeare motioned toward the intact stallion's underbelly. "Are you going to geld this beast, or must I do it myself?"

Horrified, Sir Francis Bacon walked straight up to the playwright. "Master Shakespeare . . ." he spat close enough for the bard to taste every syllable, "absolutely *no harm* will befall Aston in your care, do you understand? His line runs straight to the two horses gifted to Richard the Lionheart by Saladin. They saved Richard at Arsuf and stayed with him throughout the holy wars. It took four centuries of patience and husbandry to reincarnate them into the magnificent creature you see here. So, mark my words, master bard, and mark them well for one time in your life: You will return Aston to these stables *alive* and unharmed, and if you even *think* of taking a knife to him, I swear to every god and every faith that I will castrate you myself!"

Bacon then shoved his leather book into Shakespeare's chest with so much violence that it knocked the playwright back a step. "That codex contains all the necessary instructions—"

"Wait. . . . Instructions?"

"Yes, instructions to save his life! If Aston sustains any injuries on your mission, it will be your job to repair him."

"You're mad!" Shakespeare gasped. "I'm a playwright, not a . . . zoo doctor!"

"AS. I. SAID! If Aston is injured, consult that codex! It cost nothing short of your previous horse's life to fill its pages."

Dumbfounded, Shakespeare looked down at the leather tome in his arms and flipped it open . . . to a lifelike drawing of his beloved horse's severed head. The codex was a handwritten, hand-illustrated atlas on equine anatomy: every bone, every muscle, every organ, and every vein that had made up the pained playwright's former companion. "Bentley . . ."

"There's more, master bard. We trained Aston to neither trust nor work with unfamiliar faces. It's the reason he spurned you earlier; it's a safeguard against theft. You have to establish a bond with Aston before he lets you ride him, so starting tonight, you will sleep with him in his stall for the next several months."

"What? *Months?*"

"As long as I deem necessary," Bacon pressed.

"You can't do that! I . . . I have a home!"

"We all do, master bard. It's called the Ordnance Office, so get used to spending more time than you'd like here."

"But this is not what I came here for!"

"You read the letter, master bard. If you plan to take Aston, these are my terms."

"But, I—"

"Master Bacon?"

The scientist, the playwright, and even Aston turned their heads to a squire who unexpectedly entered the discussion. "Shakespeare can't sleep with Aston tonight. I'm sleeping with him."

The bard grinned with triumph while the snubbed scientist turned his back on the squire. "Tomorrow, then," Bacon sneered. "As for now, come with me. There's one last thing we need to do before the dusk."

"What is it this time?" Shakespeare scoffed. "Do I have to clean the Augean stables?"

"You are welcome to clean Aston's stall when you get there. Until then, you and I have business atop the White Tower." Bacon turned his back on the bard and marched toward the castle while the puzzled playwright scratched his head. He looked once more to Aston, but then gazed skyward to the conspiracy of ravens circling the Tower of London.

Chapter VII

Joining the Conspiracy

I t had previously occurred to Shakespeare that London's raven population had increased dramatically within recent years. The more superstitious part of the playwright took this as an ominous sign—another bout of plague, perhaps—but the truth was quite the opposite. These ravens did not arrive to curse Britain, but to save it.

Bacon's footfalls echoed up and down the White Tower's spiral stairs while Shakespeare followed behind him carrying two wooden pails. The reeking buckets were overflowing with an odd assortment of animal parts: chicken livers, beef kidneys, sheep lungs, ox hearts, pig intestines, tongues, eyeballs, and several clumps of dead rats. The bard was unsure what Bacon's plans were after their recent row over Aston, but he had neither the time nor the energy to protest the mad wizard. The blue skies outside the Tower's arrow slits were darkening, and Shakespeare was very much looking forward to fleeing the fortress before someone locked him inside it. Since the only way out of this quandary was up the castle's twisting steps, up, up he climbed to the top of the Tower of London.

"Do you always feed them like this?" the bard put to the scientist.

"No, but this is how we train them."

"Train them for what?"

Bacon paused mid-step. He turned with his lamp raised so that he could clearly see Shakespeare's face. "What I am about to tell you does not leave this castle. It's a secret to everybody."

The amused playwright smiled and acquiesced with a bow. "Please proceed, Master Bacon."

Placated, the man of science continued his climb while speaking over his shoulder. "Several years ago, I began testing the limits of animal intellect in the interest of training birds superior to carrier pigeons.* My research brought me to Aesop's fable about the crow and the pitcher,† and from there to Pliny's writings on the remarkable interactions Romans enjoyed with their ravens.‡ I determined that if ravens could learn names and faces, solve puzzles, and even serve as lookouts in antiquity, we could train them to serve the realm far more effectively than as mere messengers."

"How so?" Shakespeare asked. "Can you make them sing for the king on his birthday?"

Bacon hitched his lamp onto a hook, silhouetting the scientist as he looked down at the playwright. "Imagine powers greater than Saint George commands, master bard. Imagine observing the Scottish Highlands and the Cliffs of Dover in one blink; being able to distinguish all your friends from all your foes in an instant; never failing your allies, and never forgetting your enemies. Imagine all this from a creature with eight thousand claws, two thousand eyes, and one thousand hearts. In all your years, master bard, and with all your proud faculties, tell me: Can you imagine that?"

Shakespeare took a long look at the philosopher eclipsing him

---

*Francis Bacon, *Francisci de Verulamio, Summi Angliae Cancellarii, Instauratio magna* (Londini: Apud Ioannem Billium typographum regium, anno 1620), Lib. II, Aphorismvs XXXV.
†Avianus, *Fables*, 27, "The Crow and the Pitcher."
‡Plinius Secundus, *Historia naturalis* (Venetiis: Johannes de Spira, 1469), book X, chapter 60.

with his shadow. Although he could not see his face, the bard could feel the intensity coursing through the man's veins. "I have a good imagination," the playwright acknowledged, "but imagining is not the same thing as believing."

Behind his silhouette, Sir Francis Bacon was smiling. "That, master bard, is why you *lack* imagination." The shadowy scientist pushed a door open and disappeared onto the White Tower's rooftop. As Shakespeare followed, an unusual noise filled his ears: a deep, sustained cacophony that almost sounded like gasping, or gurgling. No . . . groaning.

The bard froze. His gray eyes widened.

Atop the White Tower, William Shakespeare and Francis Bacon stood ninety feet in the air, offering both men a spectacular view of London and its surroundings. To the bard's left, the River Thames snaked left and right, north and south, past St. Katherine's Docks and Says Court, around the Isle of Dogs, along Greenwich and the Palace of Placentia, and then off into the east. Straight ahead of the bard was the castle's southwestern turret, which bisected his view of Southwark into Barnes Street on the left and the Globe's own Bankside on the right. Connecting Southwark to London proper, Shakespeare could see the full expanse of London Bridge stretching more than eight hundred feet across the Thames with twenty arches and four clusters of tenements squeezed together like bellows. About two miles beyond the bridge, the River Thames bent southward, past the royal Palace of Whitehall and the larger Westminster complex. Guy Fawkes was down there, the bard noted, as he focused on the buildings by Westminster Abbey. To his right, Shakespeare surveyed the setting sun behind the countless spires sticking out of the walled city. More than two hundred thousand Londoners fell under his eyes. Farmlands, windmills, and country homes dotted the pastoral landscape in the distance. It was a spellbinding viewpoint for reexamining the world where he lived.

And then there were the ravens. . . .

One by one, two by two, wave by wave, a vast conspiracy of black ravens descended upon the Tower of London. The bard had never seen so many of the huge birds in his life. They appeared as long as his legs and had wingspans as wide as his arms. The ravens formed a swirling black cloud that completely blanketed the castle's battlements. As they swooped down to perch on the roof top, every one of their onyx eyes and sharp beaks honed in on the bard at its center.

"You have been busy. . . ." Shakespeare remarked to the scientist.

"More than you can imagine." Bacon walked up to the playwright amidst a crescendo of croaks from the birds. "Hold out your hands." The bard set down his buckets and outstretched his fingers as if playing a clavichord. Bacon turned the playwright's palms upward and stacked them high with meat. As Shakespeare's hands became laden with entrails, he could not help but glance nervously at the ravens around him. There was a violence in their voices that the bard found disquieting, but once Bacon stepped away from the playwright, their tones changed completely. Most of the ravens fell silent, some turned their heads, and a few even called out to the birds around them. It was almost as if they were discussing the playwright with a communal curiosity.

"What is this?" Shakespeare asked. "Why have you brought me here?"

"Need I repeat myself, master bard?" asked Bacon as he set down his buckets.

"You never mentioned this part. Whatever part it may be." The bard winced at the carrion in his hands. "What are you trying to do? Feed *me* to them?"

"As I explained, master bard, this is their training." Bacon removed a wooden flute from his belt. "Don't move."

Shakespeare turned his head to the scientist in near-panic. "What are you doing!"

The wizard raised the wooden flute to his mouth. "It's a secret to everybody."

The flute whistled.

The ravens froze.

There was silence and stillness. And then, flapping.

The bard shut his eyes.

The ravens washed over Shakespeare, engulfing the playwright in a frenzied swarm of black feathers. The bard could no longer see London. He could no longer see daylight. He could no longer hear anything other than the whirlwind of screaming ravens surrounding him. The bard peeked through one eye to see the birds tearing the entrails in his hands to ribbons. Some of them perched on his wrists as they ate, weighing them down. Others flew onto his shoulders. One even tugged on his beard as if to make sure it was real. One after another, the ravens studied Shakespeare's face as the bard stared in shock at the blood-covered beaks.

"No matter where you go," said Bacon, stepping into the storm, "you will never be alone. You will always be followed, and you will always be guarded. These ravens will watch over you with all-seeing eyes. All their relations and offspring will be told who you are. Ravens from every corner of Britain will know you by your face; even those who have never seen it themselves. As long as you are friendly to them, these ravens will protect you with their lives. They are your secret weapon. They are your patron saint. They are your guardian angel."

"Remarkable," Shakespeare observed as several ravens broke away, carrying news of the bard's into the horizon. "Just remarkable."

"No, they're not," the mad wizard corrected. "They are nothing. *This* is nothing. This afternoon never happened. Do you understand me?" Bacon filled the playwright's hands with more meat, and the conspiracy engulfed them once more.

Shakespeare nodded. "It's a secret to everybody."

Chapter *VIII*

The Mating Call

It was dark outside when Shakespeare finally reached his apartment; too dark for him to notice the raven following him home or the other, more ravenous bird waiting for him by his window.

The bard's London lodgings in 1604 was a three-story town house on the northeast corner of Silver Street and Muggle. It was a large, spacious building in the affluent neighborhood between Cheapside and Cripplegate within the northwestern edge of London Wall. As with most homes on Silver Street, this one was oak-framed with gray timbers on beige loam—not exactly colorful, but quaint nonetheless. The bard's lords were the Mountjoys, a prosperous Huguenot family whose downstairs business supplied the Globe Theatre with fine wigs and headdresses. Their storefront and workshop filled the ground floor of this building, their apprentices and servants the top floor, and the Mountjoys enjoyed the middle—save for when Madame Mountjoy sneaked to Swan Alley for her affairs with "Mr. Wood." Shakespeare's apartment was a single room on the same floor as the family, which was where the playwright found his landlord anxiously pacing the halls this evening.

"Master Mountjoy?" asked the bard as he crept up the stairs.

Christopher Mountjoy jumped. "Master Shakespeare! Thank heavens you're here!"

"I'm sorry I startled you. Is something wrong?"

"William, there's a man here for you!"

The playwright went rigid. His thoughts immediately returned to Guy Fawkes. "Is it a great man with red hair?"

"No. This one's a small fellow with white hair. Very nice hair! It would make a fine wig." The dimly lit Mountjoy seemed to stare off for a moment, but then remembered: "He says he's from the government."

The bard groaned.

"William, what have you gotten us into! If this has anything to do with my daughter—"

"It has nothing to do with your daughter," assured Shakespeare, who had recently agreed to nudge one of the upstairs apprentices into marrying Mary Mountjoy, for a fee.* "The gentleman is here for a private matter regarding one of my plays. It is of no concern, Master Mountjoy. You can go to sleep. All is well."

"Do you swear it?"

"I swear on Madame Mountjoy's good name," the bard promised, his tongue firmly in cheek.

The naive landlord exhaled. "Whew! What a relief! Have a good night, William."

"I will. . . ." Shakespeare sighed with less confidence. Once the dunce Mountjoy exited the scene, the bard drew his new rapier and rushed into his bedroom. *"Who's in here!"* he whispered with his tempered blade raised.

A white raven was perched on the bard's windowsill. It turned from its view of St. Olave's across the street and stared straight at the playwright. All of Shakespeare's candles were lit, which baffled him since the room had appeared dark from outside. Someone must

*PRO, Court of Requests, Req. 4./1 (11 May 1612).

have lit them only seconds ago, and said someone was seated beside the raven at the bard's writing desk.

Shakespeare took a step forward. "Those candles cost money," he said in a firm tone. "Put them out!"

"I want to see your handsome face," the figure replied in a feminine voice. She stood up and removed her hat, sending long, shining locks of silver hair cascading onto her shoulders.

The bard lowered his rapier. "Penny?"

"You said you would be seeing more of me, Will. Here I am!" She playfully curtsied in her men's clothing, bowing low with her shirt open.

The bard was petrified.

"What? Aren't you going to welcome me with a kiss?" The woman sashayed toward Shakespeare in the candlelit apartment while seductively stroking her white beard.

"Why are you wearing that?" The bard grimaced while sheathing his sword.

"William Shakespeare!" Penny laughed. "Surely an actor like you appreciates a convincing disguise." The woman twirled a finger through her fake beard and removed it with grace. "Deception is a lady's best defense at this hour, especially in a city overrun with wolves like yourself." Penny closed in and slipped her fingers beneath Shakespeare's shirt. As she pressed her body against his, the bard could feel the bulge of her codpiece brush against his inner thigh.

Shakespeare pushed her away. "Don't tease me, Penelope."

"I am not teasing you!" Unable to control herself, she then teased the bard's beard until he smacked both her hands away. The pained woman grinned.

"What are you doing here at this hour?"

"I knew Bacon would keep you late. I just wanted to make sure it wasn't too late." She traced her finger around the smooth head of Shakespeare's steel pommel. "I'm the reason you're not sleeping at the stables tonight. I sent that squire to rescue you from the Tower."

The bard tilted his head. "Really?"

"Of course! You may be a *beast*, Will, but only I get to treat you like one. And whip you like one." The lady coiled herself around the playwright as she spoke.

Shakespeare looked down at the silver-haired siren beckoning him with bedroom eyes. As he bent down to kiss her, she slid her hands down his waist until the bard heard something click.

Penny turned away from Shakespeare and robbed him of his belt—along with all the weapons and inventions Sir Francis Bacon had given him. "A belt this nice you should wear of one hip." She modeled. "And what are these? Playing cards?"

Outraged, the bard stormed up to Penny and spun her around. However, once he seized her, he found her dangling his deadly time-piece by its fatal pin in his face. "Ah, ah, ah!" she chided. "Would you rather spend the next seven minutes in heaven this way?"

"Lady Percy!" Shakespeare gasped as she dropped the bomb into his hands. "Are you trying to kill us? What the devil is the matter with you!"

"No, what's the matter with *you*, Master Shakespeare? Disarmed and deprived of your dignity so easily? And by a mere woman! Oh, how your enemies must cower in fear of you!" she taunted.

"You are a devil-woman!" Shakespeare swore as he ripped his belt off her waist. "A succubus!" The woman smirked with her arms akimbo as the bard's temper cooled. "That was a waste of fine leather," Shakespeare grumbled. He tossed the broken belt onto his bed.

"It may not be a complete waste. The night is young and full of pleasures! I'm sure we can find another way for you to embarrass yourself."

"You made your point, Lady Percy. I will exercise better caution. Now *please* leave. It's been an unusually long day, and I don't know how many months it will be before I sleep in here again."

"Don't worry about Bacon. As long as you visit Aston regularly, I have no doubt you two will be friends."

"Me and Bacon?"

"No, you and Aston. Bacon thinks you're a pimp and a traitor."

Exhausted, the bard collapsed into his chair by his desk. Outside his window, the half-moon was already dipping over the southwestern horizon. He did not need to consult his new timepiece to know that it was late. "I appreciate your concern for my well-being, Penny, but if you don't mind me asking: Why are you here? More specifically, why are you *still* here?"

Penny pulled over a second chair and produced a piece of parchment from her pants. As she crossed and uncrossed her legs, the bard noticed and just as quickly looked away from her codpiece. "I won't lie to you," she began. "My reasons for being here are quite personal."

"How personal?"

"Carnal."

The bard raised his eyebrows.

As Penny was about to speak, a black raven settled on Shakespeare's windowsill, attracting the white raven nearby. The two called to each other, moved closer, and began necking. Penny smiled at the two lovers. "They mate for life. Did you know that?"

"Most people don't have a choice these days." Shakespeare sighed from experience as he poured a cup of wine from a pewter bottle. He offered some to Penny, but she turned it down. However, she did help herself to a quill and some ink from the bard's desk, and in the process filled Shakespeare's face with her rosewater-scented breasts. "So, what's the real reason you've come calling this evening?"

"I need the names of all the men and women you've been with since the Earl of Essex debacle."

The bard squinted his tired eyes. "Been with?"

"Made with, laid with, and died upon. The names of everyone you have slept with."

Shakespeare sat up and stared straight into Penny's unflinching gaze. She was dead serious. "Thomas sent you, didn't he?"

"Why else do you think I'm here, Will? To make the beast with

two backs?" she teased. "W wants to know who you've been consorting with since your discharge and whether you shared any sensitive
information with them."

Insulted and injured, the playwright gulped down his wine.
"Where do you want to cut first?"

"Let's start with Anne. Have you made love to your wife at any
time within the last three years?"

"You know we don't enjoy that kind of marriage," he deadpanned.

"So I've heard," Penny replied with a smirk. "But have you shared
anything with her that she might have spread to some of the merry
wives of Stratford she frequents?"

"No."

Satisfied, Penny took her feather and scratched Anne Shakespeare's name from her parchment. "Viola?"

The playwright's face changed. "How do you know about her?"

Penny tried—and failed—to suppress her smile.

"Of course. Thomas," the bard reasoned. "No, I haven't seen her
in ages."

Another name, gone. "Emilia?" she continued.

"No. At least . . . not anymore." The playwright let out a soft sigh.

"Aw. My poor Will!" Penny moaned while holding her hands
against her chest. "It's all right."

"Continue," the bard growled.

Penny struck a line through Emilia Lanier's name as well. "How
about the Earl of Southampton?"

Surprised, Shakespeare sat up in his chair. "That was all a misunderstanding!"

"Ah!" she delighted. "So, you have *never* been intimate? Not
once?"

"Not physically. He . . ." The playwright struggled under his in-
terrogator's eager eyes. "I regret to say he became infatuated with
me. He confessed his feelings, and I had to reject them. It was embarrassing for us both."

"Well, I cannot blame him." Penny grinned.

The bard rolled his eyes. "Is that your aim for the evening? To reopen old wounds?"

"There's just one more name, love, and then you can do with me as you want."

"Out with it."

"Bianca." Penny looked up from her parchment.

The playwright froze. There was silence.

"Will? Have you been with Bianca?"

The bard clenched his jaw and made a fist with one hand. "You know her, don't you?"

"We're social," Penny acknowledged.

"Then you know what we've been through?"

Penny nodded. The playfulness in her eyes faded, and her smile became forced.

A deep pain swept over Shakespeare's face like a veil. "Then you know I have nothing more to say to you."

"Will, I—" Penny pleaded, reaching forward.

The bard shut his eyes and turned his head. "Please leave me."

Her mission completed, Penny took her things and hurried out the door while the unmoving, unspeaking playwright remained at his desk. Once she was back at the crossing of Silver and Muggle, Penny turned around and looked up at the bard's window. One by one, all the fires she lit for him were extinguished.

Saddened, Penny put her fake beard back on and walked home while her white raven reluctantly returned to her post.

Chapter IX

The Crossing

While Lady Percy spent her morning reconnecting with an old friend, Shakespeare spent his plotting what amounted to a mental war with Guy Fawkes. It was a battle of wits the famed playwright knew he could win, but only if he took the time to appreciate his adversary no differently than any one of his villains. Fawkes was a formidable opponent with a sharp mind and strong build, the bard noted, but he was also someone who started his day just like everyone else: with a trip to the privy. As long as Fawkes continued to go about as if his trips did not stink, the advantage was Shakespeare's—and on this particular morning, it was.

After waking to church bells and changing into some fresh linens, the bard breakfasted with his landlords on cold handfuls of leftover meat pie, white manchet bread, and a pewter goblet of home-brewed beer. Their otherwise chatty tenant might have seemed somewhat quiet this morning, but the veteran actor masked this by smiling at all the right moments. Beneath his facade, the bard was weighing whether or not to seek Fawkes in person or to wait for his challenger to approach him at the Globe. The latter, he decided, granted his opponent too much power. Shakespeare wanted to surprise his adversary. Nay, he wanted to impress him. He wanted to show that he too could be brazen, especially after being bested by Fawkes at the Mermaid. Shakespeare finished his ale with the matter settled in his head: he would cross the River Thames not for Southwark but for Westminster this morning.

Shakespeare bid the Mountjoys good day and stepped onto Silver Street, where he noticed a raven take to the skies over St. Olave's church. The bard smiled. He turned left and was monitored from on high as he entered the busy intersection at St. Alban's church to the east. The raven followed from St. Alban's to St. Michael's to atop the towering Cheapside Cross monument as Shakespeare walked south on Wood Street into the Cheapside bazaar. The bard maneuvered the bustling market overflowing with sights, sounds, smells, wares, horses, hagglers, beggars, thieves, prostitutes, clowns, jugglers, jargon, gossip, and swearing, pausing only to purchase a plum from one of countless women hawking food from baskets. The bard bit into his fruit as he made his way onto Bread Street, where he crossed the same contemplative spot he had found himself on the previous day. He once more walked past the twin-finned siren outside the Mermaid on his right as well as All Hallows church on his left. He then passed Watling Street, Salters' Hall, St. Mildred's, the malodorous Pissing Alley, and the not-quite-so-foul Old Fish Street until he reached the crowded waterfront on Thames Street. His raven observed from the busy skies over Queenhithe harbor before settling beside another raven on a wooden post at Salt Wharf. Here, the waiting ravens watched their target as he passed rows of English warships—some of them veterans from the war with Spain, the bard admired—as he scanned the dockyards for something smaller to cross the Thames with.

"Ho thou!" the playwright hollered to the edge of the pier.

A grizzled waterman looked up from his antediluvian wherry. "Where you going, master?"

"Westminster," the bard replied as he stepped onto the bobbing skiff.

"Eight pence."

Shakespeare laughed. "Eight pence is robbery! I'll give you three-pence and not a penny more." It was the duty of every Englishman to haggle prices. Including watermen.

"Eight pence. The tide is going out."

"And it just might take your customer with it," the playwright cautioned in between the final bites of his juicy plum. "Threepence."

"You want threepence? Go to Blackfriars."

"How about I walk to Blackfriars and meet you there for a half-penny?"

"How about you jump out of my boat and swim to Westminster?"

Parried, the slighted playwright shook his pit at the pilot. "How about I give you threepence and this stone to suck on!"

"Done." The waterman popped the remains of Shakespeare's plum into his mouth and rowed his creaking vessel into the Thames. The bard raised his eyebrow with surprise but otherwise did not protest. He wiped his hands and noticed his raven's replacement already following him from the skies.

And so, moving westward along the Thames, surrounded by swans, ships, and more than two thousand wherries, the bard leaned into his cushioned seat and turned his thoughts back to Guy Fawkes. Within his mind's eye and ear, the pensive playwright improvised how his encounter with the man would unfold: Fawkes would greet Shakespeare, shake his hand, and likely introduce him to Thomas Percy. But then, why should Thomas Percy be there? Fawkes said the two were in a building adjacent to the House of Lords, but for what purpose? Something political? Location suggests this since it would be unusual for Fawkes and Percy to be working there otherwise. It might also explain why the two were requesting a political drama. Perhaps they were planning to sway the public and Parliamentary sentiment against . . . what? Witchcraft? Or perhaps this play was in protest to the new Witchcraft Act. Perhaps their intentions were noble! Nevertheless, witchcraft was still a dangerous subject for any theater to tackle, so Shakespeare would have to keep his eyes open for anything suspicious at Westminster. But again, why Westminster? Even if he inquired about their location, the bard already anticipated their excuse: they were renting the building from John Whynniard, the Keeper of the King's Wardrobe.

But . . . why share this? What business was it to Shakespeare who owned the building? A play is a play. It should not matter to any playwright whom a paying patron rents from. Was Fawkes trying to intimidate the bard with Whynniard's name and title? Possibly. But then, why pressure the playwright so heavily? Fawkes was already threatening Shakespeare with his knowledge about the bard's Catholic past. Why bring up John Whynniard? Was it so Shakespeare would not ask about it later?

No, the bard realized. That line about the Keeper of the King's Wardrobe was rehearsed! It was something Fawkes used to make himself sound grander. It sounded like it carried weight, but it was meaningless. It was all an illusion. Deception. A mask. Guy Fawkes was hiding something, and whatever it was, he was hiding it right under the noses of all the king's men in Parliament. But what could it be? And what did it have to do with this strange play?

Ah yes . . . the play. The bard smiled as his boat dipped south and his thoughts turned to his role in this drama.

Shakespeare knew there would be no rush for him to write Fawkes's play. In truth, he might never even write it if Fawkes was indeed plotting something illegal. But then again, the bard liked a challenge. Surely he could set an interesting story in Scotland. He would have to consult Holinshed's *Chronicles* when he got home, but he had no doubt he could find something worthwhile in the annals of Scottish history. After all, Fawkes was right. Witchcraft would be a good draw. All the bard had to do was accept his commission.

Shakespeare stroked his beard. How would he do it? How should he accept Fawkes's offer?

I accept your offer. The bard gestured. But then he narrowed his eyes. *Also, do not threaten me ever again.*

Threaten you? Ha! The bard imagined Guy Fawkes would laugh. Of course he would deny it. That would make Shakespeare appear weak and timid for suggesting it. *You must be mistaken.*

No. The bard needed to start with something more tantalizing. Something that would pique Fawkes's interest.

I accept your offer, he tested. *Also, I have one request.*

He expected a different response from his opponent this time. *What would that be?*

Shakespeare put his gloved hand on Fawkes's shoulder. *If I can be of any other assistance, brother, please let me know.*

That was it!

Guy Fawkes knew the truth about Shakespeare's family, or at least some of it. It was well known that the bard's native Warwickshire had been a hotbed for Catholics. The Jesuit priest Edmund Campion blanketed the region with Catholic texts before he was hanged, drawn and quartered—texts such as the pamphlet young Will's father, John Shakespeare, had kept hidden in Stratford.* The bard's mother was cousin to the same Edward Arden who was executed for plotting to kill Queen Elizabeth.† The bard was wed to a three-months-pregnant Anne Hathaway at Temple Grafton by John Frith, "an old priest and Unsound in religion"—i.e. a Catholic—to appease both their families.‡ Whatever Fawkes knew, it was enough for him to believe he could threaten Shakespeare with it. Or more specifically, it was something Fawkes would have found threatening himself. Why?

---

*Edmund Campion, *The Contract and Testament of the Soule.*
†*Report of the Deputy Keeper of the Records*, vol. VI, PRO (Ms. 9 and 10).
‡*Minutes and Accounts of the Corporation of Stratford-upon-Avon and Other Records, 1553–1620*, vol. 10, xvii.

Because . . . Guy Fawkes was also Catholic! That was the only explanation for why he knew so much about Shakespeare: the Church had told him. It was why Fawkes disappeared from the Mermaid's logs so many times. It was why he operated under so many names, presently "Guido," a Latin name. A Catholic plot was afoot just outside of Parliament, and as Shakespeare entered Westminster waters, he knew whatever was at work there threatened to destroy everything he had built at the Globe.

If Shakespeare told Walsingham to continue the investigation from there, Guy Fawkes would be killed and whatever loyalists he had hidden would seek revenge. If Shakespeare chose not to meet with Fawkes, there was no telling how far this covert Catholic would go to keep whatever the bard knew about him a secret. Shakespeare could be killed. His actors slain. His wife and daughters murdered at Stratford. *W was right*, the bard realized. By involving the Globe in their plot, Fawkes forced Shakespeare into a position where the only way to expose this conspiracy was to join it. The playwright had to betray England in order to save it.

"We're at Westminster," croaked the waterman.

"Take me to King's Bridge."

"Aye."

The bard crossed himself.

It would take months, Shakespeare realized, but he would see this through to the end. He would not be intimidated. He would not have his actors used as puppets. The Globe was the closest thing to a democracy in authoritarian England, and Shakespeare would not have it turned into a crucible for civil war again. The playwright was prepared to defend it with his life. He would meet Fawkes, he would greet Fawkes, and then he would defeat Fawkes.

Once more, the fate of England would be decided by a play. But this was not *Richard II* and the Essex affair. It was the Catholics this time, trying to succeed where the Earl of Essex failed.

Once more, the world would hinge on what took place at the Globe.

Also, for whatever reasons, this play would involve witches.

"What will you do if Shakespeare does not show?" Thomas Percy asked from his desk.

"Then I will have to pay him a visit where he works," Fawkes replied.

"Will you need me to come?" inquired Jack Wright as he sharpened a dagger.

"Only if I need to visit him where he sleeps."

"Jack, you shouldn't be up here. Go back to your hole."

"Aye, Percy." The swordsman pushed himself up from his barrel and went back to work in the tunnels.

As for Fawkes: "Guido?"

The bearded man turned his head.

"Are you sure we can trust Shakespeare? How do we know he hasn't alerted the government?"

Guy Fawkes smiled. "Because he hasn't! One of the sisters followed him home yesterday. She says we have nothing to worry about."

"Oh? Which sister?"

A knock at the door interrupted the men.

Meanwhile, across the river . . .

"Penny?"

"Sister!"

Outside the office of the most gifted barber-surgeon in Southwark, two friends who had not seen each other in ages shared a loving embrace.

"All of God's blessings upon you!" the elder spoke as they hugged. "It has been too long, Penny. Are you all right, love?"

"All is well." The Secretary smiled to the woman who saved her life as a child. "May I come in?"

"Of course! We have the whole house to ourselves."

"Perfect," appraised Penny, who hoped to make this encounter as painless as possible.

As with most barber-surgeon shops in the city, this one was marked by a wooden pole—an old spear painted red and topped with a brass washing basin. The bowl contained leeches and sat atop a pair of white, and blood-covered bandages. Since the white bandages were often wet, they sometimes stuck to the pole when carried by the wind. The pole served as an advertisement of sorts: an exhibit of familiar tools of the trade. Some even displayed a collection of human teeth suspended from strings to showcase the surgeon's dental skills. Judging from the many molars Penny passed on her way through the door, she could tell that business had been good for her friend. The bloodied floor she found inside served as further confirmation, as did the tools she saw. One of them, an iron forceps, was freshly mottled with red pulp.

"I am sorry we have not spoken in so long," Penny sighed as her friend whisked her into more private quarters.

"Fie, fie! Think nothing of it. You have your work, and I have mine." The lady surgeon smiled with large, caring eyes that contrasted brightly against her raven hair and dark skin. "Please, sit! Can I get you anything?"

"No, thank you," Penny replied with diminished enthusiasm.

"Nothing at all? I have some white wine you will love!"

Penny had no doubt that she would, but instead she said "Perhaps later" knowing that a second chance would not come.

"Well then, tell me everything!" The dark lady sat with the silver-haired secretary at a table containing nothing but a shrunken red rose. "What brings you here, Penny?"

"Business, I'm afraid." Lady Percy removed her gloves and sat upright without smiling.

"Is somebody injured?"

"No," Penny replied. She had no hint of friendship left in her voice.

All the brightness on the dark lady's face faded as if a passing cloud obscured the sun. "You know I don't do your type of work anymore."

"I know you *haven't* worked for the government in a long time," Lady Percy corrected. "Also, both you and I know that the government still very much works for you."

The dark lady's back stiffened and her surgeon's hands clenched into fists. "What's this about, Penelope?"

"It's about business, Bianca."

With half her face masked in shadow, the dark lady's eyes glowed with anger.

Act III

1604~1605

Chapter X

Paradise

When the great Christopher Marlowe met his inconvenient demise, he was carried off to a distant land that might as well have been Heaven. The dining was finer and the weather more sunny, the parties more festive and the wine cost less money! The air was tinged with a whimsy equally mingled with mystery, which electrified the dead poet's heart like a thunderbolt. Some of the most interesting people in history were his neighbors, and those with the best secrets wore them proudly behind decorative masks. Every vice and virtue was Marlowe's for the tasting; every sin and sensation, every pleasure and pain. And books! An entire library overflowing with freshly pressed texts awaited his fingertips like a learned man's harem. If knowledge is paramount, be it carnal knowledge or higher, Marlowe was on top of the world in the floating city of Venice.

Or at least he was until the Carnevale of 1605, for there was trouble in paradise.

From Constantinople to Calais, all ports pointed to Venice—even if the city had lost some of its shimmer by the seventeenth century. The steady stream of trade ships that flooded its markets with treasures also brought plague rats in 1575, which quartered the city's population in two harrowing years. Those who survived this great mortality lacked their ancestors' acumen, for lives of excess dimmed the city's fortune during an already tumultuous era. The Spanish Conquest plundered the New World while Venice stayed bottled up in the Old. The rise of English and Dutch traders surrounded Venetian merchants with fresh new rivals. The Ottoman Empire was in decline and threatened to destabilize the Venetian half of Europe. The Catholic Church hobbled back from the Reformation determined to purge the Venetian Republic of her sinful ways. Venice, La Dominante, the Queen of the Adriatic had dark waters on her horizon, but she was still the most powerful, intellectual, and free-thinking city in Europe when Marlowe crawled into her embrace.

The floating city was the perfect place for men like Marlowe to disappear, and for good reason: beneath all its fortune and splendor, Venice was also a city of ghosts. Spies, exiles, and assassins lurked beneath its shadows, some with no intention of leaving and others with no choice but to stay. Transit occasionally resulted in permanent isolation within the city for reasons ranging from political upheavals to illness to even the occasional romance. No matter what their story or duration of stay, these anonymous exiles were the Venetian walking dead. They were shades, specters, sleepers, the lost souls of countless dead men and women from accross the continents. Marlowe was not their most recent addition, but he was unquestionably one of the happiest.

Being trapped in the most serene city in history tends to make for beautiful friendships. While many of these ghosts hailed from warring kingdoms, they often found themselves too busy enjoying Venice to continue fighting. Many settled their differences over pipe weed and fine wines. Others agreed to work together for their mutual benefit. After all, when so far away from their native lands and with little hope of return, where should their loyalties lie if not to themselves? Besides, information was a valuable commodity in the city, which made murdering a spy a complete waste of money. Any information could be sold to foreign markets at inflated rates. This is why the wisest Venetian exiles pooled what they knew from their former lives to make large fortunes. It was a wholesale information exchange, it was a barter of brains, and it was brilliant. It was what any impartial observer would call a lasting peace among all nations in the most beautiful city in the world.

Yes, Venice was paradise—until trouble finally found the name of Christopher Marlowe, deceased.

Chapter XI

The Dragoman

Several months after Shakespeare rode the River Thames into Westminster, another man with another mission entered Venice's Grand Canal at night.

He was a towering figure, almost a head taller than anyone else in the city, and that was without wearing any of his fantastic hats. On this particular evening, the stranger wore a brilliant white turban with matching silk robes and a fur-lined, gold-embroidered, kermes-red kaftan made of *çatma*: Ottoman silk velvet, the finest and most expensive cloth in the world. His coat alone made him one of the wealthiest men in the city, and he wore it like armor as he sat erect in his gondola with a burning torch in his gloved hand.

His gondolier rowed silently through the vast expanse of the sleeping city. Rats bobbed here and there, but otherwise all appeared to be quiet. It was past midnight, and there were few people to bump into on Venice's Canałasso at this hour. That is, save for one gondola that drifted dangerously close to the men. The vessel carried two young women wearing beautiful masks and laughing merrily. The ladies passed the men and disappeared into the darkness behind them.

Carnevale was fast approaching, the dragoman noted.

The tall man turned away from the laughing ladies and focused on the Rialto. Countless gondolas were tied up in the waters, some with boatmen sleeping inside them like watery cribs. And then there was the bridge; that grand structure connecting Venice's San Polo on the west to the San Marco *sestiere* on the east. Antonio da Ponte's beautiful contribution to the floating city was only thirteen years old at the time. As the dragoman's gondola passed through the marble archway, his glowing torchlight illuminated its immaculate underside. The dragoman lifted his chin and let his eyes run like fingers over the smooth white surface. It had been six months since he had last seen the enchanting creation.

Once the dragoman emerged from the bridge, he directed his gondolier into the narrow *calli* that would take them to the Carampane di Rialto. Venice's famous Ponte delle Tette was there, "The Bridge of Tits," where prostitutes were required by law to expose their breasts to all young men. Although Marlowe was not as young as he used to be and the bridge's legendary ladies were indoors, the dragoman knew the late poet's ghost would be lurking someplace near.

According to tradition as well as government records, dragomans played a unique role in shaping matters between the Ottoman Empire and the Venetian Republic for centuries. Although essentially an interpreter, a seasoned dragoman also used political cunning coupled with a mastery of foreign languages to sway dealings at their own discretion. No one understood the chaotic climate of world affairs better than they did, and through something as simple as a choice of words, dragomans wielded more power than kings or sultans during dialogues. Ambassadors were helpless without their wisdom. The fates of nations could be dictated by their hand gestures, their posture, a raised eyebrow, a pursed lip, or even by a well-timed cough. Every inch of their body was a psychological weapon, which made these strange figures as prized as they were feared and venerated. To be a dragoman was to be counted among the most powerful people deliberately kept off the pages of history, and the tall figure searching the Carampane di Rialto brothels for Christopher Marlowe was unlike any dragoman the world would never know of.

During the twenty-year war between Protestant England and Catholic Spain, Queen Elizabeth found an indispensable friend in the most unlikely of places: a Turkish harem. Safiye Sultan, consort to Sultan Murad III of the Ottoman Empire, was taken by tales of England's Virgin Queen and enjoyed a personal correspondence with her for years. The two swapped gifts and trinkets, but more important, they shared a unique connection: both women found themselves in seats of insurmountable power during a most unlikely century for their gender. Neither the king of Spain nor the pope in Rome could wrest Elizabeth from the English throne, and all the armies and navies of Europe could not drink from the fountains in the sultana's palace by force. The ladies delighted in each other and busily brokered a peace across the fifteen hundred miles separating their mighty empires. It was an alliance that could have tipped the scales of power to England's favor in Europe, and all it required was an English-speaking dragoman to meet these queens at their midpoint: Venice.

Unfortunately, this remarkable union between the British and the Ottomans never came to fruition. Murad III died in 1595 just before Elizabeth's greatest gift could be delivered: a jewel-encrusted clockwork organ, along with an entire convoy of ships. The sultana tried to repair the situation through her son Mehmed III, who was interested, but dark forces quickly descended upon Istanbul. The sultana's dragoman Esperanza Malchi, a woman whom Safiye Sultan had relied on for years, was brutally murdered in 1600. Three years later, Mehmed III mysteriously died on the winter solstice, the darkest day of the year. Cut off from the world and surrounded by enemies, the sultana was forced from power and banished by her son's successor, Ahmed I, who as a final insult destroyed the magnificent clock Elizabeth had gifted his predecessors. Any possibility of an alliance between England and the Ottoman Empire was shattered, and with the Virgin Queen dead, her dragoman had little choice but to join the multitude of undead in Venice.

This dragoman remained a man of great influence and access despite his background being a mystery. The only clue to his true heritage was a single scar on his shaved head, which though invisible to the world was long and painful to its wearer. This was why the tall man wore so many fine hats: he preferred keeping his greatest secret hidden in plain sight no differently than the Venetians with their masks. He was the dragoman who accompanied the English fleet when they delivered the queen's clockwork organ to the Ottomans. He was the man who accepted the sultana's letters from Esperanza Malchi before the woman was murdered. He was one of countless men and women with no true homeland, and among them, he was regarded as a master of exiles.

The dragoman's name was unimportant, although it did translate quite beautifully across tongues. Here in Venice, however, he was simply dragoman. Or, as the late poet liked to call him . . .

"Drago!"

"Cristoforo." The dragoman bowed.

Chapter XII

The Exchange

Within the festive walls of one of the Carampane di Rialto's brothels, the late playwright known everywhere except in Venice as Christopher Marlowe appeared alive and well—endowed. He was sitting upright in a filthy, fluid-stained bed with both his hands behind his head and a tobacco pipe bouncing up and down in his mouth. A slush of white wine and pink vomit was dripping from his chin, mixing into a soup of several other liquids stuck to his chest. Beneath his nipples, a writhing blanket containing several young men and women was still moving after hours of competitive gambling. From the dragoman's perspective, everyone appeared to be winning.

"I see God has already bestowed his blessings upon you," the tall figure said.

The dead poet smiled dreamily with drunken eyes at the dragoman. "My dear friend, *urrt—*" he slurred with a burp, "you have no idea how lucky I feel to be myself right now."

"I understand. Cristo, I have some information that I need to share with you in private."

"Do I have to get up already!" Marlowe protested.

The dragoman looked down at the bumping bodies beneath

Marlowe's blanket. He then gestured with his head that the paramours needed to leave.

"As you wish, love." The poet clapped his hands. "Go to sleep now!" the happy patron sang in Venetian.

The stirring beneath his covers stopped, but only briefly. "I think he wants us to leave," a female voice whispered. "Are you sure?" replied another. "I thought he wants us to go to sleep." "He does, but not here." "What about us?" asked a male voice. "What about you? You're both leaving as well." "Says who?"

The poet looked up at his tall friend and shook his head. "Can you believe these people?" Marlowe puffed his pipe and scratched his messy mane of brown hair as the quarrel continued, and it took nothing short of a well-timed fart for the poet to put the matter to rest. Once the prostitutes escaped with their clients, Marlowe wrapped himself in a bedsheet and threw open a window. "I apologize for the odor," he acknowledged as the dragoman held a scented handkerchief to his nose. "So! How's Constantinople?"

"Istanbul," the dragoman corrected. "We can discuss the situation there in due time. For now, I need the documents you are carrying."

"You said you have information!"

"I do," the figure sounded. "And you would like me to share it, but I will need those papers in order to do so."

The poet furrowed his eyebrows, but then narrowed his eyes and grinned. "Oooh . . ." Marlowe reveled. "I love seeing you work! You could talk the Devil into giving you his pitchfork!"

The dragoman smiled softly, but then reminded: "The documents?"

"Of course." Marlowe hopped into action. The poet took a red lamp from the window and searched the floor until he found a leather satchel filled with books and papers. He emptied the bag onto his bed and rooted through its contents until he pulled out a handful of parchment, which he handed to the dragoman. "Compliments of the Biblioteca Marciana!" the playwright offered with a theatrical bow.

The dragoman examined the pages against Marlowe's red lamplight. They were the original handwritten accounts of Marco Polo's travels into the Orient; the writing Rustichello da Pisa obtained and translated into Old French. These notes in particular covered Polo's encounter with Chinese astrologers at Khanbaliq, the Mongol capital of the Yuan dynasty.

> The astrologers of each separate sect annually examine their respective tables, to ascertain thence the course of the heavenly bodies, and their relative positions for every lunation. From the paths and configurations of the planets in the several signs, they foretell the state of the weather and the peculiar phenomena which are to occur in each month. In one, for instance, there will be thunder and storms; in another earthquakes; in the third violent lightning and rain . . .
>
> Their annual prophecies are written on small squares called takuini, which are sold at a moderate price to all persons anxious to search into futurity. Those whose announcements prove more generally correct are accounted the most perfect masters of their art, and consequently held in the highest honor.*

Unlike the eventual printed work, Marco Polo's original manuscript contained hand-drawn illustrations of Chinese star charts and astronomical equipment.

The dragoman reached into his kaftan and handed Marlowe a leather purse filled with one hundred pounds in Venetian *zecchini*. It was as much as an English merchant made in a year—or an En-

---

*Marco Polo, *Livres des merveilles du monde*, XXXIII.

glish spy. "You have done well. It looks like we'll be enjoying at least one more year in each other's company."

"And a *buon anno* to you!" Marlowe clapped his tall friend on the shoulders and hopped up to kiss him on his cheeks.

The dragoman slipped the pages into a leather folio concealed within his coat. "Were you able to find any of these 'prophecies' Polo mentioned? The *takuini*?"

Marlowe shook his head. "The library doesn't have any of them. I imagine people discarded them at the end of every year."

"That was my assessment as well. I was unable to find any almanacs he described in Istanbul."

"Constantinople," Marlowe corrected.

The dragoman ignored this.

"So! How are all things Ottoman?"

"I do not think this is the best place to discuss that." The dragoman ran his eyes over the room. "If you don't mind my asking, why are you here?"

Marlowe giggled and hiccupped. "One of the men beneath the blanket was the doge's nephew!"

The dragoman raised his eyebrows. "Did you learn anything from him?"

"Yes! I learned that he comes here!" Marlowe picked up an empty wine bottle and shook its last drops down his throat. "What's new in Constantinople?"

The dragoman carefully checked the door behind him and looked behind the paintings on the wall. After finding no peepholes or passages, he closed the room's window and pulled the only clean-looking chair he could find next to Marlowe. "The Ottomans are going to lose the war in Hungary."

The poet squinted while gorging on fruits and cheeses from his bedside. "The Ottomans are in Hungary?"

The dragoman sighed. "The Ottomans have been in Hungary longer than you or I have been in Venice."

Marlowe shrugged and continued stuffing his face with both hands like a baby. With wide eyes, the poet waited for the dragoman to continue his story.

"Several months before Sultan Mehmed's death, he beheaded his grand vizier, Yemişçi Hasan Pasha, and replaced him with a more capable man. That man, Yavuz Ali Pasha, died in Belgrade six months ago."

"You are just learning this?" Marlowe snickered. "I heard that *five* months ago!"

"Yes. I know. From me."

"Ah yes! That was you!" Marlowe spit some seeds onto the floor and wiped his mouth with his bedsheet. "Is that why you went to Constantinople? To make sure that the dead man was still dead?"

The dragoman moved closer to Marlowe. "I spoke with Safiye Sultan."

His stupid-looking friend dropped his act and sobered up instantly. "How is that possible?"

The dragoman would not say. All he could do was continue. "She told me Yavuz Ali Pasha was murdered while planning a sweeping campaign in Belgrade that could have won the war for the Ottomans and severely cripple the Habsburgs."

"Did she do this?"

"No. But she told me she suspects the vizier was killed by a female assassin."

Marlowe's eyes widened. "Women still do that?"

The dragoman drew very close. "Safiye Sultan suspects that her son Mehmed was poisoned by one of his concubines, and that her husband Murad was poisoned by one of his wives as well. The sultana believes these same harem girls were responsible for her dragoman's murder before she could finalize an alliance with England."

Marlowe scratched his chin and found a sticky piece of something on his stubble, which he flicked off. "Why does she suspect that?"

"She was head of the harem. No one knows what transpired within those walls better than she does."

"But . . . has anything like this happened before?"

The dragoman sat back in his chair. "It is possible, but unlikely. One harem girl? Maybe. Perhaps motivated by religion or revenge. But several girls over the course of a decade? And none of them with sons to install as sultan? That is a tale I have never heard told."

"Who were these women?" Marlowe asked. "Could they have been working together?"

"I cannot imagine how such a situation could be possible. These women were slaves purchased from all over Europe. They had neither family nor loyalty connecting one another. No sisterhood. If one concubine approached another to hatch a plot, that girl would have told the sultan to gain his trust and have the plotter killed. There is simply too much for these women to gain in betraying one another. It's a safeguard designed to prevent such conspiracies from happening."

"And yet these women assassinated sultans and viziers? In bed, I imagine." Marlowe grinned.

"Not necessarily. However, if these assassinations were carried out by harem girls over the course of several years, it is without precedent in history."

"Well, either way, I like the sound of these lethal ladies! It's not every day you encounter a woman who could lay a man dead! Well, besides this fine establishment."

The dragoman smirked and folded his hands. "Which brings me to why I am sharing this with you. Cristo, do you think such women might already be in this city? If what Safiye Sultan tells me is true, then these female assassins operate all the way to Belgrade. A lot of money could be made if we exposed who they are to their next targets."

Marlowe made a silly face. "What makes you think there will be 'next' targets? Let alone rich ones we could find."

The dark figure stared straight into Marlowe's eyes. "My friend, whoever wanted the Ottomans to lose the long war in Hungary were likely the same people who sabotaged the alliance between England and Turkey. If they are all taking orders from whom I imagine they must be, then I will need your help to find these assassins. Here. In *La Serenìsima*."

Marlowe stared blankly at his serious friend. "Well, you do have a knack for being right all the time. Sure! I can help. The only problem is, Drago, I have no idea where to start looking! There are too many whores in this city. Care to sleep on it, my handsome friend?" Marlowe drunkenly beckoned the dragoman to his bed.

The great man looked his filthy friend down and up. "Have you been exercising?"

Marlowe laughed. "For what! I'm little more than an illegal librarian these days!"

"You need to start exercising. For your own safety."

The bashful poet looked away. "Drago, you know I don't do that kind of work anymore. I thought you just wanted me to poke around in some brothels."

The dragoman once more leaned close to his friend. "If you are to help me with this, I need you to be fit. You're the only person in the city I can trust with this mission. I cannot afford to lose you."

"Awww!" Marlowe moved in to kiss the dragoman—or at least try—but was distracted by a wine bottle at the foot of his bed. "I love when you talk to me like that. Tell me again why you trust me so much!" Marlowe reached for the bottle, but the dragoman seized it and placed it under his chair. The poet groaned.

"I trust you because if the Ottomans have been twice bested by carefully timed and planned murders, then it means your government had nothing to do with them."

"*My* government!" Marlowe laughed. "Believe me, those wretched isles no longer bother my buttocks. The Protestants are hypocritical asses, and the Catholics just as rear-ended."

"The English Crown had more to lose from these assassinations than any other kingdom in Europe. Circumstances lead me to believe that the Vatican orchestrated the murders. They have the most to gain from unrest in the East."

Marlowe's ears pricked up at 'Vatican.' "You're not hinting at what I think you are, are you?"

The dragoman locked his brown eyes with Marlowe's and nodded.

The poet rubbed his hands together. "So, you think the Church is using their nuns to harvest men's souls again!"

"No one would know this better than you, my experienced friend."

"I disagree!" Marlowe grinned. "I may have caught one of their birds in the act, but she slew a friend of mine deader than I'll ever be!"

The dragoman smiled. "What was her name again?"

Marlowe's eyes were awash with happiness. "My old friend and I used to call her the Dark Lady."

Chapter XIII

The Dark Lady

Many years ago, before the storm that shattered the Spanish fleet, a young woman was pulled into a grand conspiracy at a time of gods, wars, and rogues. It was a thrilling tale of intrigue and of global consequence. It was a lesson on survival, true love, and betrayal. It was one of history's greatest mysteries. It was the adventure of a lifetime, her lifetime. And it was all born of a young woman's desire to read.

Her name was Bianca.

White, shining, pure. Perfect.

Bianca.

Like the chiming of church bells in the notes of B, A, and C: *Bi-an-ca, Bi-an-ca, Bi. An. Ca.*

Just to be clear, her name was Bianca even though her olive skin was quite dark.

Bianca was born in southern Italy to a family of converted Jews around the time that Shakespeare and Marlowe were speaking their first words. Bianca's parents were poor and suffered prejudice in the Spanish-ruled Kingdom of Naples, but their daughter was rich in resourcefulness and determination. She possessed height, strength, and guile that would serve her well in life, but more than anything, Bianca wanted to learn how to read. Since her parents had no money for books or tutors, she was allowed to leave home with what little they saved for her marriage and joined the first convent she found. To be a nun was a life of prayer and poverty, but it offered Bianca precisely what she was looking for: an education.

The dark lady learned to read and write in many languages, which earned her the esteem of her order. When coupled with her natural beauty and tenacity, she became too valuable for the Spanish to keep locked up during wartime. Her kingdom, just like England, needed spies to fight and die for their faith, and as a converted Jew, she was perfect—i.e. expendable. As expendable as a Catholic schoolboy in Protestant England? Yes, although Thomas Walsingham had never told this to young Kit Marlowe.

Bianca was transferred to Rome and was given an extraordinary assignment. According to the Holy See, it was her duty as a bride of Christ to protect the Church by catching and unmasking English spies throughout the city. She was allowed to use any methods necessary to accomplish this task, including the dark art of seduction. Bianca was tempted by this, but not so she could assume the role of Salome or Delilah. Instead, she took advantage of this opportunity to study alchemy, anatomy, archery, and poisons to become a far more efficient killer. The dark lady was good at what she did. Very good. That is, until a certain Jesuit from Florence turned out to be much, much better.

Young Marlowe proved a challenge for Bianca the moment he showed up in Rome. Although she was supposed to treat all new faces with suspicion, this "Cristoforo" she encountered appeared all too convincing. He looked Italian, spoke Italian, Greek, and Latin with fluency, and he presented himself as devoted to his fraternal order. The young Jesuit gave an impassioned defense when one critic questioned his faith in a display that left listeners and onlookers applauding. The young priest seemed destined for greatness;

sainthood, even. And the language he used, the words . . . Bianca had never seen such declarations in person; she had only read about them. However, she soon realized that something was off about this "Cristoforo": Jesuits had to forswear ambitions for higher ranks within the Church.* This one carried himself like a future cardinal. In reality, the masked Marlowe was unabashedly auditioning to be the next pope.

Bianca's suspicions were eventually confirmed in the Vatican, which she routinely visited disguised as a priest. Within the Cortile del Belvedere courtyard of the Vatican Palace, the tall, bearded Bianca spied her target in conversation with other Jesuits in front of the great Laocoön statue. The young priest said one line in particular that resonated with his eavesdropper: how Helen of Troy possessed "the face that launched a thousand ships" and brought Laocoön, his sons, and all Ilium to their doom. Bianca had heard Marlowe use those same words to a cardinal days earlier while admiring the *Venus Felix* at the Cortile delle Statue. At that moment, the incognito lady realized why this mysterious Jesuit was so well spoken: he was reading lines. Everything he said and did was a performance, an act designed to distract and dazzle. And as far as actors went, this wolf in priest's clothes was greater than any she had ever encountered.

Had he heard these thoughts, the great Christopher Marlowe would have agreed.

Now that Bianca had identified her opponent, the dark lady went to work on him with her deadly art. She started by staring at the Jesuit with looks that would have pierced any man's holy armor. He never noticed. She then crossed paths with Marlowe and dropped a scented handkerchief for him to find. He walked around it. Frustrated, Bianca chose a more aggressive means of disposal than she preferred: she cornered "Cristoforo" alone in the Vatican Library

*Constitutions S.J., Part X, N°6 [817].

with an illuminated copy of Boccaccio's *Decameron*. She looked her adversary in the eyes and demanded that they read the tale of Masetto da Lamporecchio and his lusty nuns. Amused, Marlowe took the book, glanced this way and that way to make sure they were alone, and agreed—but only if they retreated to his apartment. The dark lady grinned, and was then rudely knocked over the head by the heavy tome. After looking around one final time, Marlowe dragged the dark lady behind a bookshelf and into one of the many passageways hidden throughout the Vatican. After being carried across the Passetto di Borgo—Marlowe killed the guards there without difficulty—Bianca woke up bound by her own rosary in a prison cell at the Castel Sant'Angelo. Her captor, who found a stiletto blade hidden in her habit, pressed the dagger against her breast and threatened to do "what Menelaus could not do to Helen" unless Bianca quit acting and started singing.

Understandably, the dark lady was outraged. She had never been bested by anyone, never mind a man as impudent and patronizing as Marlowe. Furious over her failure, she chose death and spat in the Englishman's face. She then threw herself onto her own dagger, but Marlowe pulled it back in time to deny her suicide. Aside from the incident with Boccaccio, Marlowe had no desire to see the dark lady harmed. "If I wanted you dead," the unmasked spy explained, "I would have strangled you at the basilica and thrown your body into the tomb of some unimportant pope." It would have been centuries before someone discovered her body. Instead, Marlowe wanted to barter for Bianca's life. She resisted and shouted for help, but her brash captor explained "everyone in Rome is used to hearing screams from the Castel." He then opened a leather bag and offered the dark lady some wine. She refused, so Marlowe made himself comfortable on the dungeon floor and began negotiations. He did not care if it took all night; Marlowe was determined to have the dark lady leave with him for England instead of becoming a permanent resident in the Castel. Bianca refused to speak. Fortunately,

Christopher Marlowe *loved* to talk. And so, for the dark lady, the torture began.

After spending the next few hours regaling her with his life's story, the rogue got down to business and explained that he had already finished his undercover work in Italy. A boat along the Tiber was waiting to carry him out of Rome and off to sea at any moment. Marlowe was just biding his time for research and for love of art since he figured he would never be coming back to the city. He then emptied his bag and showed Bianca everything he had on him: purloined letters, state documents, cipher keys—both his own and stolen—a list of English double agents, some souvenirs, and even a list of friendly spies in Italy. Several of the names, Marlowe mentioned, that belonged to men the dark lady murdered. It was more information than Bianca could be kept alive with. "You do not know it yet," he taunted, "but I have already killed you." If he left the dark lady with just one of these documents in her cell, she would be executed for treason—that is, assuming someone found her before she starved to death.

Marlowe promised Bianca anything she wanted if she would join the English: wealth, land, a new life, anything she desired or believed she deserved. "Even love! Does that interest you?" The dark lady turned away, and the poet smiled. After several more hours of negotiating and . . . well, lots of wine, an increasingly drunk and desperate Marlowe came back to his personal items, which he presented to his captive as if holy relics. After failing to entice the dark lady with his unwashed linens, Marlowe finally got a word out of her when he offered her a stack of poetry.

"Poetry?" she asked with an equal hint of sarcasm, exhaustion, and—if Marlowe heard correctly—*curiosity*? The spy's eyes brightened. He scooted over and read the poems aloud, first in English and then translated into Italian. Once he was out of pages, Marlowe asked Bianca if she enjoyed the writing. She did not answer. He then asked: "Would you like them more knowing that I had no hand in them? They're from a friend of mine back in England."

At long last, the dark lady turned her head.

"He's a bright lad!" Marlowe touted. An "upstart crow" in London who had sent Marlowe letters once he learned of his plays. Not unlike Dante and Cavalcanti, whom Marlowe correctly guessed Bianca was familiar with, the two poets enjoyed a friendly exchange, swapping sonnets in exchange for each other's feedback. Quite a few of these poems detailed his friend's wish for a happy marriage. "If you come to England with me, I can offer you this man. You may meet him, you may appraise him, and if you desire, you may have him." Marlowe asked the dark lady to think this over while it was still dark enough for them to escape. He folded his arms and leaned back to nap.

However, as Marlowe rested, Bianca reread the poems. She then kicked her captor awake. "I choose to live," she decided. Marlowe lifted the young woman onto her feet, cut her free from her rosary, and led her out of the Castel by torchlight. Once at sea, the former nun and false priest left Rome with the sunrise behind them.

And so the dark lady came to England. She met the legendary Sir Francis Walsingham, to whom she told everything that could be useful to the English spy network. She shared what Vatican ciphers she knew with Thomas Phelippes, Sir Francis's chief cryptographer. She outlined every method used by Spanish spies and assassins, including where they operated and what they earned so that they could be bought or disposed of. And, perhaps most important, Bianca was able to make sense of the conflicting reports Walsingham had on the movement of the Spanish Armada. She looked over the letters Marlowe brought from Walsingham's chief informant in Florence, Pompeo Pellegrini, and filled in their holes with what she knew: that the Spanish were not planning to invade England until 1588. It was the greatest breakthrough in English intelligence throughout the war, and Bianca's insight provided Walsingham with the fore-knowledge he needed to adequately prepare England's defenses. The dark lady was rewarded with a pension, her own building in Southwark, and even the identity of a man so that she could legally own her property. It was more than any English spy ever received for their services, including Marlowe, who seemed satisfied with his prize: a license to write and perform his plays free from censorship. "This license," he bragged to Bianca, "will be what kills me!" He was right.

For the moment, all seemed well. For the moment, Bianca was happy.

But for only a moment.

No matter what her compulsion within the Castel, Bianca became genuinely interested in the poet Marlowe spoke so highly about throughout their two-thousand-mile trip back to England—when he was not talking about himself. The mysterious bard behind those sonnets that ultimately saved her life was already in London when she and Marlowe arrived. With Marlowe as her matchmaker, the dark lady got to meet the young crow in person. She found him seated by himself, writing in the Mermaid Tavern on Cheapside. Once the bard and dark lady locked eyes, what happened next was the stuff of sonnets: poetry that Bianca coauthored.

Within her lover's embrace, Bianca was happier than she ever dreamed possible. That is, until she learned that this "upstart crow" longed for a loving marriage because he was trapped in an unhappy one, and with children. Marlowe had deliberately hidden this from the dark lady with his silver-tongued logic since he was so desperate to bring her to England as a war spoil that would win him artistic freedom. It was a trick made more painful by how Bianca learned this: from the bard. Although he knew nothing about Marlowe's grand schemes, the playwright left out certain details about his life when he and the dark lady met. Once he told her the truth, it was too late for his past actions to amount to anything other than betrayal.

The dark lady was trapped in England, and her new home became her prison. The Walsinghams would never let her leave London after what she had learned of their spy network. Bianca had become a traitor to her homeland and to her Church, and as a Catholic captive in England, could never return to either. She never saw her parents again or learned of their fates. She could never thank them for the life they gave her or apologize for how she squandered it. Instead of the pastoral fields of Italy, she was condemned to the stinking, plague-filled squalor of London.

And worst of all, during all these tormenting years trapped in England, Bianca was smothered in the growing fame of her primary offenders. She saw Marlowe conquer London with the same theatrics that won him the Vatican. She lived through his successes, his excesses, and, after his "death," his eclipse. She watched Marlowe's partner outshine his predecessor and just as quickly rule the Globe. All of London knew his name. Everyone who she worked with admired his plays. His renown was enough for the Earl of Essex to recruit him for rebellion, for Guy Fawkes to attempt the same, and for Thomas Walsingham, England's nearest spymaster, to make sure that the bard completed his task.

Yes, even if it meant sending his secretary to reopen every wound in Bianca's heart by giving her a secret mission involving the man who had wronged her so many years ago. The bard who, wrought with guilt, filled page after page of poetry in memory of the love they lost. The playwright who named more than one character in his plays after her. The man whom Bianca was staring at right now.

She, the Dark Lady, disguised as a man in black, seated by herself in the darkened corner of a Westminster tavern. Her eyes and ears were focused on William Shakespeare, a man she had not seen for fifteen years.

Understandably, she was not smiling.

Chapter XIV

Reunion at the Duck and Drake

W ithin the Duck and Drake Inn on the Strand, between Covent Garden and where the Thames bends into West-minster, five friends who had not seen one another in many months were reunited where it all began. It was a cold February evening and fresh snowflakes filled the windows, but the cozy inn had a fire going and, quite appropriately, a large pot of duck soup cooking—even though the soup contained no duck at all.

As one surreptitious figure monitored the scene from her dark corner, the boisterous group that met at this same spot on May 20 the previous year exchanged their blessings.

"Guido!"

"Robert . . ."

The man who Shakespeare now knew well enough to no longer call "John Johnson" threw his arms around Robert Catesby, the leader of the gang and its current master of ceremonies. He was a tall, gentlemanly-looking fellow in his early thirties, just like Fawkes, only with longer hair and a more pointed beard. Both Robert and Fawkes were dressed alike in thick cloaks and large hats, except Catesby wore a shiny metal breastplate over his doublet. Due to the nature of their meeting, the bard surmised, Robert had deemed it necessary to travel in armor.

"All God's blessings upon you, Guido." Guy Fawkes then shook hands with Tom Wintour. He was Robert's financial expert, a well-connected lawyer, and cousin to the dashing swordfighter rising from his seat.

"Jack," Tom added. "You're looking sharp this evening."

"As are you, brother." Jack Wright, one of the best swordsmen in England and Guy Fawkes's former schoolmate, threw an arm around his cousin while keeping a tight fist on his rapier.

"Master Percy." Robert bowed. "You have my deepest thanks for these arrangements."

"Appreciated," a seated Thomas Percy replied with a modest nod. He was a more serious man than Catesby, prematurely gray and afflicted with a hideous skin condition that made physical contact painful and most clothing uncomfortable for him to wear. He was an angry, unpredictable man quick to quarrel and criticize, but the bard nevertheless found something eye-catching about him: despite his distance from the fireplace, Thomas Percy's doublet was already soaked through with sweat. However, Shakespeare knew this was on account of the man's malady and not the matter of the hour. Beneath his unpleasant exterior, the sweaty Thomas Percy was dangerously fearless.

With all blessings exchanged, Robert Catesby turned to the gentleman who everyone braved cold and curfew to meet. "And *this* must be our playwright!"

The bard bowed his head.

"Master Catesby . . ." Guy Fawkes announced, "I give you William Shakespeare!"

"Will," the playwright offered.

Robert shook the bard's gloved hand tightly and pulled him closer. "*Will,*" he purred. "It is a pleasure to meet you in person!"

"The pleasure is mine as well."

Robert grinned wide with triumph. "I understand you have something you'd like to share with us this evening?"

"I do, sir."

"In due time," Fawkes interrupted. "Make yourselves warm! Enjoy yourselves some food and beer!"

As the six sat at their table and made their merry over double beer and tavern fare, their dark observer disappeared from their periphery and left the inn without anyone noticing. Not even Shakespeare.

"You know, my father was friends with your father," Robert Catesby waxed with nostalgic eyes.

"A good friend," Shakespeare confirmed. "I also know that your father shared some writing with him."

Robert's eyes sparkled. "Did he?"

"Indeed. It was Cardinal Borromeo's *Contract and Testament of the Soule.*"

Guy Fawkes narrowed his eyes with satisfaction as the conversation treaded into forbidden waters.

"Ah yes!" Robert chuckled. "The Borromeo testament. I remember my father reading that booklet to me."

"As do I. My father transcribed your father's copy." The dramatist spoke in a caring, almost gracious tone. "I was just a boy at the time, but I was old enough to know the risk involved." Shakespeare paused to let the sentiment sink in with the other men at the table. "Robert, your father made my father the hero he was to my family."

Robert leaned forward in his chair, flush with confidence. "Do you . . . still have your father's copy of the testament?"

Shakespeare considered sharing that the pages were at his home in Stratford, a lie, but he just as quickly realized that it would be best to keep his loved ones and his wife out of the discussion. Instead, the bard looked straight at Robert and affirmed: "It's somewhere safe."

Robert smiled and nodded. Tom Wintour scratched his beard.

Guy Fawkes was grinning, Percy silent, and Jack Wright slouched deeper into his old wooden chair. Although these last three men had already heard Shakespeare share this story, it was nevertheless bold of the bard to broach it once more. His words were tantamount to a confession that he, just like everyone at the table, was a covert Catholic living in Protestant England. And thus, a criminal.

"Edmund Campion gave his life to spread Borromeo's word throughout the country," Robert told the assembled. "He died a traitor, but not to God. Not to the church. He was a saint who martyred himself for our souls."

"To Campion," Fawkes toasted, raising his beer.

"And . . . the rest," Jack added, raising his.

"Amen." The men bowed their heads and drank. However, Percy refused to take his eyes off the playwright.

"So, how much has Guido told you of our plans?" Robert Catesby put to Shakespeare.

"He's not a dullard," Percy interrupted. "The playwright knows his job is to write our play."

"Ah yes. The Scottish play!" Robert's eyes shifted from Thomas back to the bard. "Is it finished?"

"Not yet," Shakespeare acknowledged. In truth, he had not even started it. "But I promise you it will be the greatest work I have ever written."

Robert beamed with delight. "Wonderful! What can you tell us about it? Does it have a title yet?"

"Well . . ." the bard fumbled.

"Is there a swordfight in it?" asked Jack while surreptitiously admiring the playwright's rapier.

"Yes, there are several swordfights in it," Shakespeare answered. He then dropped his coat over his specially modified weapon.

"Several swordfights!" Guy Fawkes gasped. "You never shared that much with me."

"Yes, he never tells us anything," Percy grumbled. "Master Shakespeare, when do you think we will actually see this play?"

"When it is performed, of course." The bard replied somewhat curtly.

"You've had more than six months to write it," Percy prodded, "and so far, we have not seen a single page for our investment."

"Tom," Robert scoffed, "there is no reason for you—"

The bard raised his hand. "Master Catesby, please. Master Percy . . ." Shakespeare turned his chair to face the sweaty skeptic. "As you know, I had been working with a February deadline. Also as you know, all the theaters in the city are closed due to the plague. The Revels Office, which reviews my plays, is closed. The Globe Theatre, *my* theater, is closed. I am unable to meet with my actors and read through what I have written, never mind acquire the necessary props, costumes, and decorations for us to stage the drama. And even if we somehow performed it, the entire city would be barred from seeing it." Shakespeare's tone was polite but affirmative. He needed everyone at the table to take him seriously, even though he was actually improvising. "I have been writing this play with all my energies and improving it with each passing day, but I am not a Johannes factotum—a 'Johnny Do-It-All.' Until this plague passes, we must all be patient and maintain our senses."

"Hear, hear!" Robert cheered, raising his cup while motioning Fawkes and Wintour to do the same. "This is why we hired you, Will! We knew you would be professional."

The bard bowed his head. "My many thanks, Master Catesby." The situation appeared to be diffused.

However, the more combative side of Thomas Percy was unconvinced. "Those were some mightily perfumed words, Master Shakespeare. But how do we know you will have this play we paid for ready when we need it?"

"Well, when do you need it?" the playwright countered.

"As soon as possible." A drop of sweat flew off Percy's upper lip and landed on Shakespeare's gloves.

"'As soon as possible' is not a date on the calendar," the bard chided, noticeably shaking the droplet from his leather.

"Will, how much more time do you need?" Robert inquired.

Shakespeare thought on this, but mainly just to look like he was thinking. "Master Catesby, due to the issues raised by the plague, I think it would be more helpful if I knew what date you desire to see the play premiere."

Robert turned to Fawkes. "When is Parliament scheduled to reconvene?"

"The third of October."

Dismayed but optimistic, Robert Catesby looked back at Shakespeare. "I trust that will give you plenty of time to finish your writing, rehearse the drama, and stage it? Preferably . . . on the day before Parliament reassembles?"

"Without a doubt," the bard promised. "Until then, if I can be of any other assistance, brother, please let me know."

The men at the table exchanged glances. Robert and Fawkes were smiling while Thomas Percy remained incredulous. Tom Wintour looked like he had no opinion, and Jack Wright was picking his fingernails with a table knife. "For the time being," Robert appraised, "the best thing you can do for us is focus on the play. Make it the greatest drama this city has ever seen! Make it something special, Master Shakespeare."

"I will," Shakespeare promised with a faux smile. Beneath the mask, the bard was disappointed. He had hoped to learn so much more from this encounter. However, beyond the play and Shakespeare's father, Robert Catesby remained wisely silent. The bard looked at Fawkes, but he only simpered with satisfaction. Wintour was useless. Jack Wright was beginning to get under the playwright's skin. And as for the man with the blotchy, unhealthy flesh, Shakespeare did not even bother looking back at Thomas Percy. The man had sweat dripping off his nose and onto his food. The bard knew Percy did not trust him, and it was beginning to obstruct his mission.

There were still so many questions Walsingham needed answered without Shakespeare asking: Who else were these men working with? Did they have allies abroad? Was Spain, France, and/or Rome somehow supporting their efforts? Why were these men determined to have the play premiere when Parliament opened even if it meant delaying their plans for nearly a year? A revolution could be launched at any time. Why wait? Why Parliament? And again, why witches? The bard had nothing but his own uncertainties to work with, and it was beginning to look like his welcome at the Duck and Drake was expiring. If he was to learn anything more about these men and their motives, he had to ask them. And fast.

However, with a nod from Robert Catesby to Guy Fawkes, the bard realized that his time was up. "Well," Robert opted, folding his hands, "I guess that's all we have to discuss! Thank you for your time, Will. If we need you within the next few months—"

"Just a moment," Percy interrupted. The scabby man locked eyes with the unproductive playwright. "Master Shakespeare, when you performed that play for Essex's men, did you know what they were up to?"

The bard swallowed.

This time, a drop of sweat began to trickle down Shakespeare's back. Out of the corner of his eye, he noticed Jack Wright sit up in his chair and move his hand under his cloak. "Are you referring to his rebellion?" the bard asked.

"What else would I be referring to?"

"Tom—" Guy Fawkes pleaded.

"Silence!" Percy spat. "Master Shakespeare, tell us what you knew."

"That's enough, Tom!" Robert reprimanded. "Will, please accept my apologies. Master Percy had a lot to drink, and—"

Percy snapped his sweaty fingers. Jack Wright drew a dagger and stabbed it into the table, silencing everyone. The situation became crystal clear to Shakespeare: he was not leaving the Duck and Drake until he answered Percy's question.

"That won't be necessary," the playwright explained while looking at the dagger, and then at Percy.

"Who're you to tell me anything?" Jack growled menacingly. The swordsman popped his rapier an inch out of its sheath hoping Shakespeare would do the same.

Instead, the playwright looked to his side and raised his gloved left hand. "I wasn't talking to you," he corrected with conviction.

Shakespeare turned back to Percy and stared at him, undaunted. His opponent's eyes widened madly, but the bard's narrowed with focus. He was no longer sweating under his shirt, and his pulse had steadied. Within his mind's eye, the dramatist turned the Duck and Drake into his stage. "'That won't be necessary.' That's what I told Essex's agents when they asked me to perform *Richard II*. I knew it was a dangerous play; I wrote it that way, and the earl's men wanted me to perform what we both knew was its most dangerous scene. I had every idea what they were up to, and they offered me some extra silver to do the job. Instead, I handed them their money back. 'That won't be necessary,' I said. I told them their performance was on the house. I *wanted* them to succeed."

Seeing that he had his audience's attention, Shakespeare looked at everybody at the table. "Do not think me soft, my brothers. I know what your intentions are. I know how you plan to use my play, and I am happy to play my part in your endeavor. Just know that if you wish to succeed where Essex failed, it will take a lot more than just a play. You will need an army to deliver England from the Protestant rabble defiling her."

With those words, all six men seated at the Duck and Drake fell silent. The falling snowflakes in the windows and flickering fires were the only movement in the room. Shakespeare breathed slowly through his nostrils to quiet his quickening pulse. The bard was gambling with his life to win the information Walsingham needed from these men, but he refused to show it. The veteran actor masked his fears behind a face that exuded nothing but total confidence. It was the only way he could steal the stage at the Duck and Drake from his critics. Without saying a word, the dramatist had to convince these men that the performance they had just witnessed was not an act.

The gambit worked.

If Robert Catesby had any doubts about William Shakespeare before they met, they had just been obliterated. A smile spread across his face. The bard had completely won him over. "We ride for Warwickshire in two days to meet with our northern allies. Would you care to join us, brother? A man of your esteem could serve us well there."

The intensity faded from Shakespeare's face. "Warwickshire?"

"Of course! It's as much my homeland as it is yours. Come with us! We could continue our fathers' legacy. We could finish the work they started there."

The playwright hesitated. "But there are no armies in Warwickshire. If we knocked on every door in every town and village, we wouldn't be able to recruit enough fighters to fill this tavern."

"Who said we were visiting towns or villages?" Guy Fawkes smiled.

Shakespeare stared at the grinning men, bewildered. "Where else is there to go?"

"Into the wild," the conspirator replied.

"We're going into the woodlands to meet the cunning folk. We've met with them before." Robert's eyes were glowing with excitement. "They are with us!"

The bard breathed deeply at this revelation. "Witches?" he whispered. "You recruited witches?"

Robert and Guy Fawkes nodded. "They have an army," the

latter boasted. "They've been amassing one for years; ever since King James forced their sisters out of Scotland. They use their healing arts to attract countless followers throughout the country, people we never could have recruited otherwise. All the travelers, outlaws, highwaymen: the cunning folk united them into a single horde. They can outlast plagues and winters, and their numbers thrive while England's dwindle. They are everywhere, and they are nowhere. No one will see them coming!"

"I have no doubt," the bard replied with an uneasy smile. "But . . . even if you conquered the entire Isles with your allies, how would the world react to such an army? The Church will think us blasphemers. All the countries of Europe will invade England!"

"No, they won't," Fawkes assured. "We have an ally in the Vatican."

"Who?"

"Cardinal Alessandro de' Medici," Robert touted. "He has already assured us that the Church will protect us from any enemies."

"De' Medici?" Shakespeare gasped. The architects of the St. Bartholomew's Day Massacre, the bard did not need to mention. It was the worst of all the religious massacres in the past century, claiming tens of thousands of French Huguenots. Francis Walsingham was Elizabeth's ambassador in Paris at the time, and he had only barely escaped with his life as the city was strewn with Protestant bodies. Due to the French queen mother Catherine de' Medici's prominent role in the atrocity, the House of Medici had become synonymous with mass murder in England. "You are working with the Medici?"

Robert grinned brightly. "They have blessed us!"

"Rest assured, Master Shakespeare . . ." Guy Fawkes hissed smugly, "once we have control of our homeland, we will decide what role the cunning folk play in it, if any."

At that moment, the bard was convinced that these men were playing too many games of political chess at once. They carried themselves like knights and bishops, but in reality, Shakespeare was sitting at a table peopled with pawns. "And who exactly is Alessandro de' Medici?"

"The next pope," said Guy Fawkes. "Believe me, my brother, there are greater forces at work right now than even you can imagine."

Shakespeare smiled softly at the faces leering at him. Fawkes was not bluffing, the bard realized. *Walsingham was right!* Something foul was afoot in England, and whatever it was, it extended far beyond the Duck and Drake. The bard had to ride with these men to Warwickshire. But . . . He glanced at Thomas Percy. . . . Would that mean riding into an early grave? Percy had the audacity to silence Fawkes and even Robert throughout their meeting. The man was clearly mentally unwell and far beyond their control. If the bard committed just one error under his watch during their trip, Percy would have Jack Wright murder Shakespeare on the spot. The bard knew he was no match for Wright with steel: he would have to fire the pistol hidden in his rapier, revealing his identity to everyone. And even if Shakespeare somehow killed all the conspirators at Warwickshire—or that night at the Duck and Drake— the conspiracy would continue. If the Medici were involved, actors like Fawkes and Catesby would be easily replaced.

The bard had no choice but to monitor the conspiracy from a distance. "You say you ride in two days?" he asked Robert.

"Yes. On Friday the twenty-second. Our journey to and from Warwickshire should take us a little under two weeks."

Shakespeare grimaced. "That's a long time to travel. Can this meeting not wait until it gets warmer?"

"No," entered Fawkes. "The cunning folk insisted that we meet them on March first. It has something to do with our calendar."

The bard raised an eyebrow. "*Our* calendar?"

Fawkes raised his hands and shook his head. "I don't know. It probably has something to do with the moon and stars. They're mystics, you know."

"Bloody heathens . . ." Percy grumbled.

". . . who insisted that we meet them during the first hours of March," Robert reminded to preserve the peace with their unseen allies.

"And they expect us to meet them in the woods? In this weather?"

"Alas," Robert sighed, "we have no choice. These are their terms. Will you ride with us?"

The bard slowly rubbed his hands together to pantomime the approaching cold. "If that is the case, my brothers, then I know where my work will be more useful. It is not in Warwickshire, but here." Shakespeare then turned to face his sweaty adversary once more. "Master Percy, your concerns are fair and justified. I apologize for my tardiness and I humbly beg your pardon." The bard looked back at Robert. "With your permission, Master Catesby, I would like to stay in London to continue my writing. If the cunning folk are our allies, then I will give them a more prominent role in our play."

Robert smiled and looked to Percy. "Are you happy now?"

The unhappy man sneered at Shakespeare but acknowledged: "Aye."

Robert nodded. "In that case, may God bless you on your work, Will. I have no doubt you will make me proud." The master of ceremonies rose from his chair and walked up to Shakespeare with open hands. As the bard hurried onto his feet, every other man stood up as well. Robert clasped the playwright with both arms and grinned brightly. "Let's make our fathers proud as well, Will. You do your part, and I'll do mine."

The bard offered his hand. "Brothers?"

Robert looked down at the gloved hand and then up with teary eyes. "Master Shakespeare!" The leader of the conspiracy threw his arms around the playwright, and all the men watching broke out in applause.

William Shakespeare, the greatest playwright in England, was now officially a part of their plot. It was a union that Guy Fawkes made possible, and which the conspirator proudly presided over as godfather.

He was one of them now, the bard realized. Finally, he was in.

With Shakespeare's mission completed, the Dark Lady turned away from the tavern windows and spurred her horse back to the city.

Chapter XV

London Under Lockdown

After a heartfelt farewell at the Duck and Drake, the bard left
the inn and stepped into the cold embrace of the winter evening. Although Robert had invited Shakespeare to spend the night
with his men, the bard convinced him that he had already made ac-
commodations elsewhere. It was a lie the playwright needed in order to leave the building alive, for if he told Robert the truth, that
he was heading home, he would have been murdered at the Duck and
Drake. London was under lockdown due to plague, and only someone well connected with the government could pass through its
gates at this late hour. Guy Fawkes and Thomas Percy would have
known this, which meant the bard had to be even more careful with
his words in the coming months.

Across the street, a lone raven took to the darkened skies and
monitored the bard from the snowy heavens.

Shakespeare wrapped himself in his black cloak and pulled down
his hood. Once he was out of sight from the conspirators, he hurried
along the icy Strand and into a nearby stable. He looked inside with
a waiting lantern to find an old friend resting upright and snoring
softly. After sweeping his footprints with a broom, the bard crept

into the stable and patted the magnificent horse on his neck. "Sorry to wake you, Aston," the bard whispered, "but it is time for us to leave." Aston, rudely interrupted from his dream, snorted with frustration but otherwise obeyed his rider's request. The stallion walked out of his stall and, with Shakespeare mounted, the two disappeared like warm breath into the winter's wind.

When the plague first came to England in 1348, it killed nearly half the population. When it resurfaced twelve years later as the "children's plague," another quarter of the kingdom perished. Death and disease had since become a reoccurring nightmare for the British Isles. The bard survived two outbreaks in his lifetime and was even born after a particularly deadly year. The most recent plight, in 1603, claimed more than thirty thousand Londoners, so with the disease back after so short an interlude, the government was taking no chances. The landscape was not yet pockmarked with plague pits, but the bard did notice more than one death cart collecting bodies for London's cemeteries. Shakespeare covered his mouth and nose as he passed a creaking wagon piled high with blackened corpses. When he saw one worker carrying a shovel over his shoulder, the playwright shuddered at the thought of digging graves in frozen soil.

The pestilence was everywhere.

Shakespeare spurred Aston along the Strand and continued eastward toward London. As he passed through the wooden archway of Temple Bar, he could hear the chains of shivering prisoners locked in the gatehouse. The bard left Westminster behind him at Temple Bar as the Strand turned into Fleet Street, which he followed across Fleet Bridge until he came to the torches of London Wall. As watchmen spotted the playwright approaching, Shakespeare lowered his head so that his hood completely concealed his face.

"Ho there!" one of the watchers of the Wall called out. The man stepped out from the Ludgate with a flaming torch in his hand. "The way is shut. Get out of here!"

Without a word, Shakespeare reached beneath his cloak and pulled out a piece of parchment. The bard sat motionless in his saddle with the note outstretched while a raven swooped down onto his shoulder. Bewildered, the sentry slogged through the falling snow and snatched the document from the silent rider. The guardsman was illiterate, but seeing Walsingham's wax seal on the paper was all it took to make his heart jump. The watcher looked at the rider and the raven, and then spun around waving his torch. The Ludgate raised it portcullis, and Shakespeare retrieved his paper from the stunned watchman as he rode past him.

As one of Walsingham's informants, the bard was permitted to enter London without so much as showing his face.

Back in the city, Shakespeare's raven took flight and disappeared alongside the tall and striking St. Paul's Cathedral, which was silhouetted against the glowing sky. Although fire destroyed its mighty spire decades ago, St. Paul's remained one of the largest churches in the city, stretching from one corner of the bard's eye to the other. He passed the cathedral on his right as he rode through its churchyard back onto Cheapside. The bard followed the otherwise teeming boulevard bumpy with frozen excrement and dead animals for three blocks before turning left onto Wood Street. Almost at home, Shakespeare quickened his companion for this final length in their ride. "This should warm you," the bard encouraged as he and Aston galloped past four blocks of sleeping, snow-swept London until they reached the Cripplegate. Now at the northwestern edge of London Wall, Shakespeare reined his snorting charger beside a waiting watchman with a lantern. The man was one of Bacon's squires, and he was there to take Aston back to the Tower stables.

"Master bard," the burly squire greeted with a nod. "Did Aston give you any trouble?"

"None at all! I think we're friends now—or at least friendly." Shakespeare climbed down from the animal and swapped Aston's reins for the squire's lamp. "I am ready to take him on longer trips. I ride for Warwickshire in two days."

"He'll be ready for you," the squire assured him as he hopped into Aston's saddle. "Sleep well, master."

"I hope I get to," Shakespeare exhaled. On nights as cold as this one, he was relieved that he no longer had to sleep in Aston's stalls. As the magnificent horse and its squire galloped alongside the Wall and out of sight, the bard treaded through the snow past two houses in the opposite direction. He walked westward onto Muggle Street, which dipped southward from the London Wall in a curve. It was just a short walk past five more houses until the bard was back on the corner of Silver Street and Muggle.

As Shakespeare smacked the snow from his boots and hurried indoors, his raven perched on a rooftop across the street. The bird rested alongside another raven and another figure that had been waiting for the bard's arrival.

Chapter XVI

The Discovery

Shakespeare rushed upstairs to his apartment, this time grateful that he did not bump into his landlord on the way. Once inside his darkened room, he cracked his lantern open with frozen fingers to start a fire without the trouble of wrestling with his tinderbox. The playwright needed to warm his hands, but more important, he needed light. After what he had learned at the Duck and Drake, the bard would be writing tonight.

Shakespeare lit the ancient candle fused into the corner of his writing desk. After thawing a frozen inkwell over its flame, he dabbed a ready feather into the liquid and scratched away onto a waiting parchment.

> *If thou*
> *doest Marry, Ile giue thee this Plague for thy*
> *Dowrie. Be thou as chast as Ice, as pure as Snow,*
> *thou shalt not escape Calumny. Get thee to a*
> *Nunnery. Go, Farewell. Or if thou wilt needs*
> *Marry, marry a fool: for Wise men know well*

enough, what monsters you make of them. To a
Nunnery go, and quickly too.
Far-well.

W
Catesby plots rebellion. I will follow to Warwickshire.

                                          W.S.

The bard set down his quill pen and looked the message over for errors. Finding none, he rose from his chair and approached his window with the parchment and a wooden whistle, the latter something Bacon had given him during one of their subsequent trips to the White Tower. The bard opened his window and blew the whistle, which emitted a long, low note. In less than a minute's time, a raven appeared on his windowsill and greeted Shakespeare with a squawk.

"Good evening," the playwright welcomed.

"Good e'vən," the raven croaked.

Shakespeare smiled, but was then surprised to see a second raven perch on the windowsill. "Two of you?"

"Good e'vən." "TOO əv yə?" "TOO əv yə?" the ravens mimicked in the playwright's voice.

Shakespeare raised an eyebrow. He had not seen more than one bird in his apartment since Penny's visit the previous summer. His curiosity awakened, the bard looked behind the ravens and down at Silver Street, but he did not spot anyone in the snow or any footprints, save for his own. Confused but otherwise unworried, Shakespeare shrugged and tied his note onto the foot of the more familiar-looking raven, the one saying *"Good e'vən"* repeatedly.

"Shh!"

"Ssh!"

"Better." The playwright threw the chatty bird out the window, and the raven soared back to its home atop the Tower. As for its companion, Shakespeare politely shooed the bird and closed his window to retain what little heat remained in his apartment.

Back at his desk, the playwright mulled in his seat. Although his official work for the evening was over, something troubled him. The bard unbuckled his weapons as his thoughts turned to Thomas Percy and their repeated rows at the inn. The villain had always been distrustful of the playwright, but this was the first time the bard ever feared for his life in the man's presence. The encounter upset his equilibrium; otherwise, Shakespeare would have gladly traveled to Warwickshire with Robert's men. Instead, he now had to follow them on his own and find a way to eavesdrop on their meeting. Percy's suspicions had become a problem the bard could no longer ignore. They were interfering with his mission, and Shakespeare knew there was only one way to defuse the problem.

The bard stared at the blank pages on his desk. It was time for him to write his play. *The* play. The Scottish play.

Instead of picking up his feather, the playwright folded his arms and took a nap.

It was not that Shakespeare was a lazy man. Quite the contrary; he wrote *Henry V*, *Julius Caesar*, *As You Like It*, and *Hamlet* all within the course of one year. It was the same year that the Globe opened, and the playwright accomplished this while acting in his plays, touring the country with his company, and juggling duties both in Stratford and to Thomas Walsingham. Those were the good days, the bard remembered. The busy days. Back when he was free to pen his plays with impunity. It was what life was like before the Earl of Essex fiasco. Before Shakespeare's falling-out with Walsingham. Before the plague of 1603. And, of course, before Guy Fawkes.

Once more, Shakespeare was permitted to write his plays however he wished. He just did not know where to start on this one.

Oh yes. He did.

The bard opened his eyes.

Shakespeare picked up his pen and scratched down the ten words Fawkes made him memorize months ago:

> *Double, double, toile and trouble;*
> *Fire burne, and Cauldron bubble.*

The playwright wrote the words in the middle of his page. Parchment was expensive, and he planned to revisit this paper later. Perhaps much later.

Shakespeare's plays always began with what were called "foul papers": a handwritten draft of the script that he would share with his actors. After hearing their thoughts and making changes—which, in truth, almost never happened—Shakespeare sent these pages to a professional scribe so that a "fair copy" could be written. However, to save time and money, the bard made an effort to write his plays in good handwriting and free of errors to skip this process altogether. This was part of the reason Shakespeare had held off from writing the Scottish play for so long: the bard preferred to compose, revise, and finalize his plays from start to finish in his head.

In either case, this finished manuscript, commonly referred to as "the book of the play," would be submitted to the Master of the Revels, a royal censor. The official would review the manuscript, strike out whatever he found inappropriate, and then return the book to its author with a signature of approval. These "allowed books," as they were called, were the Holy Grail to acting companies. They were officiated copies of their plays which served as prompt books that could be carried and performed throughout the kingdom. They could be copied onto scrolls for their actors to memorize. They could even be published and printed. And, if the play-wright was clever—or suicidal, in Marlowe's case—the plays could even be changed without anyone noticing. That is, unless someone did notice, as was the case with *Richard II.*

This is what made Shakespeare's license to work free from censors so valuable. It allowed him to write his plays with full prompts and stage cues rather than being forced to add them later. It permitted him to visualize, direct, and script his plays all in one sitting. It liberated him as a writer, freeing him from the oppressive world that he was forced to call his homeland. It was how Shakespeare had written all his greatest plays and how he hoped to write many more.

But, for the time being, his priorities were set in Scotland.

Scotland.

That required research, the bard nodded.

Shakespeare glanced at the dusty books piled high on the chair beside his desk. It was a modest library the bard routinely consulted throughout his writing: his Geneva Bible[*] and prayer book;[†] a *Cooper's Dictionary*[‡] and Baret's *Alvearie*;[§] copies of Garnier's *Cornelia*,[¶] Lucan's *Pharsalia*,[**] and Thomas Digges's *Foure paradoxes*;[††] Arthur Golding's translation of Ovid's *Metamorphoses*[‡‡]—the bard's favorite

---

[*]William Whittingham, et al., *The Bible and Holy Scriptures Conteyned in the Olde and Newe Testament, translated according to the Ebrue and Greke, and conferred with the best translations in divers languages, with moste profitable annotations upon all the hard places, and other things of great importance as may appear in the epistle to the reader* (Geneva: Rovland Hall, 1560).

[†]*The boke of common praier* (London: Richard Grafton, 1559).

[‡]Thomas Cooper, *Thesaurus Linguae Romanae et Britannicae* (Londini: Impressum, 1584).

[§]John Baret, *An Alvearie or Quadruple Dictionarie, containing foure sundrie tongues: namelie English, Latine, Greeke, and French* (Londini: excudebat Henricus Denhamus, 1580).

[¶]Robert Garnier, *Cornelia*, trans. Thomas Kyd (London, 1594).

[**]Lucan, *Lucans first booke translated line for line*, trans. Christopher Marlowe (London: P. Short, 1600).

[††]Thomas Digges, *Foure paradoxes, or politique discourses* (London: H. Lownes, for Clement Knight, 1604).

[‡‡]Ovid, *Metamorphoses*, trans. Arthur Golding (London: W. Seres, 1567).

since his schooldays; a collection of Samuel Daniel's essays, which
Shakespeare purchased primarily for *Musophilus;*[*] a tattered copy
of William Painter's *Palace of Pleasure,*[†] which consulted while
writing *All's Well That Ends Well* the previous year; a new translation of Plutarch's *Lives*, which the bard was currently rereading
for *Antony and Cleopatra*;[‡] Samuel Harsnett's *Declaration of egregious Popish Impostures,*[§] which the bard started but had not finished; and, of course, a carefully cared-for copy of *Hero and Leander*
by Christopher Marlowe, deceased.[¶] Seeing that one made Shakespeare smile. Although stacked unceremoniously on a broken
chair and stained with wine and candle wax, these books comprised one of the most consequential collections in history. They
were Shakespeare's sources for nearly every single one of his
plays.

However, for the moment, the playwright needed something different. He reached beneath Harsnett's *Declaration* for his copy of
Holinshed's *Chronicles of England, Scotland and Ireland*, which would
have familiarized the playwright on Scottish history months ago
had he not accidentally flipped through its pages to the legend of
King Leir of Britain. Fortunately, such was not the case this evening. On this snowy night in London, Shakespeare cracked open
Holinshed's *Chronicles* precisely where he needed to: its detailed

---

[*]Samuel Daniel, *The Poeticall Essayes of Sam. Danyel* (London: P. Short for Simon
Waterson, 1599).
[†]William Painter, *The Palace of Pleasure Beautified, adorned and well furnished, with
pleasaunt Histories and excellent nouelles, selected out of diuers good and commendable Au-
thors* (London: John Kingston and Henry Denham, for Richard Tottell and William
Iones: 1566).
[‡]Plutarch, *The Lives of the Noble Grecians and Romaines*, trans. Sir Thomas North (London: Richard Field for Thomas Wight, 1603).
[§]Samuel Harsnett, *A Declaration of egregious Popish Impostures, to with-draw the harts of
her Maiesties Subiects from their allegeance, and from the truth of Christian Religion pro-
fessed in England, under the pretence of casting out deuils* (London: Iames Roberts, 1603).
[¶]Christopher Marlowe, *Hero and Leander* (London: Adam Islip, for Edward Blunt,
1598).

passage on the illnesses afflicting Duffe, king of Scotland in the mid–tenth century.

The word "witches" made one particular passage stand out to him.

> Howbeit the king, though he had small hope of recouerie, yet had he still a diligent care vnto the due administration of his lawes . . . But about that present time there was a murmuring amongst the pople, how the king was vexed with no naturall sicknesse, but by sorcerie and magicall art, practised by a sort of witches dwelling in a towne of Murrey land, called Fores. . . .*

The bard smiled. But *of course* it was witches!
He continued reading with a skeptical smirk on his face.

> The souldiers, which laie there in garrison, had an inkling that here was some such matter in hand . . . by reason that one of them kept as concubine a yoong woman, which was daughter to one of the witches as his paramour, who told him the whole maner vsed by hir mother & other hir companions, with their intent also, which was to make awaie the king.

Shakespeare's smile began fading.

> The souldier hauing learned this . . . shewed it to the kings messengers, and therewith sent for the yoong damosell which the souldier kept . . . . Wherevpon learning by hir confession in what house in the towne it was where they wrought their mischiefous mysterie, he sent foorth souldiers about the middest of the night, who breaking into the house, found one of the

*Raphael Holinshed, *The Chronicles of England, Scotland and Ireland*, (London: Henry Denham, 1587), vol. II, 233.

witches rosting vpon a woodden broch an image of wax at the
fire, resembling in each feature the kings person . . . *

What sorcery is this? the bard wondered.

. . . made and deuised (as is to be thought) by craft and art of
the diuell . . .

Shakespeare's eyes hovered over those last two words.

the diuell.

"The devil," he spoke aloud.

---

*Holinshed's *Chronicles*, vol. V: Scotland, 234.

Chapter XVII

"Who the Devil . . . ?"

S vejàte," the dragoman ordered in Venetian—"Wake up."

"Oh, it's you," Marlowe mindlessly mumbled with sticky lips. "Not tonight."

The poet rolled in his blankets and went back to sleep while his well-dressed guardian shoved the doge's naked nephew out the door. After handing some silver coins to the brothel madam, the dragoman locked himself in with Marlowe and swept through the room via candlelight. *"Wake up!"* the shadow whispered with added urgency.

Instead of rising, the sleeping poet burped, snored, and farted.

With his patience evaporating, the towering figure seized his friend by his filthy hair and pulled him out of his even filthier bed.

"Fine, fine! I'm awake! I'm awake!"

The dragoman dropped the drunk poet. "We need to talk."

A naked and dehydrated Marlowe struggled to stand on the brothel's grimy floor. "Didn't we talk the other . . . day?" he asked before collapsing onto all fours. It felt like the city was sinking faster than the poet had gotten used to.

"That was three weeks ago."

"Really? It's been that long?" Marlowe lifted his head and raised his eyebrows even though both his eyes were shut. "Is it still February?"

The dragoman gently helped Marlowe up and seated him on his bed. Once the inebriate was steadied, his gigantic attendant pulled over the same clean-looking chair from their previous exchange. The dragoman flattened the fine fabric of his *zhiduo* robe—Ming dynasty—and sat within whisper range of the departed playwright, albeit far away enough to keep his silk from touching the stinky bed. "How many people know who you are?" the figure asked.

"Lots!" Marlowe smiled. "I'm more popular than the pope around here. You know it!"

"I do." His friend exhaled. "And that gives me pause. How many people know your name? Here. In Venice."

The dragoman's tone and stare were beginning to upset poor Marlowe, who by now was wrestling with the sensation that the room was both spinning and sinking. "Nobody, Drago! I haven't told anyone my real name since I got here. Honestly! It's the one thing I know I can't do."

"You told *me* who you were."

"Yes! But . . . that was because I love you! We're like brothers, you and I. I knew I could trust you!"

"You told me who you were less than an hour after we met."

"Drago . . ." the poet pleaded. "My brother! I—" Marlowe suddenly grabbed his friend's garments and made an unpleasant face. He looked like he was about to vomit straight into Drago's silken lap.

Prepared, the dragoman moved quickly. "Drink this," he offered, producing a glass vial from his robe.

Marlowe stared with confusion at the whirling bottle before him. "What is it?" He reached for the vial several times without success, so the dragoman mercifully grabbed Marlowe's hand and placed the vial in it. The flask was warm and filled with a mysterious black liquid.

"It's medicine," said the dragoman. "Please drink it."

Marlowe grimaced when he uncorked the bottle, but his expression changed once he lifted the vessel to his lips. The fluid was fragrant, returning life to the poet's senses with a pleasant aroma akin of roasted chestnuts and fresh caramel. Intrigued, Marlowe took a sip. The mysterious drink slipped down his parched throat, soothing it while restoring warmth to his cold fingers and toes. As Marlowe moistened his mouth, a swift alertness seized his mind. Enchanted, Marlowe swallowed some more. His stomach settled, the room steadied, and his pounding headache began to dissipate. But then, something strange happened. Something the late poet had never experienced. A burst of energy shot back and forth between Marlowe's brain and body like lightning. It started as gently as a wave, but then engulfed him with the enormity of an ocean. Marlowe's pulse jumped and his pupils dilated. His imagination screamed obscenities. Addicted, Marlowe guzzled the rest of the black stuff as if it were mother's milk. "What is this?" he demanded.

"Kahveh," his tall friend replied.

It was the first coffee Christopher Marlowe had ever tasted. "I need more of this."

The dragoman smirked. "I will provide it when you require it. For now, all I need in return is your honesty." The speaker adjusted his boxlike *si-fang pingding jin* hat and leaned forward. "Am I the only person in Venice who knows your real name?"

"More *kahfey*," Marlowe mispronounced.

The dragoman furrowed his brow.

"Drago, *kahfey!*" Marlowe begged. "Please!"

His tall friend produced one more vial from his robes. "This is the last of it."

"You're greater than God!" Marlowe praised as he downed the

black stuff. As the miraculous elixir went back to work, the poet closed his eyes and took in a deep breath. "Infinite pleasure, and in so small a bottle," he mused.

"Cristo?"

Marlowe's eyes opened. "Oh yes. You're the only one who knows that I'm here. I swear it. Whenever I meet someone, I always tell them something different; whatever makes them drop their pants or share a few secrets." Marlowe was hoping to get a smile out of his friend with this aside. Instead, the dragoman's eyes narrowed and the dead poet's smile departed.

"One of my contacts put me in touch with an anonymous client this afternoon," said his opposite. "You know I don't work with anonymous parties, but I trusted my source on this one. The client asked me to hire someone for an assassination."

The poet tilted his head. "I thought you were out of that business."

The dragoman's brown eyes bored into Marlowe's. "As I said, I was asked to hire someone for an assassination."

"Oh?" the poet chirped, feeling somewhat embarrassed. "Well, I imagine they came to the right person! So, who are they after?"

"Christopher Marlowe."

The poet nodded, but then jumped out of his bed in terror. "No . . ." he gasped while backing away from his ascending friend. As the dragoman lunged at Marlowe, the poet's eyes shifted onto the two empty vials on his bed. Marlowe fell against the wall and grabbed his throat. He had the look of death in his eyes and was only seconds away from fainting.

"Quiet, quiet!" the dragoman ordered. "This client didn't want me to kill you! She was recruiting me to hire *you* to murder someone else."

"Crazy Mary of mercy!" Marlowe gasped as his friend seated him back on his bed. The poet's heart was pounding so hard that his eardrums throbbed with each beat. "Who do they want me to kill?"

"She would not say."

"Then how am I . . ." At last it registered. "Wait a minute—a *woman?*"

The dragoman nodded.

Marlowe stared off in disbelief. "O me!"

"Oh yes," his friend agreed. "O *you.*" The dragoman returned to his seat and folded his arms, allowing Marlowe to absorb the severity of the situation.

The poet propped himself up with his arms, aghast, and still completely oblivious to his nakedness. "Do you realize what this means, my friend?"

The dragoman raised his eyebrows. "You tell me."

"This means . . ." The poet slowly rose to his feet. "That you and I are going to be *rich*! Rich as king—nay, pirates! As rich as pirates!" Marlowe spun toward his friend with his eyes alight with ideas. "This is it, Drago! Our ultimate prize! Our Golden Fleece! All we have to do is figure out who this wench wants me to murder, sell her out to who she wants dead, and then get drunk as popes off both dullards! Oh, my friend, this is a perfect arrangement! Let's celebrate with some *kahfey!*"

The dragoman's face dropped in horror.

Marlowe found his friend's reaction sobering. "No *kahfey?*"

"Please sit," he instructed. "And cover yourself."

The nude poet obeyed.

"There is no reason why this woman should know you exist, never mind that you are alive and friends with me." The poet smiled, flattered, and the dragoman continued. "If what you say is true, that you never shared your identity with anyone other than myself, then we are entering dangerous waters with this woman. What she knows could destroy you."

"But . . . *money!*" Marlowe pleaded. "Is this not better than what we described earlier? These are them! The killer women! Just like in Belgrade and Istantinople."

"Those women killed their targets themselves. This is something different. Anyone can hire murderers, Cristoforo, and there are much more seasoned killers in this city than you."

"That's not true," Marlowe protested. "I have more seasoning than the East and West Indies!"

"You are out of shape *and* out of season. You have the balance of a sinking ship in a hurricane. Your reflexes are slow, your instincts poor, and your mind has become a mass grave to past wisdom. You possess none of the desired qualities for any sort of assassin, yet to this nameless, faceless woman, you are somehow champion of the Venetian underworld. I find that suspicious and even more dangerous. Especially since, if what you tell me is true, the only way this woman could have learned of your whereabouts was from someone on your home island. England."

"Impossible!" Marlowe scoffed. "Aside from you and me, only two other people know I'm here. They're reliable and trustworthy. They would never betray me!"

The dragoman was unmoved. "Are you so sure of that?"

The poet scowled. "Of course! I wouldn't be here today if it weren't for them. They were my dearest friends in the world until I met you!"

The dragoman nodded incredulously. "And who were they?"

For the moment, Marlowe was hesitant. "I told you about the one." He paused. "My former master, Thomas—"

Marlowe's inquisitor raised his hand, silencing the poet. "And the other man?"

"I . . . I shouldn't tell you his name."

The dragoman's gaze intensified. "Tell me."

Marlowe lowered his eyes. Feeling vulnerable, he covered his nipples with his bedsheet.

"Was it the friend you introduced to the Dark Lady? The one with the sonnets?"

Marlowe refused to answer.

"Cristo," the dragoman whispered, "I need to know if your life is in danger. I need to know who to trust. Please tell me your friend's name."

The saddened poet at last mustered the courage to look the dragoman in the eyes. "He would never betray me. Never! Especially now that I'm dead to London. My friend has supplanted me from this planet." Marlowe whimpered. "That's all I have to say."

Satisfied, the dragoman leaned back in his chair. He was impressed. Even while helpless, distressed, and cornered after a night of excessive drinking and decadence, the late Christopher Marlowe was capable of keeping details about his former life a secret—and from his closest ally in Venice, no less. There was no doubt left in the dragoman's mind: Marlowe had successfully kept his identity from the Venetians. The situation was indeed as dangerous as the towering shade anticipated. "Whoever this woman is," the dragoman continued, "she is clearly well connected. That puts her at an advantage over us. You could be walking into a trap by responding to her, my friend."

Marlowe shrugged. "We work with people like her all the time."

"No, we don't. *I* do. And you work for me whenever I need something from the Biblioteca Marciana. Naturally, political gossip is always welcome, but not when it is about you and your former life in England. If you were to meet with this woman, she will know your greatest secret. She could tax you for all you're worth, my friend. Keeping such a secret could cost you a lot more than your gold. She could force you to do this assassination for her, no matter what the danger. And then another. And another. You could be her slave and prisoner for the rest of your afterlife."

The poet's mood lifted. "I actually like the sound of that!"

The dragoman's eyes fell to his friend's bedsheets. "Cover yourself."

"Oh." Marlowe complied. "Sorry. Well, if this she-beast is indeed as poisonous as you paint her, then tell her to fly on her broomstick and find someone else! Tell her I'm out of that game. The only foes I lay dead are those who are brave enough to join me in bed!" The poet patted his mattress, which emitted an unusual squeak. Surprised, Marlowe looked down and drew his hand back.

The dragoman shook his head. "You have to meet her."

"What? You just said that meeting her would be bad—for some reason."

Frustrated, the dragoman pushed himself up to full height. "You fail to grasp the danger surrounding you. When I met this lady, she refused to tell me her name or even show me her face. The entire time I spoke with her, the woman wore a leather mask. She requested to meet you in person so you could kill whatever target she names. That could be anyone! It could be the doge, the pope in Rome . . . she could even ask you to murder me! I find it troubling that she would share so much information with me when she could have requested to meet you under your alias, or perhaps recruit you for something less dangerous. I might have permitted that, but the methods she's using guarantees that you will meet her in person. She's extorting you, Cristo, coercing you into her service, and she is leaving no room for error. You must meet with this woman, and when you do, you must be prepared to do whatever is necessary to keep what she knows about you a secret."

Marlowe sat with his hands in his lap and both eyes agape. "Then it is settled. Give me enough *kahfey*, and I will kill this woman for you."

The dragoman's face twisted. "No. We do not know who this woman is or who supplied her information. Besides, murdering her would be difficult considering where she wants to meet you."

Marlowe raised his eyebrows. "Where will it be?"

The dragoman stiffened. "At la Piazza this Tuesday, the first night of Carnevale."

The poet gasped. "*What?* We'll be in the middle of the festival! There will be people everywhere!"

"I know."

"And guards!" Marlowe added. "The doge's palace is *right there!*"

"*I know,*" the dragoman stressed.

Shocked, Marlowe turned away and ran a shaking hand through his hair. "Drago," he began, clinging to his guardian in fear, "I haven't killed anyone since I got here! Also, I really, *really* need more *kahfey!*"

The unsmiling shade shot his friend a dark look. "No. You've had enough for the evening. Carnevale begins in two days. . . . No." The dragoman checked a timepiece attached to his belt. "Tomorrow. That leaves us with less than twenty-four hours for you to reclaim your former fitness. You *need* to exercise, Cristo. Your life could depend on it!"

"*Oh . . .*" Marlowe sighed with relief. "We still have time then. Sure! I can do that." The poet stretched out his arms and fell backward into the repellant embrace of his bed. "Good night, my tall friend! I will see you in the morrow."

"Get out from there," the figure thundered.

The cheery poet looked up at his serious-looking friend. "Why so serious?"

The dragoman drew a Damascus sword from his robes and took a mighty swing at Marlowe's bed. Horrified, the poet leaped out of the path of the blade, which sliced his malodorous mattress in a diagonal deathblow. Marlowe fell to the floor and rolled back onto his feet in time to see a family of rats come pouring out of his mattress. The dragoman looked down his nose at the screaming vermin, dried their blood from his shining blade, and then turned to his friend staring speechlessly at the rodents. "From now on, you will stay with me at the Fontego dei Turchi. And you will bathe. And with every hour we have left in this city, you will exercise."

Wide-eyed and in the nude, a reawakened Christopher Marlowe turned to his savior. "Will you make me some more *kahfey?*"

The dragoman nodded, and Marlowe followed him from the embrace of the defeated bedroom.

Chapter XVIII

The Scream

Shakespeare flipped through Holinshed's *Chronicles* with increased aggravation. Although Duffe's encounter with the dark arts piqued his interest, the bard knew that he could not use it. The tale of King Duffe was a triumph, not a tragedy, and the playwright imagined that his strange patrons would not take kindly to a drama about a Scottish king's victory against black magic. The bard needed his drama to injure England's King James; not celebrate his legacy as a witch-hunter. Especially since Robert Catesby and Guy Fawkes had an alliance to preserve with their Warwickshire cohorts, the cunning folk: midwives, folk healers, and fortune-tellers.

White witches, the playwright reminded himself.

Shakespeare needed something different from Scotland's turbulent history to deliver the political messages his patrons requested. He needed a dark main character; someone who could captivate audiences like the bard's greatest villains. He needed a Scotsman who could share the same stage as Richard III and Marcus Brutus. He needed a tragedy so treacherous that it would terrify London.

And in the middle of this maelstrom, the bard also needed witches. Three witches.

Fading quickly, the tired playwright closed his eyes and wandered inward. Within his mind, he could already picture his players walking onstage in kilts. He could hear the laughs their Scottish accents would draw. He could already see Richard Burbage mesmerizing the crowd as the play's title character. Shakespeare knew what he wanted; all he needed now was a name. Unfortunately, it had been six months and England's greatest playwright had not even accomplished that much.

Wracked with frustration, the bard opened his eyes and returned to the *Chronicles*.

After Malcolme succéeded his nephue Duncane the sonnne of his daughter Beatrice: for Malcolme had two daughters, the one which was this Beatrice, being giuen in marriage vnto one Abbanath Crinen, a man of great nobilitie, and thane of the Iles and west parts of Scotland, bare of that mariage the foresaid Duncane; the other called Doada, was maried vnto Sincell the thane of Glammis, by whom she had issue one Makbeth a valiant gentleman, and one that if he had not béen somewhat cruel of nature, might haue been thought most worthie the gouernment of the realme.*

Shakespeare paused at the end of this passage.

Makbeth
a valiant gentleman . . . cruel of nature . . .

The playwright continued.

*Holinshed's *Chronicles*, vol. V: Scotland, 264–5.

Banquho the thane of Lochquhaber, of whom the house of the Stewards is descended, the which by order of linage hath now for a long time inioied the crowne of Scotland . . .*

The corner of Shakespeare's mouth curled upward. King James hailed from the House of Stuart, formerly Stewart, making him a direct descendant of the Scottish thane Banquo.

After reading of the rebellion Macbeth and Banquo subdued for King Duncan . . .

Makbeth and Banquho iournied towards Fores, where the king then laie, they went sporting by the waie togither without other companie, saue onelie themselues, passing thorough the woods and fields, when suddenlie in the middest of a laund, there met them thrée women in strange and wild apparell, resembling creatures of elder world . . .†

Shakespeare's eyes widened.
Three women?

the first of them spake and said—

"*TOO ǝʋ yǝ?*"
The playwright spun in his chair. "The devil!" he cried. Behind him was the same raven from earlier rapping on his window with its beak. Bewildered, Shakespeare rushed over and let the bird inside. The room was suddenly filled with a cold gust of snowflakes and feathers. Candles were blown out and pages flew into the air as the raven darted in and perched atop the bard's writing desk. Before the stunned playwright could speak, the bird opened its beak

*Holinshed's *Chronicles*, vol. V: Scotland, 265.
†Holinshed's *Chronicles*, vol. V: Scotland, 268.

and emitted a low, sustained scream. It was a disgusting, unnerving sound that chilled the bard even more than the cold, and it was not long before the siren woke up everyone in the building.

"What the hell is that!" a voice hollered from the halls.

"It is nothing!" Shakespeare shouted to his landlord as the bard tried to silence the animal. He made a reach for the raven, but the bird flew away from his fingers and swooped straight out the window. The playwright rushed to the windowsill only to notice similar cries emanating throughout London. In a matter of seconds, a swirling fury of ravens descended over Silver Street and Muggle.

Almost instantly, the bard then heard a different scream—a woman's scream.

Shakespeare leaned forward and stuck his head out the window to spy a small figure running away from his intersection. The figure was surrounded by a black cloud of shrieking ravens. The birds assaulted their target with their claws and beaks, filling the neighborhood with cries that echoed noisily against London Wall. Dogs began barking. Startled neighbors rushed to their windows with candles. And then, out of the corner of his eye, Shakespeare saw something glowing across the street from him.

The bard turned his head to see a dark, haunting figure looming over the rooftops. The figure stood tall with a flowing black cape and hood, and was holding a lantern that glowed brightly amidst the snowfall. The playwright's jaw dropped. The figure was staring straight at him and disappeared just as soon as Shakespeare noticed.

"The Gods!" the playwright gasped as he ducked from the window. With his mind alert and pulse jumping, the bard lunged across the floor for his belt and weapons. After drawing his sword and securing his gear, Shakespeare surveyed the situation from the ground. It was too dark and cold for him to meet his observer outside, he had no footprints to follow, and Sir Francis Bacon's ravens were clearly busy elsewhere. The bard was alone and exposed in his apartment, but he had no safer place to retreat. Resigning himself to his situation, Shakespeare turned around and peeked out from his window. There was nothing but darkness and snow to behold. Even the woman's screaming had stopped.

Relieved, Shakespeare shut his window and sank back to the floor. But then, just as his pounding heart quieted, his thoughts turned to the men he met at the Duck and Drake. "Oh fig," the bard realized. If a spy had been sent to follow him home, he would have seen Shakespeare ride Aston through the Ludgate. The conspirators would know the bard had lied about having lodgings on the Strand. They would know he had government access during lockdown. Shakespeare's entire mission could be compromised, and, with one whisper, so would his life.

Overwrought with stress and wary of being seen through the windows, the hapless playwright remained confined to the wooden floor. He looked at the lone candle on his desk, but he decided against snuffing it. If he was still being watched, Shakespeare wanted his enemies to think that he was still awake. It was his only safeguard against someone trying to murder him in his bed—that is, aside from his weapons and his current view of his door. Realizing he was in for a long night, the bard scooted over to his desk and pulled his copy of Holinshed's *Chronicles* into his lap. The book closed as it fell, but a stray raven feather shut inside it conveniently marked the bard's place.

Using the modest light he had, Shakespeare opened the book to the feather and revisited Macbeth and Banquo's encounter with the strange women.

the first of them spake and said; "All haile Makbeth, thane of Glammis" (for he had latelie entered into that dignitie and of-fice by the death of his father Sinell.) The second of them said; "Haile Makbeth thane of Cawder." But the third said; "All haile Makbeth that héerafter shalt be king of Scotland."

No cruelty. Not black magic. Neither good nor evil. These were not the same witches who cursed Duffe. These women were mystics: diviners no different than the cunning folk his employers planned on meeting.

The bard kept reading to keep himself awake as his candle burned down. By the time it was spent, so was Shakespeare. The exhausted playwright was slouched forward. He had fallen asleep with his sword in his hand and his book in his lap, but he had finished his reading. Within his sleeping mind's eye, the bard shared the same sorry fate of Macbeth.

He now knew of Macbeth's scheming and manipulative wife, of King Duncan's murder, and of Macbeth's deadly ascent to the throne.*

He saw the treachery of Banquo's murder and the escape of his son.†

He shared in the prophecy that Macbeth would never be slain by any man "borne of anie woman, nor vanquished till the wood of Bernane came to the castell of Dunsinane."‡

He witnessed Macbeth's descent into madness, the massacre of Macduff's family, and the spectacle of Malcolm's men wearing Birnam wood as they assaulted Dunsinane hill.§

And lastly, the bard went to sleep with his mind afire over the tragic fall of Macbeth. How the prophecies that led to his rise also led to his death. How Macduff was "neuer borne of my mother, but ripped out of her wombe."¶ How Macbeth met his death due to hubris, the machinations of his vain and ambitious queen—Elizabeth, perhaps?—and the words of three witches.

Words, he dreamed. *Words!*

---

*Holinshed's *Chronicles*, vol. V: Scotland, 269.
†Holinshed's *Chronicles*, vol. V: Scotland, 271.
‡Holinshed's *Chronicles*, vol. V: Scotland, 274.
§Holinshed's *Chronicles*, vol. V: Scotland, 276.
¶Holinshed's *Chronicles*, vol. V: Scotland, 277.

The playwright jerked from his slumber and made a blind grab for his desk. Unfortunately, he missed both his quill and paper, managing only to spill his inkwell all over himself the floor. Irritated, Shakespeare groped through the darkness until he found the raven's feather sticking out of his book. After dabbing the floor for ink, the bard wrote:

THE TRAGEDIE OF MACBETH.
Actus Primus. Scæna Prima.
Thunder and Lightning. Enter three Witches.

Despite being written on floorboards with an unsharpened quill in the dark, Shakespeare attempted his best handwriting. Even with his secret license, the bard had no intention of sharing this project with a scribe.

He then went back to sleep on the floor using page 277 of Holinshed's *Chronicles* as his pillow:

> This was the end of Makbeth, after he had reigned 17 yeeres ouer the Scotishmen. In the beginning of his reigne he accomplished manie woorthie acts, verie profitable to the commonwealth (as ye haue heard) but afterward by illusion of the diuell, he defamed the same with most terrible crueltie. He was slaine in the yéere of the incarnation, 1057, and in the 16 yeere of king Edwards reigne ouer the Englishmen.

The ink-covered playwright woke that morning to the cawing of crows. Once he realized he survived the evening, Shakespeare pushed himself up off the floor and groggily looked out of his window. Aside from some ravens, no one was watching him from the rooftops. Relieved, the playwright staggered to his bed only to slip on the cold floor's frozen ink.

Had Shakespeare looked to where he had heard screaming the prior night, he might have noticed black feathers sticking out of the snow.

Although invisible from the distance, the white snow was also speckled red with blood.

Chapter XIX

The Complaints Office

Your birds are not working."

Sir Francis Bacon looked up from his reading. "They work harder than you, master bard."

"I beg to differ," Shakespeare replied. "Also, I beg your pardon for my appearance." The playwright had black ink on his face and a throbbing bruise on his forehead.

"I have no time for beggars," Bacon snapped. He put the papers he was reading facedown under an astrolabe on his desk and once more threw a cloth over the chalkboard behind him. Although Shakespeare had been a Double-O operative for more than six months at this point, it did not make England's greatest scientist any happier to see England's greatest playwright this morning. Quite the contrary, Bacon preferred knowing when the bard would be visiting weeks in advance so that they could meet on the Tower Green without setting foot in his workshops. In a way, the renowned thinker's distrust of the playwright was prudent. Although Shakespeare had no intent to cause trouble, he did enjoy reading everything on Bacon's blackboard before it was covered.

912	1456
Annála Uladh	Vitæ Pontificum
987–989	1531
Gesta regum Anglorum	Petrus Apianus
1066	1606–1608
William	?

"1066 William" stood out to Shakespeare for obvious reasons. He had to keep them to himself, however, for Sir Francis Bacon was in no mood to talk.

"Why are you interrupting me this time?"

The bard looked away from the blackboard. "Your birds are not working."

The unwelcoming scientist stared back at the playwright. "And what, in all frankness, is that supposed to mean?"

"It's the ravens, Master Bacon. They are not doing their job."

"Yes, they are. You may leave."

"But I *can't* leave," Shakespeare fumed. "Someone was stalking me outside my building last night. Your ravens alerted me to his presence, but they did not attack him. Instead, they went after someone else: a woman for the sounds of her screams."

"Did you get a look at this woman?" the scientist inquired.

"No."

"Well, the ravens did, and it sounds like they deemed her a threat. You can thank me by leaving. I have work to do, playwright." Bacon shoved Shakespeare aside and returned to his desk.

"What about the person who was spying on me?"

"Why should I believe this other person even exists?"

"Because I saw him!" Shakespeare shouted with his bloodshot eyes throbbing. "He was staring at me from the rooftops last night. In the cold! Does that not alarm you?"

"How could you have seen this person if you say it was nighttime?"

"He was holding a lantern."

"Are you sure of it?"

"*Yes,*" the exasperated playwright groaned. Still weak with sleeplessness, he stared helplessly at the uncaring scientist. "I need help, Master Bacon. I met with the conspirators last night. If they had someone follow me home, my entire mission could be compromised. Our security breached. My life forfeit!"

Shakespeare tailored this last line at his own expense so that the scientist would ridicule him some more. It was the best approach, the bard gambled, for getting what he needed out of Bacon. Eventually, the man would have nothing more condescending to offer than his condescending assistance. However, the scientist stunned Shakespeare by returning his saddened looks with sincerity. The steely glare in his eyes softened while the bard's brightened with hope. "I never thought I would say this," Bacon sighed. The great thinker folded his hands and leaned forward as he disclosed with disappointment: "You are a poor player, playwright."

Unmasked, the bard grimaced. "You do realize my investigation could be impeded if I am even *slightly* killed."

"The ravens have safeguarded you thus far, master bard. If you don't like being alive enough to complain about it, then I suggest you start liking the other side of my door."

"But my life is in danger! And it is all because your birds failed to intercept my assailant!"

"If the ravens considered him or her a threat, you would have been the first to know."

"But I *did* know!"

"Master bard, you wouldn't know an obvious fact if it hit you in the face." Bacon glanced at Shakespeare's bruises as he said this. ". . . Again. So please, for your sake, don't let the door hit you on your way out. Good day." Considering the matter settled, Bacon picked up his papers and resumed his reading.

"This is worthless. . . ." Shakespeare scoffed.

The scientist remained silent.

Seeing the situation lost, the bard turned away. As he was about to walk out of the building, however, he hesitated. "How good are the ravens outside of the city?" he asked.

"Do I need to summon the guards, master bard?"

"Master Bacon," Shakespeare continued, "I have to leave for Warwickshire tomorrow. While there, I need to somehow spy on these conspirators from afar, through a forest. I don't know how I will do it or what to expect, but before I go, can you assure me that your ravens will keep me safe?"

Once more, Bacon looked up from his documents, which he held close to his chest so that Shakespeare could not read them. "You are leaving the city?"

"I just told you."

"No. *Why* are you leaving the city?"

The bard bit his lip, not knowing how much he could share. However, realizing he was out of options, he shared: "The conspirators will be meeting with witches."

At last, William Shakespeare had Sir Francis Bacon's attention. Albeit reluctantly, the scientist set down his pages and studied the bard down and up. "You said you met with your adversaries last night. Correct?"

"Yes."

Bacon raised an eyebrow. "Did you dine with them?"

Shakespeare's brow wrinkled. "Yes?"

"Were any of these witches present?"

The bard shook his head. "I don't think so."

Bacon's face intensified. "Did you see who prepared your food? Did you pour your own beverage?"

Confused and alarmed, Shakespeare replied with a soft-spoken "no."

Apparently, "no" was not the right answer. The scientist stood up from his chair with both arms at his sides. "How feel you, master bard?"

Shakespeare's heart was jumping. "I feel tired."

"Just tired?"

"I had very little sleep last night."

Bacon's concerns shifted to the bump on Shakespeare's forehead. "That's not a bubo, is it?"

The bard raised his stained hand to his brow. "No. I just had a tumble this morning."

"And your skin?"

"It's ink, Master Bacon."

"All of it?"

"*Yes,*" the bard grumbled. "I also had an accident with my inkwell."

Satisfied, the scientist nodded. "Follow me, master bard." Bacon led the way through the building's labyrinth of laboratories while the silent playwright worried whether he had somehow contracted the plague.

Shakespeare followed Bacon back to the Double-O's medical stores, where they found several assistants hard at work force-feeding poison to prisoners. The playwright winced at their screams, which apparently had no effect on the doctors—including Bacon. The scientist briskly moved in and out of the scene for a leather pouch he took from one of the vomit-strewn tables.

"Do you know what this is?" Bacon asked as he handed the pouch to Shakespeare.

The bard looked the leather purse over. "Dog skin?" he judged.

The scientist narrowed his eyes and untied the bag's strings. The purse was filled with a fine, rust-colored powder. "This is *terra sigillata,*" Bacon explained. "Medicinal earth. It's used as far off as the

Americas,* and research shows that the soil can successfully counteract poisons.† Mix a spoonful with wine and take it whenever you eat or drink with your enemies. You should be able to survive a double dose of whatever they give you—provided you take the proof quickly, of course."

"How quickly?" Shakespeare asked.

"As soon as you realize that you have been poisoned. The sooner you take it, the more effective its powers will be. Just be warned, master bard: even if taken correctly, the experience can be unpleasant. You will suffer great pain, but tests show you will likely survive the ordeal."

"That doesn't sound like something to look forward to," said Shakespeare as he tied the pouch to his belt. "What if I take the soil before I am poisoned? Will that ease the experience?" The playwright's eyes shifted to and from the prisoners writhing behind Bacon.

"If you wish to experiment on the subject, you are welcome to, master bard. Just make sure you die someplace close enough for us to examine your corpse."

"I'll remember," Shakespeare agreed as Bacon led him into the armory.

"I assume you'll be taking Aston."

"I assumed I would as well."

"How long will you be gone?"

"At least a fortnight. I have to ride out tomorrow."

"It will be cold out there. Here . . ." Bacon handed Shakespeare a heavy pelt of white fur rolled into a bundle. "Take this with you, and make sure you use it."

---

*Thomas Hariot, *A Briefe and True Report of the New Found Land of Virginia* (London: Theodore de Bry, 1588), 11.
†Andreas Bertholdus, *The vvonderfull and strange effect and vertues of a new Terra sigillata* (London: Robert Robinson, 1587).

"It looks warm!" the bard piped. "Thank you."

"It's for Aston," Bacon sneered. "This one is for you." Shakespeare was then handed a white cloak heavier than the black one he was wearing. "Make sure you wear this when you travel by day. Wear your black cloak over it at night. As long as you keep a safe distance from your targets, no one should be able to see you or Aston in the snow."

"That will have to be some distance," Shakespeare grumbled. "Master Bacon, I don't think this will be enough. I need a better way to spy on my targets."

Bacon paused. For the moment, the great thinker did not have a solution. "You said they will meet in the woods?"

"Yes."

"How many of them?"

The bard shrugged. "I don't know. It could be a few people, or it could be a horde. The conspirators boasted that the cunning folk have many allies. If their numbers are great, I have no idea how I will be able to spy on them without being discovered."

Bacon squinted in thought. He then glanced at the playwright's moving mouth. "Do you know how to read lips, master bard?"

"Of course," the actor replied.

Checkmated, Bacon resigned himself to the only move he had left. "Very well." He led Shakespeare back to his laboratory, prepared to part with his most treasured possession. "The farther you travel from London, the fewer ravens you will have to act as your guardians. In consequence, I must advise that you stay as far away from your targets as possible during their meeting."

"Then why bother going?" the bard fumed. "Master Bacon, how will I learn anything during this meeting if you keep telling me that I must keep my distance the whole time?"

Bacon opened a drawer and pulled out an uncanny invention. It was a long, shining cylinder of retractable brass with a glass lens fitted onto both of its ends.

"What is that?" asked Shakespeare.

Bacon pulled the contraption until it extended to the length of both his arms outstretched. *"Magia naturalis,"* he answered. "This clever device was put together by one of our Italian counterparts.* It uses convex and concave lenses to allow its user to view distant objects as if they were closer. Test it before you leave, master bard. You will be able to make out the farthest windmills from atop the White Tower." The scientist closed the device, wrapped it in its leather sheath, and then handed it to the stunned playwright.

"Remarkable," Shakespeare observed. "It should make for an interesting tour of the country." As the playwright threw the device over his shoulder, however, Sir Francis Bacon caught him.

"Master bard, I do not think you understand the situation you have just put yourself into. That device is precisely what I said it is: *magia naturalis*—natural magic. This is no power that any witches or wizards obtain through a pact with the Devil; it is the natural philosophy of how the world functions. It is God's handiwork, master bard. It is the closest thing the Double-O has to Divine weapons, and it is the best defense we have against the dark arts. If you can use this tool to learn more about our enemies, then I will gladly part with it. But I cannot stress this enough, master bard: you *must* bring it back to us. And preferably in one piece. There are only two of these devices in the entire kingdom."

Shakespeare turned his head sideways. "Really? I could have sworn that I've seen one of these before. In W's office."

Bacon nodded. "The one you hold is its brother. Do not break it, master bard. And above everything else, *do not* let it fall into the hands of the enemy."

"I won't," Shakespeare promised with a smile. He offered Bacon his hand, but the scientist turned his back on him and returned

---

*Iohn Baptist Porta [Giambattista della Porta], *Magia Naturalis: in xx Bookes* (Naples, 1558).

to his desk. Seeing that his time was up, the dramatist bowed and exited the Ordnance Office to try out his newest toy.

Bacon waited until Shakespeare closed the door before resuming his reading: a handwritten account of Marco Polo's encounters with Chinese astrologers. Much like the manuscript that made Shakespeare's telescope possible, these pages were also a recent arrival from Venice.

Chapter XX

Exercise

O h no . . ."
Just when things were looking up for the doubled-over Marlowe, the poet vomited all over the toes he was desperately trying to touch. Fortunately, the dragoman was familiar with such afflictions due to a past that he kept hidden, which was why he insisted there would be no coffee until the dramatist finished his stretching. It was Marlowe's first attempt at exercising in more than a decade, and although the experience was unbearable, the dragoman's residence was the perfect place for exorcising the poet's demons.

The hotel colloquially known as the Fontego dei Turchi, "The Turkish Inn," was a tall, stately building that served as headquarters to Ottoman merchants in Venice. Although not as large as its future site at the Palmieri Palace, the Fontego at San Polo's all'Angelo was a welcome haven to Turkish travelers when the dragoman first came to the city. The complex tripled as a residence, storehouse, and marketplace that opened into the Rialto's international epicenter at Campo San Giacomo. The hotel was a Turkish microstate within the Venetian Republic, keeping the city supplied with exotic goods while providing its occupants with every possible comfort from home. This latter detail was why the dragoman insisted on having his inebriated companion with him that morning, for unlike any of the casinos or brothels Marlowe frequented, the Fontego dei Turchi had a *hamam*: a Turkish bath.

After Marlowe's capsized stomach was righted thanks to a remarkable substance called "*yoyurt*," he and his friend sat for a *kahvaltı*: a "before coffee," the dragoman translated. The intricate breakfast consisted of white bread and a wide selection of stuffed *börek*, some cheeses—*beyaz peynir*, as well as both *eski kaşar* and *taze kaşar*—fresh butter, imported honey, *sucuklu yumurta*—a baked egg served with large slices of spicy beef sausage—black and green olives, jams, fresh vegetables, and several cups of a bright red liquid called *tavşan kanı çay*—rabbit's blood tea. Once the two finished their eating, the dragoman permitted the imploring poet one cup of coffee, but only if he drank it in small sips while they walked. The poet complied and was finally reunited with his precious elixir in the Fontego courtyard.

After sharing a pleasant conversation about hospitality and reciprocity, the dragoman learned forward with his *kufi* cap and whispered that he and Marlowe must part. When the wide-eyed poet asked why, the dragoman explained that he had business at the Jewish ghetto that was relevant to their appointment at Piazza San Marco. The dragoman made it clear that he would return, but until then Marlowe would have to remain with the Fontego staff. The poet smiled and inquired what sort of pleasantries such preferential treatment entailed. The two set down their cups, the dragoman nodded, and a pair of enormous hotel guards seized Marlowe by his shoulders. The terrified poet resisted, crying "Drago!" as he was dragged into a darkened room. His tall friend checked his pocket watch as he left the hotel.

Marlowe kicked and screamed his way across a beautifully tiled floor until he was shoved into a regal rotunda decoratively adorned with bright quartz. The room was low, wide, and hot, and had a large, octagonal marble platform at its center. The air was unimaginably humid, causing the sunlight piercing through the ceiling's innumerable starburst windows to waft in the air like misty ribbons. Marlowe had never been subject to such exotic surroundings, which surprised him since he thought he had already sampled every pleasure that the afterlife had to offer. But then again, within the cozy womb of the Fontego dei Turchi *hamam*, the late Christopher Marlowe was not exactly in Venice anymore.

"Remove your clothes," one of the hotel staff requested.

Amused, the poet pivoted on his sticky toes and invited the burly men to disrobe him themselves. The guards exchanged a glance and then moved on Marlowe with their *yatağan* knives drawn. Before the poet could explain that he was jesting, their shining blades flashed like mirrors all over his body. The shredded remains of Marlowe's undergarments fell to the floor, except for several stinking clumps stuck to his filthier parts. In the nude and abashed, the poet covered himself. The guards threw Marlowe onto the marble slab and held him down so that the hotel staff could get on with their assignment.

After being forced to sweat out an entire lifetime of alcohol, the poet was scrubbed vigorously until stripped of enough dead skin to fill a small sock. Marlowe was then lathered from head to toe, doused with warm water, and thrown back onto the slab so that the hotel's even larger masseurs could go to work on his fossilized muscles. Every naked inch of the poet was pulled, pounded, and twisted, resetting his skeleton and yanking out every tangled knot in his body. Outside the *hamam*, the Fontego echoed with the violent screams of a man being reborn. At the nearby San Giacomo di Rialto, a flock of pigeons took to the sky as a new hour tolled. And then another. And then another until, finally, after being submersed in pools of steaming hot and freezing water, Marlowe was bombarded with cloths, handed a cup of tea, and told by the hotel staff to take a walk.

With every joint in his cadaver loosened and every muscle in his body throbbing, Marlowe staggered out of the Fontego in such a daze that he did not even notice that the hotel staff had dressed him. All his old clothes had been discarded and replaced with only the finest: splendid white linens, an expensive doublet of red silk and shining silver, a pair of freshly stitched brown leather boots—doeskin for extra comfort—a white cape clad with crimson, a shining sword and parrying dagger, a new belt with a silver buckle, and a large, floppy red hat the bewildered poet unconsciously discarded as he scratched his head.

Marlowe's back had been bent, but now it was straightened. His eyes had been vacant, but now they reawakened. A bright, blinding light beckoned Marlowe forward, back into the world of the living. The poet squinted and shielded his eyes until the shining setting faded back into clarity. Marlowe lowered his hand and looked around: he was standing in the swirling center of the Campo San Giacomo. The loud bazaar was alive and moving, yet all its people seemed distant. The Venetian cacophony sounded dimmed and muted, as if the poet were somehow listening from underwater. The entire world around him looked and sounded indistinct, save for one timbre that made him pause: the plucking of a mandolin. The poet stopped walking and listened blissfully to the strumming strings until the angelic notes of a singing woman made him turn his head. Wide eyed, Marlowe looked straight ahead so that he could listen to both sounds with sharpened senses. The woman's vocals started swelling, and the mandolin strings jumped with electricity.

The reborn poet's heart was pounding.

A forgotten vigor from Marlowe's youth started surging through his body. Reunited with his former self, young Kit took a step forward, then another, and another, once more, then again, and again . . . With increasing speed and energy, the poet sprinted straight out of the Campo faster than the Fontego guardsmen watching him could follow. Marlowe ducked and dodged his way through the *mercato*, never losing momentum. When a merchant's table blocked his path, the nimble poet bounded over it. When a heavy wagon rolled in front of him, he dove under it. Marlowe maneuvered the congested center of one of the busiest cities in history as effortlessly as the sounds around him or the wind and the birds above him. Revived and revitalized, the reborn poet felt like he had wings for feet.

Once he reached the Grand Canal, Marlowe decided he wanted a challenge. The Rialto was too packed with people for him to lope through; many of them were already wearing their evening masks. Rather than get in line to cross the water, the poet raced up the Rialto Bridge's balustrade and leaped off its edge as stunned Venetians looked on and gasped. Marlowe jumped into the first archway he saw and climbed up using its unshuttered window's wrought-iron bars. As his awestruck audience both laughed and cursed, Marlowe pulled himself atop the marble structure no differently than the Roman walls he scaled in Canterbury. After taking in a breath of triumph, Marlowe sprinted eastward across the bridge, slid up and over its central arch, and leaped off its sloping roof towards a window at eye level. Although he was hanging on by just one hand, Marlowe had crossed the Canałasso in a manner higher than any Venetian in history.

After pulling himself over the window's balustrade, Marlowe dusted his hands while looking upward, curious if he could repeat this modest feat on the window above him. The poet stood on the balustrade, jumped, and succeeded, so he tried this again until he was standing victoriously atop Riva Ferro. Marlowe was more than sixty feet in the air now, offering him a spectacular view of the Grand Canal. The famous Fondaco dei Tedeschi was to his right: the first of nearly a hundred palaces stretching westward for a mile along the Canałasso. Directly across from Marlowe, the peach facade of the Palazzo dei Dieci Savi was facing him. The poet had to smile at the realization that he was now standing taller than the bronze of Saint James atop the San Giacomo di Rialto. To the poet's left, the Canalasso stretched more than two thousand feet west-southwest in a nearly perfect line of gondolas, merchant vessels, and cerulean water before bending southeast into the teeming Bacino di San Marco. Beneath his dusty boots, many of Marlowe's onlookers from Riva Ferro to the boats bobbing in the water were losing interest in the crazy poet who had just vaulted from the Rialto Bridge. Losing interest in them as well, Marlowe turned his back on San Polo as he took in his view of San Marco from its northernmost point.

It was a lovely sight as well, but . . . not high enough. Marlowe's view of the *sestiere* was obstructed by the nearby spire of San Bartolomeo. Since the spire was at the opposite end of his rooftop, the poet wandered over to examine it. After teasing its surface with his fingers, Marlowe drew his newly acquired parrying dagger and stabbed the structure. The dagger held, giving him enough leverage to climb even higher until he was able to shinny up the remaining distance. Now at the church's highest point, the poet was more than seventy feet in the air. An easy victory. Marlowe held on to the spire's point and looked for further conquests. From the nearby *chiesa* of San Paterniano to the distant tower of Sant'Elena, there did not appear to be any higher structure standing between the triumphant climber and his view of the floating city. Except for . . .

Marlowe set his sights on the Campanile di San Marco: the great bell tower rising 323 feet just next to St. Mark's Basilica. The lofty structure was a mighty column of red bricks crowned with a commanding belfry, alternating icons of the Lion of St. Mark and la Giustizia, and a pyramidal spire of emerald green framed in marble white. The massive structure was topped by a golden weather vane fashioned into a statue of the archangel Gabriel—or at least it should have been. The statue was the highest point in all of Venice, making it a frequent victim to lighting strikes. This meant that Marlowe would have some scaffolding to work with if he wished to temporarily take Gabriel's place. Especially since the guardian angel had recently been taken down for repairs.

After examining the sea of shingles between himself and the Campanile, Marlowe slid down his shorter spire, sheathed his dagger, and took a running leap from the rooftop.

That night . . .

After spending an entire afternoon scaling Venetian churches and palaces; after enjoying a meal along with some lovemaking from a coquettish soprano singing from her window; after sitting atop the four bronze horses Venice sacked from Constantinople in 1204; and after sharing a few choice words with Mark the Evangelist atop his cathedral; Christopher Marlowe, the man who had spent his youth scaling battlements erected by Roman generals, the fallen priest who admired Rome from atop the Castel Sant'Angelo and the Colosseum, the murdered poet who spent his afterlife wallowing in Venice as if the city were still a swamp, had finally conquered his demons. He had finally ascended to something higher.

With the sun asleep and the stars ablaze, with the evening alive with music and laughter, with Piazza San Marco overflowing with partygoers dressed in their finest costumes and masks, with every voice in the city cheering, with every church bell in Venice tolling, and with a barrage of fireworks filling the night sky around him with explosive colors, Marlowe lowered his head from atop the highest point in the floating city, outstretched his arms, and offered a benediction in Latin so that even God could hear it: *"Deus mea est fortitudo, atque quod me nutrit me destruit."*

"God is my strength," he whispered, a literal translation of the Hebrew 'Gabriel.' "And what nourishes me destroys me."

The late Christopher Marlowe was back from the dead, and just in time.

The Carnevale of 1605 had begun.

Chapter XXI

Shakespeare & Aston

R obert Catesby, Guy Fawkes, and their fellow conspirators departed the Duck and Drake during the early hours of February the twenty-second, 1604—more on this last detail later. It was not yet daylight, but the bard had little trouble spotting their lamps as their carriage crawled north-northwest from Westminster into the snow-swept landscape. It would be a long journey across one hundred miles of frozen, unpaved roads to Warwickshire, but Shakespeare took the same route every summer to be with his family in Stratford. Even though it was winter, the bard was confident that he could complete this ride, and for good reason. For the first time, he would be taking a vastly superior vehicle into the English countryside.

Once the conspirators reached the distant windmills of Hampstead, the playwright sheathed his brass spyglass and slid down from his rooftop. Within a familiar Strand stable, Shakespeare found a saddled Aston rested and ready for him. Clad in fur and cloaked in white, the two embarked on their journey while a familiar raven took flight as well.

For seven days and six nights, the bard closely followed his distant targets. He stalked their tracks, monitored their movements, and disappeared into the same towns where they rested. The bard never betrayed his position, nor did he observe any suspicious activity. Quite the contrary, the most extraordinary aspect of this cross-country endeavor was how ordinary it appeared on both ends of Bacon's telescope. Shakespeare and Aston encountered no difficulties for nearly the full length of their trip. The weather was cold, but not unbearable; the two were well equipped for the winter. Their ride was unhindered by wolves, which had long ago been eradicated from England. Also, the countless bodies they found frozen to gibbets gave Shakespeare confidence that the local marshals were keeping the peace. The playwright's raven was quiet, and Aston appeared to be in good spirits. As such, it should not be too surprising that the horse and rider became quite chatty by the tail end of their travel.

The discourse started while the two rode through Buckinghamshire en route to what the bard imagined was Aylesbury. They were in the Chilterns—or at least what remained of them. Many of the region's beech forests had been cut down in recent years to deny them to thieves. When the conspirators accidently veered into this impassable wall of tree stumps, the bard took Aston behind the veil of what little forest remained. Seeing this would take a while, the playwright dismounted and patted his partner. However, something unexpected happened. For the first time into their journey, the silver stallion flinched at Shakespeare's touch. "What is it, cousin?" the bard asked with surprise. He slipped off his leather glove and felt under the horse's winter fleece. Aston's neck was not too terribly knotted, but the magnificent creature cringed when Shakespeare ran his hand over the animal's inflamed croup. "Oh, Aston . . ." the playwright chided. "You shouldn't keep these things to yourself!" Shakespeare removed Aston's saddle and rummaged through the kit Bacon had given him for repairs.

Inside, Shakespeare found two wooden mallets and Bacon's codex on equine anatomy, which the bard no longer looked upon as a painful reminder of Bentley. The playwright flipped through the indexed ailments and compared them with the book's detailed drawings, which he mentally projected onto his injured companion. Shakespeare set the book on a large stump and he traced his fingers along both sides of Aston's spine. Once he came to the animal's lower vertebrae, he put his hands together and gave Aston a hard shove with his palms. There was an audible *pop* as the vertebrae properly realigned. He then tapped the sore spot with his mallets—to Aston's delight, the playwright gathered—and then semicircled the shining creature to finish things in the front.

Shakespeare gently stretched Aston's neck to the left and the right, and then threw his arms around the animal in an almost loving embrace. The bard locked his fingers together just behind Aston's ears and gave him two hard, quick yanks. This time, the forest filled with even louder cracks than before. "Better now?" the playwright asked even though he knew the answer was yes. After giving Aston a few more therapeutic taps, the bard patted his partner and packed his kit. "See? This is why you should tell me everything!" Once he was back in the saddle, the playwright treated his gracious companion to a one-man performance of *Much Ado About Nothing*.

And then *Richard III*.

And then, so long as Aston appeared interested, the bard decided to go through the rest of his repertoire: *The Two Gentlemen of Verona*, *The Taming of the Shrew*, the three Henry plays, *Titus Andronicus*, and so on. The playwright recited them line by line, play by play in the order that they were written, including *Love's Labour's Won* but with the understandable omission of *Sir Thomas More*. It was not as good as a performance from the King's Men—the bard was working with just one costume—but it was nevertheless a cathartic reading after months of pent-up aggression. Every theater in London had been closed for months due to the plague, and the Globe was no exception. "A plague . . ." the playwright seethed halfway into *Romeo and Juliet*. "They have made worms' meat of me!" It was the most exhaustive performance of English drama in history, and the bard would not have shared it with any other horse. Only Aston.

Overhead, the playwright's stately raven continued to monitor the duo.

By the last legs of their journey, the curtain fell on *A Midsummer Night's Dream* as the conversation shifted with the scenery to something serious. The two finally crossed into Warwickshire on February the twenty-seventh a little less than an hour after departing Banbury. The timing of their entry revealed the conspirators' plans to the playwright: they were less than a day's ride from Warwick, which was precisely where their carriage pulled in for the evening. After crossing the Avon on Aston, Shakespeare rented a room under an alias and monitored the conspirators from across the street where they slept. Once their windows went dark, the bard went to bed convinced where they would be riding in the morning. They were north of the River Avon, they still had at least a day's travel ahead of them, and his targets planned to meet with the cunning folk. Their final destination had to be the Forest of Arden.

It was.

After waking somewhat later than the bard expected, the conspirators returned to their coach and rode north five miles into Kenilworth. The men rested and lunched, swapped their horses for sturdier mounts, and continued north until bending with Finham Brook in a northwesterly direction. Shakespeare watched through his spyglass as the carriage crossed the frozen River Blythe and journeyed deeper into the winter's heart of the Hemlingford Hundred. With Aston and their resting raven awaiting their next move, the bard shouldered his telescope and ventured forward into the barren north-northwest.

The Hemlingford Hundred was a wide, sweeping landscape that had also been home to extensive forests before falling to English axes. It was the ancient edge of the Arden, a vast wilderness so unknown and unexplored that even the Romans avoided it. The

Arden was a mysterious place with no definite borders, especially with so much of the woodlands disappearing every day. There were still a few lonely trees scattered across Hemlingford like twigs, but otherwise, these icy fields served as a graveyard to the native lands that ancient Britons revered as "Albion" in dead tongues.

The conspirators rolled westward in their wagon over the Arden's frozen shores while freezing rain beat down on the playwright behind them. As they passed Bickenhill and Solihull, the towns became fewer and the clumps of trees increased dramatically. The wind was rustling and the skies darkening when the carriage at last approached the wooded halls of the Arden. From Shakespeare's viewpoint on the very edge of the Hundred, both the conspirators and the forest in front of them were silhouetted in the setting sun. The bard tried to observe through his telescope, but the cylinder was stuck shut with frost. By the time he opened the contraption, his distant targets were already swallowed up by the veil of trees. Alarmed, the playwright shouldered his spyglass, scanned the woodlands left and right, and charged Aston across the ice before he lost the conspirators completely.

Once the two were inside the frozen fortress of Arden, Shakespeare slowed Aston to a trot while his raven perched atop a branch. There was no sight or sound of the conspirators to follow. "These are an ancient wood," the playwright whispered to his partner. "A mystic place. A living link to a distant past my grandparents used to tell me about. Lighthearted stories and dark deeds have taken place in here. The woodland welcomes children with laughter, but by nature is made for rapes and murders." An owl hooted, and the playwright's observant raven turned its head. "Such is the Forest of Arden, my dear Aston. It is ruthless, vast, and gloomy. Such is the dark heart of Warwickshire, my home."

With these words, the bard's raven swooped down and screamed. Two cloaked figures stepped in front of the bard from behind the trees.

As a startled Shakespeare reared his whinnying mount, his shrieking raven raked a red line across the faces of both bandits. The injury caused one villain to drop his knife and double over in pain while the other looked up and swung his sword at the violent bird. Alarmed, Shakespeare turned Aston to flee the forest only to find a third man blocking their escape. The cheery figure was brightly dressed and wore a hideously repulsive mask.

The bard reached for his rapier but fumbled desperately. The stubborn sword would not draw! Frustrated, he looked down only to realize that his frosted blade was stuck in its scabbard.

His grinning adversary, however, was more familiar with the effect of weather on weapons. With a single swipe from his sword, the villain slew the playwright's raven.

Severed from the outside world, Shakespeare and Aston were trapped inside the Arden.

Chapter XXII

The Hobgoblin

F *ee-fie-fo, fellow English! What fortune finds you alone? You sing so sweet of your homeland, yet you are so far from home!"*

The grinning figure swaggered forward across the bloodsplattered stage; his tall boots crushing the feathers of the playwright's fallen raven. The villain carried himself with a joie de vivre of an almost theatrical nature, bending low like an actor proudly addressing his groundlings. He curled his fingers in intricate gestures like a mime as he walked. His short cape was jet-black with an inner lining of gold and black diamonds. He wore a thick, rumpled ruff atop a decorative doublet flamboyantly checkered in a harlequin pattern of colors. And crowning it all was a black velvet cap with a long feather and a gold medallion that Shakespeare imagined was stolen.

And then there was his face. Or more specifically, his mask.

Staring back at the bard was the same twisted visage that every English traveler in the countryside dreaded. What did the mask look like? In one word: grotesque. Stories about the mask varied from person to person, but every single one of them could attest to its ugliness. You would know it when you saw it, particularly if its wearer was leering at you from the forest. Under such circumstances, perhaps you could turn tail and flee before his toadies, Snell and Shorthouse, shot you full with their crossbows. However, if you were instead riding peacefully until an owl hooted at an odd time of the day, as Shakespeare was, then it was already too late. You just walked into a trap set by men who lived in the forest drinking nothing but beer and eating nothing but old meat and toadstools. Such a dangerous lifestyle has a toxic effect on the mind, which was why these particular highwaymen had an overactive imagination with their hapless victims.

If you found yourself trapped between the masked man and his toadies, you were theirs. All of you. Every part of your body was now their puppet to play with. They once forced a Cambridge scholar to give a lecture with a puukko knife held to his neck. Another time, they forced one of Shakespeare's own actors to perform a scene from *Hamlet* in the nude. No one knew what to expect from these outlaws or their twisted ringleader, save for that one detail: it was a truly grotesque mask, as Shakespeare now knew for himself. Such was the legacy of Gamaliel Ratsey, the former nobleman now feared throughout England as "the Hobgoblin."

The playwright narrowed his eyes and shook his head at the villain. "Do you spend your days practicing on little birds, Ratsey?"

"Little birds and little boys! With little throats and little toys."

Shakespeare smirked with skepticism while one henchman wailed madly behind him. The bard's fallen raven had taken out one of the highwayman's eyes.

"How be thee, matey?" the Hobgoblin asked Snell.

Enraged, the bloodied henchman rushed over to the raven's remains, screaming "Thou demon!" as he slashed the slain bird with his sword. "That beast took my eye!"

The Hobgoblin turned away as bloodied bits of pink snow stained his costume. *"I would weep for you, brother, but you still have another."* The maestro wiped a red tear from his eye as he returned to the bard.

"As you see, the cruel Fates be unkind to my friend. Perhaps kindness from you will make his sorrows end."

"You must be jesting," the playwright replied.

"Ah! I may laugh, I may leap, I make merry; it's true! But to think me a jester? Such a joke is on you!" The Hobgoblin pointed at Shakespeare with a devilish leer. He then looked to Shorthouse and said: *"Bind his hands, brother."*

"What do you want from me?" the bard grumbled while tightening his grip on his reins.

"Nothing of consequence. Just your silver, of course. And your gold and your garb. Maybe even that horse."

Shorthouse threatened Shakespeare with his crossbow since Aston would not let the bandit approach. "Unhorse you'self," he ordered while the silver steed stomped his hooves.

"I suggest you stand back," the dramatist cautioned. The more Aston bucked, the less control he appeared to have over him.

Shorthouse looked to his leader for the go-ahead to kill Shakespeare. Instead, the entertained Hobgoblin cackled with laughter. *"You persist and resist! I must say, my dear brothers; this one fights with more boister than Ralph Roister Doister!"*

"Do you have the courage to say that to me face to face?" asked the bard, who was beginning to see flaws in Gamaliel Ratsey's act.

"With a smile and guile!" The masked bandit raised his sword and stepped closer. *"Now, would you kindly—"*

Aston reared onto his hind legs, kicking Gamaliel flat onto his back. The blow knocked the Hobgoblin's mask off, revealing the villain's surprisingly handsome face underneath. The bard spun his mount and tried to flee, but instead had to pull on his reins. Snell was done mutilating the bard's raven and had a crossbow aimed at Aston. "Dismount!" the toady screamed with blood and eye fluid dripping down his face.

Shakespeare struggled atop his angered stallion. "You can see that I can't!"

"Can't, or shan't!" Gamaliel shouted as he tied on his mask. *"I will teach your damned horse how to kneel!"* The Hobgoblin staggered onto his feet and raised his sword. *"Restrain the beast, or I'll slaughter him. I swear we'll make him our next meal!"*

Seeing no other option that would safeguard his friend, Shakespeare raised his hands and quickly studied the snowy setting around him. He moved Aston under a tree and tied his reins to a tall branch—one that none of the bandits could reach without climbing into his saddle. He then patted his partner and slipped his boots from his stirrups. Shorthouse violently pulled the bard from his saddle before he could dismount. Aston, infuriated over seeing his rider fall, tried to free himself from his harness while Snell kept his crossbow pointed at the magnificent horse.

Shorthouse kicked Shakespeare on the ground and threw the playwright's hood back. As the bard looked up from the snow, his enemies got their first look at his uncovered face. The Hobgoblin's eyes widened with recognition, filling the edges of his mask's furrowed slits. *"Welly!"* he chirped. *"Welly, welly, my felleys! It seems that our victory's won . . . against none other than the great Bard in Avon!"*

Shakespeare wobbled onto his feet with one boot strategically placed in the snow. "None other," the famed playwright confirmed while Shorthouse stripped the bard of his rapier and telescope, which were both thrown to Snell. "Shall I perform for you?"

The masked villain guffawed. *"Do you hear this, my brothers? By all means, please do! Perform* The Jew of Malta *for us. Act one . . . er . . . scene two."*

The playwright's face froze. *"The Jew of Malta* is not one of mine," he clarified. "It's Christopher Marlowe's."

"Is Marlowe a no-no?" the masked bandit teased.

The bard straightened himself and angrily smacked the snow from his cloak. "I won't do it."

"You perform Morley poorly," the outlaw critiqued, shaking his head with sardonic disappointment.

"I knew Marlowe. He was a good man. . . ." The bard paused. "Actually, no. He wasn't. But he was a greater man than you are. And if he were here now"—Shakespeare's voice trembled—"he would have *laughed* at your ridiculous mask."

The Hobgoblin slowly tilted his head. Shakespeare was trying to get under his skin with that comment, and it worked. The lecherous creature slinked up to the dramatist and pressed his bloodied sword to his cheek. *"What if I cut off your face, then? It would not be so hard. I could cast down the Hobgob' and henceforth be the Bard!"*

Face to face with his enemy, the veteran actor did not budge; not even when the severed feathers from his former raven grazed his face. Instead, Shakespeare narrowed his eyes and smiled. Although Ratsey was wearing a mask, the playwright saw straight through his facade. The man was acting, and poorly. He relied too much on props which, frankly, paled in comparison to the ones his would-be victim had on him.

"How about some magic?" the dramatist offered instead. Shakespeare did not need to see Gamaliel's eyebrows to know that this lure hooked its prey.

The Hobgoblin asked. *"A magic trick?"* The bard nodded, and the bandit took a step back. *"Make it quick."*

Shakespeare straightened his sleeves and reached for the playing cards in his cloak. Although Shorthouse caught the bard by his hand, the dramatist was not threatened. "It's just an ordinary deck of playing cards. . . ." he offered with the usual flair. Shorthouse looked to his leader with suspicion, but the Hobgoblin allowed the playwright to continue. "A deck of cards . . ." the bard pledged to the men. "Each one filled with surprises." Shakespeare tore open the knave of diamonds and emptied it into his palm. "Precious spices!" The bard poured the fine powder into the Hobgoblin's hands.

Gamaliel and Shorthouse sampled the spices and then looked up with surprise. *"Be there more, troubadour?"*

"My dear sirs," the bard grinned, "this whole deck contains spices galore!" This time, Shakespeare opened a few packs of poisonous spades and emptied them over the pile the Hobgoblin had. However, the bandit let the deadly stuff fall through his finger and seized the rest of the deck. *"We'll take your word for it, brother."* Gamaliel handed the purloined prize to Shorthouse. *"That was a laugh! Do another!"*

Although Shakespeare was smiling, his heart sank. He stared speechlessly at the bandits until Shorthouse poked inside the bard's cloak with his sword. "And what's that?" the bandit asked, tapping something hard with his saber.

"Something aglitter?" the Hobgoblin hissed with a slither. The masked bandit stepped closer. *"It is gold! Bring it hither!"*

The veteran actor successfully suppressed his smile. Shakespeare took his pocket watch from his belt and presented it to the mesmerized highwaymen.

"Amazing . . ." Gamaliel gasped as he and Shorthouse beheld the machine. *"How does it function?"* asked the Hobgoblin as he reached for the trinket.

"With gumption!" Shakespeare smirked as he pulled the device back to wind it. He then offered the watch to the bandits while covertly removing its pin.

The Hobgoblin snatched the gold timepiece, and the bard innocently dropped its pin with an "Oops." As Shakespeare bent down to pick it up, he seized the puukko knife Snell had dropped earlier and which the bard had been standing on this whole time. Shakespeare stabbed the Finnish blade straight into Shorthouse's boot, severing his Achilles tendon and bringing the hulking brute down.

The Hobgoblin cradled his timepiece. *"Kill him!"* he cried as the playwright made a mad dash back to Aston. As Snell turned his head from the horse, Shakespeare threw the puukko knife at the villain, striking him in the one eye he had left. The bandit stumbled backward and screamed while Shakespeare picked up his spyglass and sword and leaped back onto Aston. The bard freed his reins and spurred the charger out of the woods while pulling on the branch above him until it slipped from his grip. The branch swung backward and struck its neighbors, dropping a thick cloud of snow onto the bandits while Shakespeare and Aston made their escape.

However, just before the duo could emerge through the forest, the bard reined his horse to a harrowing halt. A second raven was flying in from the distance and screeching. And behind the raven, Shakespeare saw a dark figure riding toward him with a bow raised and drawn. The rider loosed an arrow straight past the playwright, striking Shorthouse in his ear. Horrified, the bard looked behind him and understood there was only one pathway left. He charged Aston back into the woods just in time to see Sir Francis Bacon's deadly watch detonate.

The timepiece exploded directly under Gamaliel Ratsey's face, blasting his jaw into jagged shards that embedded themselves onto the roof of his mouth. The villain screamed in agony and reached for his injuries only to realize the hand holding the watch had been reduced to a mangled stump. Ratsey could hardly see and barely breathe. Nearly all his teeth were blasted out of his skull. His whole mask had been blown off, taking his nose but otherwise preserving the upper half of his face. The once silver-tongued bandit could now only speak in mad gasps, for the tattered remains of his tongue were hanging free from his head. At long last, Gamaliel Ratsey was the hobgoblin he had always pretended to be, and as Shakespeare galloped back onto the scene, he had no choice but to run Ratsey over with Aston.

Deep down, the playwright hoped Aston's hooves might put the mangled man out of his misery. Instead, they only added to the Hobgoblin's torment within the frozen walls of the Arden.

Chapter XXIII

The Curse

"Do you hear that?"

"Hear what?"

"That poor soul has been sobbing for hours now."

"No, that's not it. I heard a sound of thunder outside."

"Thunder?"

"In this season?"

"These are a haunted woods, Robert. We should never have come here."

"*You've* been sobbing about that for hours now. And sweating and stinking."

"Shut your noise, Wright!"

"Make peace, you two! And Guido, please sit. You're upsetting the carriage."

"I think we're close."

A bright flash of lightning illuminated the forest, making all five conspirators turn their heads to their windows. It was snowing outside their carriage in white streaks that changed violently with the wind. The night skies pulsated in purple, and then erupted with a loud thunderclap that shook the coach and startled its horses.

"How is this possible?" Tom Wintour gasped.

"Black magic," replied Percy. "Robert, God will condemn us to Hell for consorting with these demons."

Robert stared sympathetically at his partner. "You know it is too late for us to turn back."

Suddenly, a red glow filled the windows. The carriage stopped.

"We've arrived," said Guy Fawkes.

"God save us," sighed Robert.

Behind them, a snow-covered William Shakespeare lowered his spyglass.

For many years, the cunning folk were allowed to practice their arts throughout England without fear of reprisal from Parliament. All that changed under Henry VIII with the passage of the Witchcraft Act of 1542, which targeted England's witches and cunning folk with equal severity: death.* It was the first law in English history to define witchcraft as a capital offense, and although it was repealed five years later for its cruelty, first blood had already been drawn. A Reformation-fueled frenzy of witch hunts swept over England, taking many of the kingdom's thousands of cunning folk with it.

Although Elizabeth tried to remedy the situation with a more moderate stance against witchcraft,† the government and the church had become too dangerous for the cunning folk to contend with. Some disappeared into what remained of Britain's once plentiful forests. Others fled north only to be claimed by the even deadlier frenzy fanned by Scotland's King James VI. With Elizabeth dead and James now king of England, Ireland, and Scotland, Parliament's campaign against witchcraft had reached

---

The Bill ayēst conjuracōns & wichecraftes and sorcery and enchantments (33 Hen. VIII. c. 8).
†*An Act against Conjurations, Enchantments and Witchcrafts* (5 Eliz. I c. 16).

its greatest intensity. The Witchcraft Act of 1604 broadened the laws of King James's predecessors, making any consorting with the cunning folk more dangerous than ever.*

As a result, it was no surprise to Shakespeare that Thomas Percy was not the only man sweating when the conspirators finally met with their Warwickshire allies.

By the time the bard caught up with his targets, night had fallen, bringing in storm clouds with it. Shakespeare did not know if he had eluded the dark rider hounding him, but he was too close to his enemies to risk revealing his movements. He found the conspirators by following an enormous fire in the forest, which he imagined had to be their final destination. It was. The men were so deep in the Arden that Shakespeare did not even know if they were still within Warwickshire. The skies crackled with electricity as a cold wind bellowed down from the heavens. A chaotic downpour of snow and ice coated his cloak. The bard had to wipe his lenses repeatedly as he studied the scene through his spyglass. Beside him, Aston was securely tied behind a tree lest a sudden flash of lightning reveal him to their enemies. Fortunately, just as Bacon promised, the silver stallion was unaffected by the storm and its thunder.

In the distance, the conspirators were standing outside of their carriage within a glade centered by a tall, roaring fire. A great stone lay flat in the melted snow by the flames, serving as an altar for the crucible and human skull atop it. As Shakespeare studied the skull, he could see the faint flicker of a candle inside it. A silhouetted wall of large men stood in front of the bonfire brandishing clubs, axes, and other cruel-looking weapons. And beside the men, three aged figures stood limply in tattered robes that seemed to resemble

---

*An Acte against conjuration Witchcrafte and dealinge with evill and wicked Spirits (2 Ja. I c. 12).

monks' habits. Although their hands were not bound, their heads hung forlornly as if already condemned.

And in front of them all, facing the conspirators and undeterred by the elements, stood two women.

The women held their heads high in the storm with unblinking eyes fixed on the conspirators. The taller appeared slightly older to Shakespeare: her hair a thick mane of dark brown with a single streak of gray. Her younger companion was shorter, skinnier, fair-haired, and possessed a piercing stare that made the conspirators too terrified to take their eyes off her.

Down on one knee and concealed behind a wall of frozen rose bushes, the bard focused his skills and spyglass on his targets' mouths as they moved.

"Are you controlling this storm?" Robert Catesby hollered over the wind.

"We agreed to meet againe," the elder answered, "in Thunder, Lightning, or in Raine."

"When the Hurley-burley's done," the younger barked, her hair blowing. "When the Battaile's lost, and wonne."

Robert's worried eyes wrinkled with confusion. "What hurly-burly? The fighting has not started yet."

The women fell silent. The high hiss of their swirling fire was their response.

Believing their powers, Guy Fawkes entered into the dialogue. "We have our requests," he called out, removing three sealed letters from his flapping cloak.

The elder woman stared at the conspirator and raised her left arm to her side.

Fawkes stepped forward to deliver the letters, but then stopped once he saw the burly men behind the women move. They disappeared behind the bonfire and returned carrying a large cauldron that had been hidden behind the flames. As the men moved around the fire, the bard noticed that their faces and arms were intricately tattooed with blue dye. The remaining men pushed their swaying, seemingly sedated three captives forward. Once the languid men were standing beside their mistresses, one of their brutes placed a curved blade in the elder's hand. The woman clenched the knife and lowered her arm, the whole time without breaking eye contact with Fawkes.

As thunder cracked and the wind intensified, Robert hustled over and snatched the parchments before they became lost in the storm. Robert turned the first letter over to open it, but before he did, his eyes moved up. The younger woman across the glade threw back the hood of one captive and held his head over the cauldron.

"What are you doing with him?" Robert asked.

"A deed without a name," the elder answered.

Robert took a step forward and squinted at the captive. "I know that man. He's a Jesuit priest!"

"They all are," Fawkes gasped. "Those are Father Garnet's men!"

Robert's mouth was agape.

"You said you needed these men for your spells! Not for your—"

"Calm yourself!" Robert cautioned.

"Bloody heathens!" Thomas Percy shouted.

Catesby spun around. "Quiet!" He looked back at the women with desperation on his face. "My ladies, when we entered into this pact, we did not know such sacrifices would have to be made."

The two women stayed silent, completely unmoved by Robert's pleas. Behind them, their large bodyguards began batting their weapons.

Seeing this, Jack Wright put his hand on his sword, which he was beginning to think would be useless against so many enemies.

Terrified, Robert turned to Guy Fawkes. "Guido, what have you gotten us into?"

Fawkes shook his head, speechless.

"What do I do?" Robert asked with urgency.

Fawkes tried to rationalize the hopelessness of the situation. "If we succeed . . ." he stammered, "then God will forgive us."

"And the priests?" Robert added.

Fawkes thought for a moment, but then nodded with confidence. "They will die martyrs," he decided. "These men are saints, Robert. We will build churches to them."

Robert looked once more to the limp Jesuits, and then back to his parchment. "God wills it," he said.

The conspirators crossed themselves, and the elder woman lowered her knife to the priest's throat.

Robert broke the first parchment's wax seal, which bore the coat of arms of Spain's Philip III. "We ask that you sever England from all her overseas allies," he read aloud through the tempest.

The elder sliced the priest's throat, emptying his blood into the cauldron.

The bard held a glove to his mouth as he watched the carnage unfold.

Once the bleeding man fell forward limply, the younger woman dropped the priest to make room for their next captive. Like his predecessor, the Jesuit neither screamed nor struggled, nor did he offer any other sign of resistance. He had the look of one already dead.

Robert came to the next letter, which bore two seals: one Italian and the other French. After breaking them both: "We ask that Cardinal Alessandro de' Medici be made the next pope."

Once more, a Jesuit had his throat slit.

The conspirators had to turn away, but Shakespeare had no choice but to look on. He forced himself to study how the body fell and its blood spurted. This was no drama, the bard realized. This was not theater. It was real.

Finally, Robert broke the seal to his last letter, one that he and his fellow conspirators composed. "And lastly," he read, glancing up at the women, "we ask that you bless us on our endeavor: That we purge these isles of the Protestant pestilence defiling it. We ask this in the name of our Lord Jesus Christ . . ." Robert closed the letter. "And yours."

The elder woman slew the final Jesuit.

Once this third body was discarded onto the two in the snow, the elder woman handed her bloodied knife to her younger assistant.

"What now?" asked Robert. "Is it done?"

"In God's name, may we *please* leave!" Percy begged.

The women did not respond. Instead, the younger set the bloodied knife down on the stone and returned to the cauldron with the skull and crucible. The elder woman checked the skull, which still had a candle burning inside it, and carefully placed it deep within the cauldron. She then took the clay crucible, which was about the size of a tankard and similarly topped with a lid. The elder turned the crucible over and emptied its contents, spilling a fine orange powder atop the skull. As the wind carried the orange powder inside the skull's glowing sockets, it flickered.

Their deed done, the women stepped away from the cauldron, as did their bodyguards and the frightened conspirators.

As Shakespeare watched through his lenses, nothing appeared to be happening. But then something stirred within the belly of the iron beast.

An ashen mound began to rise out of the cauldron that burned violently at its center like a volcano. As its flames shot out and spiraled into the wind, the women turned their eyes to their stunned spectators and smiled.

"Is this it?" Robert gasped while backing away.

"This is it," Guy Fawkes answered. "This is their magic."

Seemingly out of nowhere, four fiery arms erupted from the cauldron and began writhing like tentacles.

"Sorcery!" Percy screamed. "This is black magic!"

"Fly, brothers!" Fawkes shouted as he and Robert ran away from the flames. "Fly!"

The conspirators hurried back into their carriage and whipped their terrified horses. The coach fled from the ceremony while Shakespeare sheathed his spyglass as quickly as his arms could move. If he was to have any chance of escaping, he had to follow the conspirators' carriage out of the Arden. He untied Aston in a hurry while taking one last look at the fiery spectacle. He was speechless. Although the bard was familiar with a wide array of special effects, he had never seen or even heard of anything such as this. No matter who these women were or how their spells worked, Walsingham needed to know about them. Their cauldron appeared to function as a gateway to Hell.

Shakespeare leaped onto Aston and spurred out of the forest completely oblivious to the deadlier storm he was riding into. For you see, in England, although it was a few minutes after midnight on March 1, 1604, it was actually March 11, 1605, in the rest of the world due to the difference between the Julian and Gregorian calendars. The cunning folk knew this, which was why they insisted on meeting Guy Fawkes and his men when they did so deep in the country. Although the conspirators could not have known it, two of their three curses had already been carried out more than a week ago.

It was now only a matter of time before word reached the British Isles that Pope Clement VIII was dead, and that the Carnevale of 1605 had ended in horror.

Chapter XXIV

La Volta

Marlowe floated down the stone steps of the tallest tower in Venice with his arms swinging, his spirits soaring, and a winning smile spread across his satisfied face. The carefree poet felt reborn—nay, resurrected—after his hours of exercising. Its most recent feat alone felt like it had added another hundred years to his life. The daredevil inside him wished Venice had more summits to scale and more skies for him to own. However, his day was over, the sun had set, and Marlowe's energy was waning. Fortunately, he could think of no better nightcap to his evening than some coffee with his dearest friend in the city. With his mind made like the feather bed he was looking forward to crawling into, Marlowe clicked his heels and hit the floor of the mighty campanile he had conquered.

The poet strode through the triumphal arches of the Loggetta del Sansovino as if all of Venice were heralding him as their champion. In truth, they were celebrating, but for reasons Marlowe was too in love with himself to remember. The poet took two steps from the Loggetta and was swiftly seized by the same hands that had abducted him earlier. "Such service!" he applauded as the guards from the Fontego whisked their complicit captive to a darkened corner of the Piazzetta di San Marco.

Beneath a secluded section of the Biblioteca Marciana arcade, a large figure met Marlowe with a deathly glare. The man was cloaked in a thick robe of ultramarine silk festooned with a pirate's treasure of pearls and silver charms. His head was topped with a magnificent hat made to resemble a ship crashing against a rock. His visage was hidden behind a ghostly volto mask that had a single teardrop painted on its porcelain cheek. Despite his foreboding appearance, Marlowe immediately recognized the man from his height and headwear. "Drago!" The poet greeted his friend with wide-open arms.

The dragoman grabbed Marlowe by the shoulder and forced him to start walking. "What on earth is the matter with you?" he whispered as the two hastened through the lively Piazzetta.

"Nothing's wrong with me," the poet protested. "I'm feeling better than ever! Although I am a bit tired—"

"You were not at the Fontego," the dragoman interrupted. "You were not even in the same *sestiere* when I returned from the *ghèto*. The guards told me you raced across the Canalasso and began leaping from buildings."

"You heard that?" asked Marlowe, flattered.

"The whole city heard about it! People thought you were going to jump from the Campanile at midnight. It's the only reason I was able to find you." Behind his white mask, the dragoman's eyes shifted anxiously over Piazza San Marco.

"Leap?" Marlowe laughed. "And land on what? That little hay cart of death over there? That would have been suicide, my friend, and you of all people know I don't play that game—anymore."

"This is no game." The dragoman stopped walking and spun the poet around. "Cristo, do you have any idea how much danger you're in? Your entire day has been a suicide for us both! Do you even remember—" As Marlowe scratched his head, his keeper noticed something. "Where is your hat?"

The poet looked up at his shaggy hair. "I had a hat?"

"The hat I gave you. Where is it?"

Marlowe checked inside his cloak and then shrugged. "I must've lost it."

Beneath his mask, the dragoman's eyes bulged. The tall figure snapped his head over the teeming sea of Venetians circling the two like sharks. Once he found what he was looking for, he seized Marlowe's wrist and dragged him to a merchant by the Four Tetrarchs. The guardian purchased a Zanni mask and a floppy red hat for the poet. "Put these on," he ordered.

"What for?"

"For security. Also, it's Carnevale."

"Sure it is," the poet scoffed as he tied on his Zanni. "You said it wouldn't be until Tuesday."

"It is Tuesday. Carnevale started at midnight."

"Yes, midnight on . . ." Marlowe checked the clock on the Torre dell'Orologio and counted on his fingers until he came to the dreadful conclusion. There were more people out than usual for a Monday night in the city. Everyone was wearing their finest clothes and most extravagant face masks. The evening was aglow with fireworks, colored lanterns, torches, and an enormous bonfire in Piazza San Marco's center. The square was packed with revelers from San Geminiano to the golden Basilica. Carnevale was everywhere. "Oh no . . ." The poet groaned and collapsed to his knees in distress. "I think I'm going to be sick."

"You are too late for that." The dragoman yanked the faint poet back onto his feet. "You have an appointment to keep."

"I thought Carnevale was tomorrow. . . ." Marlowe muttered in disbelief.

"Today is tomorrow. Keep your wits about you. You have not lost them completely."

The two moved closer to the fiery heart of the piazza. "Why are you taking me here?" the poet asked.

"To dance."

Marlowe's eyes widened. "With you?"

"No. With the woman you're meeting." The dragoman straightened up his disheveled friend and wiped him with a perfume-scented handkerchief.

Marlowe nervously turned his head to the masked men and women circling the roaring bonfire. "Drago . . ." the poet whimpered. "They're dancing La Volta out there."

"Is that a problem?"

Marlowe's mouth gaped. "A problem? Drago, I've been exercising all day. I'm *exhausted* right now! You want me to dance La Volta? I don't have the life in me to lift someone up. Just thinking about it is killing me!"

The dragoman ignored this. His cautious eyes were scanning the skies.

Suddenly, an idea hit Marlowe like a bullet to his brain. "*Kahfey!*" The poet threw himself into his friend's silken robes. "Drago, *please* tell me you brought some *kahfey*! I need it now more than ever!"

With these pleas, the towering figure froze. It had previously dawned on the dragoman that he had forgotten something at the Fontego in his race to find Marlowe. With the question of what he forgot to bring answered, the grand guardian shut his eyes and lowered his head.

"*Nooo!*" Marlowe sobbed as he slid down his tall friend. All his strength was fading. Marlowe felt like he was disappearing. The late poet was convinced he was going to die—permanently.

"Enough of this." The dragoman picked Marlowe up and stood him on his wobbly legs. "You survived deadlier situations than this before we even met. Just go out there and, *somehow*, this woman will find you. When she does, gather all the information from her you can while promising as little in return as possible. If any danger befalls you, I will be here. Do you understand?"

The poet was speechless. The tired eyes behind his mask were looking death in the face.

"Marlowe!"

The ex-spy snapped back to reality and looked to his tall friend. "You're the first person to call me that in almost twelve years."

"I won't be the last," the dark man in the white mask warned. The dragoman patted the poet on the shoulder and then shoved him into the fiery circle.

Marlowe staggered backward and spun on his heels as he was bathed in the heat of the bonfire. He regained his footing only to find himself in a spinning configuration of dancers: a rotating series of wheels within wheels moving in a clockwork motion. The men and women stepped, skipped, stepped, skipped, and then *la volta*: "the turn," where the men would lift their ladies straight up by their corsets on their fifth step. It was a risqué dance, which was why it remained popular in the city. The men pranced like proud horses and smiled behind their fixed faces. The ladies laughed and cradled their partners' necks as they circled the fire again and again. It was a whirlwind of merriment and enchantment, and Marlowe was trapped inside it. There was no escape. The Carnevale of 1605 was here.

As this fiery carousel closed in on Marlowe, the poet was pulled into the inferno by a slender, unseen hand. "Christopher Marlowe?" a woman whispered in a faraway accent.

The poet turned to have his mask pushed off his face by a pillowy mound of soft, scented skin. Marlowe bent like an old bow and strained to catch the woman leaping into his arms while at the same time trying to hold on to his mask and hat. The poet saved the beret, but his Zanni shattered against the floor and was trampled under the high heels of more than two hundred dancers. With his full face exposed, a wild-eyed Marlowe took his first look at the mysterious woman who, for some reason, knew his real name.

The young dancer was wearing an emerald-green gown that shined vividly against her fair skin and long red hair. Her rich ornaments suggested a courtesan—or a highly accomplished jewelry thief—save for one necklace of simple leather bearing a pendant of three interwoven silver spirals. This modest charm stood out to Marlowe among all her gemstones and gold if only because it appeared Celtic; not exactly the type of jewelry one could purchase in Venice. Out of all her ornaments, this triskele was bound closest to her neck.

Marlowe followed her neck to find two green eyes staring back at him, and nothing more. The woman was wearing a jet-black *moretta*: a round, strapless mask meant to be held in place at the mouth. The *moretta*'s only openings were two circular eyeholes, and aside from its slight bump for the nose, the mask completely robbed its wearer of all features. It was a vast departure from other Carnevale masks, which were embellished with intricate details and bright colors. The *moretta*, on the other hand, was so simple that it almost looked like no mask at all, especially in the evening. Up close, the poet's mysterious dancer appeared to be nothing more than two eyes floating in an enormous hole in her head.

Marlowe was surprised that his mystery lady chose to meet him wearing a mask designed to render its wearer mute. The poet knew she had plenty to talk about. Namely, himself. "How do you know that name?" he whispered.

"Because you're the only one left," she replied in English.

Marlowe stared into the dancer's jade eyes in disbelief, and not because she somehow spoke without removing her *moretta*. Her English had an unusual accent to it; a slight hint of Gaelic that Marlowe could not pinpoint. After looking again at her pendant, the poet asked: "Where are you from? And how did you—"

The woman grabbed Marlowe and silenced him with a kiss so violent that, even with her mask on, the poet began to taste blood on his lips. The two were so close that their eyelashes touched. Neither Marlowe nor his dance partner blinked. This was no longer La Volta, he realized. This was something more primal, more carnal. With his eyes wide open, the poet glanced over to some of the other dancers. Quite a few men had taken their masks off as well, but whenever they tried to unmask their partners, the ladies grabbed their hands and pressed them onto their bodies.

The poet's pulse raced. Every single woman was wearing the same haunting mask.

Suddenly, Marlowe realized something that made him groan in despair. One after another, he began to recognize nearly all the unmasked men around him. One was Jacopo Manucci, an informant who once worked for the legendary Sir Francis Walsingham. Another was Antony Standen, an ex-operative who worked in Florence under the alias Pompeo Pellegrini. Although the poet did not know it, both Standen and Manucci were still on Thomas Walsingham's payroll. Marlowe had no idea that either man was in Venice, and he just as quickly hid his face to keep them from recognizing him. Nearly everyone the poet knew was in that circle: friends, drinking partners, fellow ghosts, gamblers, smugglers, and countless assassins. To Marlowe's surprise, even the doge's nephew was there.

Why were so many of the Venetian walking dead together? Why were they unmasked? And armed? And why were they surrounding Christopher Marlowe?

The poet turned away from the shades and looked back at the masked lady. "My friend says you are interested in an assassination. Is that true?"

The leather woman did not reply, but her unblinking green eyes said "yes."

"Who is the target?" he demanded. "And why must I be involved?"

Once more, the poet's expressionless partner remained mute.

Marlowe ran a finger up the woman's chin to unmask her, but her black *moretta* did not budge. Instead, the woman took his hand and pressed it to her breast. Angered, the poet pulled his hand free and grabbed her head. He tried to yank the mask off, but the woman winced and slapped him back. As Marlowe raised his hand to his cheek, he noticed spots of blood on his fingers. Shocked, the poet looked once more to the anonymous dancer glaring at him.

Her leather mask was stitched onto her face.

The Torre dell'Orologio chimed even though it was not the top of the hour. Several smoke bombs were thrown into the circle, blanketing the dancers in a misty veil. Marlowe stared agape at the woman as she lunged back into his arms. She pressed her hips into his and guided him for one last dance.

Outside the circle, the dragoman looked up to his stately raven. The watchful bird was quiet.

Then, a strange sound filled the piazza.

Marlowe reached for the hands embracing him only to feel a sharp pain on his fingers. He yelped and kicked the dancer away. Her hidden blade had only found the nape of Marlowe's neck. Furious, the woman unleashed a Celtic war scream and charged at the poet with her dagger unsheathed.

After years of disuse, Marlowe's defensive training kicked into action. He blocked the woman's arm with his own and wrapped her hand up in his cloak. He then drew his parrying dagger and buried it up to its hilt in her corset. The woman's eyes bulged, but the injury did not kill her, nor did it cause her to drop her weapon. Instead, a feral spell fell over her that seemed to carry her generations away. Tears watered her emerald eyes and they closed. They then reopened with a renewed vengeance; an ancient hate. The cunning woman, fueling on the anger of her ancestors, sliced herself free from Marlowe's cape and made a final lunge for his heart.

This time, Marlowe let go of his dagger and knocked his attacker with both arms, bending her elbow back until her knife was pointing at her. The poet rammed into her with all his weight and shoved her own dagger into her body. The blade buried itself in her throat, severing her necklace and causing its silver pendant to fall to the crimsoned floor.

The woman let out a breathless gasp and fell backward, but Marlowe caught her. "I am sorry!" he cried. "Please tell me what's happening! Where do you come from? Why are you doing this? And . . . why me!"

The woman stared back at the Englishman and tried to curse him in Old Brythonic, but she had no breath left.

Desperate for answers, Marlowe pressed his fingers against her *moretta*. The openings around her eyes were not stitched, so he extracted his dagger and cut away at the leather without touching her skin. As the clouds around the two cleared, the poet cast aside the woman's veil and looked down. He was speechless. The woman in his arms was spellbindingly beautiful; a *leannán sídhe* in the flesh.

And then she became death.

As Marlowe backed away from her lifeless body, a loud cry filled the air. A raven swooped down and began circling the unmasked villainess, screaming madly.

"MARLOWE!" a voice cried.

The exhausted ex-spy turned his head. The dragoman was charging straight toward him with his sword drawn and his guards from the Fontego branding their *yatağan* blades.

Suddenly, another body fell down next to Marlowe. And then another. And another. And then they fell dead by the dozens.

The poet looked around and discovered that every single man who had been in the dance circle with him was slain. Every one of their throats had been sliced during their last *volta*, and their fallen bodies now wreathed the bonfire in a circle of death and blood. Not even the doge's nephew was spared. They were all murdered.

Except Marlowe.

The cunning ladies turned their black masks onto the last man standing. They saw that one of their sisters had fallen and that her killer was still looming above her. They realized that she had been unmasked. And lastly, they heard the raven shrieking just like so many of their sisters had warned. Prepared for this, the women hid their blades and pointed at the blood-covered poet. *"Assassino,"* they cried. *"Assassino!"*

Marlowe jumped backward with his bloodied blade still in his hand. "No!" he pleaded. "This is not what it looks like!"

"Assassino!" the women screamed, whipping their thousands of stunned spectators into a frenzy. "Killer! Murderer! Demon!"

Marlowe cowered beneath his red cap and looked to his friend. "I err'd!"

The dragoman surrounded the poet with his two guards. "We need to flee! Follow me!"

The swordsmen flashed their weapons and sprinted to the Torre dell'Orologio so that they could take the Merceria all the way back to the Fontego. However, while the panicking Venetians watching them backed away, the women assassins threw themselves against the men to deny them their escape.

"Drago! Help me!"

The masked guardian turned around and found Marlowe being pulled back by his cape. After he cut the poet free with his sword, the mob descended upon the dragoman as well. *"Assassino!"* they screamed while seething "Kill them!" in dead tongues.

But then, the unthinkable happened. Amidst the melee, one of the women managed to knock off the dragoman's face mask *and* his hat.

The spectators gasped. A large, shining *P* had been branded on the dragoman's forehead.

The guardian's eyes bulged with horror.

"Pirata!" the mob shouted with renewed energy. Now the Vene-

tians joined the fighting, quickly overpowering the dragoman's guards. "Pirates!" the people cried. "PIRATES!"

Out of options, the dragoman pointed his rapier into the air and pulled on its hidden trigger. A large explosion shook the piazza, forcing the frenzied crowd to back away.

"*Mago!*" they shouted. "Sorcerer! *Stregone!* Magician!"

The dragoman's life was now in more danger than Marlowe's. Fortunately, this was precisely what he was aiming for. "Follow me!" he shouted, and the two men ran westward.

"Why are they trying to kill us?" Marlowe cried as they hustled toward the church of San Geminiano. When they passed the bonfire, the dragoman took a handful of playing cards from his robe and threw them into the flames. The clubs exploded in rapid bursts, forcing their Venetian pursuers to flee.

The cunning assassins, however, were undeterred by such illusions.

Once the duo reached San Geminiano, the dragoman pulled the pin from his pocket watch and lobbed it straight into the screaming killers. He pulled Marlowe behind a pillar and the bomb exploded, knocking nearly every one of the cunning folk down.

"We need to get to Cannaregio," said the expert. "You should—"

"DRAGO!" Marlowe screamed.

The doge's guards joined the fighting by shooting two flaming arrows into the dragoman's back, bringing the guardian to his knees. As Marlowe watched his friend fall in horror, other arrows began flying in his direction as well. Terrified, the poet rushed to San Geminiano's doors and, finding them locked, threw himself through one of the church's stained-glass windows. "Drago, this way!" he pleaded.

The dragoman removed his robe to smother the flaming arrows. However, once he was back on his feet, he looked at Marlowe and shook his head. "You're on your own. Get to the *ghèto!*" he thundered. "Find—"

"Behind you!" Marlowe shouted.

The dragoman turned his head directly into a dagger belonging to one of the cunning women. Half the lady's mask had been blown off, exposing her bloodied face underneath. With her injury returned on the dragoman's eye, she raised her long knife for the kill. But then Marlowe heard a screech and looked upward. The dragoman's raven swooped down on the woman and ripped off the other half of her false face. The assassin dropped her blade and screamed madly while the dragoman staggered back onto his feet and fired the last bullet in his rapier at her chest. "Go!" he shouted over his shoulder. Marlowe nodded and disappeared into the church while the dragoman removed a tiny brass cylinder from his belt. He threw the shiny object in the air, and his raven swooped over it. The bird caught the canister in its beak and flew off, leaving the dragoman on his own against what was coming.

A multitude of Venetian soldiers descended upon him.

The tall figure threw down his sword, fell to his knees, and bent forward in prayer.

Marlowe could not see his friend once he reached the top of San Geminiano. The doge's guards were on the scene with their weapons drawn, trying to prevent the evening from escalating into an uprising. Nearly all the masked assassins were dead, and those who were not had no trouble disappearing into the evening.

Assuming the worst, Marlowe wept into the red cap his fallen friend had so recently given him. But then two flaming arrows whizzed past his face. The poet turned his head, and the manhunt resumed across the moonlit rooftops of Venice.

Far away from it all, the dragoman's lone raven carried word of the Carnevale of 1605 back to London.

The message arrived on March 1, 1604, just in time for the coming storm.

Intermission

Chapter XXV

The Cunning Wind

It took the bard more than two weeks to ride back to London on account of the fierce thunderstorms besieging Britain. Although it was neither the worst storm in a century nor the first the Isles saw of thundersnow, the tempest seemed perfectly timed to cause as much damage to the English government as possible—which it did.

The conspirators parted ways outside the Duck and Drake on a disagreeable day for good-byes, particularly for the weather-beaten playwright monitoring them in the rain. Shakespeare had been following Guy Fawkes and his cabal for nearly a month now, and both his patience and endurance were beginning to wane. His preoccupation turned to self-preservation, which was prudent considering the horror he had witnessed within the Arden. The bard had grim news to report back to London, and with so few ravens flying due to the storm, Shakespeare had no choice but to carry the message himself. Such a burden made the bard a ripe target for murder, which only added to the nightmares keeping him up at night. Not only did he have the conspirators and now the cunning folk to contend with, but the frequent flashes of lighting that haunted

Shakespeare confirmed his worst fears: He too was being followed, and likely being watched at that very moment outside the Duck and Drake.

He was.

With his mission accomplished, the bard sheathed his spyglass and spurred Aston back to the city. He crossed Temple Bar and once more arrived at London Wall, where he presented his pass with Walsingham's seal to the familiar-looking guard at the Ludgate. As the bard awaited reentry, he noticed there were more soldiers outside the gate than the last time he passed through. He then glanced up at the column of crossbowmen looking down on him from the Wall. Shakespeare was feeling less than welcome and a lot more than exposed in the rain, especially since the only raven that he saw swooped down to cozy under his white cloak for warmth. The playwright stared ahead and exhaled, fretful that the added security was due to a deteriorating situation with the plague. Although the plague was still present in London, something even more sinister awaited Shakespeare on the opposite side of the Wall.

"I'm afraid you'll have to ride with us, horsemaster."

The hooded playwright looked down at the guard with surprise. "For what reason?"

"Orders." The watchman handed Shakespeare his pass and then a second letter bearing Thomas Walsingham's seal. As the bard examined the envelope, several soldiers surrounded him and Aston. The Ludgate remained shut.

"Where are we going?" Shakespeare asked while steadying his horse.

The watchmen shook his head. "We don't know." He then pointed to the sealed letter, and the bard opened it.

> *Flavit Iehovah et Dissipati Svnt.*
> *He blew with His winds, and they were sca-*
> *tter'd.*

SEETHING LANE

W

Penny opened the portal to the cold and candlelit Seething Lane mansion that, at least from the outside, appeared to be vacant. Like Shakespeare, she too had been working for nearly a month without rest, and it showed. Her eyes were red, her face was pale, and her silvery hair less kempt than she usually wore it. Once she saw who had come knocking on her doors, however, her face brightened and her eyebrows rose in surprise.

"Lady Percy," the bard greeted with an exhausted attempt at a smile.

Her lips parted.

Shakespeare moved in to kiss her, but Penny stopped him with her hand and slowly, almost mechanically, pushed him to an appropriate distance. "It's a plague year," she reminded him, her right hand pressed against the playwright's left breast. After so many late nights at the mansion, she needed to make sure that she was not dreaming and that this visitor was not William Shakespeare's ghost.

"Of course." The sodden playwright straightened himself. "I apologize."

After feeling Shakespeare's heartbeat, Penny lifted her tired eyes and stared deeply into his.

"Are you all right, m'lady?" the playwright asked. "You look like you have just seen a ghost."

With these words, Penny's eyes narrowed and a smile returned to her face. "Still so formal," she teased.

"Yes. May I come in?"

"Well, that depends." Once more, Penny blocked her open door with her body. "Would you mind explaining why you took so bloody long to report in? W thought you were dead."

"I had a raven cut down," Shakespeare sighed. "And the storm delayed me. Also, I think I'm being followed. May I please come inside?"

A slight smirk curled up the corner of Penny's lips. "Would you like me to walk you home when you're finished?"

"No," he replied curtly, standing in the rain. "Please let me in."

"Of course."

Penny pulled Shakespeare in by his shirt and kissed his face while spinning backward and kicking the door closed behind her. Once the two finished their dance, the bard noticed something out of the corner of his eye: the dark, seemingly empty mansion was filled with royal guards. The men were armed in full regalia.

"What's going on here?" Shakespeare asked.

"You must be jesting," Penny laughed somewhat uneasily as she escorted the playwright past the guards.

"I'm afraid I lost my appreciation for jesters along with my watch in the Arden."

"Bacon will be disappointed," the lady chided as she hung up Shakespeare's wet cloak to dry.

"My lady, please." Shakespeare pulled Penny over by her arm and closed the door to her study. "Why are there royal guards here? Why the darkness? Why is the city under such tight security?"

All the playfulness on Penny's face disappeared. "Are you serious? You really don't know?"

"Know what? Is it the plague, or—did something happen while I was away?"

The lady secretary breathed heavily as the thunderstorm battered her windows. "I think you should see him now," she replied nervously. Penny returned to her desk in a tizzy, leaving Shakespeare where he stood: beside W's heavily armored door.

"Should I knock first?" he asked.

"Just go in." Penny dabbed a quill pen and then looked up from her desk. "Good luck, Will."

Once more, the bard stepped into the spymaster's office. What he saw made him immediately regret entering without knocking.

Sir Thomas Walsingham, forty-four years old, was standing at his desk with a spent pipe in one hand and a large leaf of parchment in the other. His back was straight, his chest puffed, his clothes black save for the white ruff around his neck, and he had the stern look on his face of a man interrupted. And opposite him, seated, wearing a brown fur cape over a white doublet with matching stockings and shoes, sporting a short, goatlike beard, and staring back at Shakespeare with a thin face and sunken eyes, was the thirty-eight years old James I, king of Great Britain, France, and Ireland, Defender of the Faith, etc.

In desperate need of a remedy, the bard bowed his head until the farthest retreat of his receding hairline was nearly touching the floor.

Seeing no chance of rescuing the situation, Walsingham turned to King James and asked: "Would Your Majesty mind if we continued this discussion later?" The king mulled this over, and then exited the room without saying a word. Thomas Walsingham bowed, and Shakespeare dutifully held the door open for the monarch as he left.

"Close the door," Thomas ordered.

The bard complied, and W threw his parchment into the crackling fire behind him. "Where have you been, Will? We've been busy."

"As have I, W. Believe me."

"I never doubted it," remarked Walsingham while refiling his pipe. "What's the news from Warwickshire?"

"Frightening," Shakespeare answered in disbelief. "Wicked."

"Of course it is. The news has been nothing but terrible all month." The spymaster lit his tobacco with a rolled-up report.

"What happened?"

"You tell me your story, and I will follow with mine." Walsingham pointed Shakespeare to the king's chair with his pipe.

The upholstered seat looked like a feather bed after hundreds of hours on horseback. However, the bard turned his back on it. "W, I need to know—"

"No, you don't," Walsingham interrupted. "Not yet. This is not the Globe, master bard. I give the directions here, and you act out the modest roles you are given. It is a lovely alternative to anarchy." The spymaster took a few puffs from his pipe. "Don't you agree?"

The levelheaded Walsingham reined in the playwright's anxiety. With his better senses restored, Shakespeare nodded with gratitude, and W returned the gesture. The two men sat, and within the warm office, the bard felt something akin to comfort for the first time in weeks.

Sensing this, the spymaster tested, "May I offer you something?"

Shakespeare followed Walsingham's finger to a pewter pitcher surrounded with fruit on a small table. "I am a bit thirsty," the playwright acknowledged.

Shakespeare reached for a vessel, but Thomas stopped him. The spy-chief rose from his chair and poured a large goblet of wine. After handing Shakespeare the chalice, Walsingham walked back to his desk while opening his pocket watch to a hidden mirror. Behind him, he saw the bard drop a small clump of *terra sigillata* into his claret. Satisfied, W closed his timepiece and returned to his seat. "I see you're looking out for yourself," he commended.

"Someone has to," Shakespeare responded, taking the hint. "Someone could have been trying to poison the king just now. Or perhaps the king had planned to poison you."

"That type of thinking will save your life one day," said Thomas. "So, what wicked news this way comes out of Warwickshire?" Walsingham returned to his pipe while Shakespeare gulped down his wine.

"Guy Fawkes has recruited cunning folk to aid the conspirators. It looks like this was their plan from the beginning. It is the reason they insisted that I include witches in their play."

"How is that coming, by the way?" Thomas asked with a genuine interest.

"I have my subject. The play will cover Macbeth."

Walsingham raised his eyebrows, intrigued by the choice. "Well, that settles that. The conspirators got what they wanted: your very first Scottish play. Congratulations."

The playwright smirked. "So it is, I have only begun to write it. Also, I think the conspirators want it performed when Parliament reconvenes."

"In October?"

The bard nodded.

Walsingham picked up a quill pen and scrawled "October" onto a parchment. He then scratched a long line through the word. "And what of their cunning folk allies?" he asked as he set down his feather.

Shakespeare's voice deepened. "I spied on their ceremony at the Forest of Arden. There were sacrifices; human sacrifices. I watched as three Jesuit priests had their throats cut open."

"Did you know who they were?"

The bard shook his head. "No, but the conspirators recognized them. Through a . . . Father Garnet, I believe."

W picked up his pen and wrote "Henry Garnet," the Jesuit Superior for England. He then crossed a line through that name as well. "And why were they killed?"

"It seemed to be part of the ceremony. Robert Catesby gave the cunning folk three requests: that England be severed from her overseas allies, that Alessandro de' Medici become the next pope, and that the conspirators successfully eradicate the Reformation from England."

The stable spymaster's pipe trembled with the sound of thunder outside. Seeing this, he removed the pipe from his mouth while the playwright continued.

"After each request, the cunning folk slit one of the priests' throats over a cauldron. They then performed . . ." The bard struggled. "Some sort of a spell unlike anything I have ever thought possible. There were no wands, no incantations; only ingredients. They used a skull, blood, and powder to make their cauldron bubble black ash. And then I saw it spout large, burning limbs!"

"Calm down," Walsingham entered. "Pour yourself some more wine."

"W," Shakespeare replied with a steady voice and level head, "I am not giving in to fancy right now. I know what I saw, and it was no illusion: their cauldron erupted branches as wide as my waist, and as red as hot coals. And I saw these limbs writhe across the ground like fiery snakes."

Walsingham's brow furrowed. "Could this have been alchemy?"

"I don't know what to believe," the bard sighed while rubbing his forehead. "I was always skeptical of witchcraft, black magic, the dark arts. If you spend enough time on stage, you learn how to see through anyone's act. In all my years, W, I have never seen a display such as this. Whatever these women conjured, it looked like it was not of this earth."

The spymaster's eyes narrowed at one particular word. "Tell me more about these women."

The bard drew a breath. "Well, there were two of them. An elder performed the ceremony while a younger woman assisted. They were accompanied by a group of men in blue paint. The men never spoke, and they followed orders without being asked."

"Blue paint?"

"Yes. Intricate markings, like chain mail on their flesh."

Walsingham paused. "Were they Celts?"

Shakespeare shrugged. "Anybody can cover themselves in blue paint."

The spy-chief nodded, accepting this. "How old would you say these women were?"

"Not that old. The elder appeared about as old as us. Forty? Perhaps older? The other woman was closer to my daughters' ages. I'd say she was no older than thirty."

Another pause. "Was she blond?" Walsingham whispered. "And the elder witch brown of hair?"

The bard's mouth gaped. "How did you know that?"

Walsingham leaned forward in his chair. "Did the older witch have a scar across her neck?" he asked, making a motion across his with his pipe.

Shakespeare shook his head. "I don't know. I could not tell."

The spymaster scowled. "And what of their accents? Was there anything peculiar about their speech? Did it have a guttural sound to it?"

"I would not know. The storm was too loud, and I was too far away to—"

"The storm?"

The playwright paused. "Yes?"

Walsingham sat up in his chair shocked. "Will, when exactly did this meeting take place?"

Shakespeare, put on edge by the disquieted spymaster, replied, "Around midnight, between the last of February and the first of March."

"The first night of the storm?"

The bard nodded. "Yes. Shortly after the first flashes of lightning."

Walsingham processed this with intensity. "William, is there any way you can assure me that the storm *preceded* the arrival of the cunning folk to the meeting ground?"

Shakespeare raked his mind over this, but then shook his head. "No. The cunning folk were already in the forest with a fire going when the conspirators arrived. With the wind and snow as they were, their fire had to have preceded the storm."

A deathly glare fell over Walsingham's face. Without explanation, the spy-chief rose from his desk and hustled into Penny's study. The busy secretary looked up from her desk, where she was transcribing W's conversation with Shakespeare. "That will be all, Lady Percy. Would you leave us, please?" The secretary put down her feather and handed Walsingham her parchments. She then walked out of the room and closed her door just as the spymaster closed his.

W strode past the playwright and threw his pages into the fireplace.

Shakespeare jumped from his chair. "Enough of this. What's going on, W? Why is everyone on edge? You would think that we're being invaded right now!"

"We're always being invaded!" the spymaster spat. "It's a pastime as old as Julius Caesar. You of all people should know that!" Walsingham turned from the fire and squared shoulders with the playwright. "Do you know why I keep that up?" he asked candidly, pointing to his painting of the Spanish Armada.

Shakespeare glanced at the great portrait of English and Spanish warships in battle. "As a trophy?" he guessed.

"As a warning. I look at that painting every day to remind me of what swept me into this office."

"Bad weather?" Shakespeare snickered, hoping to lighten the mood with some humor.

Walsingham was not smiling. He turned his head and looked back to the painting. "During the war, my cousin obsessed over how to shore up our defenses for the Spanish invasion. He estimated more than fifty thousand men would come at us from Spain and the Low Countries." The spymaster directed Shakespeare toward a mess of maps on the wall. "The most we could ever muster was half that, and spread over more than ten thousand miles of coastline. Unless we stopped the Armada on the high seas, this kingdom would fall."

"Well." Shakespeare nodded. "I guess it's a good thing that you stopped them." The bard took out the letter Walsingham left for him at the Ludgate. *"Flavit Iehovah et Dissipati Svnt."* Shakespeare looked up from the note, smirking. "Is that why you summoned me? To remind me that God blessed these lands with foul weather? You've made me a resident expert on the subject. If I spent three more weeks in these elements, I'd be Noah."

The spymaster puffed his pipe, ignoring the playwright's indignation. "You remember the role I played in the war, correct?"

"Did you blow God's horn?"

"Watch yourself, playwright."

The bard exhaled, feeling a bit more at peace with himself. "I cannot say I remember because I was too busy not getting involved. But . . . I do remember a former friend of ours sharing something on the subject."

W nodded, grateful that Shakespeare heard what he did from Marlowe. "And what did he say?"

"He said you worked for your cousin during the war. That was all."

"In this very building," Thomas emphasized. "My cousin worked there," he said, pointing to the desk beneath his late cousin's portrait, "and my office was there." This time, he pointed to the adjoining room, Penny's study. "I was the only person Francis trusted as his last line of defense, and if anyone wanted a word with him, they had to speak to me first."

"How loquacious of you," the bard praised.

W sucked on his pipe and walked toward a large map of the Isles. "You remember those three men who were watching Kit the first night that we met?"

"Of course. I was actually there that time."

"Indeed. One of them, Poley, was a bit of an expert at the intelligence trade. He would meet with the type of people I chose to keep away from. He was my filter for them." Thomas paused, blowing a thick cloud of smoke. "Once word reached this office that we repulsed the Armada at Gravelines, Poley said a cunning woman wanted to meet with my cousin. She apparently traveled all the way from Scotland to London just for the occasion. I wasn't interested, but Francis was. The woman offered England the opportunity to defeat the Spanish fleet once and for all."

"Thomas . . ." Shakespeare muttered, piecing the bigger picture together. "What did you do?"

"I did nothing!" the spymaster insisted. "As I said, Francis, my predecessor, had made it his mission to defend these isles with every resource at our disposal! This woman said she and her sisters could sink the Armada. Not defeat it in battle, but crush it against rocks! She promised a hurricane the likes of which no son of Spain would soon forget."

The bard swallowed. "And whose throat did she slit to seal this deal?" he sneered.

Walsingham walked into the playwright's face. "One of her own! All the woman requested was a private ceremony here, at Stonehenge." W pointed to a small drawing of the stone structure on a Wiltshire map. "The women would allow only one witness, so my cousin requested that I attend. I did not want to, but I trusted his judgment." The spymaster stared straight at Shakespeare. "I was there, Will. I saw the same women that you did. It was a hideous day. Gray, dreary, lifeless; you know the kind. I watched that elder witch stab her own sister in the throat: a lovely lass with brown hair. She did not appear any older than I was at the time. The dark deed was carried out at sundown while a young girl watched and helped. A blond girl. She could not have been any older than six."

"The woman had her throat slit, and she lived?"

"It was not a deep cut. She bled and collapsed, but the elder witch saved her life." W puffed his pipe. "The women were cunning folk. They had no homes, so I just left them where they were. By the time I returned to London, word had just reached the city that a terrible storm wrecked the Armada off the coast of Scotland."

"The Protestant Wind. . . ." Shakespeare chided, shaking his head. "That's magnificent, Thomas. You made the whole world believe that God saved us and preserved the faith. But in reality, you entered us into a pact no differently than if Faust had been our king."

"It was war, Will! We were already living in Hell." W turned away and puffed an angry cloud of frustration. "No one knew of the ceremony. Francis died two years later."

"Was he murdered?"

"I don't think so. He had been ill for some time, but . . ." The spymaster hesitated. "Something strange happened around the same time as his death."

Shakespeare's eyes widened. "What was it?"

Walsingham turned to his map of the Isles. "In the spring of 1590, King James, the man you just saw in this room, was nearly killed in a storm while returning from his wedding in Denmark. A tribunal was put together to investigate, and as king of Scotland, James personally questioned the woman accused of causing the tempest: a cunning folk healer named Agnes Sampson. James was *not* convinced of her guilt and was prepared to rule in her favor. However, to the shock of everyone, the woman confessed to her crimes! She then looked the king in the eyes and repeated the same words he shared to his queen on the night of their marriage.* James was shocked by this and had the woman put to death. Her execution set off an entire wave of witch trials throughout Scotland. It was the largest witch hunt these lands have ever seen." W turned away from the map and looked back at Shakespeare. "That sorceress, Agnes Sampson, was the woman I met."

"You are sure of this?"

"Positive. I was at her trial as an observer. The only reason I did not enter my experience with her as evidence was because I could not risk exposing the Protestant Wind for what it was."

---

*Dæmonologie, James R[X] (Edinburgh: Robert Walde-graue, 1597).

Shakespeare bit his lip anxiously. "And what of the two other women? The younger ones?"

"I never learned their names or fates. I had never even seen them before the ceremony. Poley knew nothing of them either. The eldest witch approached him alone."

The bard raised an eyebrow. "And what was his fate?"

"Poley went missing years ago. I have not heard from him since."

"Well . . ." Shakespeare surmised, "it sounds like you got quite a bargain. You made a deal with a Devil, and now you're expecting me to get us out of it."

"Honestly," Thomas exhaled, "I am not expecting it so much as I am hoping it." Walsingham finished his pipe and looked down at it dejectedly. "Two weeks ago," he continued, walking over to his master map of Europe, "a raven arrived bearing news that our spy network in Venice had been compromised. And after that, nothing. Dead silence from every one of our overseas stations. Paris"—he pointed—"Hamburg, Prague, Vienna, the Low Countries, Spain, Algiers . . . All of them."

"There's no word?"

"They're all down. All their reports ended on or before March first. If the stations were still operational, we would have received updates from them by now."

"Could this be due to the storm?"

Walsingham shook his head. "I sent some men across the Channel to Calais to investigate. They said all four of our agents in the city had been slain."

"Slain!" Shakespeare gasped.

The spymaster nodded. "Murdered during the French revelries on Fat Tuesday. I swear, Will, it's like St. Bartholomew's Day all over again." Walsingham shook his head and stuffed his spent pipe in his mouth.

"Who could be behind this?"

"Who do you think! My men also heard some news while in

Calais: Pope Clement VIII is dead. A secure source says he was found unresponsive in his bed on March the third."

"Was he murdered?"

"I don't know yet. However, Alessandro de' Medici is expected to win the papacy since he enjoys French and Italian support. The cardinals should be convening right now."

"You think the Medici are behind this?"

The spy-chief did not respond. Instead, he let the playwright figure it out for himself.

England's entire international spy network had been severed.

The pope was dead, and Alessandro de' Medici was only days away from becoming his successor.

Shakespeare's heart skipped a beat. "God save me," he groaned.

"Yes. God save us both," said W.

"This is real?" the bard asked. "It all feels like a dream."

"That's because you've been asleep to the truth your whole life. The world you know is a stage; a drama. This is the world as it is, Will. These are the villains we are forced to fight."

The bard had to steady himself against the wall. "And what am *I* supposed to do against women who control storms and can shift the tales of entire kingdoms?"

The spymaster emptied his spent tobacco into the fire. "Conspiracies are like weeds, Will. You need to rip them out by their roots. We have plenty of time to uproot Fawkes and his men, but these cunning folk can no longer be ignored. They clearly possess a power that Bacon has yet to catch up with." Walsingham noticed the bard's spyglass slung over his shoulder. "How does his magic hold up on the field?" he asked.

"Pretty well," the stunned playwright responded.

"Well, I want to see if you can use some of his magic again."

Shakespeare swallowed. "How?"

"I need you to go back to the cunning folk and kill every last one of them."

The playwright absorbed this, and then turned to the pewter pitcher behind him. "I think I will need some more wine." Shakespeare filled his cup with a shaking hand and then fumbled for the leather pouch in his cloak.

"You need not worry. It's not poisoned."

"It would be so much easier if it was," the playwright sighed with a gulp.

Chapter XXVI

A Dramatic Entrance

The Jewish ghetto—or *ghèto*, meaning "foundry"—was not easy for Christopher Marlowe to find. Fortunately, this worked to the poet's advantage after eluding authorities across more than a mile of rooftops.

When the Venetian government created the first ghetto in 1516, they went out of their way to keep its location as inconspicuous as possible. They chose Ghetto Nuovo, a small island in the Cannaregio *sestiere* that was being used as a waste site for the adjacent Ghetto Vecchio, a copper foundry. Despite covering less than two acres and with nowhere to build but upward, this tiny fragment of slag became home to thousands of Jews. The ghetto was enlarged in 1541 to include the Ghetto Vecchio as well, and the sites were enclosed within high walls under constant security. The ghetto's iron gates closed at sundown and remained locked until dawn, and its canals were patrolled by Christian sentries at night. The ward was both a prison and a refuge for countless Jews throughout Europe, and much like the city they shared, business and scholarship thrived within the Venetian Ghetto's community.

To the dragoman's credit, the location was a wise choice in the event of extraction. All Christopher Marlowe needed was a way in. Atop the Calle Farnese, the puzzled poet scratched his head as he planned his next move.

He thought about jumping, but the Ghetto Nuovo was encircled by too wide a canal. The only part he could reach was Ghetto Vecchio, which was surrounded by too high a wall. He then considered hiring some prostitutes as a distraction—not for the guards, but for himself. Unfortunately, the poet's pockets were empty, which also meant he could not attempt to bribe his way inside either. Running out of clean options, Marlowe's diligent mind turned to murder. Yes, he could kill the guards without difficulty, but that could prove disastrous for the Venetian Jews, whom Marlowe imagined would get blamed for the indiscretion. *Drago would have disapproved*, he acknowledged with difficulty. It was the first time the saddened poet had ever thought about his friend in the past tense.

As Marlowe brooded, he heard movement over at the Ghetto Vecchio's gates. After creeping across several buildings, he was surprised to find an old man in a red, pointed hat walking out of the ghetto. The man was stopped by guards, but he identified himself as a doctor, which reminded Marlowe of the rare instances when he came across Jews outside of the ghetto at night. Most often, they were doctors, but there was one other fine industry that employed quite a few Jews throughout the city at this hour. Particularly on festive evenings such as the first night of Carnevale.

Marlowe climbed down from his rooftop and stuffed his parrying dagger under his floppy cap so that it more closely resembled the red hats all Venetian Jews were required to wear. Once he tied the blade in place with his long hair, the still blood-covered poet strutted up to the Ghetto Vecchio as if he were the man who paid the guards' salaries.

"Lo!" a voice hollered as Marlowe approached the ghetto's gates.

Two sentinels descended upon him with torches. "The gate is closed! *Vai a cagare!*"

"But I'm a Jew!" replied the poet, pointing to his red hat.

The men scrutinized Marlowe. "What are you doing out at this hour? It's forbidden!"

"I'm an actor!" he answered, throwing out his arms with an "Eh?"

The ghetto guards were unconvinced. "He's armed!" one of them shouted. The two sentries drew their swords while Marlowe kept his hands in the air. "What are you doing with a weapon?"

The poet looked down at the Venetian *schiavona* he had nearly forgotten about. "Oh, *this*? It's just a prop! You can take it, if you like!" The poet undid his belt and let the weapon fall to the ground. He then returned his hands to the air with a generous grin on his face.

One of the guards picked up the sword and unsheathed it. The fine blade was sharpened. Alarmed, he showed the weapon to his partner, and the two guards closed in. "We could have you arrested for this!"

"As I said, it is yours! Need to repeat myself, do I?"

The other guard grabbed Marlowe's shirt. "There's blood on him."

"Let me explain! I was performing with my actors at a party this evening! They're all goys. You would love them! Anyway, they offered to walk me home, but I told them: 'What are you talking about? On a night such as *this*? And in a city this *safe*? If this wasn't my home, I could live in this place!'"

"Who were you performing for?"

"For the doge's nephew! We know each other quite well. He lives at Piazzetta dei Leoncini. I could tell you more about him! He is a *grave* man, I assure you."

One of the guards was unconvinced while the other remained taken with the poet's *schiavona*. "What were you performing?" asked the former.

The poet stood tall and proud. "*Doctor Faustus*, by Christopher Marlowe!"

"Never heard of him."

The poet's eyes widened. "You've never heard of me?" he asked in his real voice.

The guards raised their eyebrows as a nervous smile spread across Marlowe's face.

"Who are you?" asked one of them.

The poet thought for a second. "Gabriel!"

Satisfied, the sentry with Marlowe's sword returned to his prize. The skeptical guard, however, needed more convincing. "You say you acted today?"

"Yes! The performance concluded around midnight. The doge's nephew had a dance to attend."

The skeptic narrowed his eyes and pulled his torch back. "Show us a scene from the play."

"With pleasure." The poet bowed, and then he shot up with a look of profound surprise on his face. He raised his hand in the air and slowly, dreamily . . .

Marlowe drew back his hand. "Do any of you speak English?"

The guards remained silent.

Marlowe shook his head. "Never mind." He got back into character and translated his lines into Venetian.

> *Was this the face that launch'd a thousand ships,*
> *And burnt the topless towers of Ilium?*
> *Sweet Helen, make me immortal with a kiss!*

The poet moved toward the skeptical guard as if to kiss him. The man drew back in disgust while his partner laughed and applauded, his new sword tucked under his arm.

"There's more!" Marlowe offered.

The skeptic reached for his keys and unlocked the Ghetto Vecchio's gates. "Get the hell inside!" he ordered.

"May God bless you." The poet bowed once more, and then sauntered into the Venetian Ghetto.

Chapter XXVII

Life

Marlowe strolled down Calle del Ghetto Vecchio as its iron gates closed behind him. The narrow street ran through an urban valley of tenement houses nearly one hundred feet high, forcing a chilling breeze to billow through the poet's cape. The buildings were as expressionless as empty faces and all featured the same simple facade: a vast departure from the lavish palaces beyond the ghetto's walls. Nearly six thousand Jews from all over Europe were packed into these apartments. They surrounded Marlowe, sleeping, eating, praying, arguing, coughing, and adding to the population. Such was the Venetian Ghetto, and the English poet found it fascinating for a most unlikely reason. It very much reminded him of London, sans the horses, filth, and the unfriendly weather, naturally.

Two young men converged on the poet until they were walking right next to him. "Hello, boys!" he greeted.

"Please lower your voice. I am Azariah," said Azariah Figo, a twenty-five-year-old rabbinical student, "and this is Simone."

"Shalom! How did you find me?"

"We heard you shout your name from the gates. Voices travel far here, so please lower yours."

"Oh!" Marlowe covered his mouth. "Sorry."

"Where's your large friend?" Azariah asked.

All playfulness slipped from the distressed poet's face. "I don't know. We were ambushed by female assassins at la Piazza. They turned the whole crowd against us!"

"Is he dead?"

"If he is injured, we have doctors," entered the twenty-one-year-old Simone Luzzatto.

"I don't know his fate. From what I saw, I . . ." Marlowe whimpered. "It looked like he fell in the fighting."

The two students exchanged anxious glances as they entered Campiello delle Scuole. They turned left at the ghetto's modest piazza, guiding Marlowe past a tall yellow building: la Scola Spagnola. The elder student unlocked its doors, and the three men entered.

La Scola Spagnola, "the Spanish Synagogue," was a clandestine temple erected by Venetian Jews who survived the horrors of the Spanish Inquisition. Although its interior paled in comparison to its later renovations by Baldassare Longhena, Marlowe was nevertheless surprised by how large the candlelit temple appeared from the inside. All four floors of the building were one enormous place of worship crowned with a single continuous balcony not unlike a London theater. It was the largest synagogue in Venice, and one of the largest temples left in use in the world.

Azariah picked up a waiting lamp while Simone took Marlowe's bloody cloak. Not knowing what to do as a sign of respect, Marlowe crossed himself as Azariah led him through the temple. Three older men were seated on its wooden benches: rabbi and merchant Joseph Pardo, Rabbi Judah Leib Saraval of the ghetto *beth din*, and Ben Zion Sarfati, the chief rabbi of Venice. The three rabbis took one look at the blood-covered poet and gasped: "What is *this*?" "*This* is a *disaster!*" "*What* have we *done?*" "Why is *he* here, but *not* the drago-man?" "We *never* agreed to *this!*"

"I can hear everything you're saying," Christopher Marlowe interrupted in Hebrew.

The three men turned their heads, as did Azariah and Simone.

"Where did you learn Hebrew, young man?" asked Rabbi Pardo.

"At Corpus Christi College in Cambridge." In truth, Marlowe had taught himself Hebrew during his semester abroad, but he figured Corpus Christi would elicit more of a reaction out of the rabbis. Which it did.

"Come forward," the head rabbi asked in an old, wispy voice.

"But please accept our apologies if we ask you *not* to sit," added Rabbi Saraval.

"You're covered in blood, young man," Rabbi Pardo explained.

"Yes, I know," Marlowe sighed as he looked down at his crimsoned garments. "It's not mine."

The rabbis looked at one another in an unspoken acknowledgment of the dangerous waters they were entering into.

"May I sit?" the bloodstained poet asked.

After a moment's hesitation, "Yes," Rabbi Pardo replied.

". . . provided it is on the *floor*," Rabbi Saraval clarified.

The head rabbi overruled them. "Sit next to me, young man."

Marlowe, already down on one knee, looked up with surprise as Ben Zion Sarfati waved him over. The poet rose from the floor and approached the rabbis while young Simone hustled over with some cloths to cover the benches with. Marlowe sat, and the four men spoke in whispers while Azariah and Simone guarded the sepia temple.

"Your great friend told us about you," Rabbi Pardo began. "Is he still alive?"

Marlowe shook his head. "I don't know."

"Do you *think* he is still alive?"

Marlowe's lips flinched speechlessly until he painfully acknowledged: "I think he's dead. It is possible the doge's guards captured him, but even if they did, he will probably be executed. I do not expect to see him again. Ever." The poet sniffled.

Rabbis Pardo and Saraval looked to each other and then turned to Ben Zion Sarfati. The head rabbi's eyes appeared absorbed in thought, so Pardo asked: "Do you know *why* we agreed to help you?"

Marlowe shook his head. "I know my friend worked with more people than I could ever keep track of. It was just easier to assume he knew everyone in the city."

"So, you do *not* know what he did for *us*?"

Marlowe shrugged. "An information exchange? Some other business?"

"This is not about *business*," said Rabbi Pardo. "We are speaking about *life*!"

Marlowe paused, confused.

"Your friend," the head rabbi spoke in an ancient voice, "filled these walls with hundreds of people over the course of a decade. Men, women, little boys and girls from throughout the Continent. People who needed *hope*."

"People?" asked Marlowe. "You mean for this synagogue?"

"For survival," said Rabbi Pardo. "Your friend approached us ten years ago and offered to help us bring displaced Jews to Venice. We let your friend know where they were and who needed help the most. He arranged their safe passage here at great risk to himself. It is because of *him* that every one of these people are still alive."

Marlowe scratched his head, at which point he realized he was still wearing his parrying dagger in his hair. "Just so I know, how was something like that permitted? Shouldn't the government have disapproved?"

"The Venetian government *paid* him to do it!" Rabbi Saraval explained. "As a dragoman, he was able to persuade the Council of Ten about the *boon* that dispelled Jews had been for Istanbul. He told them how commerce increased thanks to Jewish merchants under Ottoman protection, and he read them a letter signed by the Sultana Safiye herself praising her *Jewish* dragoman, Esperanza Malchi! This convinced the council that more Jews should be brought to Venice, and that those already living here should be given more liberty. And the reason the Venetian government attempted this with your friend was because they knew he was *not* the government!"

"It was a secret," Marlowe realized. "They did not want the public to know."

The rabbis shook their heads.

"Well," the poet exhaled, "that was certainly nice of him! So . . ." Marlowe paused to rub his hands together. "My friend helped you, and . . . you Jews will help me?"

"We are helping *him*," the head rabbi clarified, "by assisting you at this dark hour."

The poet shrugged. "Just as good. Thank you! What's the plan, then?"

"There is a rabbi in Ferrara named Leon Modena whom I will send you to," said Rabbi Pardo. "You are welcome to stay with him or live elsewhere with the money the dragoman has left you."

"Money?" asked Marlowe, raising his eyebrows. "How much?"

"Three thousand ducats."

The poet's eyes widened. "Well . . ." he gasped, "that's a nice even sum. I'll take it! Also, just so I know, is there a chance I could maybe . . . retire here?" Marlowe's eyes wandered over the clandestine temple.

The three rabbis fell silent.

"No," Rabbi Saraval answered flatly. "It is too dangerous."

"The entire ghetto would be at risk," said Rabbi Pardo.

"It was our agreement," the head rabbi grunted, "to get you *out* of Venice."

The poet's face sank with disappointment. "How much time do I have left in the city?"

"You leave at dawn," said Pardo.

Marlowe gaped. "Oh no, no, no! That's not enough time! Drago could still be alive! If he's captured . . . You just said he's cut deals with the doge! I have, too! Well, the doge's nephew, but . . . still! I can't just leave him here! Drago has to come with me! I'll rescue him from prison and cut him free from the gallows if I have to!"

"It is too dangerous for you to go *anywhere* other than where he said," Rabbi Saraval grumbled.

Marlowe grimaced. "Someone—nay, *someones*—tried to kill me tonight! Some gang of killer women operating from here to Belgrade to Istanbul! They killed *hundreds* of people in one deadly dance! You expect me to leave my friend against *them!*"

"You said yourself that he's dead," Azariah Figo interjected from across the synagogue.

"I said it *looked* like he was dead!"

"You told us that you did not expect to see him again," Rabbi Saraval added.

"Young man . . ." The head rabbi spoke with sympathy. "The loss of your friend is a painful loss to us as well! There is *no* replacing him. His life was a world of life to us."

Marlowe shook his head, still not ready to surrender. "Did he leave any sort of message for me? A clue, or a codex? A cryptic sentence? Some silly puzzle box I need to solve?" he asked, flicking his fingers together.

The rabbis were silent.

Marlowe scratched his stubble and glanced at Rabbi Pardo. "You said he left money for me."

"Yes. Three thousand—"

"Do you handle his finances?"

Rabbi Pardo was caught off guard by this question. "No."

Marlowe cursed in English.

"That is . . . not me personally," the rabbi continued. "But I know who does. His name is—"

"Does he live in this ghetto?"

"Yes."

Marlowe snapped his fingers and pointed to the students. "Go wake him up!"

Act IV

1605

Chapter XXVIII

The Man Who Bested Walsingham

G iotto's Campanile stands a towering 278 feet over Florence, making it fifty-five feet shorter than the angelic summit that Christopher Marlowe scaled in Venice. But for all the beauty the poet bathed in atop the Campanile San Marco, he appeared to be enjoying his current viewpoint even more. Saint Mark's Basilica was no Brunelleschi's dome—or at least not from the outside. The Palazzo Ducale lacked the Palazzo della Signoria's impressive clock tower. The Lion of Venice was but a stray cat to Benvenuto Cellini's heroic bronze of Perseus. And none of Sansovino's sculptures or Titian's paintings could compare to Michelangelo's *David*. Yes, the Queen of the Adriatic still commanded the cyan sea from her marble throne, but returning to the Tuscany that inspired Dante reawakened Marlowe to the floral world he had forgotten. It had been more than a decade since the English poet had set foot on solid ground, but there he was, basking in the Tuscan sun atop a tower of red Siena, white Carrara, and green Prato marble.

It was a beautiful afternoon to reconnect with Florence, the city that reinvented history.

As the seven bells of Giotto's Campanile tolled beneath him, the poet lowered his gaze and returned to the task at hand. It was Sunday, April 10, and Easter service had just ended. The Santa Maria del Fiore's doors were opening, and somewhere through its throng of distinguished Florentines was Marlowe's target.

It had taken Marlowe several days to find Roberto di Ridolfi after arriving from Ferrara. According to the dragoman's banker in the Venetian Ghetto, Roberto deposited a fixed income into his friend's account on a routine basis. The payment always arrived the day before the dragoman would hand Marlowe his monthly pension, which made the poet suspect a deeper connection between the two, especially considering the name involved. The Ridolfi family was the most prominent banking house in Florence, and at seventy-three years old, Roberto had become their patriarch. He had spent decades setting up shop overseas, including spending more than fifteen years in London. He enjoyed the service of kings and popes, and had recently been made a senator of Florence.

Roberto owned a palazzo across the Arno on Via Maggio, which was where his stealth pursuer was looking forward to having him. You see, Christopher Marlowe had known the name Roberto di Ridolfi his entire life. In 1571, Roberto masterminded a plot to assassinate Queen Elizabeth.

The poet's doeskin boots hit the ground before the Campanile's bells had finished chiming.

The Ridolfi plot was an international conspiracy involving the king of Spain, the pope in Rome, coconspirators from Norfolk to the Netherlands, and none other than Mary, Queen of Scots. Engineered by Roberto himself, the scheme called for a Catholic rebellion in northern England to coincide with Queen Elizabeth's murder, restoring Mary to the English throne. Ridolfi personally financed the plot for years, and it nearly succeeded despite a chance encounter with a man whom Roberto would later boast should have beheaded him twenty-five times over. In 1569, a thrity-seven-year-old Roberto was put under house arrest by the Privy Council so that they could have someone question him. The man specifically chosen by Elizabeth's secretary of state, Sir William Cecil, was a thirty-seven-year-old Francis Walsingham.* After being interrogated by the official who would soon become one of the most powerful men in history, the Italian spy and the English agent shared a conversation of enormous consequence but of little record. Ridolfi, to the shock of everyone, was released from custody, and shortly after, Walsingham recommended Roberto to the Privy Council as an upright man both wise and honest.† It was, to any observer, the single biggest failure in Francis Walsingham's career. The Ridolfi plot continued without interruption for two years, and its godfather went down in history as the only person to ever best England's greatest spymaster.

And on this Easter Sunday, Christopher Marlowe was there to kill him.

After racing across the Arno through the Corridoio Vasariano, Marlowe exited the secret passage at Santa Felicita, whose gate he had unlocked earlier. The poet scaled the church with a waiting ladder, which he used to ascend the higher parts of the surrounding rooftops. Marlowe had plotted his path days in advance to avoid being seen in daylight. The poet peered over the edge of the rooftop to look upon the busy crowds on Via Guicciardini. To his right, he saw his target approaching from the Ponte Vecchio. Marlowe stepped back and stalked his target across the rooftops until they were both outside the Ridolfi home on Via Maggio. Roberto unlocked the palazzo doors while his pursuer entered through the windows, unnoticed. By the time the old man had climbed upstairs

---

*State Papers, Domestic, Elizabeth I, PRO SP 12/59 nos. 3 & 11.
†PRO SP 12/74 no.12.

to change his clothes, the English poet was already waiting for him in his empty bedroom.

Roberto entered the wooden chamber, and Marlowe quietly closed the door behind him.

The old man heard a floorboard creak. Slowly, he turned around. Silence.

"Buona Pasqua," the poet ultimately offered in Tuscan.

"Happy Easter," Roberto replied. He then drew a breath and asked: "Am I dead?"

"That depends," said his assassin.

The old man leaned forward and squinted, his eyes barely visible beneath his enormous eyebrows. "Are *you* dead?" he asked politely.

Marlowe was not expecting that. After thinking it over, he exhaled and said: "I don't even know anymore."

"Ahhh . . ." The old man spoke with familiarity. Returning to that matter in a minute, "May we talk first?"

The poet nodded. "Yes, we may."

Marlowe took a step back and leaned against the door behind him while his captive limped feebly across the room. After Roberto collapsed into an ancient chair, the poet noted: "You're healthier than you pretend, old man."

Once more, Roberto froze, but this time his eyes narrowed out of anger. "What makes you say that?" he asked in a clearer, stricter voice.

"If you were so decrepit, you would have moved your bedroom to the bottom floor. And you would at least have had a servant working." The poet smirked. "I have been following you for days."

Unmasked, Roberto di Ridolfi's face completely morphed. Instead of appearing weak and fettered, his eyes homed in on Marlowe's like a falcon's. The senator scowled and straightened himself, sitting upright in his seat as if his bedroom were the Salone dei Cinquecento. "Who sent you?" he asked.

"I did." Marlowe kicked himself off the door and swaggered

forward, his right hand clenched into a fist on his parrying dagger's grip. "You're not expecting anyone this afternoon, are you?"

"No," the senator scowled. "I am expected somewhere else, though."

The poet batted his eyelashes. "You'll be keeping them waiting quite a while, then." Marlowe leaned against a dresser with his elbow out and his cape unfurled as if posing for a portrait. "I know who you are, old man, and I must say: seeing you up close is a disappointment."

"I am not sorry to hear that."

The assassin raised an eyebrow. "Are you not surprised by this, then? Your death?"

The senator shook his head. "No. I knew this day would come."

His killer smiled. "You should be surprised that death didn't get you sooner! I know that *I* am! If I bested you so easily, so should have Francis Walsingham."

With that name, a sea change washed over Roberto's eyes. He looked deep into the poet's features. "You're an Englishman," he deduced.

Marlowe wrestled with this in his mouth. "It's been a long time since I called myself one, but yes."

The old man nodded. He considered staying this subject, but since it was not in his killer's interest, he asked: "Why are you here?"

The poet flicked the tip of his dagger's pommel with an itchy thumb. "You've been in contact with a friend of mine in Venice for quite some time. You send him money every month."

The senator nodded very, very slowly. And then he parried: "Did you know his name?"

The slight smirk on Marlowe's face vanished, stolen by his opponent. "I . . ." he struggled. "I know it's difficult to pronounce. I've only heard him say it once. And I . . . was tired," the sobered-up poet lied.

Roberto's face wrinkled with skepticism. "You know so little of your friend, then."

The poet popped his dagger from its scabbard. "Don't talk about Drago that way."

"Drago?" asked the senator.

Marlowe gripped his weapon. "He liked that name."

Roberto processed this with a blank canvas of emotions. "You knew him, then?" he asked, deliberately using the *imperfetto* to upset Marlowe.

"Yes," the poet sneered. "Very well. We were friends for years. We ran an information exchange in Venice. I purloined documents when he needed them, and he shared whatever he had with me." Marlowe's thoughts took a detour for a moment. "Which reminds me: Do you have any *kahfey*?"

The old man's brow furrowed. "*Café*?" he asked.

Marlowe's mouth opened. "YES! If that's what you call it, sure!"

Roberto shook his head. "I am sorry. I used the last of mine this morning."

Marlowe grimaced and stomped his boot, shaking the building. "If you had some, I would drink it even if it were poisoned."

The old man smiled. "If I shared some, it would not be poisoned."

Marlowe snorted. "I don't believe you."

"It's true."

The poet rolled his eyes. "Well, just so I can find some when we're finished here, where did you get your *kahfey*?"

"From your friend," replied Roberto.

Marlowe's blood boiled. "You're getting under my skin, old man." He drew his dagger. "Perhaps it's time I get under yours."

"I am only speaking," said the senator.

"No, you're *torturing* me and embarrassing yourself. I know how you work, old man. Only someone like you could have organized a massacre like the one in Venice."

Roberto's eyes clouded. "Massacre?"

Marlowe took a good look at his adversary: his hands, his feet, his face. Roberto's brow was not perspiring, for he was precisely in his element. The poet walked straight up to the senator and leaned down until their faces were nearly touching. "You know *exactly* what I'm talking about."

A silence fell over the room that was quashed only by the sound of chirping birds. Neither man blinked. However, the senator was the first to move. He nodded, not in acknowledgment, but out of respect for the spy before him. Roberto knew better than anyone that it took talent for a man or woman—or lady—to survive what Christopher Marlowe must have suffered. "What do you know about my 'encounter' with Walsingham?" the old man asked. "Sir Francis Walsingham," he clarified.

Marlowe raised an eyebrow. "Should I have him confused with someone else?"

Roberto di Ridolfi wisely kept his mouth shut about Thomas Walsingham.

The assassin shrugged. "Very well. I know that you and Walsingham had a nice chat with each other, and . . . somehow, you walked away the victor."

"Do you know what we talked about?"

"Old man, I did *not* come here to hold your hand and reminisce about your younger years. I came here for information: Who tried to kill me, and why did those same people want Drago dead?"

The old man smiled. "And what if I told you that your friend is still alive?"

Marlowe's face froze. "Say that again?"

Roberto raised his eyebrows and turned his head, looking out the window. Down in his garden, he could see the two birds that had been chirping. "There comes a point in everyone's life when they look back on the road they've taken and question whether that was the path their life was meant for, or whether a wrong turn led them astray. Most people confront this quandary midway upon their journey. I, alas, was not so fortunate. I only came across it recently."

"Tell me what you said *before* all that, old man, and I might let you die of old age."

The senator looked back to Marlowe. "If all you have to threaten me with is death, then you are seventy-three years too late."

"If you insist." Marlowe clenched his dagger and stepped forward, prepared to claim the old man's life.

"If you kill me, you will never see your friend again."

Marlowe put his shining blade to Roberto's neck. "I don't expect to."

"But you will wonder whether you could have. It will haunt you every day, every minute, every heartbeat that you have left until you are as old as I am: so old that the entire world you lived in is just a memory. However, you will not remember the sweeter things: your mother's voice, a lover's laugh . . . You will not even remember your dear friend's face. However, you will remember this moment: the moment when you turned your back on him. And with your dying breath, your last words will be: 'What if . . . ?'"

Marlowe gritted his teeth as his blade trembled against the old man's skin. However, he could not cut it. In doing so, Marlowe knew he would be killing Drago.

The poet looked into Roberto's eyes. "Is my friend alive?"

The old man nodded. "Yes."

"How could you possibly know that!"

"Because he told me in a letter."

Marlowe nervously turned his head, searching the room for parchment. "Where is it?"

"I burned it."

The poet's eyes rekindled with hated. "Then you are a liar!"

The old man shook his head. "Not to you."

"Yes you are! You lied to me, the dragoman, Walsingham—"

"No, no, and no."

Enraged, Marlowe shoved the man onto the floor before he risked killing him. The poet panted angrily and threw his dagger, impaling it on the bedroom door. "How on earth did a troll like you ever outwit a man like Francis Walsingham!"

Roberto coughed from his dusty floor. "That . . ." he groaned, "was one of the greatest tricks he ever pulled." The senator slowly pushed himself back onto his feet while addressing his would-be killer. "When Walsingham confronted me those many years ago, he never threatened me. He did not need to. I knew from the moment he sought me out that one look from him would mean my death. I had no loyalty to Tuscany, and all my sacred faith had failed me. So, I told him everything, all my plans and schemes, to save my life. I was on my knees, begging him for mercy." The old man looked down and dusted himself. "I was convinced Walsingham would kill me, but what he did instead was extraordinary."

Marlowe sniffled, and then he sneezed. "How extraordinary?" he asked, rubbing his nose.

The senator stood tall, resting his knuckles against his windowsill to keep his balance. "Francis Walsingham did not want me dead. Instead, he asked me to continue my conspiracy. He wanted it to unfold, uninterrupted, drawing in as many people as it could. He wanted every corrupted citizen in the country to be a part of it so he could catch them all at once."

"Your conspiracy to kill the queen?" The poet gasped. "He let it happen?"

Roberto nodded. "Rather than face some unforeseen danger in the future, Francis allowed my plot to continue until the time was best to stop it. He cultivated it like poisoned fruit. It was smart of him. And he was friendly about it, too."

"*Friendly*?" Marlowe laughed. "Francis Walsingham? Friendly?"

"We maintained a correspondence for many years and helped each other in our own ways. It kept us ahead of the larger powers trying to manipulate us into war. Unfortunately," Roberto sighed, "as

I got older, I realized I spent too much time abroad when I should have been here in Tuscany. The Medici have turned this lovely land into yet another squabbling monarchy. The people weep for the Florentine Republic that only men as old as me are sons of. It is the reason I joined the senate. I want to give the people their country back."

Marlowe narrowed his eyes. "And what of the Medici? Were they behind this massacre?"

Roberto smiled and shook his head. "No. But as with Walsingham, they allowed it to happen."

Marlowe grimaced and looked away, at which point he noticed his dagger sticking out of the door. He walked over and extracted it. "You said my friend is alive. How did that happen?" The poet sheathed his blade. "And where is he?"

"Your friend surrendered himself to the doge and used his wealth and wits to secure his release."

"That's very vague of you," Marlowe scrutinized. "How do I know you're telling me the truth?"

"The truth is he was vague about it!" Roberto parried. "Surely you can respect him withholding information from me. The only other detail I know is that he left Venice on a boat bound for the New World."

The poet's heart sank. "Well," he sighed, "one way or another, I . . ." Marlowe's voice faltered. "I will never see my friend again."

The man who bested Walsingham allowed a moment to let this fate sink in.

Until . . . "Not necessarily," Roberto tempted. "Your friend's journey is long, and he should be arriving in Messina shortly. A simple message tied to a pigeon could arrive in time to redirect him to your location."

Marlowe's watery eyes brightened. "Is that possible?"

The senator smiled, narrowed his eyes, and slightly raised his chin. He then gently grazed his cleanly shaven cheek with his fingernails, the whole time keeping his littlest finger raised.

The poet got the message. "What do you want from me?"

"There are rumors going through the senate that the Medici sold their souls to the devil to secure the papacy. Whether it be true or not, my people could use this information to bring down the House of Medici once and for all. It could help us rally the people so that we may forever banish them from this city. For that to happen, and for you to see your friend again, I must ask that you go to Rome."

Marlowe's jaw dropped. "And do what?" he scoffed. "Assassinate the new pope? They're supposed to be crowning him today!"

"I am not asking for murder. All I require is your assistance. You say you obtained information for your friend, yes? I would like you to do the same for me. Come with me to Rome and find me evidence of this conspiracy so that men like me can die knowing that we liberated Italy from her enemies."

Marlowe bit his lower lip. "That sounds too dangerous. I was only lucky to survive in Venice. And what of Drago? Where is he in all this?"

"Your friend can meet us in Rome! We can ride south as he sails north. It will guarantee that you see him in the shortest time."

Marlowe took a breath and thought this over. He always wanted to return to Rome, and he still remembered the city well. "I will need some equipment."

The old man's eyes lit up. "I have plenty! Here!" Roberto led Marlowe to a nearby room filled with chests and cabinets. He threw them open to reveal a vast arsenal of Italian weaponry: broadswords, halberds, dussacks, stilettos, harquebuses, and wheellock pistols. Marlowe even saw a ribauldequin and a lantern shield propped against the wall. "I see you're prepared for everything," the poet complimented Roberto di Ridolfi.

"These are relics from my younger years. If you assist me, then they are yours."

"And what is that?" asked Marlowe once he came to what looked like a suit made out of leather. The outfit had large, round lenses in place of eyeholes and a mess of tubes sticking out of its mouth.

"Ah! You should be familiar with that one," the old man teased. "Leonardo developed this diving apparatus while he was in Venice. It was made for surprise attacks against boats from underwater."

"Are you expecting us to run into trouble with the papal navy?"

"To be safe, I will give you everything."

Marlowe turned around to take in all the possibilities open to him. So many weapons, so many ideas whispering to him like iron muses of epic poetry.

"So, can we help each other?" Roberto asked, offering the English poet his hand.

Marlowe had no doubt he would regret passing up this opportunity. "To Rome," he vowed, accepting it.

The old man smiled. *"Va bene."* He then led Marlowe downstairs for some coffee, which the poet was overjoyed to learn Roberto actually had plenty of.

As he promised, it was not poisoned.

Chapter XXIX

The Fog

I t was springtime in London; or at least it was supposed to be. The cunning wind persisted through the New Year and eventually transitioned into April rain. By the time the storms were spent, a thick fog fell like a curtain over the sodden, plague-strewn city just before the first of May. With London obscured behind this veil, the bard worked at his desk on Silver Street with only the gossip of a chatty conspiracy of ravens for inspiration.

> *The Rauen himselfe is hoarse,*
> *That croakes the fatall entrance of Duncan*
> *Vnder my Battlements. Come you Spirits,*
> *That tend on mortall thoughts, vnsex me here,*
> *And fill me from the Crowne to the Toe, top-full*
> *Of direst Crueltie: make thick my blood,*
> *Stop vp th'accesse, and passage to Remorse,*
> *That no compunctious visitings of Nature*
> *Shake my fell purpose, nor keepe peace between*
> *Th'effect, and hit. Come to my Womans Brests,*
> *And take my Milke for Gall, you murth'ring Ministers,*

> *Where-euer, in your sightlesse substances,*
> *You wait on Natures Mischiefe. Come thick Night,*
> *And pall thee in the dunnest smoake of Hell,*
> *That my keene Knife see not the Wound it makes,*
> *Nor Heauen peepe through the Blanket of the darke,*
> *To cry, hold, hold.*

Shakespeare's words were no more a compliment to London's raven population than to its weather. The rancorous birds outside his windows had become a nuisance ever since the fog descended. Although he was alarmed by their cries at first, the bard stopped trying to make sense of their strange behavior once he realized that they, like he, had nothing to observe but endless gray. Perhaps they had found an adversary, or maybe the blinded birds were just communicating through the mist. In either case, the playwright could think of no better crutch to fall upon than apathy. As long as Bacon's ravens kept his enemies at bay—

There was a pounding on his door. "Will!" a voice cried out.

It was Guy Fawkes.

Shakespeare turned his head, stunned that the conspirator had somehow found a way to his apartment. The bard glanced once more to the droning ravens, and then back to his door with alerted eyes. As the pounding continued, he then looked to his sword.

"SHAKESPEARE!"

"Just a moment!" The playwright hid his few belongings and opened the door for the hatted, bearded man waiting for him on the other side.

"Will!"

"Guido," the playwright nodded.

Fawkes put a gloved hand on Shakespeare's shoulder. "Brother. May I come in?"

Before the bard could ask him not to, the conspirator had already rushed inside. "Please be my guest, my friend."

"Bless you, brother!" Fawkes's eyes raced across the room like a cornered animal.

"Is everything all right, Guido?" Shakespeare asked as he closed the door. "You look—"

"Will, we need to get out of here!" Fawkes interrupted.

"What! Why?"

"We have to go to Westminster. It's urgent! I tried to reach you yesterday, but . . ." The conspirator instinctively pulled his hat over some of the scratches on his face. "The birds are a menace in this part of town!"

Shakespeare's eyes shifted to the clouded windows. "Yes, they tend to be."

The conspirator nodded nervously. "Very much so. Now, come! Fly with me!"

"Guido!" the playwright pleaded, catching the conspirator by the arm. "What is this about? You're acting mad."

"You know we can't talk about this here!"

"Of course we can."

"Will! I—" Several footsteps from the floor above them silenced Fawkes. The conspirator looked back to Shakespeare and grabbed his hand. "Come. We're leaving!"

"Guido, I don't have my sword!"

"You'll be safe with me." Fawkes pulled the playwright through the door.

"Would you at least tell me what this is about!" the bard protested as he yanked his hand back.

The conspirator stared deeply into Shakespeare's eyes. "I'm only sharing this much with you because I know you can be trusted. My brother, we have been betrayed!"

The bard's heart stopped. "By whom?"

Guy Fawkes's nostrils flared. "By the witches!"

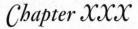

Chapter XXX

The She-Wolf

Christopher Marlowe and his Florentine accomplice arrived in Rome two weeks and two days after Alessandro de' Medici was crowned Pope Leo XI. The date was April 26, 1605, and although Alessandro's papacy was in its infancy, neither the poet nor the senator could have guessed how literally. Not in their wildest dreams or their darkest nightmares.

Marlowe had to discover it for himself.

As a visiting senator and head of one of Italy's most prestigious banks, Roberto di Ridolfi proved a valuable companion the moment he and Marlowe bribed their way into the Eternal City. The spies passed through Nanni di Baccio Bigio's triumphal Porta del Popolo at the Aurelian Walls towing an entire wagon of weapons that was neither stopped nor searched. Their arrival had been completely unhindered and their grand designs were untraceable. They took up lodgings at separate locations from Campus Martius to Trajan's Column, and after a day's rest and planning, the two descended upon

Rome like eagles. Roberto worked the political scene, coaxing friends and contacts for information while Marlowe went back to doing what he did best. Once more, the English poet took the cloth and disappeared among the city's clergy.

Marlowe walked out of the Collegio Romano wearing a Jesuit robe Roberto procured for the occasion. It was a beautiful Wednesday afternoon, and the wide piazza outside the school was filled with students and brimmed with light. Marlowe took a moment to enjoy the setting, reflecting on how he used to be one of these undergraduates. Sort of.

After scanning the square for a familiar face, the Jesuit raised an eyebrow, finding none.

"*Padre*," a familiar voice called out behind him. Marlowe turned around to find Roberto covertly waiting beside the ivory school's wooden doors.

"*Senatore*." The Jesuit walked over and blessed the man.

Roberto bowed his head while using his hand to hide the smile on his face. "Follow me," he whispered in English. The men left the Jesuit college behind them and walked toward the ruined tower atop the Quirinal Hill. "So, what did you find?" the senator asked the Jesuit once they crossed Via del Corso.

"You first," replied the priest.

"No, I insist," Roberto begged with dignity. He wanted to save what he had learned for later.

The Jesuit shrugged. "Very well. That name you provided caused quite a stir. Henry Garnet requested the transfer of three Jesuits to England sometime last year. According to Padre Clavius at the Collegio, the three priests were his students."

Roberto's brow wrinkled. He was familiar with the name. "Mathematicians?"

"Astrologers," Marlowe corrected. "Clavius said they were brilliant, too. Gifted students. He was sorry to see them go."

"Did Garnet provide a reason for needing them?"

"Nope! In fact, Clavius became mad as a bull when I asked for one. The fat man huffed and puffed about how dangerous England is and how he hadn't heard from the boys in months. He thinks their lives are in danger, and I don't blame him! England is a popular place for priests to die."

The senator thought on this. "A few students were sent to England. That's all you found?"

"From how it sounds," Marlowe snickered, "I don't think *anybody* is going to find them!"

Roberto grimaced. On the whole, he was disappointed. "Nobody in Tuscany is going to care about a few dead priests in England."

"Don't worry. Aside from fat Clavius, I don't think anybody cares around here either. Martyrdom is a fate with its own reward." The incognito Englishman fell silent as their busy street slowed to a near stop. "So, what did you learn from *your* friends?"

"*Che bella giornata di primavera,*" the senator replied to throw any listeners off course. "*Camminiamo.*" Marlowe understood Roberto's concerns, and the conversation shifted with the scenery to Rome's Trevi district. However, this locale proved even more crowded due to construction projects in the area. After inspecting the noisy square, the senator led the poet to Jacopo della Porta's *fontana* so that their words would be drowned out by the Acqua Vergine's rustling waters. "I spoke with several people today, and they all told me the same thing: the pope is gravely ill."

"Oh?" Marlowe snickered. "Does this one have gout as well?" Leo XI's predecessor, Clement VIII, spent the last years of his life bedridden with the rich man's disease.

Roberto shook his head. "It is more serious than that. He's been getting weaker every day since his coronation. They fear he may be dying."

Marlowe raised his eyebrows. "Are you serious? After less than a

month in the hat? He only barely edged Pope Urban!" Pope Urban
VII died in 1590 a lucky thirteen days into his papacy. "I don't believe it. Three different popes in less than half a year—again!"

"That's what they told me," Roberto continued with frustration.
"A lot of people who campaigned for Alessandro's candidacy are
angry. He is the first Medici pope in half a century, and it cost a
fortune to make that happen. Cardinal Aldobrandini told me that
Henry IV of France spent three hundred thousand *écus* on Alessandro's behalf during the conclave. The House of Medici hinges on
Alessandro's survival."

"Do you think he will?"

The senator shook his head. "I am not sure. I was hoping *you*
would find out for me."

Marlowe's eyes widened. "Me? How?"

Roberto smiled and then guided his companion two blocks eastward. The senator and the Jesuit left the Trevi district as they ascended Rome's highest hill.

The men turned right at Via della Panetteria and walked toward
one of the newer additions to the city: the creamy white Palazzo del
Quirinale, the pope's recently constructed Roman residency. Marlowe put his hands on his hips and smirked at the impressively ironic
building. For such an important stronghold, its outer wall was just a
perimeter of simple houses. Its modest facade more closely resembled a papal prison than a palace. Its "Courtyard of Honor" was
somewhat dishonorably closed to the public. Its papal gardens came
off as simple shrubbery compared to the Vatican's. And, of course,
Marlowe took some satisfaction in the knowledge that its current
occupant, Alessandro de' Medici, apparently bribed his way into
the building just so he could die in there.

It had been nearly twenty years since Marlowe saw the palace,
and he found it more amusing now than ever. "Do you want me to
take a look inside?" he asked the senator.

"Not in the manner which you are thinking. My sources tell me that His Holiness was moved from his bedchambers to the Torrino for his health." Roberto pointed to the small, box-like Torre dei Venti, or "Tower of the Winds" atop the palace.

Out of all the rooms in the palazzo, the Torrino appeared to be the easiest for a man of Marlowe's skills to access. "How convenient," he appraised. "How are the airs treating him up there?"

"Not well," replied the senator, "which is unfortunate, since I've been told that he is now too weak to be moved out of it. Also . . ." Roberto moved in closer. "There are whispers that the pope requested this so that he could be alone with a certain priest."

The poet glanced at the senator. "A priest?"

Roberto nodded.

The Jesuit smirked. "Is it a young priest?" he surmised. "Beautiful? Pure? Innocent?"

Again, confirmed.

Marlowe grinned with delight as he looked back to the tower. "Well, at least he's dying happy!"

"My friend, this is serious. The pope is the Vicar of Christ. If this one is destroying himself through decadence, then it is the best news we could have hoped for. The Medici will *never* return to the papacy! They will become as vilified as the Borgia."

"And that's good for you?" Marlowe asked with a raised eyebrow.

"It will be good for the people of Toscana. All I need is for you to confirm these rumors before the Medici weave their own mythologies when the pope dies."

The poet bit his lip in thought as he looked up and down the palazzo.

"Will you need anything to accomplish this?" asked Roberto.

"Yes, I will." Marlowe turned his head and squared his shoulders with the senator. "My friend, the dragoman. Why is he not here yet?"

"I don't know," replied the politician. "He is traveling a great distance. Perhaps he encountered some bad weather. Perhaps—"

"Perhaps that pigeon you sent never made it to Messina." Marlowe grabbed the Florentine by his arm and forced him into a secluded alley. "Perhaps it arrived here, alerting the Medici to my presence. Perhaps my friend is dead, and you always knew it. Perhaps you led me here to die as well."

"My friend . . ." Roberto smiled, raising a hand. "I thought we already established trust with each other."

"I am not your friend, *Senatore*, so don't pretend I am just because I spared your life. We are accessories to each other. You are using me, and I am using you."

The senator smirked. "I thought you were used to this type of barter. With your friend."

"Don't provoke me, old man. You're asking me to crawl into the wolf's mouth right now. How do I know you're not just another fang waiting to come chomping down on me?"

Roberto narrowed his eyes and scoffed. "You truly are rarity, Marlowe. You are boorish and hedonistic by default, but also resolute when you need to be. It is so clear to me why your friend holds you so highly. You are a greater survivor than he ever was." The senator deliberately chose these words to disarm the poet. He wanted to raise Marlowe's hopes only to cast them back into a sea of doubt.

The poet glared at his companion, but then blinked. His eyes fell forlornly.

The man who bested Walsingham stood tall, brimming with victory. "I will be at the Pantheon while you work, same as last night. If you encounter any trouble, meet me there and I will take care of you." The senator put his hand on Marlowe's shoulder. "May God be with you."

The Jesuit's eyes glowed angrily in the darkened alley. "I don't need God right now. What I need is proof that you're not my enemy."

The senator smiled. Seeing no other course of action, he grabbed Marlowe's face and kissed him. *"In bocca al lupo,"* Roberto pledged. "Into the wolf's mouth."

Not convinced, the poet left his ally in the alleyway. *"Crepi il lupo,"* he threw over his shoulder. "May the wolf die."

That night.

Since Marlowe had done reconnaissance work at the Quirinale during his younger years, he knew his way on and off its ground without being spotted by the Holy See. Thanks to his watchful eyes and careful planning, the only sentry he came across was one of the city's countless cats. Marlowe watched and waited until the half-moon was eclipsed behind the Vatican cupola, allowing the Eternal City to darken even more. Still dressed in his black Jesuit cassock and *ferraiolo* cape, the stealthy poet took a breath and went to work on the papal palace, operating almost entirely by memory.

The Quirinale's outer wall was easy enough for Marlowe to climb. Since it was comprised primarily of tenement buildings, the poet scaled its weakest point in less than half a minute. The palazzo itself, however, did not have any easy points of entry, and Marlowe knew this. After zigzagging his way across the palace grounds, he ascended the palazzo's mammoth base with a grappling hook and rope launched via crossbow. It was one of several such devices from Roberto's armory that the men agreed might prove useful. Once Marlowe was on the palazzo's marble balcony, he collected his rope and shot it again, this time over the narrow wedge jutting out of the palace's northernmost point. The grappling hook cleared the shortened roof and secured itself, allowing Marlowe to climb the remaining distance to the top. The poet pulled himself over the palazzo's tiles and onto his feet, and then raced across the building's spine to the Tower of the Winds. All eleven of the Torrino's windows appeared to be dark, but as Marlowe circled the ivory tower, he glimpsed some firelight emanating from its southern corner. The poet paused, deeming it too risky to use his hook to scale the structure. Instead, he climbed its ledge at its lowest point, allowing him to peer inside one of the tower's windows.

At first, things appeared precisely as Marlowe expected within the tower. A bed had been arranged against its southeastern wall, the only wall with just two windows instead of three. The pope was barely visible to Marlowe; nothing but a darkened lump against a white pillow. But as the poet's eyes adjusted to the room, he began to see Alessandro de' Medici more clearly. The man did not look well at all. His skin was ghostly pale, even against the room's amber light. His white beard was a disheveled cobweb. His face appeared twisted in fear. The pope groaned softly in his sleep as if in pain. His covers lifted and fell with shallow breathing. If this man was the last hope of the House of Medici, then all their fortunes appeared as dim as the candle by the man's deathbed.

And then, beside the pope, there was the other person.

Marlowe quickly pulled his head back once he saw movement. It was nothing in particular; just a shadow cast by someone with a candle. After seeing the shadow settle, Marlowe leaned once more against the window. Just as Roberto reported, a lone figure in a priest's habit was present with the pope. The figure was seated and watched Alessandro as he slept. The priest's posture was straight and strong, statuesque, and his demeanor almost territorial. The poet could only see a hint of the figure's face. Once more, all appeared precisely as Roberto had heard. The attending priest looked to be young, and quite attractive.

Marlowe studied the two for nearly an hour, but little happened. The pontiff stirred in his bed occasionally while his attendant's gaze remained unflinching. As the poet's eyes shifted from the pontiff to the sentinel, he began to notice that the priest did not seem to move at all. He drew no visible breaths, and he did not even appear to blink. After deciding that nothing would change for the entire evening, Marlowe drew away from the window and stepped back onto the palazzo. He sat on the tiled roof and took a breath while gazing over Rome. The poet raised his head as if to consult the stars for guidance, but finding none, Marlowe sighed and let his eyes fall.

But then he saw something move across his doeskin boots. The poet ran his hand over it, casting a shadow. Marlowe looked over his shoulder. There was movement in the Tower of the Winds.

The poet pushed himself up and once more climbed the tower's ledge. This time, he was a bit more impatient than he should have been, looking inside with nearly his entire body in the window.

Marlowe's mouth fell open.

The priest beside the pope had unbuttoned his cassock and let the cloth slide down his shoulders, revealing that the young man was actually a woman. A smile curled across Marlowe's lips at this revelation, but then the smile faded. Confusion washed over Marlowe's face. And then, speechlessness. Shock. Horror.

Fire danced in the woman's eyes as she ran her fingers through the dying pope's silver hair. The old man's face wrinkled with worry and his lips moved as if to scream. The woman's face, meanwhile, intensified. A seriousness fell over her. A hateful, ancient anger. The woman leaned forward and pushed the groaning man's pallid face into her breast. As the dying man's lips latched onto her, she raked her nails again and again against his scalp. Ensnaring him. Trapping him. He, delirious and mad with hunger, and she, overflowing with a deadly toxin she ingested every morning since she was a child, immunizing her. Saturating her. Corrupting her every morsel with the same poison she was now feeding into the pontiff's mouth, just as she had been doing every day for weeks. And to his predecessor.

It was a weapon unlike any wielded on the battlefield. It was Roman charity, made wicked.

Christopher Marlowe was petrified.

And then there was a din: the sound of metal tapping against glass. The tip of Marlowe's parrying dagger accidentally bumped against the window he was watching from. The woman snapped her head toward the sound; her wild eyes burning with a madness that Marlowe had seen before. It was the same look of the woman who he unmasked in Venice. Livid, the woman grabbed her bedside candle and blew it out.

Horrified, Marlowe tried to slide away without falling off his ledge. However, just before he could leap to safety, two hands came crashing through the window. The bloodied arms seized the poet and pulled him into the tower.

"NO!" Marlowe cried as his arms and legs were pierced by glass. The poet landed hard on the floor, embedding his palms with painful shards as well. Marlowe groaned and tried to stand while a deathly gasp suddenly filled the room. In need of light, the poet removed a small pouch from his pocket and threw it against the wall. The pouch exploded in a bright flash that caused one of the tower's curtains to ignite. The spy pushed himself up to see the woman atop the pope, stabbing him repeatedly with a dagger. The bare-breasted villainess screamed like a banshee with every thrust, splattering herself and Marlowe with blood. Her howls attracted the attention of every guard in the palazzo, who turned their heads to the Tower of the Winds and came running. Injured, Marlowe reached desperately for his parrying dagger, but could only find an empty sheath. The blade was gone; stolen by the woman who pulled him inside. She had just killed the pope with his weapon.

Covered in blood, the lady assassin lowered her arms and turned to Marlowe.

Amidst the spreading fire, the poet staggered onto his feet while unsheathing a throwing-knife from his boot. "Who are you?" he demanded, his blade shaking in his bleeding hand. "Why are you doing this? Tell me!"

The woman did not say a word. Instead, she lowered her head and stared deeply into the Englishman. Marlowe had used his native tongue. Her face wrinkled like a wolf's snout and she flashed her teeth like fangs, some of them still pink with carnage. The woman squeezed her stolen dagger, screamed a Celtic curse, and then tore her own throat open with her blade. Marlowe's mouth hung open while the woman's neck erupted all over her body. She then lowered her gaze, stared straight into the poet's eyes in triumph, and fell backward into the blood-soaked bed. Both she and the pope were dead; murdered by Marlowe's dagger.

"Oh no . . ." the poet realized as the entire room filled with flame.

The Torrino began to thunder as papal guards raced up its spiral staircase. *"Proteggete il papa! Assassini!"*

Realizing he was in trouble, Marlowe jumped straight out the window that he had been pulled through.

A modest donation was all it took for Roberto to pass his evening in the Pantheon, the one building from ancient Rome still in use in the city. Specifically, as a tomb.

The senator was paying his respects to Raffaello when the tolling of church bells filled the chamber. With his prayer interrupted, Roberto crossed himself and turned around. He walked across the temple's magnificently tiled marble floor with only a few candles burning. He stepped directly under the starlit oculus 142 feet above him in the center of the temple's dome. The constellations Draco and Hercules loomed above him, and Roberto was curious what fortunes they portended. The senator stood tall and homed his eyes through the church's open doors, past its Numidian marble cantons and sixteen Egyptian granite columns. His hands were at his sides, and his pulse was steady. In his mind, he imagined it would take a younger man like Marlowe about five minutes to run from the Quirinale to the Pantheon. Maybe ten minutes if he got lost.

Instead, an exhausted Marlowe came staggering through its doors only seconds later. It took the pope's guards several minutes to sound the alarm during his escape.

"Roberto!" Marlowe gasped, limping forward. "The pope is dead! A woman killed him! A mad witch! I saw her!"

The senator used all his strength to obscure his euphoria.

"Roberto, they're after me!" Marlowe pleaded, the pope's blood still staining his face. "They think I did it! I'm injured! You have to help me!"

The wounded poet reached out with dripping palms and blood-splattered boots. Footsteps were approaching. Behind him, a host of guards and papal soldiers descended upon the Piazza della Rotonda from all directions.

Marlowe looked over his shoulder to his bloodied footprints and then snapped his head back to Roberto. "They've followed me!" he cried. "They're here! I am a dead man! Please do something!"

The senator waited until the guards were inside the Pantheon.

"Assassino!" the first guard shouted. *"È un assassino! Uccidetelo!"*

Roberto smirked. The soldier's choice of words could not have been more appropriate.

The senator grabbed the priest by his garbs and yanked him forward, ripping the buttons off his cassock so that his bare chest was exposed.

Marlowe looked down at Roberto's hands and then back to the senator's eyes in horror.

The man who bested Walsingham plunged a dagger beneath the Jesuit's robes. "Send Walsingham my regards." Blood splattered over both men, and the great Christopher Marlowe fell lifelessly.

Marlowe was dead. Again.

Chapter XXXI

"He's Dead?"

The conspirators nodded. "Murdered in his bed," said Robert Catesby. "The Italians are already calling him Papa Lampo. The 'Lightning Pope.'"

"He flew in and out like lightning," Jack Wright snickered from behind his pewter cup.

Shakespeare rubbed his beard in worry, but it was all an act. Thomas Walsingham had already briefed him on Pope Leo's murder. "Do we know who killed him?"

The intoxicated conspirators set their angry eyes on Guy Fawkes, among them several new recruits: Jack Wright's younger brother Christopher, Thomas Wintour's older brother Robert, Catesby's servant Thomas Bates, and Robert Keyes, an indebted but honest good-for-nothing. "A man was found fleeing the grounds," said Fawkes, "but—"

"A man?" the bard interrupted. That much had not been disclosed to him. "Who was he?"

"We don't know. They killed him, but . . ."

Fawkes wavered, and then took a loud gulp from his March beer—potent stuff.

"But what?"

Thomas Percy angrily stomped his boot. "A heathen witch was found on the pope's body! Her throat had been sliced like a sow's," he slurred.

"We don't know she was a witch," Fawkes countered. "She could have been a prostitute. Or a nun."

The sweaty man shook his head. "No. You told us she was wearing priest's robes. I hope you burn in Hell for what you've gotten us into, Guido!"

"Fie, fie!" chided Catesby, the only sober man in the group. "There will be no more of that."

"You wanted an army, I got you an army," Guy Fawkes growled.

"An army of hell-spawn she-beasts!"

"You couldn't recruit your own mother."

Percy's pockmarked face twisted. "Why, you . . . miserable . . ."

"Brothers, *please!*" Robert Catesby leaped up from the barrel he was sitting on. "Have we not been through enough rows already? Do I have to knock your heads together to remind you that we are a confederacy?"

"I am sorry, Robert, but . . ." Tom Wintour needed another drink to continue. "It is beginning to sound like this entire endeavor—"

"Utter one more syllable and I will dig your heart out with this cup," Percy snapped.

Threatened, Tom looked to his cousin for defense, but the sergeant-at-arms was preoccupied with his tankard. "No one quits," Jack Wright grumbled. The swordsman greedily downed some more March beer.

An uncomfortable silence fell over the assembly for reasons other than their unpleasant location. Instead of the fashionable Duck and Drake or the comfortable Catherine Wheel, the conspirators' backdrop had changed to a musty, torchlit basement that more closely resembled a catacomb. It was an enormous undercroft half a mile upstream from the Strand, and it once served as a royal kitchen for the Palace of Westminster. The conspirators rented the empty space on Lady Day, March 25, from the same John Whynniard who leased them their prior property. The Keeper of the King's Wardrobe was happy to get rid of this place: it was dank, moldy, and had noxious air with little light. Its floors were caked with centuries of dirt, its one door opened directly into the reeking Thames, and its many crevices were a breeding ground for all sorts of vermin. It was a nauseating, suffocating place, but the conspirators prized it for one reason. The wooden boards above its twelve stone pillars happened to be the first floor of the House of Lords.

The men were sitting, drinking, and scheming directly under Parliament.

"So, why did you bring me here?" asked the playwright.

The nine conspirators looked up from their cups.

"Because recent events make your contribution to our enterprise more important than ever," declared Catesby. "If the cunning folk have betrayed us—"

"Of course they have!" Percy cried. "The bloody heathens."

"*Assuming* they have," Catesby continued, "then they have simultaneously deprived us of our greatest allies. The Medici are lost to us. The French, the Spanish, the Church . . . no one will support us after what happened in Rome. We are on our own now, which means whatever chance we have of building an army rests on your shoulders. We *need* your play to rally the people behind us when it premieres."

The playwright nodded. "I will continue to do my part, and I promise that it will be finished on time."

"There are also the cunning folk to contend with," Guy Fawkes reminded.

"Don't you even think of going back to them for help!" shot Percy.

"That's not what I meant." Fawkes's bloodshot eyes shifted back to the bard. "Will, you remember when we first told you about their involvement?"

Shakespeare nodded. "Of course. At the inn."

"You said you would increase their role in our drama. That you would give them more prominence."

"Did you do that?" Catesby inquired.

The bard looked over the drunk, desperate men. "Yes, I did. I said I would."

Guy Fawkes glared. "Then you must eliminate them."

Shakespeare raised his eyebrows. "Strike them from my writing?"

"Yes."

"No!" Percy countered. "Don't you dare do such a thing!"

"Tom . . ." Robert pleaded. "What are you—"

"Quiet!" The sweaty man snapped his head to the playwright. "Shakespeare, I want you to paint these pagan mystics as the infernal demons they are! Use every power at your disposal. Make the people of London want to murder every last one of them!"

Percy's companions were stunned. "That is actually a—*urrrt*—good idea," Fawkes acknowledged with a burp.

"Of course it's a good idea! It's what we should have done from the beginning! Kill them all!"

"Hear, hear!" the conspirators applauded in Thomas Percy's imagination. He raised his drink and accepted their praise even though the table had been quiet.

But then an unlikely party reentered the conversation: "Perhaps now is the time for us to do something about that."

All eyes turned to Jack Wright. "What was that?" asked Catesby.

"These witches know what we look like, and I am assuming they know both of your names." The swordsman pointed his gloved finger to Catesby and Fawkes. "How do we know they are not going to betray us to the government? One word from them and all our heads will end up on London Bridge."

A disquieting silence fell over the undercroft, and it was followed by more drinking.

"Did you share my name with them?"

Fawkes and Catesby looked at the bard with worry on their faces. "I am afraid so," replied the former.

This time, Shakespeare was not feigning fear as he rubbed his face. "I think I'll have a beer," he said, helping himself to a pint.

"So, what are we going to do?" asked the swordsman. "Are we just going to wait here until autumn?"

After a pause, Fawkes decided: "We have to meet with the witches again."

"What? Never!"

Guy Fawkes glared at Percy. "You want to kill them all? This just might be your chance!"

"Guido, they have an army," said Catesby.

"We don't know that," Fawkes realized. "They only told me they have an army, but I have never seen it."

"What about those brutes they had with them during their ceremony?" Wintour asked.

"A couple of country bumpkins with paint is no army," Fawkes scoffed. "We have twenty barrels of gunpowder and the best swordsman in England." The conspirator's eyes flashed to his leader. "Let us go back into Warwickshire. We will meet with the sisters and find out precisely what has happened. If the cunning folk tricked us, then I say we treat them to gunfire. Let us not leave the woods until every last one of the she-beasts is dead."

"Hear, hear!" Jack Wright and Tom Wintour cheered. Percy was a trifle jealous, but nevertheless entered his vote of confidence with more drinking.

Fawkes smiled and then looked to Shakespeare. The bard was a mix of emotions, and he was having trouble masking them all. "I should probably go back to my writing now."

Thomas Percy shook his head. "Oh, no you don't!"

"Brother," Catesby begged, "as I said, we need you now more than ever! Will you fight with us?"

The bard shook his head with indecision. "I do not know. When?"

The leader looked his men over. "My coachman is waiting at the Duck and Drake as we speak. I say we drink some more and then ride out!"

The slobbering crowd cheered in their subterranean parliament.

Shakespeare could scarcely believe what he was witnessing. He thought W was being fanciful when he requested that the cunning folk be destroyed, but now the conspirators were electing to attempt just that. The two forces would meet each other and destroy each other. And for that reason, "I cannot do it," the playwright said.

The conspirators' smiles faded as they looked to Shakespeare.

"I am a writer, not a warrior," he sighed. "If I were to ride out with you, I would only be an impediment on the battlefield."

"Oh, come now," Catesby chuckled. "We need all the men we can get. Show some strength!"

"Please. This is not what I agreed to. I am only here to write your play."

"What's the matter, playwright?" Percy heckled. "Are you afraid of lifting something heavier than a feather?"

The bard clenched his jaw and wrestled with a reply. Fortunately, he did not need one. Jack Wright had noticed that Shakespeare was not wearing his sword. "The playwright's right," he decided. "He would only get in my way." He then leaned over and asked: "That lovely rapier you carry. Where is it?"

"I left it at home," Shakespeare said, and then swallowed. "Why do you ask?"

The swaying swordsman leered at the playwright. "You've never even used it, have you?"

Shakespeare did not need to oversell his response. His answer was simple because it was also honest: "No."

The swordsman slinked back and returned to his beverage. "He'd be useless."

Catesby nodded. "Very well, then. Will, go back to your writing. And please pray for us every opportunity you have."

The bard bowed his head. "I will."

"Thank you. Go in peace, brother."

Catesby hunkered down with his men while Shakespeare quit the darkened stage.

"Master Bacon?"

The scientist looked up from the cadaver he was dissecting. "What is it?"

The Ravenmaster presented Bacon a small, rolled-up piece of parchment. "This just arrived."

The scientist pulled his arms out of the prisoner and unfurled the note with red, wet hands.

> *Fiue haue I slaine to daie in stead of hime,*
> *A horse, a horse, my kingdome for a horse.*

ASTON. SILVER ST.

Bacon returned the parchment stained with fingerprints. "Send him over immediately." The Ravenmaster bowed, and the scientist turned to the surgeon beside him. "I am afraid that you must ride off as well."

Knowing what this meant, the silent surgeon's bloodied hands clenched into fists.

Chapter XXXII

The Slap

"L et me do the talking."

"*We* will do the talking."

"Pish! You're the two who got us into this mess!"

"Mind your tongue, Thomas. Your empty threats are paper-thin."

"Fie upon thee!"

"Fie *thyself*!"

"Tush, tush, tush!"

"Peace, brothers! Stop this madness!"

"We need to kill them."

"*I* will kill them!"

"How much longer must we wait?"

The conspirators had been arguing in the darkened Arden for almost an hour. It was a misty, moonlit evening, and Shakespeare had plenty of foliage to hide behind as he monitored from afar. The bard counted ten men in his spyglass: the nine from earlier in Westminster, and John Grant, a veteran of the Essex Rebellion. The conspirators picked him up at Norbrook on their way through Warwickshire. Grant was Catesby's supply man for the English Midlands, and thanks to him, every one of the conspirators was brandishing weapons.

The bard was kneeling, Aston was quiet, and a stately raven was keeping watch above.

There were no cunning folk to be seen.

Then, across the glade, the conspirators saw a spark.

Robert Catesby raised his torch. "Lo!" he hollered. The men behind him tightened their weapons.

A ring of fire surrounded the forest clearing, wreathing the conspirators in flame.

"Dear lord," Catesby muttered. The cunning folk had been present the whole time.

As before, the two women had a thick wall of woad warriors behind them.

Guy Fawkes and Robert Catesby looked at each other, nodded, and then stepped across the glade. "Sisters," began the former. "Something dreadful has happened. We beseech—"

The elder woman ignored the man and threw a torch onto a woodpile. The timber erupted into a towering fire, forcing Catesby and Fawkes to step back. As the elder stared at the conspirators, the younger woman placed three skulls onto the stone slab by the blaze. Each skull had a candle flickering inside of it.

"What have you done?" Guy Fawkes gasped.

"A deed without a name," replied the elder.

The conspirators were speechless. The skulls were from the Jesuits.

Percy stomped forward and lobbed a throwing ax at the witches. "BLOODY HEATHENS!"

Catesby spun around. "Brother! No!"

The weapon flew straight toward the women. Without blinking or flinching, the elder caught the ax and tossed it aside, shattering all three skulls with it.

Her eyes were alight with resentment. "Twice the brinded Cat hath mew'd. Thrice and none the Hedge-Pigge whin'd."

"'Tis not time," the younger taunted. "'Tis not time."

Catesby swallowed. "Ladies, Alessandro de' Medici is dead. Every one of our foreign allies has deserted us."

There was no response.

"You have cursed us!" Fawkes entered. "You betrayed us with every one of our wishes! Explain yourselves!"

"The foul she-beasts . . ." Percy grumbled to Jack Wright.

"Faire is foule, and foule is faire . . ."

"Hover through the fog and filthy air," the cunning folk replied.

The conspirators froze in confusion. "What is that supposed to mean?" asked Catesby. "You expect us to weather this? You have us at your mercy! We have—"

But with those words, Guy Fawkes's patience had run out. He sheathed his weapon and marched forward.

"Guido! What are you—"

"Let me handle this," he shot to Catesby. The conspirators watched in shock as their lone cohort tromped up to the women. Their painted bodyguards stepped forward, but the elder woman kept them back.

Fawkes looked straight into the woman's wizened eyes. "No more riddles, mistress. Tell me clearly: Why is Alessandro de' Medici dead?" The conspirator was prepared to attack if he did not get a satisfactory response.

Instead, the woman blinked. She lifted her face to his, and her lips parted.

Surprised, Guido moved in closer so he could hear her whispers. Silhouetted by the crackling fire, their exchange was obscured to everyone, including Shakespeare.

When the whispers ended, every muscle on Guy Fawkes's face cringed. He drew back and looked into the woman's emerald eyes. A smile curled across her lips.

With all his strength, Guy Fawkes slapped the woman across her face.

"RUN!" he screamed.

Chapter XXXIII

Bewitched

With that clap, the cunning warriors came screaming across the glade while an even larger horde of painted men charged through the circle's flames. The conspirators, realizing they were outnumbered, cowered backwards in fear, but Fawkes sprinted past his cohorts and leaped through their burning barrier. Seeing this, Catesby led his remaining men through the fire and to their carriages. The conspirators whipped their horses and fled the Arden, many of them leaving their weapons behind.

The playwright sheathed his spyglass. It was time for him to fly as well.

Shakespeare had lowered his lenses the instant he realized what the cunning folk were up to. The women used their wreath of flame to mask a larger army hidden in the woods around them. It created the illusion that their warriors were being summoned from the fires when they were simply lining up behind them. It was theater; not magic. The conspirators were being deceived. The only question that kept the bard from fleeing earlier was why the warriors did not surround the entire circle. By leaving their only opening by the carriages, it was almost like they wanted the conspirators to escape.

However, the bard had no time to search for answers. Warriors were converging on the clearing from all directions, and Shakespeare needed to flee before any of them spotted him.

But then, the playwright's raven came screeching down just before he untied Aston. The bard followed the bird over his shoulder to see it claw at two painted men sneaking behind him. Shocked, Shakespeare drew his rapier and cut Aston free from his binds. However, as he stepped into his saddle, a sword flashed in front of him and sliced off his stirrup. The bard came crashing down and landed on his face.

The playwright rolled over to find a hideous figure looming over him.

"Wehlsgchy, wehlsgchy!" the drooling, misshapen Hobgoblin garbled and hissed.

Although the lower half of his face was masked behind a metal jaw, there was no doubt in Shakespeare's mind that the madman was smiling.

The ring of flame had died out by the time Shakespeare was forced inside the circle. With the conspirators gone, the bard was all alone against the cunning folk. Their warriors stripped Shakespeare of his weapons and then brought him to their mistresses.

The women appeared somewhat different in person than the bard had observed through his lenses. Instead of standing tall and statuesque, the elder was sitting on their stone slab while the younger examined her bruised face. The injury was not serious, but the elder already requested that her men bring her some arnica, parsley, and cold cream to make a balm.

The bard was thrown before them, and the two women turned their heads.

"Ladies." He bowed.

The painted men grumbled something to the women, and the mistresses narrowed their eyes at the playwright.

Shakespeare shrugged apologetically, but was then interrupted by two ravens that came swooping down to defend him. Unfortunately, the bard was too outnumbered for the ravens to help him escape, but he nevertheless smiled as the bloodied birds went to work on the painted warriors. However, the women were prepared for this, and the elder jumped back onto her feet. She waved over an older man holding a hollowed-out wooden log. The man threw the cylinder into the bonfire, and as it ignited, it billowed a brightly colored smoke over the glade. The fume had a noxious smell that assaulted the ravens, forcing them to retreat. One of the black birds fell down, dead, while the other fled from the clearing.

The abandoned bard sighed with sadness. "How cunning of you," he commented.

The women were not amused. "What are you doing here?" the elder asked in a Gaelic accent as she sat down.

The playwright raised an eyebrow. "Do you normally speak like that?"

"Not normally." She then chatted something to the younger woman in Old Brythonic, an ancient tongue that the bard's trained ear could not recognize. "I ask again," she continued, "why are you here?"

Shakespeare shrugged. "I guess you could say I came in with the breeze," he replied in his natural Warwickshire accent. "This is my homeland. I was born here. The Arden is as much a part of me as my mother." The playwright was not lying. His mother had been born Mary Arden.

The women were not moved by this proclamation. However, Shakespeare saw some curiosity on their faces when one of their warriors presented them with his possessions. Some shards of glass fell out of Bacon's telescope as the elder removed it from its sleeve.

"What is that?" asked the younger. "Some sort of tool?"

The playwright smiled smugly, for the instrument had been damaged. They would never know what it was. "It's for digging," he said, thinking back to Percy's threat to Thomas Wintour.

The elder set the device aside with Shakespeare's playing cards and his rapier to examine them in more detail later. "You intruded upon our meeting," she said, "so I will ask you one more time: Why are you here?"

"Honestly, I got lost," the actor replied. "I was in the forest looking for some toadstools."

"Toadstools?" asked the younger.

"At this hour?"

"They're for my wife. She is sick. I am sorry I intruded, but I saw your fire and hoped that you would help me find my way out."

"I thought you were familiar with these woods."

The bard theatrically ran his eyes over the clearing. "Evidently, not these parts."

The seated elder sharpened her senses on the playwright.

"Did you find any toadstools?" asked the younger.

Shakespeare shook his head. "No, I am sorry to say. If you have any, I will gladly buy them off you."

The two women exchanged glances. "If that is all you need, we will give you some and help you find your way."

The playwright's heart leaped. "Thank you, ladies." He bowed.

But then . . .

"Nuuurrrrrrgh!"

A voice cried out so full of sorrow that it made Shakespeare wince. The assembled turned their heads to the writhing Hobgoblin, who hobbled into the circle like a marionette. He was mangled, mad with pain, and rendered half dead from his injuries.

The playwright had to look away from the disfigured bandit, who apparently still had a flair for rhyming even without his silver tongue. The villain spoke in rasps and wheezes behind his metal mask, but nevertheless pantomimed to the cunning folk that something foul was afoot.

The younger woman walked up to the creature and held his broken hands. "What are you saying?" she asked with empathy.

Enraged, the Hobgoblin pointed his stubby fingers toward Shakespeare, and then his sawed-off stump to his toadies: the blinded Snell and the deafened Shorthouse. The creature sneered at the playwright and then flapped his arms like a bird, shrieking.

With this revelation, the two women looked to each other in shock, and then back to Shakespeare.

The bard's eyes shifted nervously.

"So, you came here with the raven," said the elder.

Shakespeare smirked. "I told you, I came in with the breeze. Not the birds."

The women scowled.

Suddenly, a loud whinny filled the clearing. The playwright's smile faded and his heart sank. It was Aston.

The magnificent horse was being pulled toward the bonfire. The stallion resisted furiously, but nearly a dozen men had ropes tied around his neck.

"There is no need to be rough with him!" Shakespeare shouted.

Enchanted, the younger woman beheld the horse with widened eyes. After whispering something to her sister, the elder nodded and the younger approached the animal.

"Tell me more about your sick wife," the elder woman taunted the playwright. "Where does she live? Somewhere near that we may ride to?"

The bard swallowed. After weighing his options . . . "What can I say?" He surrendered. "You found me out. I'm just a vagabond. I am not even married!" the dramatist lied with all his skills.

The elder was not convinced.

The younger, meanwhile, walked straight up to the stallion and stroked his shining coat. The horse snorted fiercely and stomped the ground, nearly crushing the woman's toes with his hooves.

"I would be careful with that animal!" the bard cautioned. "He's not exactly friendly."

"No horse like that has ever existed on these isles. What are you doing with him?" the elder woman asked the playwright.

"With your permission, I would like to ride him out of here."

The stallion bucked, forcing several of the painted men to lose their grip. As Aston reared onto his hind legs, one of the glass balls from his saddlebags fell into the grass.

"What is that?" the younger asked in her native tongue. She picked up the amber sphere and studied its clouded contents.

"That's just a suppository," said Shakespeare.

The glass orb was cracked. As the younger woman examined it, it began to leak onto her hands. The woman sniffed the liquid, and her eyes lit up with recognition. She looked back at the snorting animal. "Hold him down!" she commanded. The painted warriors pulled their ropes until Aston's head was bowing. The cunning woman walked up to him and held her moistened hand under his nostrils.

Shakespeare gasped. "What are you doing?"

Aston turned his head, following the scent.

"What are you doing!" the bard demanded. He fought against his captors with so much anger that the elder slapped him across the face to calm him down.

The young mistress stared straight into the animal's eyes. Her pulse quickened. She then lifted the sphere over her head and broke it open, dousing herself in the mare urine. She stepped toward the snorting animal and let him run his nostrils over her. Aston's anger dissipated, replaced with curiosity. And then, arousal.

"Let him go," she ordered. The painted warriors dropped their ropes, and the cunning woman led the stallion off.

"Leave him alone!" the playwright cried. "Aston! Get back here!"

"He is not your horse anymore," the elder woman explained.

Shakespeare shut his eyes as tears began to form in them. "What are you going to do to him? What are you going to do to me?"

The woman whispered to her servants, and then looked back at Shakespeare. "You've been spying on us. Haven't you?"

The bard struggled in both mind and body. "I told you: I was lost!"

"Yes, you were looking for medicine. Just as I imagine you were the last time you intruded. When you mutilated our brothers here." The elder pointed her chin toward the Hobgoblin and his toadies. "You came into this forest both times when we met with the Englishmen."

The bard's nostrils flared. "You can say and think whatever you like, but please leave my horse out of this. Bring him back to me!"

The elder smiled menacingly. "No. My sister clearly wants him, so I will pay you for him."

"With what?"

The cunning woman rose to her feet. "With medicine."

The elder turned her back on Shakespeare while her bodyguards seized him. Behind their painted faces, the bard could see the elder mash a few things together in a crucible. The woman's primary ingredient was ergot, a fungus that grows on rye. She mixed the substance and then placed the crucible into the fire to stew. Once the charm was ready, she poured it into a chalice fashioned out of the skull of a Roman soldier killed in battle. She then walked back to her captive with the steamy brew and told her warriors to hold his mouth open.

"You saw me whisper to that Englishman before he struck at my face. Do you want to know what I shared with him?"

Shakespeare struggled against his captors, unable to speak.

"I told him we had no intention of killing his silly pope. We sent our sister overseas to subdue him; to force-feed him the slavery that men like you have forced upon us since your arrival. Our lands have been destroyed and our people slain under all your kings and Caesars, under all your popes and bishops, under all your lords and houses." The woman's eyes glared. "You think you can defeat us, but we will *never* leave these isles. We are Albion. We will never forgive, and we will never forget."

The woman poured her hot mixture down Shakespeare's throat, scorching it. The elder grinned and told her men to let go of their prisoner. The bard doubled over and coughed violently into the grass. As his hands covered his face, Shakespeare shoved a handful of *terra sigillata* from his cloak into his mouth. The bard swallowed with difficulty, but then looked up at the cunning woman and said: "I prefer claret."

The elder woman's brow furrowed.

And then there was a whinny, accompanied by a shriek.

The cunning woman and her bodyguards turned their heads to see Aston racing toward Shakespeare. Behind the animal, the younger witch was screaming on the ground with an arrow sticking out of her wrist.

Another arrow shot through the clearing. And then another and another nearly every second. Cunning warriors began falling in rows, giving Shakespeare the time that he needed to take his sword back and run to Aston. Sir Francis Bacon's broken telescope got left behind.

The women shouted orders in ancient tongues as the bard was reunited with his companion. However, as Shakespeare leaped onto Aston's back and fled the clearing, a painful blow nearly knocked him off his saddle.

The bard fell forward and held on to Aston with only one hand. His right arm was in excruciating pain and could no longer move. One of the cunning folk had hit Shakespeare with Thomas Percy's throwing ax, shattering his shoulder. The playwright screamed in agony as he pulled himself back into his seat. However, as he struggled to regain his breath, a great heaviness fell over him like a spell.

The potion he ingested was beginning to go to work on him. The skies began to ripple, and the Arden awakened with monstrous eyes.

Drugged and broken, Shakespeare spurred Aston through the psychedelic forest as the painted men behind him mounted horses and joined in the chase.

Chapter XXXIV

The Kaleidoscope

The Arden exploded with thunder from more than one hundred hooves as the injured playwright raced his charger through the forest. The bard had only moonlight as his compass while the screaming madmen in pursuit had flaming torches and a shimmering horse to follow. Fortunately, Aston was able to maneuver the wooded labyrinth via scent, freeing his rider to contend with the cunning warriors behind them.

Shakespeare winced with pain as he looked back at the hell-knights. The painted riders hurled ancient war cries that pierced at the playwright's poisoned mind like arrows. Every sight and sound around him was amplified and distorted due to the foul concoction he consumed. The Forest of Arden flashed wildly with every heartbeat, breath, and blink, illuminating its wooded halls in a kaleidoscope of colors.

The bard shut his eyes and wildly shook his head. He needed to keep his wits together long enough to survive the manhunt.

Although a valiant attempt, the cunning folk's mixture worked quickly.

A shriek rang through the forest that echoed against Shakespeare's ears. The bard looked up into the exploding sky and saw a demon descend over him like a harpy. It was one of Bacon's ravens, and the bird swooped straight into the face of a cunning horsemen. The rider tumbled off his mount and was trampled to paste.

As Shakespeare watched through psychedelic lenses, he remembered that he had other weapons.

The bard held on to Aston while leaning back until his injured arm could reach into his saddlebags. The awkward posture forced Aston to slow, allowing their dogged hunters to close in. However, just when their vanguard was about to swing at Shakespeare, their horses collapsed from under them. Bacon's caltrops destroyed the horses' hooves, throwing their riders face-first onto the spikes.

Seeing that he needed to inflict more damage, the sweating, gasping playwright reached for his other countermeasures. He picked up his bag of glass orbs and held the leather sack in his teeth. One by one, he tossed the shining spheres over his shoulders. They crashed against the ground, causing several of the pursuing horses to stop and smell them. Just as Bacon had promised, riders flew off their mounts and collided into one another. The maneuver blocked the forest path, forcing the remaining horsemen to choose alternate routes through the woodlands.

More than half of Shakespeare's pursuers had been defeated.

The bard exhaled and looked in front of him, but then shook his head in disbelief. The forward trail seemed to bend and swirl like water in a funnel. Horrified, Shakespeare pulled on Aston's reins and led his horse onto a different path. However, as Aston galloped, flames began to dance around the fever-dreaming playwright. Shakespeare reared his horse in horror. He was riding directly into his advancing enemies.

The bard's mind was leaving him again. The painted horsemen appeared to him as screaming centaurs.

The playwright spun Aston and charged back onto the twisting path he had come from. The night sky was rippling like water and the stars were streaking past him like lightning. The glowing torches haunting Shakespeare grew larger and brighter. The playwright began to blather incoherently.

Delirium had conquered him. His mind was lost.

Shakespeare let go of Aston just as they approached a fallen tree. The stallion tripped over the log and came crashing down, throwing his poisoned rider off his shoulders.

The playwright landed hard on his fragmented back, causing the forest to erupt in a starburst of colors and screams.

The bard turned his head helplessly toward the torches racing toward him. One by one, they drew closer.

And then, one by one, they fell.

Second after second, arrow after arrow, their burning torches hit the ground, creating a path of fire from the final rider straight to Shakespeare. The dark figure was carrying a yew bow.

The rider reined her Turcoman and looked down at the playwright as a bloodied raven circled the scene and then settled on her shoulder. The hooded woman appeared as Death incarnate.

The bard slipped out of consciousness and was taken away by the darkness.

Chapter XXXV

The Covert Operation

"M istress Shakespeare?"

The woman previously known as Anne Hathaway opened her bedroom door wearing nothing but the white smock she had been sleeping in. "What is it?" she asked her servant, who was standing in the hallway with a candle.

"There is a lady here to see you," replied the woman. "A dark lady. She says she knows you."

"What's her name?" Anne murmured, for she knew several shades of dark ladies.

"Bianca."

"Mmhmm . . ." Anne sighed with a sleepy smile until she realized she was not dreaming. "What?" she gasped. "She's here?"

"She's at the door, mistress."

Anne Shakespeare's jaw dropped. "Let her in," she ordered. "And tell her that I will be down shortly." Anne disappeared back into her room to dress.

"Mistress?" the servant added.

Anne returned with impatient eyes.

"I don't think this can wait at all. The lady—" There was a loud crash downstairs followed by heavy moaning. "It appears she has your husband."

Anne Shakespeare arched an eyebrow and rapped her nails against the doorframe. "How very interesting."

"What is it?" cooed the woman in Anne's bed.

"You need to leave," replied Mistress Shakespeare.

Anne walked down the winding stairs of New Place, the stately Shakespeare home at Stratford-upon-Avon, to find her husband sprawled on his belly across their dining room table. The battered playwright groaned with confusion while the Dark Lady cut his clothes off with scissors.

"Keep my daughters in their rooms," Anne told her servant. "And see to it that we are not disturbed."

"Yes, Mistress Shakespeare."

The servant spirited back upstairs while Anne approached the tall woman stripping her husband. "Bianca," she greeted her.

The Dark Lady locked eyes with the somber woman she had not seen in more than a decade. "Anne," she whispered breathlessly. The two ladies embraced and kissed. "I am so sorry it has been so long."

"Think nothing of it." Anne's eyes turned to the groaning playwright. "What have you done to my husband?"

"It was not me this time. I swear it." The Dark Lady whisked back to the bard while Anne lit the room's candles. "Your husband has been badly wounded."

"Doing what?"

Bianca's dark eyes shifted. "Do you know what your husband has been up to recently?"

"He doesn't tell me, and I don't ask questions. It is a mutual ignorance. I assume he has gotten himself into trouble again."

"It's worse than ever, I'm afraid. The government reactivated him last year. He has been meeting with dangerous people. The cunning folk. They did this to him." Bianca started unpacking her surgeon's kit in a hurry.

Anne sighed. "And yourself?"

"I had to keep an eye on him this entire time. Through rain and sleet and snow. It has *not* been pleasant," Bianca fumed. "The government forced me back into this."

"That's not what I meant. Are *you* hurt?" Anne corrected. "Do you need help?"

Openness replaced the anger in Bianca's almond-shaped eyes. "I am unhurt, but . . . tired. It has been a trying year, Anne. Really. I thought I was free of this life. I was moving on. But Anne . . ." The Dark Lady shut her eyes and shook her head. "I will always be a prisoner to these people."

Anne stepped closer and held Bianca's hand. "I am so sorry. For everything."

The Dark Lady exhaled with eyes downcast. "Also, please know I was sorry to hear about Hamnet." Anne and William Shakespeare's only son was just eleven years old when he died of plague.

"Bless you," his mother replied. "I have been surviving. Moving here helped." Anne looked over her lovely home, the second largest in Stratford. "I couldn't live in our old house anymore. All those memories . . . they haunted me."

"I know what that's like. All I have are memories. Nothing more." Bianca's thoughts turned to her parents back in Italy, and the two ladies embraced.

The playwright screamed.

Anne and Bianca turned back to William. "What's wrong with him?"

"Your husband was poisoned by cunning folk in the Forest of Arden. He also fell from his horse while escaping."

"What was he poisoned with?"

"I don't know. He already took something to counteract it-it-it-it."

The bard's hearing faded in and out.

"His delirium is getting worse-worse-worse-worse."

"Will he live-live-live-live?"

The Dark Lady looked the playwright over and touched his neck in several places. His eyelids flickered but then went lax. "Yes," she said. "But it will not be pleasant. I have worked under similar circumstances. He is stricken with a brain fever, and his injuries require surgery."

Anne studied her husband's naked body. "I will move my daughters to another wing and make sure my servants do not disturb you. Will you be needing anything to work with?"

"Yes, please. I need sewing needles, rope, and linens. And several plants from your garden, including all your roses."

"Be my guest," Anne replied. "They were his favorite flowers. Not mine."

Bianca smirked as she returned to her surgeon's kit. "I will also need to use one of your barns for the next few hours."

Anne's brow furrowed. "What for-for-for-for?"

"Before I work-work-work-work on your husband, I will need to operate on his horse-horse-horse-horse."

The bard fell asleep.

Shakespeare slipped in and out of consciousness for the next several hours. Whenever he opened his eyes, he could not recognize his surroundings. His hallucinations distorted everything. All his imaginings were assaulting him at once: his plays, the conspirators, Macbeth, the witches; everything. The Arden in particular haunted Shakespeare as Aston's whinnies reawakened his fears. Even inside his house, he felt ensnared by the ancient forest as if its roots were wrapping themselves around his arms and legs.

In reality, Anne and Bianca were tying the psychedelic playwright down to his table. "I heard everything from the windows."

"I fear the whole town heard," the surgeon groaned.

"How did it go?"

"*Horrendous*. That horse resisted my every move. I had to tie him down as well." Bianca's arms were covered up to her elbows in Aston's blood. "I know he's trained to be that way, but it interfered with every second I spent on him."

Anne shook her head. "Why is that beast so important?"

"Orders." Bianca scowled. "We need to bring him back to London. The government values that horse's life more than your husband's." The Dark Lady tightened the final strap on Shakespeare and then took a step back.

"You look like you could use some rest."

"I will. After this. We cannot wait any longer." The Dark Lady picked up a stack of playing cards and tore them open for their salts.

"What's wrong with him?"

Bianca opened her copy of *De humani corporis fabrica* with her bloody hands. "Your husband suffered an ax blow here," she said, pointing to the bone marked "R" in an illustration of a figure with its skin stripped off its back.* "It's called the scapula, and I may have to reset it or remove it, depending on how damaged it is."

"How damaged is it?"

"I'll find out once I get in there," said Bianca, pointing her bloodied lancet to the enormous bruise on Shakespeare's shoulder. A thick red line ran down its middle where Thomas Percy's ax had hit the bone.

The Dark Lady took a breath and then looked to Anne. "Are you sure you're comfortable seeing this?"

"Bianca, I've had three children. And two of them were twins."

"How was that, by the way?" Bianca wiped the horsehairs from her knife against her blood-covered apron.

---

*Andreas Vesalius, *De corporis humani fabrica libri septem* (Basel: Johannes Oporinus, 1543), 206.

"It was agony," Anne grumbled. "I had Judith and Hamnet in the middle of the winter. It took the midwife hours to arrive."

"I am sorry you had to suffer like that."

Anne pointed her chin at her husband. "It's his fault. I never planned on having children, but after Susanna, we were married and he insisted on trying for a son." Looking to change the subject, Anne turned and asked: "Are you in that line of work as well?"

"Midwifery?" Bianca smiled. "No. Although I have done a few caesarean sections."

"That sounds barbaric." Anne winced.

"Quite the opposite. It can be scary, though, considering the circumstances. It requires a steady hand. Could you pass that potion, please?"

Anne handed the Dark Lady her dwale, a painkiller prepared using three teaspoons each of boar bile, vinegar, opium, hemlock, bryony, henbane, and some lettuce from the garden, mixed and boiled.* Although not a wholly effective anesthetic, it was better than nothing. Bianca dropped three spoonfuls into some wine and fed the mixture to the injured Shakespeare. After waiting a few minutes for the dwale to work, the Dark Lady placed a leather braid between the playwright's teeth. "Hold this," she instructed Anne.

"What is that for?"

"So he doesn't bite through his tongue when I cut into him-him-him-him . . ."

The bard faded out of consciousness, and the operation began.

Leather.

Leather.

Leather.

"Leather?"

---

*Syndics of Cambridge University Library (MS Dd.6.29, f79r-v).

"I need all the leather in this house! Enough to make a dress with."

"Why?"

"Please, Anne. I need this quickly. If he has the plague, we have to protect ourselves."

Anne Shakespeare had the breath sucked out of her. "The plague? How do you know he's suffering from that?"

"I have no idea what these witches put inside him! If his fever and delirium persist—"

Plague!

The bard blacked out just from the thought of it.

Shakespeare opened his eyes on what felt like a different day even though it was less than an hour after the previous conversation. He turned his head and found Bianca seated at a table with a pile of leather in front of her: belts, boots, an apron, and virtually every one of the playwright's kidskin gloves. Anne was nowhere to be seen, but the bard could hear her ordering her servants to find them more. Bianca also had two drinking cups with glass bottoms in front of her. After poking the circles out, she held them up to her eyes to see through them. Satisfied, she set them down and resumed her stitching.

Behind the surgeon, a fire was burning and a cauldron bubbled.

The bard shut his eyes and fell asleep to the pleasant aroma of candle wax.

"What is that you're mashing?"

"Rose petals."

"Lovely fragrance."

"Isn't it?"

"It masks some of the stench in here."

The bard heard laughter.

"What are they for?"

"I'm mixing them with several other ingredients to make some pills. We've been experimenting with them in London. A French doctor claims they are quite effective at treating plague."*

"Are you sure that's what my husband has?"

"No. But we have to be safe."

There was a pause.

"Do all doctors wear that costume?"

"No, but I remember hearing about Venetian doctors wearing something similar. I've been trying to convince Bacon to use these in the city, but he's more concerned with shooting stars at the moment."

"Bacon?"

"Sorry. Forget I said that."

There was another pause.

"It's terrifying. You will look like an enormous crow in that dress."

The bard heard laughter.

"Would you like me to make one for you as well?"

"Could you?"

"Are you serious?"

"You said yourself we need to protect ourselves, and I am not leaving this house."

There was a third and final pause.

"I will need more leather."

Shakespeare drifted off to the sound of footsteps.

"We have to roll him onto his back. Would you help me?"

"Like this?"

Four sticky hands pressed against the bard's sweaty skin.

---

*Michel de Nostredame, *Le Traité des Fardements et des Confitures* (Lyon: Antonie Volant, 1555).

"Yes. Pull him toward you. Just be gentle."

"How gentle?"

"Argh!" Shakespeare roared with pain as every bone and muscle Bianca had been working on shifted back into place.

"That was too rough."

"Sorry, William!"

"Shhh! He's waking."

The playwright's eyes flickered open.

"Good morning, Will," said a familiar but muffled voice.

Two dark figures appeared out of focus.

The bard squinted, and then his eyes widened in terror.

Two leather-faced monstrosities were looking down at him like giant ravens. Their features were expressionless and their faces protruded outward in enormous, birdlike beaks. Their stitched-up skin was waxy and their eyes doubled as goggles. From Shakespeare's angle on the table, it appeared as if these birds were looming over his deathbed, deciding which part of his fallen flesh to strip off first.

And the most frightening thing of all: this was not a fever dream. It was real.

The playwright's mouth opened as if to scream.

"Shhh," one raven silenced, pressing her leather glove over Shakespeare's lips.

"Where am I?" he gasped.

"Stratford," replied the same. "You're at home, Will."

The playwright's eyes moved over his familiar ceiling in disbelief. "What is this? Who are you! Why—" He started panting.

The other raven moved in closer until its beak was nearly touching Shakespeare's face. "Lift him," she instructed her companion. "Please try to relax, Will. The worst is over. You've just survived the plague."

Shakespeare panted. "The plague . . ."

"It wasn't witches. You contracted it days ago while you were traveling."

The bard gazed into the raven's shiny eyes, which he was only starting to realize were human behind their lenses. "Who are you?" he asked.

The figure hesitated, but then responded: "It is Bianca."

"And I remain your wife," replied the other.

The bard looked back and forth between the ravens, and then fainted.

"I am sorry, but you cannot see him. This house is under quarantine for plague."

The bard could hear some arguing from outside the front door. The voices sounded like men.

"I understand," said Bianca. "I will give him your message."

Suddenly, the bard saw movement outside his window. He shifted his eyes onto a tall, bearded figure.

Robert Catesby, the head of the conspiracy, was staring at him.

Again, he fainted.

"Are you sure you cannot stay longer?"

"Your husband is well enough for me to leave, and I need to return to London. The horse should be all right as long as you feed him that diet I prescribed. Also, you cannot be seen outside the house until August. A typical quarantine lasts six weeks. You will need to maintain the illusion."

"I understand completely. But . . . what about us? It is so nice to see you again."

"Anne, you know I did not come here for the best of reasons."

"Neither did you the first time, and that worked out."

"Anne . . . it is too taxing for me to be thrown into the middle of this again."

There was a pause.

"Do you still love him?"

A second pause.

"You do."

"I don't even remember what love is well enough to know that."

"Bianca, if there is one person on this wretched isle you don't need to hide from, it's me."

"Anne, every man I have ever been close to has betrayed me. All of them."

"That's all the reason for you to stay here with me!"

"No, Anne. I can't be a part of this triangle. I want . . . I want the kind of love that people write about! The stories that made me want to run off and see the world when I was young. All this war, all this madness, it . . . it turns men into wolves."

"All men *are* wolves, so stay here. You will want for nothing. I promise you!"

"I want to have children, Anne."

There was a long silence.

"Is it still possible?"

"Yes, it is."

The bard could hear the sounds of fingernails tapping.

"I don't know what to say other than that I love you, and that I don't want you to go back to that awful place. It's dangerous, and I know that it's killing you. Please, stay here. Please . . . tell me that my love is enough for the two of us!"

There was a final pause.

"Farewell."

The bard opened his eyes and saw his wife and the Dark Lady kissing at his doorway. "I must be dreaming," he mumbled to himself.

He shut his eyes and had his first pleasant sleep in weeks.

Until . . .

"Wake up, you lout."

The playwright yawned and sat up for the first time in nearly a month. "What is it, woman?" he asked, scratching his head.

Anne Shakespeare's eyes were filled with anger. "This just arrived from a bird," she said, holding a page of parchment in the playwright's face.

> *Th'expence of Spirit in a waste of shame*
> *Is lust in action, and till action, lust*
> *Is perjurd, murdrous, blouddy full of blame,*
> *Savage, extreame, rude, cruell, not to trust* . . .

"Are you breaking this woman's heart all over again? Hasn't she been through enough, William! Haven't you and that damned rogue Marlowe—"

"Wife," the playwright interrupted. "It's just a bill for services."

The wife paused. "Don't lie!"

"It is. It's . . ." William searched sleepily for the right wording. "It's written in a very cumbersome way."

Anne looked at the sonnet in confusion, but then retorted: "Well, whatever Bianca's charging you, it's not enough. Pay her triple!"

"Yes, mistress."

Chapter XXXVI

Resurrection

Pope Leo XI was dead after one of the shortest reigns for any sovereign in history. The mysterious woman found mutilated atop him was sealed in the Roman catacombs to prevent a scandal. The English spy accused of both their murders was pronounced dead by a Jewish doctor and last seen drifting down the Tiber in a blood-stained sack—something his killer suggested so that no blood of his would ever stain Rome again. The city was in mourning, but behind closed doors, several of its most powerful residents sighed with relief. An even greater crisis had been averted thanks to the quick thinking of Senator Roberto di Ridolfi, the unlikely hero of this deadly affair. The veteran spy could now boast of having bested not one but two Walsinghams in his career.

"You have done the Church a great service," commended Pietro Aldobrandini, the leader of the Italian cardinals. He walked with Roberto out of the Cappella Paolina and into the Sala Regia, the Vatican's barrel-vaulted great hall. "Nobody will know the circumstances of the pontiff's murder outside of these walls—except for yourself. The Holy See is in your debt, and I must say that I am impressed by how quickly you dispatched your younger adversary."

"Your Eminence gives me great honor."

The cardinal stopped walking and presented his ring to Roberto. The old senator fell to one knee on the marble floor and kissed the holy gold. Pietro blessed the man, and then asked: "Is there anything else we can do for you?"

The senator returned to his feet. "If Your Eminence insists."

"Please. Whatever you like. Just say something, and it is yours."

Roberto took a breath and pointed to two doors on the opposite end of the enormous hallway. "May I?" he asked.

Cardinal Aldobrandini, himself a patron of the arts, permitted this with a single, stately bow. Two Swiss guards opened the crimson doors, and Roberto entered the stunning chamber he had always dreamed of seeing in his long, clandestine life: the Sistine Chapel.

Its countless works of art washed over him like a wave.

Out of all the masterpieces festooning the chapel's walls and ceiling, from Michelangelo's frescos of Genesis and the Last Judgment to Raphael's tapestries of Peter and Paul, Il Divino's rendering of the prophet Jonah caught the fellow Florentine's eyes first.

The senator smirked at the twisting figure as he turned his back and walked out the doors.

After bobbing in the same river that had carried Romulus and Remus to safety, the Tiber tugged Marlowe's bound-up body away from Rome and out to sea. The open blue of the vast Tyrrhenian shined as sapphire while the creeping dawn swept over Italy's western shores. As Marlowe's bloodstained sack mixed with salt water, a bull shark circled it with growing interest.

A harpoon smote the great fish.

A white net fell over Marlowe and rescued him from the waters. As a stalwart crew pulled the net aboard their carrack, their tall captain stomped across the deck. The figure looked down at the bloodied sack as it was cut open to reveal a breathing man wearing Leonardo da Vinci's diving suit.

Marlowe removed his leather mask and looked up at his towering friend. "I can't believe Leonardo included a pouch for urinating." The poet laughed. "And it works, too!"

Standing tall aboard his pirate ship, the dragoman shook his head.

"You look *beautiful*, by the way!" Marlowe thought the earrings and bandanna were lovely additions now that his large friend was wearing an eye patch.

The dragoman was not amused. "Do you have any idea how much gold it cost to buy you another life?"

"What does it matter? We're rich! Aren't we?"

The towering captain grumbled as he pulled Marlowe up. "Not anymore. I had to turn everything over to the Venetians to buy your freedom. All my possessions, all your books—"

Marlowe's smile vanished. "Wait, my books?"

"Yes, all of them."

"But . . . what about my poems and plays? What about my novel! Did you at least get a good price for them?"

"I had to sell them for their paper," the dragoman growled. He then walked over to the ship's bow and surveyed the horizon with his telescope.

"O me," Marlowe groaned.

The dragoman closed the spyglass. "Enough of this. We have work to do. This is not going to be a pleasure cruise. I am expecting you to do your part as a member of this crew."

"Privateering?" Marlowe asked with piqued interest. "Well, I could use the exercise. I've been mostly dead all day!" The poet grinned and rubbed his bandaged hands together.

"Not anymore. I'm taking you to London. You've been reactivated, my friend. Thomas Walsingham wants you to report in immediately."

Marlowe stopped moving. "What?" he gasped. The poet's eyes sparkled and his heart leaped. "London?" his squeaked. "Really?"

The dragoman nodded. "You're going home."

A jubilant smile swept across Marlowe's face. "Home!" he cried. "Home! We're going home!" he shouted to the crew. "Oh, Drago! Thank you! Let me bless you!" He waved his arms about. "I love you so much!"

The triumphant poet wrapped himself around his mighty friend while a stately raven monitored from the crow's nest.

Chapter XXXVII

The Bait

Shakespeare took his time before returning to London. After surviving witches, plagues, and demons, he felt he deserved some time that would not involve him fighting for his life. Walsingham permitted this via raven, but only due to the timeliness of the request. On July 28, the government announced that Parliament would not be meeting in October due to the plague. Their new date to reconvene would be on November 5, 1605.

This was bad news for the conspirators during an already troublesome time. By September, all their best-laid plans had turned to powder.

"We need more powder."

"Are you going to remind me every hour?" Thomas Percy wiped his brow beneath the sweltering sun. "Why else do you think we're here? For our health?"

Truth be told, Southwark was the least healthy place to be in the city. As the most poverty-stricken section of London, life there was cramped, polluted, and pestilent. Death and disease were ever-present, which allowed lawlessness to thrive.

Fawkes looked nervously over the rowdy crowds shoving into the Bear Garden. "We should not be here," he growled. "The garden is supposed to be closed, and the Clink is just down the street."

"Are you afraid of a little baiting?" Jack Wright baited his colleague.

"I just don't think this is the best use of our funds."

"And what, Guido, would you know about raising money?" mocked Percy.

Fawkes's summer in Spain had been completely fruitless for their conspiracy. After Pope Leo's death and the cunning folk's treachery, all their European allies, along with all their funding, were gone.

The conspirator had no response.

"That's what I thought," the sweaty man snorted derisively.

Ahead of them, within the Bear Garden, there was a thunderous roar followed by a wave of cheers and the reek of feces. The men entered the packed arena, where four foaming mastiffs were about to be unleashed against a blood covered bear.

"Ten shillings on Ursa Major!" Percy pledged to the gamblers. The bet was taken instantly.

The mastiffs ran into the ring and went straight for the jugular.

Two hours later, the three conspirators walked out of the Bear Garden penniless.

Guy Fawkes was furious. "What are we going to do? We don't even have enough coin to rent a wherry!"

"I am not walking home." Thomas Percy looked over the men walking along Maiden Lane. "Jack, go rob somebody."

"Very well. Who will it be?"

"Wait a minute." Fawkes squinted above the crowd. "Look there. It's Richard Burbage. And Will Shakespeare!"

The swordsman sized the men up. "Do you want me to kill them quickly?"

"Don't be a blockhead. Ho! William!" Guy Fawkes stepped forward and waved his arms until a raven swooped down and knocked his hat off. "You accursed bird!" he cried, shaking a fist.

Shakespeare threw some seeds he was snacking on into the street, diverting the raven. "Good morrow, sirs," he bade to the conspirators.

"Good morrow," Richard Burbage bade as well.

"Will!" Fawkes continued. "Are you all right? I heard what happened. We thought you were dead!"

"Borrow us some money," Percy interrupted, not the slightest bit interested in Shakespeare's health.

The bard ignored the sweaty man. "All is well, Guido. My health has returned to me."

"What are you doing here?" Jack Wright asked. "I thought you said all the playhouses were closed."

"They are, but I had to drop something off at the Globe. In fact . . ." The bard glanced at Burbage. "Would you gentlemen like to join us there for a moment? Richard, do you mind?"

"Not at all," replied the player.

"What for?" asked Guy Fawkes.

The bard took a step forward and lowered his voice. "The play is finished!"

Two hours later.

MALCOLM

. . . As calling home our exil'd Friends abroad,
That fled the Snares of watchfull Tyranny,

Producing forth the cruell Ministers
Of this dead Butcher, and his Fiend-like Queene;
Who (as 'tis thought) by selfe and violent hands,
Tooke off her life. This, and what need full else
That call's vpon vs, by the Grace of Grace,
We will performe in measure, time, and place:
So thankes to all at once, and to each one,
Whom we inuite, to see vs Crown'd at Scone.

With this farewell, the Globe's star player, Richard Burbage, who had just read for Macbeth, Malcolm, Lady Macduff, Fleance, two of three assassins, one of three Weird Sisters, and the delightful Porter; and the Globe's playwright, William Shakespeare, who read for Lady Macbeth, Banquo, King Duncan, Macduff, Lennox, Ross, the enigmatic Hecate, and all the remaining characters, took a bow for their spellbound audience.

Fawkes hopped up from his bench and applauded while Jack Wright and Thomas Percy were compelled to do so as well. *The Tragedy of Macbeth* was everything the three conspirators had spent the past year hoping it would be, and more.

"How was it?" asked the author.

"Brilliant!" Guy Fawkes sang and cheered. The conspirator hopped the wooden fence around the Pit while the bard and Burbage jumped down from the stage. "Bloody brilliant. Tying the plights of Macbeth to the king today? It was perfect! Precisely what we were looking for!"

Shakespeare smiled. "I made sure to keep King James's villainous ancestors true to history. Banquo conspired against King Duncan, as did Macbeth.* They both deservingly died a traitor's death."

"Bravo!" Fawkes praised, kissing the bard's hands.

Holinshed's Chronicles, vol. V: Scotland, 271.

"The witches in your play," Percy entered. "You had them proph-esize that Banquo's kin will be kings. Is that true?"

"Yes," the playwright confirmed. "It is written in the histories."

Fawkes smacked his hands together. "That's it!" The conspira-tor spun around to Jack and Percy. "That's what we need to rally the people. King James's line is illegitimate! It is the product of black magic and assassinations!"

"Bloody heathens," swore Percy.

"Guido, if you don't hold that tongue of yours, I'll have to cut it out." Jack Wright motioned with his eyes toward Richard Burbage.

"You need not worry," replied the actor. "Master Shakespeare shared me in on your endeavors. It will be a pleasure to play my part in them."

Guy Fawkes's jaw dropped. "You are willing to risk your life for this?" he asked. "For us?"

Shakespeare's star player held his head high. "It would not be the first time this wooden O served as a stage for revolution! May God be with you on your efforts. I hope you succeed to the fullest measure."

The conspirators were speechless.

"Also," the playwright reentered, "I talked things over with my friend here, and we have an idea that should attract precisely the type of crowd you are looking for."

"What is it?" scowled Percy, who remained skeptical of any idea that was not his.

Shakespeare smirked. "We are not going to announce the name of the play. Your show will be a surprise performance."

The sweaty man's eyes bulged in their sunken sockets. "You're going to keep the title secret?"

The dramatists nodded. "And with the curfew lifted, we want to make this a late performance. A nighttime show."

"What!" Guy Fawkes gasped. "This is not what we paid you for!

How could a nighttime show for an unknown play possibly be a draw in London? We need the largest audience possible!"

"My gentle masters," Richard Burbage entered in his most eloquent diction, "in all my years' experience, I can promise you that this decision will be most beneficial. The theaters have been closed all year. People will be clamoring to see this performance. And if we keep its name a secret, whispers about it will spread throughout the city like wildfire. All will wonder what it is, and all of our most dedicated patrons will attend. They will be rowdy and intoxicated. Their pulses high. Three thousand men whipped into a frenzy and already carrying torches." The actor smiled like the devil. "You will have an army at your disposal."

The conspirators were captivated. Their awestruck eyes turned from Richard Burbage to William Shakespeare, who bowed his head with pride. "We are men of action here. We are actors! We know the world's stage better than anyone."

"Bless you, brother!" Guy Fawkes hugged the playwright while Jack Wright patted him on the shoulder.

"I was wrong to doubt you," Percy acknowledged. "You clearly know what you are doing."

"Thank you for your faith, brother," the bard accepted.

"So, would you mind sparing us some silver so that we can hurry home before it gets dark?"

"Of course." Shakespeare dropped a sixpence and some silver pennies into Percy's sticky palm while Burbage flipped Jack Wright a groat. "Go in peace, brothers."

"Hail, and farewell!" Richard Burbage shouted.

The actors waved good-bye to the conspirators as they left the theater. Once they were by themselves, the bard and Burbage exchanged a glance and then retired to the Tiring House.

"You're a better liar than an actor," the star player complimented as he handed Shakespeare the book of the play *Macbeth*.

"And you, my friend, are a greater liar than every politician in

Parliament." The bard unlocked the Tiring House's cabinet and deposited the leather folio alongside all the other books of his plays. "But I meant what I said, Richard." The bard locked the cabinet. "Nobody can know that we're performing this. Not even the other actors. You must keep it secret."

"What? *Macbeth*?" Burbage teased.

The playwright winked.

Chapter XXXVIII

The Apology

The Dark Lady returned to London with little to show for her heroism. Although she proved herself as gifted with her bow as with her needles, Walsingham was infuriated that she rode after Shakespeare instead of killing all the witches in the Arden. "Such an opportunity," he reprimanded, "will *never* present itself again." He then lectured her at length on how good agents choose death over their missions, "and you know that," before turning Bianca over to Bacon for further scolding on account of Aston's injuries. Penny remained the only person in the Double-O on the Dark Lady's side, but even she could not repair the damage her friend suffered in Warwickshire. Once more, the Blanca's harpsichord, books, and stately raven were her only companions. Especially since the bard did not muster the courage to come calling at her home until October.

Bianca heard knocking, opened her door, and then slammed it in William Shakespeare's face. "Roses were your favorite flowers, not mine!" she shouted through the door in Italian.

Dejected, the playwright left his bouquet of roses outside her door, along with the bag of silver she was owed for saving his life.

The Dark Lady returned to her harpsichord and raised her fingers in frustration, but then froze once she noticed a second raven at her window. The black bird was cozying against her own.

"*TOO ǝv yǝ?*" the raven croaked in the bard's voice.

Bianca's fingers curled into fists until her knuckles cracked. After a tearful contemplation, she pounded her keyboard and stomped back to her door.

The Dark Lady threw the door open and walked face-first into Shakespeare's fist just as he was about to knock one more time.

"Oops!" he chirped as the Dark Lady stumbled backward. "I'm sorry."

Bianca rubbed her reddened forehead while staring into the playwright. She did not say anything, but at the same time she did not have to. The two knew each other well enough to read each other's eyes like poetry.

The two stared at each other for quite a while.

And then, they united.

Chapter XXXIX

Heavenly Bodies

H ow is this possible?"
It was October 12, 1605, 12:48 P.M., and atop the Tower of London, Sir Thomas Walsingham watched in disbelief as the brilliant sun was masked behind the moon. A dark shadow swept across the country like a tide, casting the entire London landscape into panic. Pulses rose, screaming spread from the northwest to southeast, animals barked, chirped, hissed, and hooted, and the watchful ravens surrounding Walsingham blathered in confusion. "We already had an eclipse two weeks ago," he added. "Why did you fail to see this coming?"

"We can only predict lunar eclipses," explained Francis Bacon. "We are still working on a method for the solar variety."

"How long will it be before you come up with one that works?"

Bacon conferred with the disquieted astronomers behind him, among them mathematician and astrologer John Dee. "Years," the latter concluded. "Perhaps decades."

"Never in our lifetime is what you're saying."

The white-bearded astrologer looked to the thirty-four-years-younger Bacon. "I am afraid so," replied the younger.

Walsingham lowered his spyglass and handed it to the scientist. "Columbus used an eclipse to subjugate an entire island. Our enemies could be doing the same right now to conquer ours."

"We understand, W."

"No, you don't, and that's the problem." The spymaster looked over at the darkened skies haunting London like a storm cloud. "The cunning folk are still a menace."

Meanwhile, at Seething Lane . . .

"O me . . ." Penny gasped from inside Walsingham Mansion. The silver-haired secretary sized up and down the tall, suntanned vagrant outside her doors. His Italian boots were specked with sea salt, his weathered cape was stained with brine, and his freshly shaven face with thin mustache appeared . . . just dashing. "Who the bloody hell are you supposed to be?" the secretary snapped, remembering her place.

"Christopher Marlowe."

"I've never heard of him."

The poet's heart sank. "Really?"

"In sooth," she sighed sarcastically. "Who sent you?"

"Well, Master Walsing—"

"I'm not interested in that. I want you to tell me the name, *full* name, of whoever told you to mosey over."

The poet's jaw dropped. Stumped, he rubbed the back of his neck. "Honestly, I don't know his name."

Lady Percy arched her sharpened eyebrows.

"Drago the . . . dragoman?" Marlowe tested. "And also, pirate?"

Penny sighed forsooth this time. "I'm sorry, but I have never heard of you or who sent you here, so please shog off." The secretary shoved her doors until they were stopped by her caller's doeskin boots.

"Please, I came a long way, and not for shogging." The sailor's sea-tested hands forced the mansion's portal open.

"Oh . . ." the corseted woman heaved, "you just made a big mistake." Penny stepped back and pounded her fist against a button carved into the wooden wall. A portcullis dropped on both sides of the doorway, but the vagabond dove under them with catlike agility and tackled her. Penny clawed and kicked Marlowe across the foyer until they rolled atop a bearskin rug.

"This is more than I can bear," he quipped. "Is this how you treat everybody?"

"You bugger!" the secretary swore. Penny stole the vagrant's dagger and plunged it at his heart.

"Ugh! What is it with you women!" He grabbed Penny's wrist and stabbed the blade through her gown. Lady Percy was unhurt, but she was also stuck to the floor by her own clothes.

"My heart has already taken plenty of abuse, m'lady. Can't we just make peace?"

Penny turned her head away and groaned. Marlowe's breath reeked of a pirate's diet of tobacco, rum, and turtles.

Infuriated, she fumbled for something else beneath Marlowe's belt.

The confused poet looked down. "That is not a sword," he noted. "At least, not now."

Penny's eyes widened. She pummeled the man on top of her with her hands and fists until, not able to resist the urge one minute more, she threw her arms around him. The two assaulted each other in a fit of passion.

"Just a moment!" the lady interrupted, kneeing the pirate off her. Marlowe writhed on the floor while Penny ran into her study, inadvertently tearing half her dress off in the process.

"I don't want to hurt you!" the poet groaned while hobbling after her. "Please, Walsingham is my friend! Tell him I'm here! My name is Christopher Mar—"

The secretary shoved a pitcher of flavored hippocras into the poet's mouth, smothering his noxious breath under the scent of cinnamon and fruits. Once the jug was empty, Marlowe wiped his face in such a stupor that he did not even notice Penny had already robbed him of his belt. She was wearing it off one hip.

The windows darkened with the eclipse, and the lady secretary's eyes appeared to sparkle.

"I thought such behavior was beneath you," Thomas Walsingham interjected shortly after. "Not directly under you." The angered spy-master slammed his crimson door while the interrupted couple leaped out of each other's arms.

"Please forgive me!" Penny pleaded as she hurried into Walsing-ham's office. "It was in defense, master! He stabbed me!"

"I did no such thing!" Marlowe stumbled in while holding up his pants. "Thomas, if this woman is your wife or daughter, I—"

"You be quiet! Lady Percy, keep such behavior outside this man-sion as long as you are a part of it. Do you understand?"

"God save you!" The lady secretary curtsied in the tattered re-mains of her dress.

"I can save myself. That will be all."

A grateful Penny rose and shot Marlowe a playful glance as she left the office.

The mutually enchanted poet bowed and watched his belt walk out the room. "So!" Marlowe opened, pivoting on his boots to his former friend. "It is good to see you again, Thomas! I love what you've done to the place."

The spymaster, like his pipe, was fuming. "Are you seriously so determined to get killed all over again?"

"If you're talking about what I'm talking about, I swear that was all her doing!"

"We have more important matters to discuss, if you don't mind." W pointed the resurrected spy to an empty seat. "Welcome back."

Marlowe exhaled with exhaustion as he collapsed into the

spymaster's chair. After admiring his new surroundings, the poet asked: "Just so I know, what exactly am I now?"

"A dead man."

The poet whimpered. "Still?"

"You can only die once. Otherwise, people stop believing it." The spymaster refilled his pipe. "We can come back to that later. As for now, I need you to tell me everything, starting with the massacre in Venice."

"Can we please settle my question first? That silver vixen outside your office had no idea who I was. She could have killed me! Twice!"

Penny agreed. She always kept a dagger at her desk, just in case.

"The current state of Christopher Marlowe is the least of our concerns," said W.

Marlowe snorted. "Maybe it is to you and the rest of England, but I want to live again! I want to publish books and plays and poems! If you don't think that's always been on my mind, well, then . . . maybe I should just work for someone else!"

The spy-chief removed his pipe. "Utter one more phrase like that and you will never leave this mansion."

Unaffected, the poet smiled and shook his head. "Thomas, we've known each other for a long time. Never, in all our years, have you not planned ahead. I know you have something to motivate me with. To entice me with. Something to keep me under control and to threaten me with. *Please* just tell me what it is! The less I wonder about it, the more I can focus on your dilemmas."

Walsingham narrowed his eyes and blew two long ribbons of smoke through his nostrils. "If you insist. Your real name and identity will be on moratorium for one year, starting November fifth. Until then, you will be a Johannes factotum in word and function. You will work for me, and you will live here. A room is waiting for you in the mansion. As long as you complete the tasks I give you and stay out of trouble, I will go through the necessary paperwork to bring you back from the dead."

Marlowe raised his eyebrows. "One year's work and good behavior?"

W nodded. "That's nonnegotiable. We need your help."

The poet shrugged. "Sounds fair. So! What's so special about
November fifth?" Marlowe helped himself to a cup of wine.

"What do you know about gunpowder?" Walsingham asked from
behind his pipe.

Marlowe looked up from his tankard. "I know that it explodes."

Penny smiled with satisfaction as she wrote that.

Chapter XL

The Last Supper

"It is a pity we will miss your play," a saddened Robert Catesby sighed. "But as you know, most of us will be needed north."

"Of course," replied the playwright. The conspirators had told him weeks ago that they planned on making nine-year-old Princess Elizabeth the new queen of England—which required kidnapping her from Coombe Abbey. "You will be missed. You will all be missed," the bard said, turning to all the men at the table.

In truth, Shakespeare had only met Francis Tresham, a veteran of the Essex rebellion, and horse breeder Ambrose Rookwood that evening. Nevertheless, the men raised their cups alongside all the other doomed conspirators in the Duck and Drake.

"It will be a bloody masterpiece!" Guy Fawkes lauded, shaking Shakespeare by his shoulder.

"We all know that yours will be the better one," Shakespeare teased. "I will make sure to stay *very* far away from the House of Lords."

"I would pay to see those fireworks." Jack Wright leered behind his cup.

"As would I. Especially since we're paying for them," chuckled

Catesby. "Guido, tell us all what we'll be missing! How will our enemies meet their infernal makers?"

"Tell us!" the drunken chorus cheered. "Speech! Speech! Speech!"

All eyes turned to Fawkes. Deep down, even the bard was curious.

The conspiracy's swaggering demolitions expert sat up with a smile and set down his stein. "My dear friends. My fellow soldiers. My band of brothers." He nodded to Shakespeare, who returned it in kind. "You see this here?" he opened, tapping on his pewter cup. "Picture thirty-six barrels pointing upward, just like this stein, each one filled with precisely fifty weight of musket powder."

"Are you sure that will be enough?" asked Catesby.

"Eighteen hundred weight of powder? I could blow the walls off the House of Lords with half that!" Guy Fawkes grinned with gleaming eyes. "The barrels will explode through their weakest point, their tops, and then outward once their iron hoops give way. Ordinarily, this would kill anyone around them, but within the undercroft of the House of Lords? Well, that's where things get interesting! The undercroft is surrounded by stone walls nine feet thick. These walls will not give as easily as the barrels' hoops. They will hold against the blast, forcing the explosion upward as if the undercroft were an enormous cannon! The explosion will knock through the floorboards of the House of Lords as effortlessly as the barrel lids, only this time with the king, his ministers, and all of Parliament on top of them!"

"What will be left standing?" asked Robert Keyes.

"Nothing!" replied the expert. "The entire building will be destroyed. Its roof, its walls; everything. We'll have blown the Scottish buggers all the way back to their native mountains! It will be raining body parts for blocks. Oh, if only you could see it!"

"And where will you be throughout this dire combustion?" the playwright probed.

"Actually . . ." Fawkes hesitated. "I was hoping you could help me with that."

Shakespeare raised his eyebrows. "What do you need, brother?"

"I plan to light the barrels with a fifteen-minute fuse. That should give me enough time to cross the river into Southwark before the powder detonates. Bankside is your territory, Will. It is where the Globe is. I imagine you will be at the theater on Tuesday morning?"

"Of course, brother. Do you wish to hide there?"

Guy Fawkes smiled. "No. A ship will be waiting for me past London Bridge, ready to sail for Flanders. When I cross the Thames, will you wait for me on the riverbank with a horse?"

The actor smirked and put his arm around the plotter. "Two horses," he promised. "I will ride with you to the dockyard."

The conspirator's eyes were watering. "You would do that for me?"

"Of course. How else do you expect me to say good-bye to you? Over cups?"

Deeply moved, the conspirator rose from his seat and stared adoringly at the playwright he had come to trust in these sixteen months. Maybe it was the lateness of the hour. Maybe it was the double beer. But at that moment, Fawkes knew that his life was in safe hands, and he loved William Shakespeare for it.

Sensing this, the bard rose from his chair, and the men embraced.

"God bless you, brother," Guy Fawkes whispered.

"God bless us all!" Robert Catesby lauded.

"Amen!" everyone but the playwright cheered.

Chapter XLI

Showtime

Monday, November 4, 1605: a day that all of London had been looking forward to and would just as soon forget.

The workweek opened with the city's quarantine being lifted. People breathed with relief knowing the plague that had haunted London for three long years finally appeared to be over. Businesses prospered, fortunes were made, and a triumphant crowd of Londoners flocked to Southwark by the tens of thousands to indulge in its many pleasures. There was bear-baiting, bull-baiting, dog fights, gambling, drinking, and whoring from one end of Bankside to the other. And farther inland, along Maiden Lane, enthusiastic crowds lined up outside the Globe for a rare late-night performance of Shakespeare's as-yet unnamed play. The city was abuzz over it: Why the secrecy? What was its subject? Was the play new or old? Why was it being performed outdoors in the cold at night? What surprises did its author, William Shakespeare, and the King's Men have in store for London?

More than three thousand people packed the torchlit Globe to find out. Huddled together for warmth and with excitement, the chatter grew louder than it ever had in the theater's history.

And then the music started. The people cheered. The play began.

Richard Burbage, the greatest actor to ever grace the English stage, emerged from the Globe's velvet curtains and stomped across its timber soil. The crowd delighted and showered their local favorite with adoration, and the master showman basked in every moment of it. He lifted his head and outstretched his arms, embracing everyone from the groundlings to the galleries. All the world was still a stage, and Richard Burbage was still its king.

Finally, after enough applause to last the king unto his death, Richard opened his hands and quieted the crowd with his palms. The audience hushed and held its breath, and the Globe's star player opened his mouth:

RICHARD
Now is the winter of our discontent . . .

There was a buzz; a muted babble of confusion. And then the audience broke into whistles and cheers. Shakespeare's secret play was an old favorite, a timely choice to commemorate the passing of the plague and the reopening of London's theaters.

Once more, Richard Burbage ruled the world as Richard III.

The playwright grinned.

Unbeknownst to Fawkes and his conspirators, the bait had just been switched.

Chapter XLII

Midnight, November 5, 1605

Guy Fawkes passed the evening beneath the House of Lords with nothing but his lantern, a pocket watch, and thirty-six barrels of gunpowder to keep him company. The timepiece was a last-minute addition, something Robert Keyes handed him at Temple Bar at the behest of Thomas Percy. The watch would make the wait more bearable, but instead, the slow-moving timepiece made its watchman more impatient. Fawkes was an anxious man; he was energized, alert, and very much awake. His motivation was the revolution that he knew history would forever connect him with. The world was crossing into a new threshold with that hour hand that night: an age when kingdoms could be undone by a lone man with a match. It would be a baptism by fire, and Guy Fawkes was proud to be its godfather.

Finally, the hour crossed into XII, and the bells of Westminster Abbey sounded November 5, 1605.

It was Judgment day. Guy Fawkes Day.

The bells were Gabriel's horn to Fawkes's ears.

The conspirator pulled his hat down, threw his cape across his chest for warmth, and leaned against the payload stacked behind him beneath a mound of firewood and coal. As Fawkes glanced one more time at his pocket watch, he began to wish that Percy had sent him a deck of playing cards instead.

But then, he heard something.

Fawkes turned his head and looked toward the undercroft's archway opening. A figure was walking through it! Prepared for this, the conspirator lowered his head and pretended to be asleep. *My name is John Johnson*, he rehearsed once more in his head. *I was sent here by Thomas Percy, a member of the Honourable Band of Gentlemen Pensioners. He is a dutiful man sworn to protect the king's life and—*

"Guido!"

Fawkes looked up in disbelief. "Will?" he whispered.

The bard entered with a lantern. "How are you, brother?"

Fawkes's face transformed itself before the playwright's eyes. "Will! My . . . brother!" The conspirator laughed unconvincingly as he got up and sheathed the dagger beneath his cape.

The two embraced. "How goes the watch?"

"All is well, but . . . Will, what are you doing here? We are supposed to meet in the morning. Across the river." Where Guy Fawkes had planned to kill him.

The bard shook his head. "I am sorry, brother, but this could not wait. I have news about the play!"

"*Macbeth?*"

Shakespeare nodded.

Fawkes wrinkled his forehead, unable to decipher if the news was good or bad. "What is it?"

Before the playwright could reply, a team of soldiers stormed into the undercroft. They were led by Sir Thomas Knyvet, Edmund Doubleday, and a third man who lurked behind them in the shadows. "In the name of King James," Knyvet thundered, "I order you to stand aside!"

"William, what have you done?" Guy Fawkes growled as he reached for his sword and dagger. This time, the conspirator was showing Shakespeare his true face, the one that had glared down at him from the windows of the Mermaid.

"Let me handle this." The playwright took a step forward and outstretched his arms. "Masters, my friend and I—"

Sir Thomas Knyvet thrust his sword at Shakespeare. Its bloodied blade pierced through the playwright's cape.

"Will!" Fawkes cried.

Shakespeare hobbled backward, clutching his chest. Blood was spurting through his fingers. "We are undone. Avenge us, brother!" The bard collapsed onto the woodpile, knocking over one of the barrels. Black powder spilled across the floor.

Furious, Fawkes seized his lantern and cracked it open while soldiers surrounded him with spears. "Stand back!" the traitor warned, holding his dripping candle over the powder. "I have enough gunpowder here to blow us all to Hades! Drop your weapons! Now!"

The line of lances wavered. "He lies," a view threw from behind them.

Fawkes's eyes glowered against his firelight. "You think I'm lying? Do you!" he cried. "Here lies your doom!"

The conspirator dropped his candle. Its flame touched the powder.

Nothing happened.

Fawkes looked down in disbelief. There was no explosion. Shocked, he bent down and brushed the deadly stuff over the candle with his hands. Not only did the powder fail to combust, but the flame became extinguished.

The conspirator's fingers were black with ash. "Useless . . ." he cursed. "Useless!"

Suddenly, the undercroft filled with the sound of clapping.

Fawkes turned his head, the soldiers parted, and Thomas Walsingham walked into the scene. "Beautiful work, my friend. Well played. We now have no doubt about this one's intentions."

The conspirator's eyes widened. "Who are you?"

"I wasn't talking to you," replied the spymaster. He nodded his head toward Fawkes, and the soldiers ensnared the villain. "Take him to the Privy chamber. I will follow shortly."

"This is a misunderstanding!" Fawkes resisted. "My name is John Johnson! I—"

One of the soldiers knocked the conspirator over the head with a wooden club. Fawkes collapsed to the floor and was carried out without further protest.

As the torches left the undercroft, Walsingham set down his lantern and puffed his pipe. "The show is over. We can go now."

The bard exhaled as he sat up from his pyre. "Will the soldiers suspect anything?"

"Not a thing. The room is dark, and all they ever see of you is in costume at the Globe, wearing wigs and makeup."

Shakespeare slid off the woodpile. "Thank you, W."

"We're out of the office. You can call me Thomas."

The playwright turned around and looked at the barrels stacked behind him. "What will become of these?"

"I'll be taking them. All the powder is in the Tower being weighed. We'll reseal it in the barrels and add them to our stores."

"Such a shame," the playwright sighed. "I was hoping to keep one as a theater prop."

The spymaster smirked. "That could be arranged, if you still wish."

Shakespeare pulled the bloodied bladder out from his doublet and tossed it to the floor. The spymaster could see that the bard was not smiling.

"Will," Walsingham added, lowering his pipe, "I know it does not matter at this juncture, but I hope you are not conflicted over the role I asked you to play tonight."

"Conflicted?" Shakespeare snorted as he and Walsingham walked out of the undercroft. "This man threatened me, my family, and my actors from the moment that we met. He paid me forty pieces of silver so that I could become his Judas. He called me his brother, he claimed to love me, but I know he never did. He was a snake in the grass. He always was." The bard narrowed his eyes at the boat drifting downstream with Fawkes. "And he wore an unconvincing mask."

Walsingham smiled. "Just out of curiosity, how do you think I would have fared if I had gone into acting?"

The playwright turned to the spymaster and snickered. "You would have made a grand Cleopatra."

The men laughed and went their separate ways: Walsingham to the Privy chamber, and the bard to the Dark Lady's.

Chapter XLIII

The Ace

November 8, 1605. The Gunpowder Plot was thwarted. Parliament was not destroyed, London was in shock, and Guy Fawkes was entering his third day of torture at the hands of Sir William Waad, the Lieutenant of the Tower. After graduating from manacles to the rack, Fawkes was finally giving his interrogators what they wanted while Walsingham observed and Penny recorded—she also "embellished" whenever W requested. With his body nearly torn to pieces across a bed of wooden rollers, Fawkes surrendered his real name on day two,* and then the names of his coconspirators on day three.†

As Lady Percy scratched these names down, it never dawned upon anyone in the Tower except Thomas Walsingham just how many of Guy Fawkes's fellow traitors were already dead.

"We are undone, and it is all their fault! The bloody heathens."

---

*"Examination of John Johnson," November 7, 1605. PRO SP 14/216/49.
†"Examination of Guy Fawkes," November 8, 1605. PRO SP 14/216/49.

"Will you *please* stop saying that?" Catesby pleaded. "As long as we keep our wits about us, we might still survive this!" Always the optimist, the leader of the conspirators went back to drying their dampened gunpowder.

On the rooftop of the stately Holbeche House, in Staffordshire, Marlowe listened through the chimney for a thorough summary on the past few days. All the conspirators had fled from London except for Francis Tresham—whoever that was. Catesby had learned of Fawkes's capture from Ambrose Rookwood, who crossed thirty miles in just two hours riding the same horse, an impressive feat! All plans to kidnap Princess Elizabeth were abandoned just as hastily as it sounded like it was planned, but Robert maintained hope of an armed rebellion even though it was unlikely anyone would join it. Apparently, it was just impossible for the man to say no to anything.

The conspirators raided Warwick Castle on November 6 for supplies and then Hewell Grange on November 7 for arms and powder. It had been pouring rain all day, so they settled in the Holbeche House for the evening. All their sodden gunpowder was lying around the fireplace, completely exposed and vulnerable.

Marlowe scratched his beard and then took an ace of clubs from his new deck of playing cards. He dropped the card down the chimney and slid off the rooftop.

The poet joined the posse surrounding the mansion just as all its windows exploded.

"What the bloody hell was that!" gasped Sir Richard Walsh, the sheriff of Worcester.

"Nothing really," Marlowe answered. "I just softened them up a bit. It should make for a shorter skirmish."

"Are you mad?" asked sharpshooter John Streete. "It's too dark out. We're not attacking them until the morning!"

Marlowe furrowed his eyebrows and looked around the midnight manor. "You honestly think it's too dark?"

"YES!" the lawmen replied.

The poet shook his head with disappointment and then turned toward the screams emanating from Holbeche House. Sir Everard Digby, the last man to join Catesby's conspirators, sprinted out of the mansion's smoking doors with his cape on fire. "I surrender!" he cried. "I surrender!" The vigilantes tossed a blanket over the burning man and took him into custody.

The sheriff and the sharpshooter turned to Marlowe in surprise. "I guess we owe you an apology. Master—"

"Factotum," replied the poet. "Johannes Factotum."

The lawmen stared at the cocky agent in disbelief. "That can't be your real name," said Streete.

"It is for the next three hundred and sixty-three days. Wake me when my *kahfey* is ready." Marlowe leaned against a tree and pulled his hat over his eyes.

A stately raven watched him while he slept.

Friday, November 8 did not dawn well for the conspirators at Holbeche House. In addition to being badly burned, half of them attempted to flee into the evening. All those who tried were shot and captured, among them Thomas Wintour. By eleven A.M., only Robert Catesby, Thomas Percy, the bad Wright brothers, Rookwood, and John Grant remained. Since Grant had both his eyes burned out in the night's surprise explosion, only five men were fit to fight against the sheriff of Worcester's force of two hundred men.

"We mean to die here!" Catesby shouted through the manor's shattered windows. Holbeche House was filled with gun smoke and riddled with bullets. There were explosions and shouting everywhere. Amidst the fighting, Ambrose Rookwood was taken down by a musket ball while the treacherous Wright brothers were reduced to one. As Rookwood writhed on the floor and the blinded John

Grant listened helplessly, Catesby, Percy, and Jack Wright became the only fighters left to kill.

Then, suddenly, at high noon, the shooting stopped.

Catesby looked out his broken window to find a lone figure moving through the mists. "Halt or I'll shoot!" cried the leader of the conspiracy.

"I know you're out of musket powder," replied the man who blew it up with a playing card.

"What's going on here!" Thomas Percy coughed as he crouched behind the window, his face covered with blood and sweat. "Is this a trick?"

"Who are you!" Jack Wright thundered.

After looking over his shoulder for privacy, the man replied, "My name is Christopher Marlowe, and I'm the man who's going to kill you."

Robert Catesby's blackened face scowled. "You call this negotiating!" he shouted.

"I'm sorry! It's nonnegotiable!"

Catesby gasped and threw his arms around Thomas Percy. "It's going to be all right!" the leader muttered.

The sweaty man was done taking orders from the optimist. "Enough of this. Jack! Go out and flay that fop!"

"With pleasure." Jack stomped out of the mansion and unsheathed his steel, shouting: "Ho there!"

Marlowe stopped walking while his raven circled overhead. "Who are you supposed to be?" the poet asked.

"My name is Jack Wright, and I'm the best swordsman in England!" he shouted, raising his blade.

The poet raised his eyebrows. "You're the best swordsman in England?"

"Aye!"

Marlowe raised his rapier and shot the swordsman dead with his hidden trigger.

"No!"

"Jack!" Robert and Percy cried from their window.

Seeing them, the poet aimed his sword in their direction and pulled his trigger one more time.

Both men were killed by the same bullet.

With his work completed, Marlowe turned around and passed through his misty curtains.

"What happened?" asked the sheriff.

A raven swooped down and perched on the Double-O agent's shoulder. "The show is over."

Act V

1606

Chapter XLIV

The Sacrifice

Robert Catesby and Thomas Percy were the first to lose their heads for their conspiracy. After falling from a single bullet, their bodies were exhumed and their heads displayed on spikes outside the House of Lords. Francis Tresham died of strangury, a painful urinary inflammation, on December 23 while still a prisoner at the Tower of London.

The remaining men were tortured, tried, found guilty of high treason, and then put to the traitor's death: being hanged, drawn, and quartered before a cheering London crowd.

Robert Wintour, Thomas Bates, Everard Digby, and John Grant went out on a cold and cloudy January 30, 1606. They were dragged through the filthy streets of London on wooden beds from the Tower to St. Paul's churchyard, more than a mile away. The conspirators were forced onto scaffolds one by one, stripped, hanged, cut down while still alive, castrated, disemboweled, and then cut into quarters amongst a symphony of jeers and laughter. High above them, Christopher Marlowe watched from atop St. Paul's Cathedral with a telescope Sir Francis Bacon had asked him to test.

Although such spectacles were fodder for countless writers throughout history, William Shakespeare was not present.

The next day, however, was a different story.

Ambrose Rookwood, Robert Keyes, and Thomas Wintour were drawn and quartered at Westminster's Old Palace Yard on January 31. It was an equally dreary day: no storm clouds, but no sunlight either. Once the three traitors were torn to pieces, one last man was forced onto the scaffold: a sleepless, battered, bruised, and waterboarded "Guido" Fawkes.

The conspirator had a noose thrown around his neck in full view of the building he had tried and failed to destroy with gunpowder. Although barely able to breathe or stand after months of torture, his vision sharpened with adrenaline. From his visage, he could see the heads of Robert Catesby and Thomas Percy: a feast for crows who had grown accustomed to their faces. The conspirator let his eyes fall and resigned himself to the fate he would soon be sharing with Catesby, Percy, and the three men whose entrails were still strewn across the stage. His gaze lifted from the blood and organs to the crowd assaulting him; the people whom Fawkes believed would have heralded him as a hero had it not been for some treason within his ranks.

There were rumors that Francis Tresham had tipped the government to the conspiracy with an anonymous letter,* but Fawkes knew it was a forgery. When it had been shown to him, the letter was still wet with ink. It was a ruse no different than when Walsingham swapped the barrels in the undercroft.

Nay. Someone else had betrayed the conspirators, and Fawkes was willing to offer his soul to find out whom.

The condemned man closed his ears to the clergyman beside him as he looked over the crowd. He knew that he, or she, had to be out there watching him. Fawkes was determined to find the person

*SP 14/216/2.

who betrayed him. His last seconds stretched into hours as he ran his eyes over the faces of his audience.

And then, he saw someone. A familiar female figure. It was the one sister who the cunning folk kept in London. Fawkes had not seen her in many months and had nearly forgotten that she existed. As the conspirator stared at her, astonished, this youngest sister turned her head to the west.

Fawkes shifted his eyes to the Lady chapel of Westminster Abbey. Although he could not see through its narrow windows, its pinnacles and flying buttresses were blanketed with ravens. The conspirator squinted at the birds, tearing his mind apart over why they haunted him like death throughout the city: at the Tower, and his execution, and . . .

Fawkes's eyes widened just as the sack was pulled over his head.

Mad with hatred, the conspirator leaped from his platform, snapping his own neck.

He offered his life to whatever god the witches worshiped in exchange for revenge against William Shakespeare.

Chapter XLV

The King's Men

T hat's disappointing," Thomas Walsingham remarked from the Lady chapel's windows. Fawkes had denied London the opportunity to see him castrated and disemboweled while still alive.

"A traitor's death is still a traitor's death," said William Shakespeare. "How we dress it up is unimportant."

The spymaster smirked and puffed a cloud of smoke as he turned around. "It is interesting that you say that. I have a letter from the king addressed to you." W reached into his cloak and produced a folded parchment bearing King James's royal seal. "There is one more traitor whose head the king would like to see on a spike."

"Henry Garnet?" Shakespeare asked as he took the document.

"Well . . . besides him."

Walsingham returned to his pipe while Shakespeare turned the letter over. King James's royal seal was unbroken. "Have you read it?"

"No."

"Then how do you know its contents?"

The spymaster snorted smoke. "Let's just say I know the secretary who wrote it down."

Shakespeare lowered his eyes and read the letter while W puffed.

The bard's hands began to shake. "You shared my play with the king?"

"Of course I did! You know I had to take it into custody."

"But . . . the king! What will he—"

"Just keep reading," said the spymaster.

The bard returned to the parchment and then looked up in disbelief. "He wants me to perform the play."

Walsingham nodded. "Parliament voted last week to make November fifth a holiday.* A day of thanksgiving to commemorate the deliverance of these lands from papists, Jesuits, seminary priests . . . et cetera," he recited. "The king wants your play to be the highlight of the evening! A spectacle that all of London can share in—since we can't kill these men again."

Shakespeare laughed uneasily. "But Thomas . . . The play is not kind to the king. I wrote it as a weapon of war for a revolution I did not want to be a part of!"

"It's a Trojan horse, is what it is! We still have the cunning folk to contend with. As long as you change the role of Banquo to one more complimentary to the king, the rest of the tragedy can be performed in its entirety. The war against the cunning folk is not yet won. Your play will help the government keep our enemies in their place and give the public something new to hold on to." Walsingham then reached into his cloak and produced what looked like a large, thick coin. "Consider this a down payment," he offered, dropping the memento in the playwright's palms.

The newly struck medallion displayed a serpent lurking beneath a bed of flowers and read "DETECTVS QVI LATVIT. S. C." around its edge.

"Interesting," said Shakespeare, tempted by the keepsake. "But I don't know. This is not what I agreed to."

"Then how about we make it the last thing we ever agree on? Do

---

*Observance of 5th November Act 1605 (3 Ja. I, c. 1).

me this favor, perform this play, and you can retire from the Double-O. The war against the cunning folk will be left to those who want to fight them, and you can return to focusing entirely on your work."

Shakespeare froze. "But what about my license? Will that be revoked as well? You're already asking me to rewrite this play."

"As I said, we can make this the last thing we ever agree on. A replacement has already been brought in for you. He will take your place the day you perform the play."

The bard's eyes widened. "Really? Just . . . like that? You're done with me?"

"After Fawkes and Essex, we're running out of conspirators for you to work with," Walsingham quipped.

The bard's voice deepened. "And what of Bianca?"

W's posture stiffened. "What about her?"

"Her war ended years ago. Let her be free of you."

The spymaster narrowed his eyes as his pipe smoldered. "So be it. We'll satisfy the king's request first, and then I promise to do everything in my power to release her." Walsingham offered his hand. "Do we have an accord?"

The playwright weighed the offer, along with the letter and the bronze medallion. "We do," he decided, shaking the spymaster's gloved hand with his.

"Very good." W smiled. "You will be missed, my friend."

Shakespeare tried to stuff the king's letter in his cloak, but Walsingham took it back. "The medallion is yours, but not the letter."

Already, the bard could feel his power fading. "Out of curiosity, who will be my replacement?"

"You will find out soon enough," said Walsingham as he walked Shakespeare out of the cathedral.

"Is it anyone I know?"

"Just remember the fifth of November, master bard." The spymaster tapped the bard's bronze medallion, and Shakespeare pocketed it.

"I will."

Chapter XLVI

A Surprise Visitor

Nine months later

A re you sure you want to go through with this?"

"Of course! Just a few more months, and I will be free of this place forever."

Shakespeare sighed as he and Bianca walked arm in arm across London Bridge. He did not think the Tower was a good place for a lady in her state. The air there was putrid. "Have you decided where you will be going?" the playwright asked.

"After Naples, I was thinking Constantinople or Rome, and then settling down in Venice. I heard such wonderful things about the library there!"

"Oh? From whom?"

The Dark Lady smiled to herself. "I can walk the rest of the way. You should hurry back to the Globe."

"Tilly-valley! I will do no such thing. Let me see you to the Tower."

"Will," she chided playfully, "I can take care of myself, and so should you."

The playwright paused with Bianca at the midpoint of the bridge, ignoring the circus of revelers rushing past them. Shakespeare ran his hands down her raven hair before settling on her swollen belly. "I know I say this every day," he started, "but Anne—"

"What Anne wants is not what I want," Bianca interrupted. "Once more, just once more, I want to be in charge of my own fate."

The bard frowned. "You could be traveling a long way for disappointment."

"If my parents are still alive, they deserve to hold their only grandchild. Being reunited with them could be the one thing that makes these past twenty years worth living." Shakespeare lowered his head, but Bianca raised his chin. "You have to let go of me at some point. For both our sakes, today would be a good day to start."

Shakespeare looked to the children running past him, which made him think of poor Hamnet. "May I kiss you before I do?"

She smiled. "Of course."

The London couple embraced and then parted ways. As did the lovesick ravens following them.

It was November 5, 1606, and the Dark Lady had just entered the last month of her pregnancy.

"Gentlemen," the bard greeted as he walked into the Globe.

"Master Shakespeare . . ." hissed William Sly in a Scottish kilt. "Where the bloody hell have you been?"

"In a nicer place than the front row if you go out like that."

William Sly looked down at his hitched-up kilt and covered his loins.

"Master Shakespeare!"

"Yes, Lawrence?"

Lawrence Fletcher rushed within whisper range. "There is a man here to see you. He says he's from the government!"

The bard raised an eyebrow. "The government?" Walsingham never came to meet him at the Globe. Ever. "Where is he?"

"Upstairs in the storage room."

Shakespeare looked up at the small hut jutting over the heavens. A silhouetted figure was staring down from its windows while a stately raven waited outside.

The bard went upstairs.

"What is it, W?" he asked as he entered the hut.

A tall, cloaked figure spun around holding a white volto to his face. The Venetian mask had a black mustache, goatee, and eyebrows painted on to more closely resemble the grinning visage of Guy Fawkes. "Boo!" said its wearer.

The playwright jumped back. "Who are you?"

"You tell *me,* master bard!"

The playwright squinted his eyes and honed his ears. Once he realized whom he was speaking to, "No . . ." he gasped.

Christopher Marlowe lowered his Guy Fawkes mask and smiled. "Yes, it is!"

Shakespeare took a step forward. "Kit?"

Marlowe threw the mask away. "William!"

The two ran into each other's arms as brothers and laughed. "You're looking good!" the poet praised. "And you're losing your hair!"

The playwright brushed this off. "Kit, what are you doing here? You're supposed to be in Venice."

"Foh! Don't mention Venice!"

"Why? Did something—" The bard froze. "No. There was a—"

"A massacre in Venice. I know. I plan to write a play about it!"

"Summer's day!" Shakespeare cheered. "You must tell me everything!"

"Why? So you can steal my ideas?" Marlowe slapped Shakespeare playfully. "I ought to have your shirt for *The Merchant of Venice!*"

The bard hid his face in his hand, embarrassed. "You heard of that?"

"Heard of it? I've seen it twice this year!"

Shakespeare's jaw dropped. "You have been here that long?"

"Yes! I am sorry I did not seek you earlier, but . . ." Marlowe held his head high. "I am a bit of a new man these days!"

The playwright grinned. "Well, it's good to have you back, my friend. Please stay for the evening! We have a new show tonight."

"Yes, the play that all London is talking about!" Marlowe teased. "The drama with no name!"

The bard could read the mischievousness on his friend's face. "You already know its name, don't you?"

The poet nodded. "*Macbeth.*"

Shakespeare laughed. "That is it! Please, you have to see it. In fact, if you want, I'm sure we could give you a small part in it!"

"I would love to, my friend, but alas . . . I'll be working in the Tower all evening."

"The Tower? What are you doing there?"

"Isn't it obvious?" Marlowe took a step back and threw out his arms. "I've been brought back from the dead! Our friend Thomas has made me the new Lazarus! Why else do you think I'm here? I'm the one who reviewed your play for the government!"

The bard shook his head in disbelief. "You're working again? You're . . . the one? My replacement?"

"If I remember correctly, you were *my* replacement!"

The two laughed cheerfully. "Yes, well, I have some stories to share as well."

"And I look forward to them with all my still-beating heart. But as of now, I must fly. We will meet again soon enough!" The tall poet embraced the shorter playwright and then dashed out of the room. "Good luck tonight!"

"Thank you! You will be missed!"

Once those words hit Marlowe's ears, the poet stopped. After a thought, he turned around and walked back into the hut. "Will, just one question before we part. You mentioned a maritime mishap in *Macbeth* about a ship called the *Tiger*."

"Yes," the bard confirmed. "The witches mention it in scene three."

The poet nodded. "I saw that was a recent addition to the book of the play. Is there any reason you added it?"

Shakespeare, somewhat surprised by this, explained: "It's just a little something for the audience to enjoy. A lot of people heard about the *Tiger* this summer; the horror. I thought it would make the sisters more menacing."

Marlowe swallowed. "Do you really think that such women can control the elements? That they can destroy ships at sea?"

Shakespeare could see that something was troubling his friend. "Kit, what is it?"

"I'm just curious."

The bard shook his head. "No. You're not telling me something."

Marlowe's eyes fell. The dragoman's ship *Sultana* had recently disappeared at sea. "To be continued," he decided.

The poet disappeared from the Globe Theatre.

Chapter XLVII

Macbeth

LEN.

Sent he to Macduffe?

LORD

He did: and with an absolute Sir, not I
The clowdy Messenger turnes me his backe,
And hums; as who should say, you'l rue the time
That clogges me with this Answer.

Shakespeare sneaked a peek from backstage. The audience was enthralled.

LENOX

And that well might
Aduise him to a Caution, t'hold what distance
His wisedome can prouide. Some holy Angell
Flye to the Court of England, and vnfold
His Message ere he come, that a swift blessing
May soone returne to this our suffering Country, Vnder a hand accurs'd.

LORD

Ile send my Prayers with him.

The players exited, the music resumed, and the Globe's enthusiastic audience applauded.

Act III of *The Tragedy of Macbeth* was over.

Actors John Heminges and Alexander Cooke hurried into the Tiring House, where William Shakespeare and the King's Men were readying act IV. The first scene promised to be a busy one: Richard Burbage's Macbeth would be reunited with the three witches from act I. Paintings and fiery torches were being readied and ghostly apparitions would descend from the heavens on ropes. Also, perhaps most important of all, a large black barrel along with a bucket of disgusting props would serve as the witches' cauldron and ingredients.

After an interlude, the music stopped. It was time for act IV to begin.

"Is everyone ready?"

"Yes, Master Shakespeare."

"Very well. Thunder?"

There was no sound from young James Sands, who was holding a frying pan and a mallet.

"I say, 'thunder'?"

Still no response.

"Young Sands?"

The boy was staring out of the left stage door window with a look of profound confusion.

"Hit the pan, boy!" William Sly stomped over and took the boy's mallet, but paused once he saw what was going on outside. "What the devil?"

"What is it?"

"Master Shakespeare," Sly muttered, "something strange is brewing in the Pit."

The bard looked out the windows beside the Discovery Space. Three dark figures in hooded cloaks were standing in the crowd. The Globe's groundlings backed away from them, thinking this strange display was part of the play.

"What's going on out there?" asked John Heminges.

The bard's eyes widened. The three figures were standing around a large black vessel.

"Is that Yorick?" asked Richard Burbage, referring to the skull one of them lowered into the cauldron.

Shakespeare grabbed a lantern and rushed out of the Discovery Room. "Ho there!" he hollered, storming across the stage. "What are you—"

The three women glared at the playwright from under their hoods.

Bewildered, the bard raised his lantern, and then he backed away in horror.

The women were wearing the tanned, leathered faces of Thomas Percy, Robert Catesby, and Guy Fawkes as masks. All three of the conspirators' skulls were in the cauldron, freshly stripped of their flesh, which, as mentioned, London's raven population had grown accustomed to.

"What are you doing!" Shakespeare gasped.

The cunning folk produced crucibles from their cloaks. "A deed without a name!" replied the elder.

The women emptied their vessels into the cauldron.

The Globe exploded with ash and fire.

Chapter XLVIII

Bonfire Night

For the first night in history, every square in London was burning Guy Fawkes in effigy atop massive pyres. It was a spectacle men like Thomas Walsingham encouraged and that Parliament passed into law. The Gunpowder Plot had been thwarted, and the people wanted to celebrate its failure with fire.

To the cunning folk, every bonfire in London was just a spark.

"Did you see that?" asked one of the watchers of the Wall, as did countless people throughout the city.

Tens of thousands of Londoners turned their heads to Southwark, where a string of fireworks shot into the sky from the Globe Theatre. The dazzled spectators cheered and applauded, completely oblivious to their impending doom.

Seeing their signal, the cunning warriors hidden throughout the city threw their innocent-looking logs into the bonfires. As in the Arden, the logs erupted with a foul smoke, a miasma that lingered overhead like a storm cloud. Revelers turned around and began to back away from the noxious vapor as it swelled into a smog stretching from the Ludgate to the Tower. Those closest to the fires began to cough and collapse. Those farther back screamed and ran away in panic. As fireworks continued to explode above Southwark like thunder, anarchy and terror swept over the city's terrified inhabitants.

"What sorcery is this?" a watchman asked.

"Sergeant, look!"

The watchers atop Cripplegate turned their backs on the screaming city to witness an even more shocking spectacle. The windmills of Hampstead had drifted in from the horizon and were slowly advancing on London Wall. An entire army of painted warriors was following behind them.

The watchmen drew his broadswords. "Prepare for battle!"

"*Archers!*" screamed an officer.

Columns of English longbowmen raced onto the Wall.

"*Archers! Ignite!*"

Archers lit their arrows with torches as the windmills crawled closer.

"*Archers! Draw!*"

The defenders of London Wall raised and aimed their longbows.

"*Arch—*"

Before the final order could be given, a cunning warrior hidden among the guards loosed his arrow into the ring of powder dusted from one end of London Wall to the other. It was the same substance the witches had used for their ceremony in the Arden; a deadly mixture that would take the rest of the world two centuries to discover.* However, instead of enough powder to fill a crucible, this was enough to fill a thousand cauldrons. The powder ignited, and a burning wave of glowing, twisting arms shot out of the ground as if Hell itself had just erupted. The watchmen coughed and choked on the deadly fumes as the branches grew as tall as trees, surrounding London in a wreath of fire no one in or around the city could overcome.

---

*Wöhler, *Gilbert's Ann. d. Phys. u. phys. Chem.*, **9**, 272 (1821) and Berzelius, *Schweigger's J. f. Chem. u. Phys.*, **31**, 42 (1821), cited in "Pyrotechnic snakes," Tenney L. Davis, *J. Chem. Educ.*, 1940, 17 (6), 268.

Except through the water.

Boats, countless boats began to drift in through the Thames, but not to rescue London's terrified inhabitants. The boats landed on both banks of the river, north and south, unleashing wave after wave of rats upon the helpless city.

Terror ruled every point of the compass within London Wall.

"Master W! The city is under attack!"

The spymaster looked up from his desk work. "Who is it?"

"I don't know!" Penny gasped. "Some sort of sorcery! A great cloud has fallen over the city!"

Walsingham's pipe fell out of his mouth. "Secure the mansion, Lady Percy. I'm going to the Tower."

"Master, shouldn't you—"

There was a crash in Penny's office as cunning warriors threw themselves through her windows.

"We cannot stay here!"

"Abandon the Wall! Abandon the Wall!"

The city's greatest defenders were collapsing on every front.

Conventional weapons were useless against the cunning folk's sorcery. Arrows passed harmlessly through the vines ensnaring London like burning serpents. There were a few watchmen who successfully doused water over the cunning weapon, but those who did suffocated in the deadly gas their heroism summoned. Unable to fight and barely able to breathe, London's watchmen had no choice but to abandon the Wall and rally behind the city's seven gates. The gates were as high as five stories and had never fallen in battle. For 1,400 years, these defenses safeguarded London from her enemies.

The city's watchmen rallied, took defensive formations, drew their weapons, and were ready.

However, the cunning warriors had no interest in attacking London's gates. The windmills approaching the city were actually siege towers being towed by teams of oxen inside them. Once the engines passed through the city's fiery wreath, their sails ignited, driving away any defenders that still stood against them.

The machines reached the Wall and dropped their bridges, unleashing wave after wave of naked, painted, screaming warriors upon the city.

"Marlowe! What are you doing?"

"What do you think I'm doing? I'm going out there!" The Double-O agent sat atop his Turcoman stallion in the Tower stables, prepared to ride into battle.

"No, you're not!" shouted Sir Francis Bacon. "Squire, bring out the Leonardo chariot!"

Marlowe lowered his rapier. "The what?"

The Tower squire ran up to the warrior poet. "Follow me, master."

"What is this madness?"

"I'm afraid I do not know, Your Majesty." Bianca hurried with Anne of Denmark through the White Tower.

Although the Gunpowder Plot had been foiled, Thomas Walsingham and England's Secretary of State Robert Cecil agreed that the Palace at Westminster was too dangerous for King James on the plot's anniversary. The risk of someone duplicating the attack through some other means was too great, especially since Princess Elizabeth had been targeted for kidnapping and James's own father had been murdered in a gunpowder blast many years before. As a result, for their own safety, the entire royal family was at Tower of London this evening—just as the cunning folk expected they would be.

The Dark Lady, however, was a factor that their wisest women had not anticipated.

"This way, Your Majesty." Bianca directed Anne and her children to the safest holdings in the keep. Once they were out of her way, the Dark Lady hurried up the spiral stairs of the White Tower to the castle's rooftop.

There was shouting and screaming everywhere in London. All of Bacon's ravens were flying in panic above the city they could not dive down to defend. The Tower's Ravenmaster and all its rooftop soldiers were dead. The thick clouds rising up from the bonfires remained a deadly weapon against the birds, as they did to Bianca once the fumes attacked her lungs. The Dark Lady coughed violently and uncontrollably as she surveyed the nightmare Bonfire Night had become.

The entire city was rimmed with living fire. Fireworks continued to flash like lightning over Southwark. A fireship packed with explosives detonated against London Bridge preventing any passage across the Thames. A column of cunning warriors breeched the Wall and were now charging through the city. The once celebratory population was now running for their lives, surrounded by painted men, plague rats, and a deadly fog looming over London. Bianca held a handkerchief to her mouth as she studied the cloud from above and the location of the bonfires, which glowed like candles through the smog.

Realizing at once what had to be done, the Dark Lady raced down the Tower's steps, coughing up blood the entire way.

Chapter XLIX

The Turning Point

G et everybody out of here!" Shakespeare shouted as the
cauldron bubbled over with flailing limbs. Terror gripped
the Globe as *The Tragedy of Macbeth* spilled into reality. The actors
ran offstage with sand buckets to control the fire, but while they
saved their theater, nothing could stop the barrage of fireworks
shooting into the sky.

Eventually, the theater quieted as the greater horror spread
to the rest of London. "Is everyone still alive?" the playwright
asked.

The King's Men were tending to some of the injured spectators,
and to their own.

"Aye!"

"Nothing serious."

"Just some bruises and burns over here."

"All is well."

Finally, the fireworks shooting out of the cauldron stopped. Its
fiery arms froze and turned into ash.

"God save us," Shakespeare sighed. "Men, keep that cauldron

under control. But keep your distance! It emits a deadly fume. I must go to the Tower."

"The Tower?" gasped the actors.

"Yes! Lawrence, fetch me the day's receipts, my sword, and my pocket watch."

"Aye, master."

"Master Shakespeare . . ." began John Heminges, "just what is going on here?"

"Aye! Why do you have to go to the Tower?" asked Alexander Cooke, who was being bandaged by young James Sands.

Torn between his loyalties, the bard looked to Richard Burbage. The experienced actor nodded, acknowledging that it was time for Shakespeare to tell with the rest of the King's Men the truth. "I would never lie to you, my brothers. I have been working for the government from the moment I agreed to write this play. The cunning folk are behind this strange attack. They are Celtic witches. Sorceresses. They want every one of us dead! I do not know how much help I can be, but as long as things are safe here, my place belongs at the Tower."

The King's Men looked at one another, many of them still in their costumes. Was Shakespeare abandoning them, or were they abandoning their greatest member?

Richard Burbage settled the matter by drawing his Scottish claymore—an anachronism, but a welcome one—as he declared: "Master Shakespeare, we would think ourselves accursed and hold our manhoods cheap"—Richard raised his sword—"if we did not fight with you! On Guy Fawkes Night!"

"HURRAH!" the actors cheered, lifting their weapons as the bard joined in as well.

"Here are your things," entered Fletcher, handing Shakespeare everything he had requested.

The bard unsheathed his sword, shouted "HURRAH!" once more, and then led the King's Men screaming out of the theater.

They were immediately stopped by a blood-covered bear terror-
izing their patrons on Maiden Lane.

"God save us," William Sly groaned.

"Master Shakespeare," reentered Fletcher. "You forgot these."

The bard turned his eyes to the bag of coins and the pocket watch
Sir Francis Bacon had begrudgingly replaced. "Stand back, men!"
Shakespeare shouted after picking up the latter.

The bear locked eyes with the playwright, and the bard pulled
the pin from his deadly timepiece.

"FIE! FIE! FIE!" Penny screamed as she stabbed the naked warrior
under her with her dagger.

"I think that's the last of them," sighed W, who was wielding
two blood-covered broadswords. The spymaster's headquarters
was littered with the bodies of countless Celtic fighters who val-
ued fear more than armor. Fortunately, they found none of the
former and plenty of the latter in Walsingham Mansion. The spymaster was wearing a steel breastplate under his doublet, and
Penny's steel-boned corset had saved her life more than once during the melee. "I should go to the Tower. Will you be all right if I
leave you?"

Penny's dagger broke in her attacker's eye socket. "I won't be
bothered," she said. She then took the fallen warrior's larger blade
as a replacement.

Satisfied, the spymaster retreated to his arsenal for everything he
needed to stroll down the road.

W emerged from his mansion carrying two eight-chambered
matchlock revolvers that his predecessor Sir Francis Walsingham
had smuggled out of the Neatherlands. He also wore two leather
straps down his shirt like suspenders, each one containing six replacement revolvers. After looking over the mess that the cunning
folk had made of his beloved Seething Lane, the spymaster put one

revolver under his arm for a far more powerful weapon. He picked a wooden flute out of his pocket and blew it.

Several warriors heard him and turned in his direction.

No effect.

Frustrated, Walsingham blew the whistle again, this time while looking at the . . . clouded skies, he realized.

"Damn it," he cursed. The only raven he summoned fell through the smog as lifelessly as a stone.

Bitter at the cunning folk for thwarting the Double-O's greatest weapon, the spymaster had to resort to his firearms as cunning warriors came screaming at him.

"Master Bacon! Master Bac—!" The Dark Lady's shouts were interrupted by retching.

"Mistress Bianca!" Bacon gasped. "What are you doing here? You look—"

"Shut it!" she coughed. "Our enemies are using bonfires to keep the ravens away. We need to destroy the fires!"

His face twisted. "You are sure of this?"

"Yes!" she hacked. "I saw everything from the top of the Tower."

Shocked, the thinker looked at the clouds above him while Bianca covered her mouth with her bloodstained handkerchief. "There is nothing natural about this," Bacon realized. "These are no storm clouds. It's a farce!"

"Bacon!" She struggled, seizing him. "Destroy the fires! Now!"

The Dark Lady sent Bacon running to the Tower stables. She then collapsed to the ground and, with a steady hand, took out her surgeon's knife.

"Take me to the Tower!"

"Master," laughed the waterman, "the city is under siege!"

"I know. But London Bridge is broken. I cannot cross it." Shakespeare threw a sack containing more than a thousand pennies into the boatman's lap. "Take me to Traitors' Gate!"

"Please tell me I'm riding that."

"You are! It needs two horses."

The squire strapped Marlowe's Turcoman and its brother into the enormous scythed chariot everyone at the Double-O thought would never see action. It was modeled after a design from Leonardo da Vinci's notebooks that Roberto di Ridolfi had leaked to the English government years before. Now in its full form and perfected as a maniacal machine, the chariot had four rotating blades on its front end large enough to cut a person in half, scythes on each of its wheels, and a final, spinning blade for any unfortunate man or horse trying to mount the monster.

The poet stepped into his horse's saddle. "Good morrow, Aston!" he bade its brother.

The silver stallion snorted.

Suddenly, Sir Francis Bacon burst into the stables. "Is the chariot ready?"

"Yes, Master Bacon."

"Good. Assemble all the best horsemen in the Tower, yourself included. You will be following Marlowe into the fighting."

"Aye, Master."

"Also, bring out some gunpowder. Small barrels. The kind that can be carried and thrown."

Outside the Tower's walls, Thomas Walsingham was in trouble. Although he walked into this fight with more than one hundred bullets, the cunning warriors outnumbered him by far greater numbers. He wanted to blow his flute again, but he did not want to risk it. He needed the skies to clear before summoning Bacon's ravens.

Also, he needed someone to let him through the Tower gates, and fast. A hideous, screaming figure had just chased him through the remains of Middle Tower, and Walsingham's last bullet bounced harmlessly off the villain's metal jaw.

"Open the goddamned gate!" Walsingham shouted as the Hobgoblin came closer.

"Open the gates!" Bacon ordered.

"Open the bloody gate!" Shakespeare pleaded.

The chariot's blades were whirling. *"Crepi il lupo!"* Marlowe cackled with delight.

Chapter L

The Passion of
Christopher Marlowe

Marlowe spurred his mount, driving both horses out of the Tower. The cunning warriors could only watch in horror as Leonardo's war machine spun toward them.

Walsingham took one look at the scythed chariot and immediately dove out of the way.

The Hobgoblin was the first villain to breach the fortress. Marlowe mowed him down like wheat.

The poet plowed a crimson path of destruction from Byward Tower all the way to St. Paul's Cathedral while the Tower's squires followed him with their payloads: the gunpowder barrels Guy Fawkes had planned to destroy Parliament with. The riders fanned out and rolled their weapons into the bonfires. The barrels exploded, destroying the pyres in fierce blasts that robbed the cunning folk of their smokescreen.

The night skies filled with white smoke, but then started to clear.

With all the bonfires around the Tower of London quelled, the riders then charged their horses toward the waves of rats scurrying through the city. The horsemen emptied their barrels on top of them and then dropped torches.

The deadly vermin were incinerated while the stunned city watched and cheered.

Unfortunately, Marlowe's chariot had its limitations. His whirling blades caught a tree at St. Paul's courtyard, injuring his horse and nearly killing him in the process. Out of options, the poet abandoned his mount and cut Aston free of the chariot. Marlowe spun around and raced onto Cheapside atop the most magnificent horse anyone in the city had ever seen.

The poet galloped back to the Tower only to see the path that he opened close. Blocked, Marlowe rode back to the cathedral to find the remaining warriors in the city converging on him from everywhere. Impossibly outnumbered, Marlowe looked over his captivated audience and attempted something drastic. "People of London!" he hollered at the top of his lungs. "Hear me!"

"Who are you?" one spectator shouted.

"Christo—er M—l—e!" he shouted among the explosions of barrels. "Yes, it is me! Back from the dead! And I have come all the way from paradise to help you as your savior! Please, help me in return!"

There was some confusion from the crowds huddled in the streets and by their windows. But then . . .

"Christus!" a voice shouted.

Marlowe struggled atop Aston for a moment, but then realized: "YES! That's who I am! I am your—" The poet interrupted his speech to fire his rapier at two warriors charging at him. The men fell down while Marlowe's audience gasped in disbelief. The poet then raised his smoking sword, heralding: "You shall see me work miracles, for I am the Christ!"

Marlowe blessed the crowd, and a mighty cheer thundered through the city.

"CHRIST! CHRIST! CHRIST! . . ." the people chanted from the streets of Cheapside to the rooftops.

Marlowe smiled with flattery, graciously accepting their worship. After passing himself as a priest and an archangel, Jesus seemed

like the only logical leap of faith left for him. "Yes!" he shouted.
"I am Christ!" Marlowe then stepped down from Aston's saddle
and announced: "My children! I have heard your prayers! I have come
from Heaven on this day of thanksgiving to deliver you from your
enemies, just as I did last year! I am here to gift you, my faithful,
with everlasting life. Believe in me!" he cried, blessing the crowd as
they kneeled. "Bleed with me!" he implored while covertly wiping
blood onto his palms. "Fight with me!" he begged with tears streaming down his face. "For tonight, I will vanquish the forces of evil
here, in your city! I will win this war against the Devil, and I will
prove to all of you my existence! All I ask in return is that you
share in this glory with me. Choose your weapons! Test your holy
armor! Taste your immortality!"

A holy roar rang through the boulevard as men and women
emerged from their homes and surrounded Marlowe from the
approaching horde. The city of London had finally joined the fight
for its own survival, and not a moment too soon. The poet side-
stepped through the crowd back onto Aston and galloped off.

And straight into an incoming throwing ax. The same one that
struck Shakespeare in the Arden.

No! the poet thought as he tumbled off Aston's back. *How can
someone die so fast?*

Unfortunately, the seemingly unkillable Christopher Marlowe
just did.

Chapter LI

The Curtain

Walsingham could not afford to wait once he was inside the
Tower's walls. Cunning warriors rushed in after him,
holding the portcullis open after Marlowe and his fellow saviors
emerged. The spymaster looked to the skies, desperate for some
sign that Bacon's ravens were still with him. Finally, with the bonfires quelled, the skies parted and Walsingham saw a black ripple
above him like fabric.

The spymaster blew his whistle.

Every raven in the city descended upon the Tower, tearing the
cunning warriors to pieces while the Tower guards finished the
rest. One after another, the painted foes screamed into the fortress,
and one after another, they were silenced. A black curtain fell over
the city, claiming almost all of London's enemies.

And then, that same curtain fell over the departed.

Marlowe was dead. Laying facedown in the street that served as
his last stage.

As Shakespeare ran into the Tower, he turned his head toward
the whinnies of a familiar friend. Aston had spotted him through

the battle and was charging straight at him, trampling the painted warriors holding open the Bloody Tower's gate.

The portcullis came crashing down on the silver stallion, bringing him to his knees.

"ASTON!" Shakespeare cried.

The playwright raced toward his companion only to see him cut down by the swords and spears of Celts unleashing centuries of anger against the most beautiful creature they could kill. Aston disappeared beneath their blows, as did the painted men behind the ravens.

But then the birds began to drop all around the bard like rain. Walsingham's weapon of last resort proved fatal for the Tower's most trusted guardians. Summoning the ravens when he did cost nearly every one of their lives.

Horrified, Shakespeare covered his head and raced toward the Tower Green. Death was all around him. Soldiers, savages, beasts, heroes, and . . .

The world stopped.

The Dark Lady lay on the ground in a pool of blood.

Shakespeare ran to Bianca and collapsed to his knees. Her eyes were closed. Her flesh was cold. Her dark skin almost completely drained of color.

But then the bard looked to her injuries.

There was no life left inside her. Not anymore. Her unborn child had been untimely ripped from her mother's womb.

Shakespeare turned his head aimlessly around him. There was no sign of the child anywhere.

Tragedy turned to anger.

Anger turned to madness.

As a black cloud of ravens fell over the bard and the Dark Lady, three figures passed unmolested though the veil.

Shakespeare looked up from his fallen love to see three women circle him, each one wearing the leather faces of his former enemies.

Two of them, the elder and the younger, had blood all over their hands.

The third figure was completely new to Shakespeare.

"Who are you?" the playwright begged with dying breath.

The three sisters locked eyes with Shakespeare as they spoke.

"We are the product of war," replied the elder. "We are the issue of our enemies."

"We are the blood that stains the ground," the younger added. "We are the corpse that feeds the soil."

"You think you can defeat us," the third one taunted in a young, almost childlike voice, "but we will *never* leave these isles."

The bard rose from Bianca and drew his rapier.

"We are Albion."

He shot the elder woman dead.

"We will never forgive."

He shot the younger.

"And we will never forget."

Shakespeare turned his sword to the last witch, who was wearing Guy Fawkes's face.

But then, to the bard's horror, he saw something familiar.

He looked into the eyes glaring back at him. The eyes peeking through their veil of stolen flesh.

Shakespeare seized the figure by her mask and tore it off.

The playwright froze.

Staring back at him was a girl no older than thirteen. Her face was scarred with claw marks, and one of her eyes had been blinded. She was the one who had followed Shakespeare to his apartment on Silver Street.

Silver.

Shakespeare's eyes widened. He backed away from the girl and dropped his sword.

The cunning youth smiled.

She was the beggar he had seen outside the Mermaid the day he met Guy Fawkes. The day he was commissioned to write the play. She was the one he threw his bag of silver to. She was the one who had haunted him from the beginning.

The cunning folk were right, Shakespeare realized. They would never leave these lands. They could not. They were the British Isles. They were the moss that covers Roman walls. Their place was everywhere. Their face could be anyone's.

Realizing the futility of his efforts and the devastation he coauthored, the bard collapsed helplessly to his knees.

"*William!*"

Shakespeare turned his head to see Walsingham racing toward him.

The cunning girl started running.

"What are you waiting for! Kill her!" the spymaster shouted. He fired a pistol at her but missed. "Will! We can end this! We have her cornered! Get up!"

"I can't," Shakespeare groaned. He buried his face against Bianca's hands and wept.

Walsingham looked down in anger but then softened at the sorry sight. By the time he turned back to the cunning girl, she was gone.

Defeated, the spymaster hung his head and then bent down to one knee. "I am so sorry, Will."

There was no response.

Bonfire Night was over.

Chapter LII

[Exit Playwright]

Thomas Walsingham did not let Shakespeare out of his sight. Although he had a city to rebuild and a nightmare to erase, the spymaster was also human—or at least he liked to think that he still was. In private, Thomas had always admired Shakespeare first and foremost as a playwright. All the same, W was not ready to lose both him and Marlowe in the same evening. The Double-O needed at least one of its greatest agents alive and well.

The two were atop the Tower of London, officially to inspect the damage. In actuality, they were waiting. Waiting for a sign of hope that would never come.

Dead ravens littered the Tower roof like broken tiles.

The spymaster puffed his pipe and walked toward the playwright, who was staring aimlessly over the misty city. "When Bacon first brought me here," shared Walsingham, "he said that we could count on a thousand ravens throughout the city. Do you know how many I've counted so for this morning?"

The bard was unresponsive.

"Will?"

"How many?" the playwright croaked in an aching voice.

The spymaster sighed as he looked down at his dying pipe. "Six. Six ravens. It looks like all the rest were dead before the dawn."

"Did they die, or quit?" Shakespeare pondered aloud.

Walsingham snorted in restrained frustration. "I don't think Bacon trained them to retire."

The bard turned away from the dreary landscape. "Thomas, why do you still have me here? What more do I have to do before you're finished?"

The spymaster raised his eyebrows. "With you?"

"No, with everything. What does it take for a man like *you* to quit? When would you consider your work complete?"

Thomas pursed his lips, but then shook his head. "The world doesn't work that way, Will. In real life, the world's a stage you only exit when you're dead."

"Or when you're killed," the bard retorted, looking once more over the blood-strewn, rain-washed city. "Or carried off."

Walsingham pocketed his spent pipe and stepped closer. "I had my men look all over the Tower. There is no sign of Bianca's child. For all you know, the infant is still alive."

Shakespeare scowled. "I don't know what living is anymore, Thomas. Everything I've been through since you brought me back; all the lying and conspiring . . . You call it living. I call it dying."

"We are all dying. Every day. All our friends, and all our loved ones." The spymaster's gaze fell to the bloodstained Tower Green, where the bard's gray eyes were staring. "It's a shame she did not survive," Thomas continued, "but she was never going to. We are all mortals, Will. And all the echoes of our footfalls upon this world will disappear."

"Then why continue?" the playwright asked scornfully. "Why press on?"

Walsingham stepped closer. "Because the more we learn about the world, the more we learn about ourselves. Pursuing that knowledge is a noble purpose. It is a life worth fighting for."

"And what did you gain from all this madness? What prize was worth the sacrifice?"

W looked over the city's silent skies. "Bacon came to me this morning with a new theory he and John Dee developed. They think the witches do not control the elements at all; they can only predict them. It is a remarkable talent, but everything else they add to it is pageantry. It's theater, Will. They're actors. And just like you, their plays can topple kingdoms."

"I slew the two women who haunted England. Why should the cunning folk be any more concern of mine?"

"Because I don't think we've seen the last of them. Will, you've been to the Double-O. I'm sure you've seen the projects Bacon is working on."

"I saw weapons of war and torture."

"There are also projects on how to predict the future, as the witches do." W checked behind his back before continuing. "Bacon believes that a comet, a reoccurring comet, is expected to return to the skies next year. It is the same comet that appeared when William conquered England. That comet is the reason I rehired you. It wasn't because of Fawkes. I share Bacon's fears that the cunning folk have something even worse in store for us once this comet comes."

"How much worse can this world get?"

W glanced around once more for security. "One of our watchers reported that a traitor ignited the demonic flames around London Wall."

Shakespeare turned his head. "So?"

"The witches could have destroyed the entire city last night. This Tower holds the gunpowder stores for the entire army and navy. That same traitor with his same flame could have leveled all of London."

The bard's eyes awakened. "Why didn't they destroy the city?"

Walsingham shrugged. "What good is a performance without an

audience? They're actors, Will, and I have no doubt that last night convinced everyone in the city of their powers."

Shakespeare's thoughts turned to the screaming crowds fleeing the Globe. "When is the comet expected to reappear?"

The spymaster locked eyes with William Shakespeare. "All Hallows' Eve."

The bard turned his head in disbelief.

Walsingham waited. He wanted the danger to sink in. "Will, I have no idea what the cunning folk are planning. You may have stopped those two last night, but if that girl of theirs returns, *anything* worse than last night is too much for me to handle."

The bard choked with shock. "Is there anyone you can hire in my place?"

W shook his head. "Alas, your replacement died last night."

The playwright froze. "No . . ." he groaned. "Not Kit!"

Thomas nodded with the unhappy news. "Marlowe is dead. England needs you now more than ever, Will. What do you say?"

The bard turned his eyes and once more looked over the city Marlowe and Bianca died defending. As he contemplated his decision, he could hear an infant crying in the distance. Shakespeare hardened his writing hand into a fist, but then relaxed it, letting life return to his ink-stained finger. "I am sorry," he put to Walsingham in a clear voice, "but I am just a playwright."

The spymaster accepted this with a single bow and turned away. "For how much longer?" he put to Shakespeare.

"For all time."

Epilogue

For All Time

On November 5, 1664, the fifty-ninth anniversary of the Gunpowder Plot, a thirty-one-year-old navy clerk named Samuel Pepys went about his morning no differently than any other. We know this because, unlike most young men in London at the time, Samuel kept a detailed diary about his seemingly uneventful life.

*5th. Up and to the office, where all the morning, at noon to the 'Change, and thence home to dinner . . . **

Although Samuel did not know it, "the office," the Navy Board, was the same Seething Lane mansion the great Sir Francis Walsingham used during his war years. Sir Thomas bequeathed it to the English government when he died in 1630, at which point a certain silver-haired secretary disappeared from history.

The apartment Samuel and his wife shared within the complex

---

*Samuel Pepys, *The Diary of Samuel Pepys, Esq. F.R.S.*, vol. 4, ed. Henry B. Wheatley, F.S.A., vol. IV, (London: George Bell & Sons, 1894), 282.

was the same that Lady Percy and Christopher Marlowe conceived their first and only child in.

. . . and so with my wife to the Duke's house to a play, "Macbeth," a pretty good play, but admirably acted.

Forty-eight years had passed since the death of William Shakespeare, a man hailed by his friends as "not of an age, but for all time."* His wife, Anne; his daughters, Susanna and Judith; and all his fellow players were departed as well.

After recording this timely performance of *Macbeth* in his diary, Samuel continued:

. . . Thence home; the coach being forced to go round by London Wall home, because of the bonefires; the day being mightily observed in the City.

Fifty-eight years had passed since the first Bonfire Night, an event suspiciously absent from the English annals of history. And if a certain fifty-eight-year-old woman with Bianca's eyes caught Samuel's gaze as he passed, he left her off his pages as well. Only the six ravens atop the Tower noticed her, along with the older and younger women standing alongside her. The elder wore a weathered, wrinkled face mask and had a pouch tied around her neck. The purse contained forty pieces of silver. The younger woman held a crucible.

As this cunning youth opened her vessel, no fires came from it. No smoke. Just a single starving rat to mingle with the local population.

One month later, a spectacular comet appeared over the city.[†]

---

*Ben Ionson, "To the memory of my beloued, The AVTHOR Mr. William Shakespeare," in *Mr. William Shakespeares Comedies, Histories, & Tragedies* (London: Printed by Iſaac Iaggard, and Ed. Blount, 1623).

[†]"So to the Coffeehouse, where great talke of the Comet seen in several places," *The Diary of Samuel Pepys*, December 15, 1664.

And then another.* 1664 passed and the New Year dawned with all of London wondering what these strange stars foreshadowed.

The plague returned in 1665, killing more than 100,000 Londoners. The next year, the Great Fire consumed eighty percent of the city.

To this day, William Shakespeare's *Macbeth* is considered a haunted play.

---

*"Mr. Hooke read a second very curious lecture about the late Comett," *The Diary of Samuel Pepys*, March 1, 1664/65.

For further reading . . .

Ágoston, Gábor, and Bruce Masters. *Encyclopedia of the Ottoman Empire*. New York: Facts on File, 2009.

Allen, Stephen. *Celtic Warrior: 300 BC–AD 100*. Oxford: Osprey Publishing, 2001.

Boas, Frederick Samuel. *Shakespeare & the Universities: And Other Studies in Elizabethan Drama*. New York: D. Appleton & Co., 1903.

Bouwsma, William J. *Venice and the Defense of Republican Liberty: Renaissance Values in the Age of the Counter Reformation*. Berkeley and Los Angeles: University of California Press, 1968.

Brandon, David. *Stand and Deliver!: A History of Highway Robbery*. Gloucestershire: The History Press, 2001.

Brooke, Nicholas, ed. *The Oxford Shakespeare: The Tragedy of Macbeth*. New York: Oxford University Press, 1990.

Budiansky, Stephen. *Her Majesty's Spymaster: Elizabeth I, Sir Francis Walsingham, and the Birth of Modern Espionage*. New York: Plume, 2006.

Chambers, David, and Brian Pullan, eds. *Venice: A Documentary History, 1450–1630*. Cambridge: Blackwell Publishers, 1992.

Cooper, John. *The Queen's Agent: Sir Francis Walsingham and the Rise of Espionage in Elizabethan England.* New York: Pegasus Books, 2013.

Crompton, Louis. *Homosexuality and Civilization.* Cambridge: Harvard University Press, 2006.

Crouzet-Pavan, Elisabeth, and Lydia G. Cochrane, trans. *Venice Triumphant: The Horizons of a Myth.* Baltimore: The Johns Hopkins University Press, 2002.

Crystal, David, and Ben Crystal. *Shakespeare's Words: A Glossary and Language Companion.* New York: Penguin, 2002.

Ditchfield, P. H., ed. *Memorials of Old London.* 2 vols. London: Bemrose & Sons, 1908.

Doody, Margaret. *Tropic of Venice.* Philadelphia: University of Pennsylvania Press, 2007.

Dursteler, Eric R. *Venetians in Constantinople: Nation, Identity, and Coexistence in the Early Modern Mediterranean.* Baltimore: The Johns Hopkins University Press, 2006.

Fraser, Antonia. *Faith and Treason: The Story of the Gunpowder Plot.* New York: Anchor Books, 1996.

Frye, Roland Mushat. *Shakespeare: The Art of the Dramatist.* London: George Allen & Unwin Ltd., 1982.

Geikie, Sir Archibald. *The Birds of Shakespeare.* Glasgow: James Maclehose and Sons, 1916.

Hogge, Alice. *God's Secret Agents: Queen Elizabeth's Forbidden Priests and the Hatching of the Gunpowder Plot.* New York: HarperCollins, 2005.

Honan, Park. *Christopher Marlowe: Poet & Spy.* New York: Oxford University Press, 2005.

Johnson, James H. *Venice Incognito: Masks in the Serene Republic.* Berkeley and Los Angeles: University of California Press, 2011.

King, Ross. *Michelangelo and the Pope's Ceiling.* New York: Bloomsbury, 2003.

Levack, Brian P., ed. *The Witchcraft Sourcebook*. New York: Routledge, 2004.

Marzluff, John M., and Tony Angell. *In the Company of Crows and Ravens*. New Haven: Yale University Press, 2005.

Nicholl, Charles. *The Lodger Shakespeare: His Life on Silver Street*. New York: Penguin, 2008.

———. *The Reckoning: The Murder of Christopher Marlowe*. Chicago: The University of Chicago Press, 1995.

Noyer, Paul du. *In the City: A Celebration of London Music*. London: Virgin Books, 2009.

Packer, Tina. *Women of Will: Following the Feminine in Shakespeare's Plays*. New York: Alfred A. Knopf, 2015.

Palmer, Alan and Veronica. *Who's Who in Shakespeare's England: Over 700 Concise Biographies of Shakespeare's Contemporaries*. New York: St. Martin's Press, 1981.

Pepys, Samuel. *The Diary of Samuel Pepys*. Edited by Richard le Galliene, introduction by Robert Louis Stevenson. New York: Modern Library, 2003.

Pizzi, Katia, and Godela Weiss-Sussex, eds. *The Cultural Identities of European Cities*. Bern: Peter Lang AG, Internationaler Verlag der Wissenschaften, 2011.

Rothman, E. Natalie. *Brokering Empire: Trans-Imperial Subjects Between Venice and Istanbul*. Ithaca: Cornell University Press, 2012.

Rowse, A. L. *Shakespeare: The Man*. New York: St. Martin's Press, 1988.

Tanner, Tony. *Venice Desired*. Cambridge: Harvard University Press, 1992.

Vries, Jan de. *The Economy of Europe in an Age of Crisis, 1600–1750*. London: Cambridge University Press, 1976.

Walker, Barbara G. *Man Made God: A Collection of Essays*. Seattle: Stellar House Publishing, 2010.

Wood, Michael. *Shakespeare*. New York: Basic Books, 2004.

Woodall, J. *The Surgions Mate*. London: Edward Griffin, 1617.

Wynn, Douglas. *Lincolnshire Villains: Rogues, Rascals and Reprobates*. Gloucestershire: The History Press, 2012.

Acknowledgments

Twenty years ago, an elementary school teacher affectionally remembered as Mrs. Raphael told her students they would be staging one of William Shakespeare's plays that year. She asked us to decide whether it would be *Macbeth* or *Hamlet*, and I enthusiastically voted "*Hamlet!*" because "there's a skull in it!" (Being an eleven-year-old boy, I acted under the authority that talking to a skull was pretty much the coolest thing actors do.) The girls in our class, however, were not so easily swayed. One of them liked the sound of *Macbeth* for reasons beyond my persuasion, the chief being that her name was Beth. She shared her amusement with the girls next to her, two of whom agreed to join her onstage as witches. The Weird Sisters had their way, and the rest of us became assassins, usurpers, soldiers and, in my case, a drunken porter.

This book exists because of everyone in that room.

Any acknowledgments would be remiss without my gratitude to these students, whom I shared the most impressionable years of my life with in the company of our beloved teacher, Nancy A. Raphael of the Central Bucks School District. Thank you.

I must also thank my parents and everyone in my family for their love and support, particularly my father, Joseph A. Calabria; my godfather, Marino D'Orazio; and my uncle Antonio Rutigliano for the unique roles they played in this project. I also thank Jonathan Maberry; my agent, Sara Crowe; my editor, Michael Homler; Lauren Jablonski; and everyone at St. Martin's Press for once again letting me share my writing with the world.

Special thanks go to Ray Errol Fox for his tireless wisdom and friendship; his daughter Lauren Fox for everything she always told me about acting; Melanie and Claire McCulley for being such inspirational towers of strength; Glyne Griffith for being such a towering friend; Erzsébet Fazekas for being there from the very beginning; Ashley E. Holley for her frequent creative and artistic insight; Bianca Rutigliano for her invaluable contributions; Daniel Eltringham and Jeff Garofalo for their chemical know-how; Eden Loeffel for her artistic input; Kate Resler for her costuming; Adrian Prockter for his extensive research on Old London; Ian Archer, Felicity Heal, Paulina Kewes, and Henry Summerson, the Holinshed Project; Dr. Philip Weller of Shakespeare Navigators; Emrah Safa Gürkan and Chris Gratien at the Ottoman History Podcast; David and Ben Crystal for all their work on original pronunciation; Rick and Diana Boufford at the Raven Diaries; Amanda Mabillar at Shakespeare Online; Dr. Victoria Buckley at Shakespeare's England; Eric M. Johnson at Open Source Shakespeare; Phil Gyford at PepysDiary.com; the team at the Map of Early Modern London; the Yeomen Warders of Her Majesty's Royal Palace and Fortress the Tower of London; the U.S. National Library of Medicine; the World Digital Library; the British Library; the Bodleian Library; the Folger Shakespeare Library; Project Gutenberg; Dr. Michael Best from the University of Victoria, coordinating editor of the Internet Shakespeare Editions; Shakespeare's Globe; the Wikimedia Foundation; the Old Map & Clock Company; the Gunpowder Plot Society; OpenCulture.com; the BBC; PBS; the New York State Writers Institute; my professors at Susquehanna

University and Syracuse University in Florence for everything they taught me; Callum MacFadyen Mellon for being Scotland personified; Anthony Losorelli for always being my first second opinion; Tim Lieb for his friendship and acumen; F. James Walton for letting me kill him onstage as Banquo; David Mitchell for always having time for me; the countless teachers, historians, actors, actresses, and playing companies who keep Shakespeare alive all over the world's stage; the mischief-makers who keep Guy Fawkes alive every Bonfire Night; everyone at Crisan Bakery; everyone who preordered this book and its predecessor months in advance; everyone who read, reviewed, and shared in *The Great Abraham Lincoln Pocket Watch Conspiracy*; all my readers at Cracked.com; and all my kind, dedicated, and hilarious Twitter followers! (Please feel free to write your names here: @_____ #PopQuizHotShot)

And lastly, I would like to give a very special thanks to my mother, Anna Calabria, for reminding me again and again to visit her students Professor John Bell, Pamela Jane, and their daughter Annelise at Villa La Pietra during my time abroad.